A GIRL, Stuck

FOUND FAMILIES BOOK THREE

KELLY ELIZABETH HUSTON

CONTENT WARNING: This story delves into the world of private detective investigation, police work, both state and federal, and the violent world of organized crime. This includes discussion, description, and brief acts of violence on the page. There is also mention of a parent's death, drug and alcohol use, and strong language.

edited by Ash White | cover and format by Watermount Publishing

ISBN: 979-8-9877885-4-7 (e-book) | ISBN: 979-8-9877885-5-4 (paperback) | Library of Congress Control Number: 2024900855

Visit www.kellyelizabethhuston.com for author information

To anyone who has done right even when it hurt, especially those who love a good dirty joke.

One

HE LAUGHED AS HE folded his tall frame into that ridiculous vintage Tahiti blue MG. He'd made a joke, a funny one, I'm sure, but I missed it while my heart crumbled in the stifling July Fourth humidity on a sidewalk in Jamaica—Jamaica, Queens, that is. The morning mist had strengthened to spitting rain, and the whole scene turned absurdly appropriate. *Warning:* this next bit won't be pretty.

"Hey, Asher." Looking skyward, I cinched my droopy ponytail, kinking in the wet. I knew to avoid his face. Better to endure the increasing pelt of raindrops on mine.

"Yeah?" He leaned out the opened window.

"*Uh,*" I sucked in hot, soggy air, wishing it wasn't. "Do me a favor, yeah?"

"What's that, Harry? Name it." Sincere blue eyes met mine when, like a fool, I lowered my gaze.

"Lose my number." It sounded more like a question. I adjusted the messenger bag that weighed me down along with the summer heat and the leather jacket I wore, intent on looking the part in some self-assured *Gloria Gaynor* moment. It didn't go that way.

"What?" Asher's shock came as a pleasant surprise, at least. "Do you mean that, Harriet? Really?"

Jesus, I hate it when people call me by my given name—except him. "Yes... Maybe... No." I tried for a chuckle, but when it fell flat,

I growled to loosen my tightening throat. "I mean, *yes*. Yes, I do. Don't call me again. Okay? Not sooner or later or—*ever*. Could you do that for me? Never call me again? Because I can't—"

"I hear you. I won't. But if you ever need anything—"

"I won't." I couldn't get those words out fast enough before I spun on the wet sidewalk to trudge through the St. John's University campus to my home three blocks south. The MG's engine rumbled to a start. "*Shit*. Shit, shit, shit, shit. I swear to God, Harry Smith, if you turn around, you will never get over the man. Just keep walking." Yes, I spoke the words aloud. To myself. I do that.

With a forceful head shake, I picked up my pace, proud of my restraint as I left the bestselling author Asher Cray, the man of my—*whatever,* in my wake. I took another damp breath and focused on getting home to email the last of that relationship out of my inbox so I could get on with the business of getting *over* the man who had unknowingly kept me under his spell for the better part of two years. *Ugh*. His *spell*? That sounded like a gooey romantic, and rest assured, I am anything but. Let's just say Asher is funny and smart and kind and an incredible, toe-curling lay, and now it's over. *Has* been over for more than a year... until he called yesterday. *Son-of-a-bitch*.

Pulled from my wallowing thoughts, I stopped short of bounding up the concrete stairs that led to my apartment when the muffled mews of one of the neighborhood's stray cats cried from under a scraggly hedge. The skittish animal didn't come out to greet me, having more sense than to step into the rain. I bent to say my hellos and pulled a folded napkin from my bag's front pocket.

"Hey, kitty. I brought you some bacon." I tore up my breakfast leftovers, placing the bits under the shrubbery for the homeless creature's easy access.

She hissed.

"To hell with you then," I jeered, but continued to rip apart the salty strip of pork. When the mangey ingrate finished eating, it scurried deeper into the privet without so much as a head bump in thanks. I remained crouched in the rain until Mother Nature urged me indoors when she sent down a harder cloudburst.

My home had the outward look of a miniature asylum rather than a residence. I'd bought the lackluster two-story brick square for next to nothing four years ago. Originally a small industrial warehouse built early last century, I had the structure gutted and retrofitted into two two-story apartments—one for me, one for a stranger who had become like family. A wise investment of an unfortunate financial windfall.

I stomped water off my sneakers, meeting a frigid air-conditioned blast when I entered the building's vestibule, and shuttered at the chill. Wet rubber soles squeaked on vintage penny tiles, announcing my arrival. I couldn't get my deadbolt unlocked and myself inside before the door across the hall flew open.

"Harry Smith." It was another hiss, but not of the feline variety.

With my forehead pressed to the still-closed door, I sighed, "Hello, Leo," preparing for the inevitable reprimand.

"Don't *'hello, Leo'* me, missy. Did I see—"

"It's not what it looked like, Nosy Parker," I cut short my neighbor's scolding with an exasperated snap.

"Oh, thank sweet baby Jesus," Leo let slip his southern accent. "Because it *looked* like that famed writer who ghosted you over a year ago showed up here last night and didn't leave until this morning, and since it took you until like last *Tuesday* to actually

get over the way-too-old-for-you-albeit-incredibly-hot man—
that would have been a gut-wrenching wound to re-open, not
to mention stupid as fu—"

"*Okay*, Leo. It was a *little* like it looked but not entirely,
and he *didn't* ghost me, and *I'm* fine, and Asher's gone for
good this time." With a slow turn, I faced unexpected silence.
My neighbor Leo, that stranger-turned-family, leaned in his
doorway with a hand on his hip, his head mere inches from the
top of the frame. He wore a look of disdain and a flowing floral
kimono identical to one I owned, thanks to a night of too much
Manischewitz and some tipsy online shopping. And dammit, if
he didn't look better in it than I did. I couldn't take the quiet.
"Jesus, say something."

"Did you—"

"*NO*." I should have guessed he'd go there. "His visit was
strictly for book research business."

"Really?"

"Well, I might have tried, but—" I confessed. I couldn't help
myself. Leo possessed a priest-like quality, though rabbi would
be more appropriate.

"*Really?*"

"Seems he's met someone," I explained.

"*Real*-ly?"

"And it's serious."

"Really?"

"As a heart attack. Asher's words, not mine."

"Well, the man is of a certain age," Leo snickered.

"Come on. He's not that old."

"Really?"

"Leopold Klein, so help me. Say *'really'* one more time. I
dare you." My glare met his pursed lips.

He didn't. He said nothing for an agonizing moment. "You all right?" The eventual soft-spoken question came laced with genuine concern.

"I'd be better if I had a summer session to teach, or my phone would ring with a P.I. case that didn't involve infidelity and the need for proof, but yeah, I'm all right." Sometimes the work schedule of an adjunct professor allowed for too much free time, and the private investigator side-hustle left me feeling dirty.

"What'll you do now?"

"I'll close out the last of the background research I did for Asher's next book—that he doesn't even think he's gonna write now— and send him his file with a *very* big invoice."

"Big, huh?"

"*Huge.* But it's the last one. Hand to—"

"I don't need to know where your hands have been, Harriet. Seriously." Leo waved his long fingers and *tsked* with a curled lip.

I laughed, relieved to find laughter still possible, and opened my apartment door.

"Hey, got plans tonight?"

"No. You?"

"Gantry Plaza. Fireworks. Independence Day?" He gave a pointed look before belting out a country song I'd like to think I'm too young to know.

"That's a hard pass." I forced a grin at my friend. "Thanks, though. Have fun."

Inside my home, I hung my messenger bag on a teak hat rack and peeled off my leather jacket before catching my reflection in a mirror. The older man's ability to say no wasn't so hard to believe when my sagging image stared back at me. A wide-receiver-on-game-day look my rain-smeared mascara provided forced an eye-roll. I wiped the smudges, toed-off my sneakers in a clumsy stumble, and trudged upstairs to my bathroom. The very bathroom Asher had showered in a few hours earlier. Last night's Macallan 18 remnants mocked me from the coffee table in the middle of my bedroom. An unexpected night of drinking had landed the best-selling author in my bed, and me—on my sofa. Yeah, not my best work.

In a blink, I found myself downstairs again and across the hall, banging on Leo's door. When it opened, I thrust the half-empty bottle at my wide-eyed neighbor. "Take it, yeah?"

"Oh, honey. I don't—"

"Take. It." I shoved it to his chest and held it there.

"You know I don't drink the dark liquor. It makes me—I mean I get—I get *wiiiild*—"

"It's three hundred dollars a bottle."

"Well, if you insist..." Leo snatched the Scotch from my grasp, and I hurried back to my solitary sanctum, shutting the door with more force than I meant. Tripping over my shoes, I beelined to the shower before any sort of "Asher Cray shrine" status took hold, and I found myself bathing at the gym for the rest of my life. *Pathetic, Harry.*

Steam filled the tiled room, and I washed away what I hoped would be the last of the memory of a man who wasn't meant to be. Well, not meant for me, anyway.

Two

I DON'T HAVE MANY friends. Days lecturing university students on investigative tactics and criminal profiling with nights spent sneaking around in a surveillance van, or worse, seedy motels and bars, don't lend themselves to a life full of age-appropriate pals who sing karaoke on Friday nights or brunch on Sundays.

Maybe I shouldn't blame my career choices for my lack of social life. I'm also a bit of a disaster and not very nice. Add to that, I'm *probably* too smart for my own good and *definitely* endowed with a firm ass and a perky rack that, when coupled with a clipboard, gain me access to just about anywhere I want to go. And as for humility, well—I might've skipped the day they gave that lesson.

People call me Harry, but my post-dated birth certificate reads Harriet no-middle-name Smith. I could tell you how I was *hashtag blessed* to be born to wonderful parents who, when they decided they *didn't* want me, dropped me at a police station instead of in a trash can. And how a young cop at that precinct fell in love with my hours-old red curls and blue eyes, so much so that, with some well-connected help, he was able to push through paperwork to foster and eventually adopt me. But none of that is very interesting. Suffice it to say, a cop raised me surrounded by more cops, and you'll never find a more loyal, protective, and supportive family. Ever. It also means I lack some social niceties, etiquette, a filter, and whether that is nature or nurture, I don't know, but Dad called it moxie. I *do* know that imparting hard-won wisdom about investigation practices and a lot of alone time in a junk food-laden, windowless van suits me. So, despite any signs of *softness*, trust that I'm a tough-as-nails badass who handles her shit with serious skill, so you can kick your concerns about any apparent heartbreak to the curb. That's for damn sure. Same with any questions about who exactly it is I'm trying to convince.

My phone rang, my business line. It helps to keep the private investigator's life separate from my personal one in many ways. I answered without looking at the screen.

"Harry Smith Investigations. How may I direct your call?" Full disclosure, people looking for a P.I, tend to have some gender bias. Shocking, I know. So, until I suss out the details of a case, sometimes even after some initial sleuthing takes place, I don't disclose my identity. The number of first-time callers who assume I'm the "front-office girl" would—well, it shouldn't surprise you. Funnily enough, once I've procured some much-needed information, often damning photographic or audio evidence, the client couldn't give a crap whether I sit or stand to pee. Investigative work is a results-driven gig, no matter who gets the goods, no matter who pays the bill.

"Hey, kiddo."

I pulled the phone from my ear and hit the speaker button, recognizing the number belonged to a local police precinct.

"Marty, why are you calling the work number? You good?"

"I'm *well*, and I debated which number to dial because this is a business call, *official* business." Martin O'Shea is one of the cops I mentioned earlier. A stickler for keeping official business *official* and his grammar correct, Marty was also my father's on-the-job partner. Harlan Smith, my dad, was shot and killed in the line almost five years ago. And I'm still not ready to talk about that yet.

"Official business, huh? Well then, *Detective* O'Shea, how may I officially be of service? And when are we doing this? Today works, right now even. I'm walking to the door as we speak." The relief at the mere prospect of something to fill my time, any length of time, washed over me, and breathing got easier.

"Slow down, Harry. Going off half-cocked won't fly with what I have in mind."

"Half-cocked is my middle name, Uncle Marty. It's part of my charm."

"I happen to know you don't have a middle name—or charm." The curmudgeon's smirk resonated through the speaker.

"Wow. With that kind of talk, you can forget the friends and family discount. Full bore for you, Smarty Marty." I flopped onto my bedroom's low sofa and kicked up my bare feet.

"I'm not looking for any special rate, kid."

"Aw, I'm just joshing. Besides, I've got a big payday on the way, and between you and me, I could use some distraction. What do you need? And when?"

"The *when* is tonight."

"Thank you, sweet baby Jesus," I mimicked Leo from across the hall. "Oops, sorry, Marty." I meant the apology.

Martin O'Shea is a devout Irish Catholic, a great man with a dry sense of humor, and he knows how to have a good time, but he prefers I keep my blasphemy to a minimum.

"What's the *what*?" I asked, eager to move on to the good stuff.

"Surveillance, but on foot, so I need you to blend in a crowd. No audio or visual evidence collection is necessary. Just follow, watch, and report back. No interaction. As a matter of fact, I'd rather you not make contact at all." The last part sounded more like an edict than a suggestion.

"*O-kay*. And who am I tailing? How will I happen upon the mark, and what am I looking for?" I took mental notes. Sometimes a paper trail gets complicated, legally-speaking.

"Let me be clear, Harriet. You're not *looking for* anything. Simply observing, watching, then reporting back to me." Marty's use of my proper name caught my attention, and I knew he wanted me to take notice.

"Okay."

"The target is a young punk. New on the scene. His name is Trey Popov. I'll send you a photo. Says he'll be at some July Fourth festivities. That's really my first question. Whether or not he shows. It could be a speedy job."

"Shows where?" I opted to focus on the business at hand and not the questionable longevity of the gig. At the moment, I'd take anything.

"Gantry Plaza. At the East River. Right across from—"

"The U. N.," I interjected.

"Yes."

"That significant?"

"No," he answered without skipping a beat. Maybe too fast.

"Marty?"

"No, Harry. He's just some young punk, and I'd like to get your take."

"How young are we talking?"

"Your age?"

"So, *very* young, then." I made the lame joke to gauge Marty's real mood.

"You wish," he teased. "He's no teenager, but it's hard to say. You're all young to me."

"Well, thirty is the new Forever Twenty-One," I quipped.

"Keep telling yourself that, Harry."

We both chuckled in a way that included more sigh than laughter. A tension Marty didn't want to concede bubbled underneath our banter, but our history said he'd tell me what I needed to know when I needed to know it, and apparently, that time was later.

"Are we clear on the particulars?" He returned to the need-to-know details.

"Got a time?"

"Let's say before dark. Easier to latch on when you can see, but it's a fireworks display, so that won't happen until well after sundown. Plus, there will be a crowd."

"Okay, blend in, just watch, note who he's with, how he acts, what he eats, drinks, smokes. Don't engage."

"Sounds about right," Marty confirmed.

"Do I follow him home?"

"No. Not this time. Just stick to Popov's social interactions."

I grinned to hear it might not be a one-time deal but kept a noncommittal tone. My eagerness was my concern. "How should I report back? Anyone else interested in my findings?" It was a bold question that may have tipped my hand, but Marty let it go.

"Let's keep this between you and Uncle Marty, okay, kid? We'll talk tomorrow. I'll call you."

"Yes, sir."

"And Harry?"

"Yep?"

"Be careful, but don't go armed. No firearm, I mean."

"Nothing but my Ivy League education, my wit, and bare hands. Promise."

"I think we both know your arsenal consists of far more than that, Harriet."

"What did you say about my *arse*?"

"Talk tomorrow, Harry," Marty O'Shea sighed and ended the call.

Three

Eager to get to work, I plotted my travel. The majority-minority neighborhood I called home prided itself on being diverse, inclusive, and *not* gentrifying. And on that July Fourth, my apartment's bedroom view included wet walkways below but parting clouds with blue sky above. The fireworks would be a go. *God bless America.*

My trek to the park, several miles west of home, included two subway rides, an Uber, and some walking in between it all, but that's just smart tradecraft. I've mentioned my education, a master's degree in criminology, but I picked up lessons in surveillance by pounding the pavement and listening to my dad. Extreme tactics wouldn't be necessary, but my path to the surveillance spot would differ from the one I took home. Having followed, listened in, videoed, and photographed more people than I care to count has instilled a healthy measure of paranoia. I take good care when I travel.

Destination: Gantry Plaza State Park. The reclaimed dockyard is a great patch of earth right on the East River with Manhattan's skyline for a backdrop, and popular with the Tai-chi-set, daily dog walkers, and seasonal concert goers. No doubt, thanks to the clearing skies, a mob would descend to celebrate the patriotic holiday, a crowd I needed to blend into, so my outfit mattered. I chose blue jeans, sneakers, and a white scoop-neck t-shirt with a red, white, and blue heart stretched across the bust. To be honest, my wardrobe lacked any flag-waving wear, and I'd bought the shirt out of necessity when I spilled coffee down my front at a café on the Champs-Élysées. In Paris. That's right, I flaunted French patriotism, not American, but a red, white, and blue heart is a red, white, and blue heart, right? I gave my reflection a reassuring nod.

After a rainy day, the hazy, sinking sun made the already steamy atmosphere downright oppressive as evening blanketed the city. A cold beer would go down fast, and I'd allow it—you know, to blend in with the crowd—more smart tradecraft. I smirked at my well-reasoned plan.

Time allowed me to take a circuitous path to my destination, and the closer I got, the denser the sidewalk traffic grew. With all I needed in my jeans pocket, including my phone, free hands could be advantageous. I had memorized the details of Mr. Popov's face best I could, but if I had doubts, I could steal a glimpse of his grainy snapshot with the swipe of a screen. Despite the sticky heat, it felt damn good to be working outside a van.

The trip, with all my zig-zagging, took nearly two hours. I didn't feel rushed, but I wondered if I had given myself enough daylight to set eyes on my target. The busier the streets became, the more finding Trey Popov felt like pinpointing a specific needle in a pile of needles. In moments like these, patience became my mightiest virtue. Patience is a teachable skill if one is willing to learn, and if not, I don't recommend a career in investigation. It's not for everyone.

I played that platitude on repeat as frustration's tune crept its way from a spot in my brain to a broader expanse in my chest. Fear of failing Marty joined in the lament, and I worried the night would end in a botched job. I breathed in more of that humid air, and my brows raised when the mugginess included the skunky aroma of some popular weed I'd noticed a lot recently. With flared nostrils, I headed straight to a line at a local craft brew truck. It was hot, and I was thirsty, and fitting in was key.

Stepping to the end of the line, I pulled out a ten-dollar bill and my phone, looking disengaged when I was anything but. A quick glance told me I had no missed calls or texts. Not surprising. The line inched ahead, and I looked forward to the cold beverage as the evening's next musical act conducted a sound-check on the nearby temporary stage erected for the event. The excruciating squawk of mic feedback jerked me to attention, and a loud groan from the crowd followed.

That's when I saw him.

I caught myself before I nearly stepped out of line with a quick reminder to the unusually jumpy investigator in me why I had come there and what I meant to do. *Focus, Harry.* Rooted in my spot in the queue, I was more intent than ever on that beer as my mouth had gone dry at finally laying eyes on the man. Now for the fun part.

From some distance, I would have said Trey Popov stood six foot nothing, maybe six-one. His build appeared slim, but I withheld judgment because of the oversized dark-blue tracksuit draped on his frame. I never would understand that fashion choice unless it aimed to provide a silhouette that disguised all sorts of things. The wardrobe preference by a person of Popov's ilk made sense, and I took mental notes about the man and those gathered around him.

Keeping his circle in my periphery, I took a seat on a bright red Adirondack chair, the likes of which dotted that area of the park. Even if you've never been to New York City, I bet you'd recognize my surroundings. Ever seen a movie or television show where a character had some hard-thinking to do— in an urban setting—while jogging, let's say? The Manhattan skyline made for magnificent scenery and the park's well-lit East River boardwalk allowed for a spectacular long-shot. Sure, they may have edited out the namesake gantry with "Long Island" emblazoned on it and the gigantic neon Pepsi-Cola sign, but chances are you've seen the place.

I snapped a few pictures, faking selfies. Again, a girl's gotta blend in, right? Casually sipping my fast-warming beer, I kept a distant eye on Trey Popov, who quickly became a bore. It didn't appear he and his friends had plans to wander anytime soon. I may have sighed my disappointment out loud.

Marty's earlier admonishment echoed, "You're not *looking for* anything..."

Good thing, Marty, I thought. Nothing to see here but a crowd of Millennials with questionable taste in leisurewear.

Enough time passed that I considered getting another drink, but a roar of laughter erupted from Mr. Popov's gang, catching more than just *my* attention. Indigo skies said the fireworks display would launch soon, and a few colorful starbursts had already shot off a barge anchored in the river. Pre-show test charges, I presumed. Curiously, Trey and his pals chose now to disperse. Why give up the prime locale with the night's main event about to begin? The group scattered a couple at a time, and I tossed my empty cup and followed the dark curls that belonged to the lone man in the navy tracksuit. With so many spectators seated and sprawled on blankets, tailing him proved easy. I kept my distance.

Things looked to get interesting when he doubled back, but he only meandered his way to a line of Port-a-Johns. I may have cursed Martin O'Shea's name for the tedium oozing from the whole affair. A few revelers waited near the makeshift bathrooms. It wasn't a place I cared to linger, but I found an out of the way knee-wall and copped a squat with a clear view of Trey's stall. I'd wait for him to do his business and follow him a bit longer, but it seemed pretty clear the night was a bust. Whatever Marty thought about our boy Trey, it wasn't happening. At least, it wasn't happening that night. My target exited the restroom. Pleased to see him wash his hands, I followed, disappointed when he veered away from the partying onlookers. Trey Popov had apparently enjoyed enough fun and headed out of the festivity zone.

I didn't enjoy having so little to report to Marty, so with the early hour and my adrenaline pumping, I continued surveilling my lanky mark. He traveled along the edge of the gathering, and I only checked-up a second when he strolled toward a darker tree-covered section of the park. My alert heightened as the population dwindled to near-nothing, but I maintained my laid-back pursuit.

Fireworks exploded more frequently, while piped-in music played on public announcement speakers hanging from light poles, replacing the earlier live bands. Behind me, the customary unison *oohs* and *ahhs* followed each colorful burst, and I worked to steady my mounting breath the further we wandered from the throng and the murkier our surroundings became.

Marty's growl calling me *Harriet* ricocheted in my ear, and I nearly tripped over my own feet when I heard my name called aloud, this time with more hiss than bark. I whipped around to see the unmistakable tall figure of my neighbor Leo and his fabulous crew. Another hurried turn and my unsuspecting date for the evening, Mr. Trey Popov, had vanished in the trees and inky nighttime light.

"Shit," I groused, then forced a smile when I faced Leo again. "There you are," I called.

"There *you* are, Miss Thing. Thought you weren't in the mood for all this frivolity."

"I wasn't, and then I was. But now, it turns out I'm not again. Think I'll head back home. Grab an Uber." I wiggled my phone.

"No! Come out and play with Auntie Leo. We're headed to a bar. A bar where I promise *no one* will hit on you. Swear to Cher, honey. It'll be fun."

"Thanks, but no. It's getting late, and I have a meeting with Uncle Marty tomorrow." I'd known Leo long enough that he was familiar with my "family," making him well-aware of who and what Uncle Marty was to me. The fact my meeting with Marty would be a phone call didn't feel too much like a lie. I shrugged.

"I won't push, since you've had a day." Leo kissed my cheek, and I waved as his gigantic, muscular frame somehow scurried to join his friends, who'd continued to a park exit.

The tempo of explosions sped up, and the impressive display wowed the audience. On the periphery, slumped on a vacant park bench that allowed a view of the show with a little solitude in an acoustical hole where the booms jarred with less intensity, I tried to enjoy the show but instead mulled over what a total failure the day had been... on so many levels.

Waking my phone, I read my recent call log and with it, Asher Cray's name. My thumb hovered over the contact icon as a bead of perspiration rolled down my breastbone. The ticklish sensation stirred memories of sexier, sweaty times when a red, white, and blue firework combination burst over the East River. "Independence Day," I muttered and hit *delete contact*.

Like some cosmic joke, another run-in with my pal Karma, the instant I confirmed the deletion, a man's voice floated out of the darkness. "You know that's a French flag you're wearing on your chest, don't you? I mean, it's America's birthday, and you're sporting some other country's flag. Not complaining, you wear it well, but…"

I expelled an unladylike huff through my nose, casually avoiding the eyes of the overconfident man who joined me on the far end of my bench. I gave an exasperated sigh. "That's quite the pickup line," I chortled, before I let my head turn to see what such a brazen man looked like.

The familiar stranger stopped my heart, and not just because of his devilish grin. The navy-blue tracksuit shouldered some responsibility, too.

"Trey Popov." He extended his hand in the introduction. "And if I didn't know better, I'd *swear* you were following me."

Four

Okay, the following are utterly legitimate questions. Firstly, how in the world did some two-bit street punk make my tail? *B.* How the hell was I going to get out of this clusterfuck? And *three.* For the love of all that is good and holy, how could those *possibly* be his real eyelashes? All right, maybe not that last one, but if anyone else had seen what I saw, they'd have asked the same question—one hundred percent.

"*Ahem,* see, this is where you shake my hand and tell me *your* name." With his cocked head and raised brow, Trey Popov waited in the dim glow of a distant streetlamp for me to gather myself, make a plan, and then execute it.

"I'm sorry. Following you? I'm—just sitting on a bench, and you sat down *after* me, so if anyone was following someone, it would be you. That's just physics." I didn't take the man's hand.

"I do love a woman of science. Maybe I only wished you were following me."

"Well, if wishes were horses—"

Mr. Popov had a charming laugh. "What?"

"If wishes were horses, beggars would ride. It's an old English nursery rhyme."

"I thought the line went, 'If wishes were fishes...'"

My turn to laugh. "That sounds like Dr. Seuss."

His dark brow furrowed, and his dashing grin vanished while I reminded myself I might be in trouble. "So, which is it?" The man in the blue tracksuit forfeited the handshake, relaxing on the bench back.

"Excuse me?" I stalled, but my brain lagged in my efforts at finding an exit strategy.

"Are you a woman of science—or poetry?"

Wow. This likely criminal continued to flirt with me. *Unreal.* "Can't I be both?" Oh, all right, so I flirted back a little. But—the grin. And the eyelashes. Then Marty O'Shea's words rebounded. *"I'd rather you not make contact in any way."* Shit. I had to get out of there.

"The total package, huh?" Did his eyes actually twinkle?

"And what does your package entail? Mr. —*Popov*, was it?" I stood and backed away.

He rushed to his feet, too. "Whoa. You kiss your mother with that mouth?"

I slipped my phone into my back pocket to free my hands while taking slow steps in reverse. "I don't have a mother."

"Oh, sorry." His apology sounded genuine.

"Don't be." I kept up my retreat.

"How about your name, then? I told you mine."

I shook my head. "Nah, I don't think so."

"Don't I look like a nice guy?"

I shrugged. "*Fronti nulla fides.*" (No reliance can be placed on appearance.)

His head bobbed side to side. "Yes. *Spectimur agendo,*" he replied with ease. (Let us be judged by our acts.)

For the second time in one day, my overheating body shivered when hit by a frigid blast. This blow came as the metaphorical sort. His Latin retort and steely stare caught me by surprise. When my gaze inadvertently fell to the ground, I feared Trey Popov would think he'd won that round. *Aw, let him*, I thought. We'd never play again anyway. I turned on my sneakered heel and hurried toward the dispersing mob of patriotic spectators. Whether he pursued or not was of no consequence; I'd be sure he didn't follow far. Smart tradecraft. *Oh, Harry.*

Two hours later, I collapsed on my bedroom sofa, cursing myself for the distraction that allowed me to get one-upped by some petty lout in the park. My stomach tightened as I looked at my unmade bed, and memories of Asher Cray in my sheets flooded my mind. And while it would have been worse if we had shared that bed the night before, the idea of climbing into it now physically hurt. Desperate to purge the image of the writer's salt and pepper hair and light blue eyes, I happened upon a new one. Dark curls and dark eyes with impossibly long, dark lashes came into focus, and for the second night in a row, I lay my head on a couch pillow and clung to another. Sometimes it's the devil you *don't* know that gets you through the night.

When my phone rang, I jerked upright, and the searing pain of a sofa-induced neck cramp radiated in every direction. The stab to my shoulder blade joined the icepick sensation at my temple, and an animalistic cry reverberated around my dim bedroom.

"*Hmm?*" I grunted the greeting. No words would form.

"Late night, Harry? I didn't mean for you to tail the guy until dawn. Thought I made that clear." Marty began with our official business meeting.

"I didn't, Marty. Just slept funny on my sofa—never mind," I groaned and stretched, forcing myself into a more professional posture.

"Didn't tail him all night, or at all? Like I said, his not showing wouldn't be a surprise."

"Oh, he showed all right." My pain allowed for a loose tongue, and I winced with regret.

"What's that mean?"

"Nothing. Popov was there, that's all."

"Harry?"

"Relax, Uncle Marty. It might not have gone down exactly as you would have had it go, but it's cool."

"You know when you say, 'Relax, Uncle Marty,' it has the opposite effect, right? I knew better than to send you, but I had questions, inklings, and I couldn't shake them." The detective exhaled. "Why don't you tell me what happened."

Still stinging from my screw-up, I may have been a bit on the defensive. "First of all, I'm damn good at my job. On my worst day, I'm better than most, and yeah, yesterday? Not a great day, but I'm *exactly* who you should send in. Just ask Penn and the FBI, NSA, and CIA." I huffed, realizing my snit-fit likely hurt my case.

Marty paused before his reply. "Uh, got any more letters you want to hurl in my direction? I'm well aware of your fancy degree and how all kinds of law enforcement tried to recruit you, but *you* turned them all down, and—"

"I turned them all down because my dad had just met the business end of a sawed-off shotgun and lost."

"That's right, kiddo. He did. Harlan should have retired a year earlier, but instead, he kept doing the only thing he loved other than being your dad. And *you* made the smart choice. Teaching and hiding behind your camera in a van."

"Hiding? Is that—?"

"I-I didn't mean hiding—" he tried to backpedal, but I wouldn't let him.

"Wow. Is that what you think I do? *Hide* in the van—and the lecture hall? Well *shit*, Uncle Marty, thanks for the wake-up call." I hung up and chucked the phone across the room. It landed safely on the taunting, unmade bed. "Shit. Shit, shit, shit, shit, shit." My stomp through the cased opening to the sleep portion of my bedroom punctuated my swearing. I grabbed at the sheets, tearing them from the mattress, and if it hadn't been for their buttery feel and expensive price tag, I'd have burned them. I like nice bed linens. Fancy sheets are my jam. Sue me. Instead of lighting a match, I balled the bamboo bedding, snatched my laundry caddy, and headed for the shared laundry room downstairs. Wash day came early.

I kept a pretty regular schedule—very regular. Blame it on my upbringing. A single cop dad with a high-spirited daughter encouraged a hectic life laden with events often out of our control. That said, the things we could manage, we did. Laundry day, grocery day, clean the bathroom day—you get the picture. We also scheduled "fun" or incorporated "down time" into the more mundane but necessary facets of our day-to-day. As an adult— and I know, even at thirty, I barely qualified— I have kept up the practice. This included bundling the ninety minutes it took me to do laundry with pleasure reading or listening to any variety of the vast number of podcasts available nowadays. I sat in the laundry room (college taught me never to leave my laundry unattended in a communal laundromat) and read or listened through both the wash and dry cycles, followed immediately by ironing if any existed.

After shoving the sheets into a washer, I turned to grab my stash of laundry detergent. In my fury, it wasn't the ideal moment to find Asher Cray's latest thriller tucked into the caddy that held Tide, bleach, fabric softener, and a stain stick. My impulse control failed me. The unread novel found its way down the old warehouse's industrial trash chute, a four-foot by four-foot steep steel duct, with a vertical tambour door that led from the laundry room to a dumpster below in the building's back alley. It happened very fast.

My phone rang. I answered but didn't speak.

"You are so like your father; may he rest in peace. Do you feel better?" Marty's calming tone and sweet words were his apologies.

"Do you?" I volleyed the question.

"Why don't you give me the rundown on last night." He knew moving forward was the best way to get over our dust-up, and without anyone claiming fault or laying blame, we left the verbal scuffle behind us.

"Well, I can see why the man gave you an itch you needed to scratch." I covered a snicker with a low cough. A flash of the impossibly long lashes triggered my own itch, but I snapped to attention when a muscle pain seized my neck and my focus.

"Do I even want to know what you mean by that?"

"I don't know what your *inkling* told you, but there is more to Mr. Popov than meets the eye. No question." As my laundry sloshed, I hopped onto a folding counter. My legs, crossed at the ankles, swung in unison.

"And what makes you say that?" Marty pressed for my professional opinion, and I could hear his satisfaction in knowing his instincts fell in line with mine.

I looked down at my t-shirt from the night before. "Between his knowledge of foreign flags, his firm grasp of Latin, and a fondness for what might be Dr. Seuss, I'd say Trey Popov is no ordinary street punk. He's also not as young as implied." I opted to omit the man's surveillance acuity.

"Harry. Not to revisit a can of worms, but if you gleaned all that from the significant distance you promised to keep—well, then I stand corrected. You are the best investigative, lip-reading clairvoyant I've ever known."

I met Uncle Marty's sarcasm with a moment of dead air.

"Harry?"

"Yeah, *soooo*, about that distance—"

Five

After filling Marty in on my observations from the night before and reassuring him that Trey Popov didn't know who I was, where I lived, or why I'd visited the park beyond my love of country, our official business meeting phone call came to an abrupt end. Some days the old man still treated me like a twelve-year-old. Riled by our squabbling, and stiff and sore from two nights of curling up on a sofa that looked better than it slept, I decided a jog to the gym would help work out some of the mental and physical knots I'd accumulated the past couple of days.

With my laundry finished and bed remade, I dressed for a workout and headed for the door with a knapsack on my back. Stepping onto the front stoop, the bright light of a new day brought some clarity and a smidgeon of shame. I slunk around to the rear of the building and tossed my small backpack on the ground beside the dumpster situated under the old chute that funneled warehouse cargo to expectant flatbeds back in the day. Two hands on the rim of the container, I hoisted myself enough to snatch the suspense novel that lay atop the mound of garbage bags inside it. Truth be told, this acrobatic scene had played out once before, a year ago. Ok, fine. *Twice.* It happened twice.

A quick stop to toss the book inside the building's vestibule, and I continued on my way in search of some stress-relief.

One perk of my flexible work-life includes going to the gym off-hours. I like to skip the early morning and late evening when the workout crowd seems more like a coffee klatch or happy hour, with more socializing than sweating. I run there and back for the cardio and do weight work on-premises. From an early age, my dad encouraged self-defense training. And when I say "encouraged," I'm underselling it. That strict and serious education began at the facility years ago and continues to this day.

My gym is also a *gym*, not a fitness center or a workout studio: no sleek juice bar, stacks of neatly folded towels, or sweet-smelling anything anywhere. Boxing rings, free weights, and some resistance machines comprise the somewhat dank but huge cinderblock and concrete-floored space, frequented by cops and other first responders, as well as locals looking for a down and dirty workout. If I want a kinder, gentler environment with a cleaner shower situation, I'd trek to the university's athletics building—lots of clean towels there. I'm a girl with options.

The day's routine proved ideal. Aside from a couple of raised chins and a nod, no one bothered me during my exercise hour. After a couple of days of out-of-the-ordinary happenings, I started to feel like myself again. While I had no qualms about *witnessing* uncommon occurrences, I didn't care to *participate* in them. Humdrum was how I liked my existence, and I didn't let much get in the way of my predictable life. For example, despite my change-up with laundry earlier in the morning, I would not miss my Friday farmers' market visit.

I guzzled the last of my water bottle and refilled it before cinching my ponytail and pushing through the gym's heavy metal door. Landing in the hot sunshine, I hoisted my knapsack to hike further away from my home, past Marty's police precinct, and farther southwest. Most Fridays, from Memorial Day to Halloween, this was what I did.

Fruits, veggies, artisan bread, and local honey were just a few examples of the weekly market's offering. Vendors traveled from all over the tri-state area and beyond to sell their wares on Fridays and Saturdays. But Saturdays often included too many children, small dogs, and love-struck couples on coffee dates coming to hear an acoustic guitar or jazz trios playing under pop-up canopies. Fridays were for the earnest shopper: restaurateurs and serious resident-foodie hobbyists purchasing fresh produce for weekend dinner specials or the at-home gourmands' experiments. And me.

I like to begin at the first aisle and do a slow survey of the week's options before grabbing a provided basket and circling back to make my choices with a fuller understanding of availability. Yes, I have a method.

"I have never seen anyone scrutinize lettuce like I have witnessed you inspect lettuce for the last three, maybe four minutes. My mother had a similar technique when it came to beets. Of course, beets require a certain amount of scrutiny, but lettuce?"

The familiar, faceless voice startled me from behind, but whether he spoke Latin on a dark July Fourth night or about root vegetables in the bright sunshine of July fifth, I recognized it. How its owner found me again, miles from our first introduction, boggled my mind. The run-in couldn't be a coincidence, which meant I really was in trouble. I opted to play dumb.

"I'm sorry, sir. Am I in your way? My apologies. Let me—" I sidestepped without so much as a glance to acknowledge the man, but he stood closer than I had gauged. My shoulder met his chest, and in the closeness of it all, I had a fleeting wish I'd showered after my earlier dumpster-diving and sweaty workout. I kept my focus on the leafy greens.

"Wow. You really *are* following me."

"I most certainly am not," I spit out too quickly.

"*Ah-ha*. I *knew* you knew it was me." A smirk colored his tone.

Jesus, I was *really* off my game.

Trey Popov didn't care to dwell on our fluke happenstance, which only made me sure he engineered it. That reality caused genuine concern. "So, what brings you here?"

I continued to shop, keeping a breezy tone. "Rain or shine, I'm here almost every Friday during the season."

"Are you a chef?" He fingered the lettuce bunches, and I noticed he wore another version of what the kids called the 'Slavic Street uniform,' an Adidas tracksuit, this one black with white side stripes. Classic.

"No. I'm—I'm a teacher." It happened to be the truth.

"Oh, that tracks." He nodded with a thoughtful frown.

"I give off the teacher vibe, huh? Remind you of earlier days?" I craned my neck to look him in the eye as he kept close.

"No. I wouldn't say that. It just makes sense you can be here in the middle of the day, a weekday. Summertime."

Trey had a point, and I ceded it with a raised shoulder.

"But if I had teachers that looked like you back then, I'd have been a much more attentive student." He delivered his outrageous flirtation with such casual subtlety that I couldn't help but roll my eyes with a snort.

"And now I also can put together the science and the poetry and the Latin. It makes sense. A teacher." He wouldn't quit.

"A gold star for you today, Mr. Popov. And what do you do?" I've found the direct approach works best.

"I, *uh*, I do lots of things." Trey moved to bushels of seasonal fruit. One vendor had made his way from New Jersey, and Trey lifted a fat, fuzzy peach to smell it.

"I see."

"What do you see?" He caught my watchful eye, and his devilish grin flickered.

"You're unemployed. It's okay. It happens." Pleased with my implied slight, I placed a couple of pieces of fruit into the plastic bin hooked on my arm.

"I'm not—I'm—I'm in security." The handsome man's surety wobbled a moment.

"Oh, like banking, bonds?" *Ugh.* Playing dumb was *not* my forte.

"No, not securities. Security. Like bodies, bullets."

"Oooh." I took a beat to look the man up and down, hoping I conveyed admiration.

"Not really," he chuckled. "I carry more Birkin bags and blown-out Bichons than anything."

Damn. The guy was funny *and* smart. Unfortunate. I let out a sincere laugh.

He appeared to relax and added, "And the letter of the day is— *B*."

I recalibrated and offered a confused head tilt, but I knew the ditzy routine wouldn't work on this one—a relief, to be honest. I'd always believed two things in life should *never* be faked—and the second one was stupidity.

"Because you're a schoolteacher? Banking, bullets, Birkin—" he attempted to explain his joke.

"Oh, I get it, Mr. Popov, and now if you'll excuse me." While the conversation seemed genial, stress sweat prickled in my pits, and my grip on my produce tote tightened. Each of us endeavored to play the other, and my confidence in who was on top faded. *Whoa.* A flashed suggestive image upped my perspiration.

"So soon? It can't be a coincidence our meeting two days in a row."

"No, I don't believe it is," came my quick reply.

He ignored my quip. "I believe in fate. I'm *destined* to know your name."

Seriously, what's with this sappy drivel? The dog couldn't be barking up a more wrong tree.

"One meets his destiny—"

"...often on the road he takes to avoid it." I finished the line of French poetry that the confounding hoodlum started. Who was this guy?

"You know Jean de La Fontaine? Do you teach poetry to your young students, Ms.—?"

"Who?" I pretended more ignorance despite being a fan of all things French. "No, I order a lot of Chinese takeout. I do *love* a fortune cookie." I hurried to the checkout, but Trey kept close at my heels. When my hands were empty, I rolled with it, taking the opportunity presented to me. Uncle Marty could surely use this in some way, right? A quick turn and I extended my hand at the stunned pursuer. "Hattie. Hattie Smith. And yes, that is my real name. Unlike yours, *Trey.*"

He neglected my hand. "What do you mean? I've gone by Trey my whole life."

"I don't doubt it, but it isn't your name. No one *names* their kid Trey. You're a *third,* yeah? I do prefer Trey over Trip. Trip is so blue blood yet white bread. I'd bring a Trey home to Mom long before I'd bring a Trip." My chatter took place half over my shoulder while I concluded my cash-only market transaction.

"You said you didn't have a mother." A new hardness edged his tone, but I ignored it.

"Well, look who's a good listener. *Two* gold stars." I gathered my purchases in my knapsack and slid my arms through the straps before I continued. "You know—when a girl stumbles out of the gate but finally gets up her nerve to flirt back, calling her out on her repartee probably isn't the surest move." I walked alone toward the outdoor market's gate to the street. For a moment, I thought I had escaped the man, and a slight pang of disappointment hit. But when hasty feet on gravel shuffled behind me, I hid a grin.

"Alvah," he said when he caught up to me, "and I don't believe you've ever had to get up your nerve to do anything, Ms. Smith."

I appreciated his observation. I appreciated a lot of what I—*Oh, Harry.* "Alva? Like Thomas Alva Edison?" I strolled down the sidewalk, and Trey followed.

"Yes, but with an *h* at the end. It's Hebrew."

"Are you Jewish? I'd have guessed Catholic with the Latin." I mentioned our Latin back-and-forth from the night before as a friendly reminder of whatever game we had been playing.

"I'm lots of things, Hattie Smith." He walked to the street side of me, and between him and the heat radiating off the brick building to my right, I'm not sure which burned hotter.

"Obviously, Trey Popov." I laughed at the same time a police cruiser *squawked* behind us. The reality of the situation registered when I read Trey's wide eyes. I spun to see which officer exited the vehicle, confident I would know him or her. I didn't.

"Easy now, Miss. Could you set your bag on the ground and place your hands on the building for me? Hands on the cruiser,

Popov." His command to Trey carried a far harsher attitude than the ones he made to me.

"I'm sorry, officer. Is there a problem?" I stepped toward the black and white, and the young cop placed his hand on the butt of his weapon. "What's your—"

"Miss, I need you to follow instructions. Drop the bag and face the brick." The officer's name tag read S. Dempsey.

I waved my hands. "You have this all wrong—"

The officer unsnapped his duty holster. "Miss, don't make me ask again."

"Hattie. Just do as he says." Trey's pleading eyes alarmed me, implying he knew more about the situation than I did. "Look, officer. She doesn't know me, we're not together. She has nothing to do with any of this. We *just* met." Another cruiser pulled to the curb, hidden by Dempsey's ride.

"On the hood, Popov. You know the drill." The officer kept watch of me as Trey faced the windshield with his hands on the back of his head. Apparently, Popov *did* know the drill.

"I'm sorry, Hattie. I didn't mean—"

"You did nothing wrong, Trey." My swift defense of him surprised me.

As the police officer clamped cuffs on Trey, he spoke to me again. "Miss, I believe I asked you to face the bricks." Mr. Dempsey had spent all of what little patience he possessed.

"Hattie, please do as he says and don't say anything. It'll only make it worse. Officer, she's really not—"

I moved to obey, wondering when the second officer would make an appearance. Surely, we'd clear up the misunderstanding as soon as he or she saw me. With a sudden shove, S. Dempsey pressed me against the hot building while tearing the knapsack off my back. "Oh my God," I gasped as he pushed my head, scraping my cheek on the brick facade, my line of sight focused in the wrong direction. "You're hurting me."

"Hattie?" Trey's angry voice held some panic as it moved away from me. "Hattie, keep quiet except to ask for a lawyer. I'm so sorry." A car door slammed.

I tried not to move, but the masonry held the heat of the July sun, and my cheek smarted with the contact. Officer Dempsey pressed his knee into my right hamstring as he cinched zip-tie cuffs on my wrists. I couldn't believe my week. The second cruiser departed first with Trey inside it before I found myself escorted to the backseat of the original SUV. My backpack rode in the front.

Officer S. Dempsey puffed up with a mild grin in the rearview. We sat for several minutes while he took notes on his mounted computer tablet and checked his phone. As I caught the mirror image of a scrape, a small trickle of blood and sweat rolled, stinging my freckled cheek. My saving grace? We headed in the direction of the precinct I knew to be Uncle Marty's home away from home. Even cuffed and bleeding, I didn't have the heart to inform the young man behind the wheel his day was about to take a nasty turn.

Six

CHANGE IN PLAN. I had a few minutes to think on the way to the precinct, and a scheme took shape. Obviously, the cops had a reason for scooping up Trey Popov on a late Friday afternoon. And whatever charming, bordering on gallant, attention the apparent criminal bestowed upon me was neither here nor there. The clever man would likely be tough to pin down, and I was well on my way to being able to help Uncle Marty if the cunning perp slipped from the law's grip. Pinning down Mr. Popov seemed the least I could do. I stifled a grin.

Relief hit me when only Officer Lina Fuego sat at her desk in the bullpen as Dempsey and I entered the station house. My uniformed friend scrambled to her feet, and the only words I caught were my name and an expletive mumbled in Spanish. My subtle headshake stopped her from intervening. Just like the pro I knew she was, she played along with my ruse.

After a quick glance at Interview Room One, she asked, "Where do you want her, Dempsey?" Lina took me by one elbow of my cuffed arms. I leaned toward Interview Room Three. "How about you let me get her settled in three while you hydrate? It's hot out there, and you're looking flushed."

"Yeah. That'd be awesome. Thanks, *Lianne*." Dempsey wiped his mottled face.

When the door closed behind her, Lina hissed while she cut my zip cuffs, "What the hell—?"

"No time," I interjected, rubbing my wrists. "Trey Popov?"

"I didn't see him come in this time, but he's in Interview One. With Marty. Popov with you?"

This time? I'd come back to that. "Sort of. But keep me out of sight. I need to talk to Marty. And I'm *Hattie* Smith for the moment, a schoolteacher, and nobody here knows me, okay?"

"Okay. Let me at least get your face cleaned up. Popov do that?" Lina headed for the door and a first aid kit.

"What? No, this is your boy Dempsey's handiwork. New guy?"

"Yeah, two of 'em. It's their second week, and I think this cowboy has got a bit of hard-on for your pal Popov." She indicated Dempsey as she closed the blind on the small room's door. "Brought him in the other day—with nothin'. Now again? Holy crap, Marty's gonna kill 'em."

"No, Marty won't lay a hand on him, and you aren't laying a hand on this. Let it fester. It might come in handy. It's just a scrape. I'll live. I could be looking for a little sympathy later and—"

"*Gurl*, your kink is weird," she snarled with an *almost* straight face.

I fought a grin. "Shut up, Lina. I'm working here."

"Seriously, Harry. You okay? Not your usual M.O." Lina twirled her index finger at me.

"No more hiding in the van."

"What?"

"Nothing. Oh, and I need to be released *before* Trey."

"Who?"

"*Popov*. I need to leave the precinct on foot, a few minutes before he gets sprung."

"And what makes you think he's headed anywhere other than holding for the weekend?"

"P.I. instincts. Can I count on you to have my back on this? With Marty, I mean. Fill him in for me?"

"I don't even know what this is, Harry. But yeah, I got you." Lina shrugged and opened the door partway. "Can I get you some water, at least?"

"That I'll take. Thanks." I lifted my chin to signal Dempsey's approach.

In a smooth move that looked like a stumble, Lina shoved the door as Dempsey tried to enter, hitting him in the forehead. "Oof, sorry, Rookie," Lina grimaced.

I looked to the frosted glass block window opposite the door to hide my smile.

Lina took Dempsey's unopened water bottle and handed it to me. "Let me show you the appropriate paperwork, Dempsey. We'll let this young lady stew a while longer before O'Shea brings the heat." She pushed the male officer out the door, grinning back at me.

"The *heat*?" I mouthed, rolling my eyes.

She covered her chuckle with a cough and closed the door behind her. I guzzled the water and continued to cogitate my forming strategy.

An hour or more ticked by before a knock rattled the door to my hideout. Marty and Lina slipped in with another bottle of water.

"Hey, kiddo." He plopped into the chair across from me. "You have an odd idea for Friday fun."

"I tell ya, her kink is weird—"

I shot dagger-eyes to shut up my friend before I had more to explain to Marty than I already knew. "Is Popov still here?"

"He is, but not for long. We'll keep him until dark, but nothing to hold him unless you want to press charges." He indicated my cheek.

"What? This? No, I tripped," I fibbed with a wink. "Rookie had him cuffed and nowhere near me. Sorry I can't help." Hanging my minor scratch on Popov didn't fit my plan and tying up an overly enthusiastic rookie? No, not my style.

"Well, the man hasn't lawyered up and seems more concerned with some dowdy *schoolteacher* he feels may have been unjustly roughed up by one of my officers than he is his own skin."

"*Aww*, nice. But like I said, I tripped. Wait, dowdy?"

"Dowdy?" Marty looked to Lina, holding in a laugh with her fist pressed to her clamped lips. "Or did he say dainty?"

"Dainty?! Jesus Christ. Oh, sorry, Uncle Marty."

"Okay, what's your plan, *Hattie*?" He let my profanity slide.

"Plan? Me? Am I supposed to have a plan?"

"Harriet. This is not some dumb crook. He's smart and probably dangerous and capable of far more than a scratch on your face, and feral creatures will pounce on a dime. You might not see him coming. Ironically, if we do this, I'm going to have to keep some distance for your safety. I can't be listening in. This is high-wire-without-a-net time, and you are not a cop. He spends time with some nasty characters, and while he might just be some low-level minion, all this is well beyond your pay grade."

"I'm not infiltrating some colossal criminal empire. I'm *maybe* grabbing a slice with a guy." Again, with the pre-teen kid gloves routine. "Uncle Marty, I want to do this. I *need* to do this. I'm capable of more than sitting in the van, snapping pictures, Googling. I realized yesterday I've been treading water for the last year. Stuck. And if I don't make a change, move in some significant way, I'm gonna drown—death by stagnation."

"This feels like an awful reckless way to get unstuck."

"You know me, Marty. Go big or go home, yeah?"

Marty nodded. "Well, with a little time, I think I can turn him. Something tells me he hasn't given over to the dark side. Not all the way."

"As a C.I.? You'd trust him?"

"I don't trust any confidential informant, Harry."

"Then it'll help if I'm on the inside. We'll have notes to compare, I mean."

When Marty got pensive, I knew I had him leaning my way. "Go slow, though. I don't want you to do anything—I mean— if he so much as touches you."

"Don't worry, Marty. I can handle myself."

As he mentioned earlier, Marty knew what talents made up my arsenal.

"Speaking of, can we get your face cleaned up?" The man lifted my chin and winced at my abrasion.

"I'll take care of it at home. Let me stick around until you're ready to cut him loose?"

"Yeah, but don't let him know where you live, okay? Not yet, anyway. Get a feel for him first."

Lina coughed with a wink.

"No plans to take him home just yet, Uncle Marty. This dainty, dowdy schoolteacher moves at a snail's pace. Promise."

Seven

"You all right, Trey?" Hours later, I spoke just above a whisper from a low cast-iron pipe railing beyond the throw of the gothic lantern fixtures outside the precinct.

"Hattie?" Trey jerked in my direction, squinting into the dark. "What are you—? You shouldn't be here. Were you waiting for—?" He scanned 360 degrees of us. "You need to go home. Is it far? Let's get you a ride. I can't believe they didn't offer—"

"Whoa. Slow down. They did offer, but I declined, and yes, I waited for you." I stepped into the light.

"My God, your face." He spun to face the building's tall, dark wooden doors. The polished shine of the brass push-plates surprised me, but then I remembered two new rookies had recently joined the squad.

"Where are you going?" My words stopped him when I thought he planned to go back inside.

"Seems like Officer Dempsey needs a lesson on what it means to be a good cop and how to respect women." He shoved his hands into the pockets of his Adidas zip-up, not hiding his quiet fury.

While I appreciated his sentiment, it also struck me as sexist, and I couldn't let the comment go unchecked. "Most cops *are* good cops, and that means they respect women, men, and everyone in between." I added, "And thank you for coming to my TED Talk," hoping to ease the sting.

Trey didn't want to laugh, but I'm a hoot. "Yeah, you're right." He relaxed. His entire face changed, like he'd just taken off a mask—or donned one, and his agreement surprised me.

"I'll ask again. You all right, Trey? What was that all about?"

"Me? I'm fine. Twice in one week. Must have me confused with someone else." He spoke distractedly, quickly reverting to the stony version with his eyes on constant lookout in all directions. "You need to go home." His gruffer tone returned, too.

"You're kidding, right?"

"No, I'm not kidding. Is it close? Got an app for a ride? Or if you go back inside, I'm sure someone will give you a lift."

"Wow. I'm sure Officer Dempsey would *love* to give me a ride." I threw up my hands and beelined to pass Trey and return to the station.

"Hattie." He caught my elbow when I came within reach.

I yanked it away. "You're the master of mixed messages, aren't you? Or I guess I read this wrong?"

He didn't reply, and his stare confused me.

"Oh, jeez, I did. *Shit. Wow.* How embarrassing." Heat crept up my neck, and I struggled to tell the ruse from reality. I really was off my game. "Sorry. I'm—" I looked to the precinct doors, unsure of my next move. I hoisted my bag full of wilted lettuce and other wasted produce and stepped toward the building.

"I'm sorry too, Hattie. You didn't read it wrong, but I'm not the guy for you." He shook his head. "Today's little disruption certainly proved—I'm not—boyfriend material. And I knew better than to—It's me—"

"Oh my God, if you say, *it's me, not* you, I'm gonna lose my sh—Boyfriend material? What are you? Fifteen? Never mind." I huffed and headed back to the bullpen. Despite the humiliation,

I knew to let Marty know sooner rather than later that our undercover scheme failed before it even began.

"Hattie?"

"Nope, I get it." I didn't face him, just waved over my shoulder, shouting. "I'm just some dowdy schoolteacher, and you're an *asshole*. Have a nice life, Alvah Popov, the Third." I stormed through the heavy doors, ashamed of my ridiculous overreaction to being jilted by a criminal I'd just met and only *pretended* to like. Dissed by two men in two days. *A personal best, Harry.*

Relieved at the news of our flop, Marty had Lina give me a ride home. I feigned nonchalance, keeping in "character" until I pushed through another door, forced to face Asher's latest bestseller staring up at me from my building foyer floor. I tossed the book and my bag on my living room sofa and headed across the hall, hoping Leo would share the Macallan 18 I'd relinquished the other day.

"Your face!" Leo gasped. I hadn't looked at it in hours and wondered if I should worry.

"I wish everyone would stop saying it like that. It's fine. Just a scratch." I described my day in roundabout terms, leaving out some of the more clandestine details. "Anyway, not my week."

"I'll say," Leo bellowed in an atypical baritone. "Let me take care of that."

"I also wish everyone would stop fawning over me like I'm some little girl. I'll clean it myself. Thank you. Now just pour." Realizing my biting response carried too much venom, I squeezed Leo's hand. "Sorry. How about you? How's school?"

He indulged me. "I'm on midsummer break, which is good, and keeping regular singing gigs. I've got a new act. Weddings and mitzvah. I'm *hot*. Well, you'll see it tomorrow night." He sipped his

Scotch. "I study during the day and sub at area hospitals whenever they call, and it works. Can't complain."

Leo moved to New York from coastal Georgia more than two years ago. He worked as a patient care tech, but after a family tragedy of his own, he returned to school for a master's degree to become a physician's assistant—the most conscientious man I knew. Leo also sang like an angel, or the devil, depending on the tune. I often joked that I thought it was a shame he planned to give up performing just to save lives. He was my confidant, my comic relief, and sometimes my conscience. Life without him would be less colorful, and I loved him for that and more.

"And as for love— I ain't got time for that foolishness," he relaxed into a southern inflection he tended to curb.

"Me *neither*." I raised my glass and clinked Leo's, but neither of us drank, startled by a knock at the front stoop. Leo scampered to the window, hiding his tall frame for a furtive peek.

"It's a man," Leo whispered, a little giddy with that dark liquor.

"Like Uncle Marty?"

Leo looked again. "Definitely *not* Uncle Marty." His brow wiggled.

"Is he in uniform?"

"Some might say."

"What's that mean?"

Leo gave a pointed look.

I wrenched my neck with a squint, then my eyes grew wide. "Shit," I mouthed, scrambling out of the beanbag chair. "Shit, shit, shit. It's him. The guy." My words made no sound.

Neither did Leo's, "Noooooo," but he did *not* approve.

I pushed him aside to look. "Yes." I nodded, recognizing Trey Popov's chiseled profile— I mean, *tracksuit*.

"Noooooo," Leo insisted with a notably more sober face.

Our silent communication escalated with back-and-forth shoulder shoves. Then we heard a timid call, "Hattie?"

"He calls me Hattie," I whispered the obvious explanation. Leo replied with an exasperated eye roll and an elbow to my ribs.

"Hattie?" Trey repeated, louder the second time.

"I have to answer." As I exited my neighbor's flat, Leo kept close, apparently not onboard with welcoming my visitor. I reached the vestibule door's push-bar as Leo tugged my other arm, almost sending my glass of expensive Scotch to the floor. I yelped, "Oops," as the door flew open.

A retreating Trey, clutching two bags, swiveled to face us.

"Trey? How'd you get here? Wait. Did you follow me home?"

"Maybe?" Trey scanned left and right.

Leo bent and hissed over my shoulder. "There's a name for that, ya know? It's called stalk—"

I bumped his chin with a gentle shrug. "Whatcha got in the bags, Trey?"

He held up a plastic Duane Reed bag as he climbed the concrete steps. "Cotton balls. Hydrogen peroxide. Neosporin. Band-aids."

"*Aw*," my supposed ally clucked, his opinion rounding a rapid one-eighty. First aid supplies were Leo's love language. I swatted at him when he squeezed my arm to pull me inside, providing an opening for a hurried Trey to enter the vestibule.

"And the other?" I asked, keeping an impartial tone. All three of us took slow steps down the hall.

"Chinese takeout with extra fortune cookies. But no pork or shrimp. Jewish, remember?"

"Oh, Jews not eating pork isn't really a thing anymore, I don't think." I thought I spoke from experience.

"For some of us, it is." Trey knitted his brow with a definite nod.

I caught Leo's eye. "Is that why you never eat my moo shu?"

Leo smirked, "Oh, honey."

I offered my now-coaxing neighbor my Scotch, but he indicated I should swallow it. I did.

"I'm gonna go now," I wheezed to Leo through the burn of the booze.

"If you don't, I will." He took my empty glass and pushed me across the hall before giving a wave with a demure hip swivel to Trey. Leo closed his door.

"I'm starving," I grinned when the mouth-watering smells of cooking grease and MSG hit my nose.

"Good," Trey chuckled in reply. "But first, your face."

I'd swear I heard another permissive sigh from the other side of Leo's door before Trey and I entered through mine.

Eight

Trey Popov stood in my apartment, *exactly* where he shouldn't have. How the hell did I allow myself to be distracted? Followed? In the surveillance game, Popov led two-nothing. *Three*-nothing? *Dammit.* Someone needed to get her head out of her ass. But the damage was done, plus he'd brought Chinese food and Neosporin.

"Make yourself comfortable." I grabbed my bag from the sofa.

"Asher Cray," Trey said the name with a trace of surprise.

"Where?" I might have gone pale.

"The book. You read Cray? Something about that guy. His detail. I mean, he doesn't always get it right, but he's better than most. His research is excellent. Smart. And he's funny too. Of course, the man's got a reputation—"

"He's not that guy." My abrupt interruption didn't read like the indifference I meant. Trey handed me the novel, and I swallowed hard, opting to move on, and fast. "So, you followed me home? Kind of creepy, don't you think?"

Trey opened the plastic bag and pulled out the first-aid supplies, lining them up on the coffee table, unphased by my allegation. "I wanted to be sure you got home safely. I also wanted the cops and anyone else paying attention to see that you and I were not something they needed to concern themselves with—that you and I were not *anything* at all. When you called me an asshole and tromped back into the police station? That was good stuff. I mean, I bought it. Anyway, I felt responsible—"

"Because ya *were,* and I meant what I said. And who else might be paying attention?"

He'd moistened a cotton ball with peroxide, and his index finger beckoned me to sit next to him on the sofa. He ignored my question, but I played along.

"You and I make quite the team," he continued while he dabbed the laceration on my cheek. I fought a wince. "You, by chance, oversee your school's drama club? You've got acting chops, Ms. Smith. The students would be lucky to have you."

"Huh?" Okay, I'll admit I got lost in his eyelashes for a moment as he gently cleaned my face. "Who'd be lucky?"

"Anyone." He reached for the Neosporin beyond my thigh, and I sprang to my feet, putting the coffee table between us. "As a teacher," he added. "The students?" Was he back to flirting?

"Thirsty? I'm thirsty. Are you?" I opened my small refrigerator and stuck my head in it, sucking up the cold air. "I've got beer. I've got water. I wasn't expecting company. Sorry."

"Water, please. And I'm not done with you."

"Aren't you, though?" I gulped.

"I meant with your face."

"Yeah, I'm good, and didn't you say you're not the guy for me? Seemed pretty clear earlier. *You* were clear. Crystal. Or was that more play-acting? Because, as I said, I wasn't." I brought him a glass of water he didn't take.

Instead, he stood and re-bagged the medical provisions, eyes only on the task. "Yeah, I did— I was. Clear, I mean. I also felt guilty for getting you into trouble today and wanted to make amends. Dinner seemed an appropriate gesture."

Setting the water on a coaster, I dialed back the brush off for fear he'd take a walk. "Apology accepted."

He lifted his chin. "And maybe I kinda wished the circumstances were—well, not what they are."

"You know what they say?"

"If wishes were horses?" One side of his mouth curled up in a mix of humor and disappointment.

"Fishes," I 'corrected' him.

"Yeah," he paused a beat. "I'm gonna go."

"Why?" It wasn't what I meant to say.

"Because I see you're okay, and it could have been worse, and I have no business turning your simple life upside down."

"Are you calling me simple, Mr. Popov?" My hands found their way to my hips.

"God, no. I—"

"Kidding. You can be so serious, Trey." I met his stunned face with a faked frown. "Do me a favor?"

"Yeah. Name it. Anything, Hattie."

My insides constricted at his use of familiar words I had heard only the day before, but I had a different scene to play now. "Save me." I almost choked on the weak plea. "From myself, this time." I pointed to the paper sack of Chinese food. "Either take that bag with you or stay to help me eat it. And I hope you choose the latter." I forced a sincere look. *Forced?* When I gestured to the sofa, he took a seat. *And the Oscar goes to...*

We ate in comfortable silence, aside from the occasional comment on the cuisine and his asking how my cheek felt. For an outlaw,

Trey Popov proved rather kind, astute, and quite the observer. Scrutiny recognized scrutiny, but Trey observed with impressive subtlety.

With a sated belly, I stuck my chopsticks into the carton of mei fun and leaned into the sofa I shared with Trey, my shoulder inches from his. Making a suspect feel comfortable in his or her surroundings, fed, hydrated, cared for— it's Interrogation 101. Well, one version, anyway. He deftly bent forward and stood. I thought he might be avoiding my closeness. Before I could say anything, his phone buzzed, and he pulled it from his jacket. One glance at the screen and his Adam's apple rose and fell. He dismissed the call and slipped the phone back into his pocket.

"Your Mom?"

He exhaled with a grin.

"Girlfriend?"

"No. No girlfriend."

"That's right. You're not *boyfriend* material." I sat up to snatch a fortune cookie before heading to the kitchen.

"I'm not sure I'm even friend material, Hattie." He followed, carrying cartons of leftovers.

"I'll be your friend, Trey. I've been in the market lately. Thinking about getting one."

"That so?" He handed me an oyster pail of beef and broccoli, and both our fingers and eyes met.

Recoiling into the open refrigerator, I stowed the food. "Not really, no. I'm not very nice." I stalled, taking a moment to rearrange the mustard squeeze-bottle, a box of baking soda, the half 'n half carton, and a mystery foil-wrapped food item; the only items that occupied the sad Frigidaire, other than beer.

"I think you're nice. Maybe too nice."

I had a sudden urge to prove him wrong. *Jesus, Harry.* It was a silent reprimand. Stretching my still-kinked neck, I barely touched his torso in the tight quarters, knowing full well I played with fire. "Excuse me. Tiny kitchen." I squeezed by him.

"Your place is nice. Not much to look at from outside, but inside, very cool. New York City is serious about small living spaces, but yours—kitchen aside—is spacious. Cramped living takes some getting used to. What do you all have against closets?"

"That's what ovens are for. Where're you from?"

"I've been all over." He paced around, anxious, like he needed to find something to keep his hands busy.

I had ideas. *Harry.* "Not a big sharer, are you, Mr. Popov?" I returned to the sofa to give the man some space.

He grimaced even before his phone vibrated again. "Uh, just not—I meant what I said before. I'm not—we're—we shouldn't," he stammered, rejecting the second call.

"Relax, Trey. I see now you're not right for me. No offense. It's an age thing."

He cocked his head, and his brows shot up under the dark curls that grazed his forehead. "I don't imagine I'm more than a few years older than you."

"Yeah," I sighed with a chuckle. "Which makes you a good ten years too *young* for me. More, maybe. You're Jewish, though; that's consistent." I casually flipped over the book that sat on the side table. I didn't need Asher's black and white PR photo staring at me. I thought Trey might comment, but his phone hummed for the third time. "You should answer that. Someone's gonna worry."

He held the pulsating device in his hand.

"Here, I'll go to the loo. Give you some privacy. And you don't have to tell her where you are. Your secret is safe with me. That's what friends do. But you didn't have to lie." In a ballsy move, I patted his chest, appreciating the muscled frame his tracksuit did no favors concealing.

"Lie?"

"It clearly says, 'MOM,' on your phone screen, Trey." I closed the door, pretty confident whoever called sure as hell was not his mother. My guest didn't make it easy, but I listened in, best I could. I heard:

"I'm fine," "Working, what else?" and "I know. I know. I'll do better."

Huh. Maybe it *was* his mom.

The surprise came when he mumbled, "рядом нет никого…"

If anyone wonders when I thought I might be out of my depth, that was it—*that* moment. Me, in my apartment powder room eavesdropping on a supposed criminal I had invited into my home as he spoke Russian to an insistent caller, who likely was not his mother no matter what the caller ID showed. I took a hard look at the reflection of my marred face—my first actual view of the damage. "Jeez, Harry. What the hell are you doing?" I splashed cold water on it and exited the bathroom, intent on getting Trey Popov out of my apartment and out of my life. For good.

"It's getting late." I focused on drying my hands on a small towel I'd brought from the bathroom. When my gaze met his eyelashes, I whispered, "Dammit." *Swim, Harry.*

"Everything all right?" No hint of an accent.

I knew I wasn't playing it cool. "Me? Yeah, one too many spring rolls, probably." No, not my sexiest moment. "Between your mom and my gurgling guts, you should maybe go. It was nice meeting you, Trey." I flung the towel onto my shoulder and folded my arms, dead set on appearing calm.

"Oh, right." Trey looked around the room like he meant to collect whatever belongings he had brought and shrugged at the abrupt end of our evening. Then he kept talking like he didn't want it to be done. "So, I was thinking about that *friend* thing. And how I'm new to town but *way* too young for you and since school's out for the summer, maybe you could—show me around. Play the platonic tour guide or something?" His sincere dark stare squeezed my lungs, and I knew my answer had to be a resounding *no*.

"*Yeah*, definitely. Sure thing. Absolutely. I'm your girl." *Oh, Harry. Welcome to the deep end.*

"Cool."

"Cool." *Not* cool.

"Can I—get your number? Like friends. Not, *hey, can I get your—*"

"Yeah, I get it. Uh. Why don't we just meet up somewhere? The farmer's market runs tomorrow too. See you there? Ten o'clock? Make it eleven." I rushed to change the time. Marty and I needed to talk before I took on the role of Tour Guide to my new Russian-speaking "friend."

"Sure. Sounds like a plan." He may have winced at the phone number snub. He'd live.

I ushered him to the exit. "Thanks for—" I gestured to the vestiges of dinner and Duane Reed, but Trey had tidied it all while I hid in the bathroom. Of course, the man cleaned too. "—everything." I finished my thought.

"Yeah. Quite the first date."

"*Not* a date," I corrected him.

"Right. Friends. Not a date." He brushed aside an unruly curl to see my cheek. His fingers met my scrape, and I sucked in air through clenched teeth.

"Sorry, Hattie." His hand moved to touch my face again, but I ducked from his gesture.

"I'll see you. Tomorrow. Ten, *uh, e-eleven.*"

The man in the black tracksuit moseyed down the hall of my apartment building. My home. The home he wasn't supposed to know existed. He spun back on his sneakered heel and gave a shy wave before putting his hands in his pockets and disappearing into the night.

Nine

My Saturday kicked-off with lots of explaining to do, and Uncle Marty had no plans to go easy on me.

"Just so I'm clear, you have completely lost any notion of boundaries. Is that what I'm hearing? I'm pretty sure that's what I'm hearing because when I told you *not* to let Trey Popov know where you live, you turned around and let Trey Popov know where you live." Uncle Marty's tone would fool anyone walking by his closed-door into thinking an amiable chat took place on the other side. As a participant in that conversation, I'd say "amiable" didn't quite capture the mood.

"I didn't tell him where I live. I didn't lure the man to my residence. He showed up unannounced." I didn't go into the details of the gifts Trey brought, but their memory sparked an inappropriate and poorly timed grin.

"Harriet Smith, is this a game to you?"

I straightened. "No, *Detective* O'Shea. It's not. I promise. But there's more, and I need you to relax."

"Relax? Then you probably should have not suggested I do that, Harry."

"Right. Noted. *Again.*"

"Spit it out, kid."

I had already informed Marty of my plan to meet Trey at the market later that morning and that a "friendly" arrangement had "developed" that involved me showing the new arrival around town, "tour guide-style." I also explained I had made it "clear" to Mr. Popov that he wasn't my "type," so, moving forward, there would be no "misunderstanding" where we stood. And yes, my fingers cramped from all the air quotes.

"He got a call while he was at my place."

"Oh. Interesting." Marty's disposition softened an iota.

"Maybe," I shrugged.

"Do you know *who* called?"

"Well, the call screen displayed, *'MOM.'*"

Marty looked at me, askance.

I read his mind. "No, I don't think it was Mama Popov, either."

"Did you get anything else from the exchange?"

"Not real-ly." I fiddled with a paperclip I had snatched off Marty's desk.

"Why is that?"

"I gave him some privacy to take the call and went into the bathroom," I explained.

Marty gave another incredulous look that demanded to know my reasoning.

"And—I don't—speak Russian." I gave a preemptive flinch.

"Jesus, Mary, and Joseph," Marty whispered.

"*Uncle Marty!*"

It took several minutes to assure Marty the scheme to meet Trey should remain in effect.

"And what if he tailed you here? What if he knows you're here right now?"

"I kinda hope he does because I'm not eager to lie to the man. That's how screw-ups happen. If he asks, I'll tell him you had more questions, and I had no answers, and I'll throw in a little distrust for the police—not out of the realm, considering my experience yesterday." I caught myself before pointing to my scabbed, bruised cheek. "You know, getting cuffed and dragged into a big scary police station for merely walking down the street. He'll trust me more for telling him, and I don't have to keep up with any lies. It's a good test, and I'll pass it with flying colors. Win-win."

"Smart. And where do you see this going? I know we don't have anything on him yet, nothing to bump up the chain. But there's just something about him. I can't put my finger on it. He shows up out of nowhere, on the periphery of some rotten apples, well-connected but has no footprints. And now he speaks Russian, fluently no less, which could definitely make him less peripheral and more dangerous than I first assumed..." Marty got lost in his out-loud thoughts.

"Yeah, I'm beginning to see the difference between theory and practicum is—a lot. Look, nothing will probably come of this. I'm sure Mr. Popov will tire of the dowdy schoolteacher who has him firmly in the friend-zone. If he's still nosing around by the end of the weekend, I'll eat my hat. You can track him some other way, come Monday."

Coming face-to-face with all I lacked in skills despite my years of education, time spent in a van, and the hours of data mining, didn't feel great. The snidest of old adages buzzed in my brain. Those who can do, those who can't... *Shit, Harry.*

"Wow." Trey Popov offered a lidded paper cup and a dazed expression.

I looked over my shoulder, unsure what provoked his amazement. When I realized that *I'd* prompted it, heat crept up my bare chest. The decision to wear sunglasses proved wise. Not only did the wide lenses obscure my scratched face but also the flicker of doe-eyes. *Down, girl.*

To play my role more convincingly, I also actually *wore* a hat, a wide-brimmed sun hat with a long, loose-fitting, spaghetti-strapped sundress in a blue that brought out my eyes—a portrait of wholesomeness. And while I had every intention of keeping close to the truth with the man, donning a *costume* I wouldn't normally wear didn't qualify as lying. No, it *didn't.* I felt pretty cute, too.

"You look—"

"Thank you." I took the beverage, interrupting what might likely be a compliment.

"I didn't know how you took it, so there's a little cream, a little sugar."

"I'm easy—I mean—" I took a sip. "It's perfect." That's when I noticed the distant acoustic guitar, and a small child ran by, brushing against the flowing skirt of my sundress. A young couple, holding hands, walked toward us, and I had a sudden urge to chuck my fresh ground, organic, free trade, sustainably-farmed dark roast into the nearest recycling bin. Dizziness hit. *What was I doing there?*

"Whoa, are you all right?" Trey took my elbow.

"Huh?"

"You good? Kinda wobbled there."

"I'm *well*, thanks." Grammatically-correct Marty flashed in my mind's eye. "Actually, can I tell you something without you getting angry?" Time to wrangle the situation.

He hadn't let go of my arm. "I can't predict how I will or won't react, Hattie, but I'm a pretty even-keeled guy and—we're friends, right? You can tell me anything."

I gave more silent thanks to the universe for the sunglasses and scrutinized Trey. The struggle to see him as the villain was *real*—as they say. My brain couldn't do the calculus. Something didn't add up. That wasn't just me; Marty couldn't figure it either.

"Let's walk, okay?" I sipped my coffee and strolled through the flower section on special display on Saturdays; part of the market I missed because of my regular Friday visits. The scents of freesia, phlox, and lavender wafted. Five-gallon buckets teemed with colorful blooms and lush greens. Not a cloud sat in the portions of the sky not blocked by the city's buildings, and the sun warmed my back in an unfamiliar way. Briefly lost in the beauty of the day, I thought Trey said my "name" more than once before it registered that he was speaking to me.

"Hattie?"

"Sorry, zoned out for a sec. You were saying?"

"No, *you* were saying. Something about me getting angry?" His face hardened some, helping me with the demure role I meant to play.

"Right. So. I had a weird morning."

"Oh, yeah?" He took a swig of coffee and strolled alongside me.

"I got a call—early. From a Detective O'Shea. And I went back to the precinct to talk to him." I kept my slow pace, but my companion had stopped. I twisted to look at Trey standing in the sun wearing a Hunter green tracksuit. How many of those things did the man own? Retracing my steps, I stood close to him, looking up from under the brim of my hat. His body shaded mine. When I removed my sunglasses, Trey winced, seeing my bruised scrape. He lifted my chin further with the knuckle of his bent index finger, and I, unlike the night before, allowed him to stroke my cheek with his thumb. My mouth went dry, but I forced myself to hold his gaze, afraid if I looked away, the man would detect my dishonesty. Then, I realized he already had.

"You got a call, huh?" Somehow he knew I lied. How could he read me so easily? My first lie, and he caught it. Did he bug my apartment when I hid in the bathroom? *Jeez, Harry. Maybe temper the paranoia.*

I shifted, knowing I had to confess. "*Uh*, no. I didn't get a call." I looked him dead on as I came clean. "I went on my own. I went to speak to the man about you of my own volition."

His stare bore into me. "And why's that?"

"Because I think what happened yesterday stinks. I think hauling you in when you did nothing wrong was—*wrong*."

"And why are you so sure I did nothing wrong?"

"Well, you're standing here now. Free. If you'd done something illegal, they'd have locked you up, right? Isn't that how it works? But they didn't. You're here, with me." I took in the scenery and some air before his dark eyes drew me back to his hypnotic gaze.

"You'd be surprised how many dangerous criminals walk the streets freely. Jails are all too full of nice guys caught with dime bags. It's the nefarious ones that get let go." Trey's hard glower almost scared me. Almost.

"Are you a bad man, Alvah Popov, the Third?" Standing too close, my demure-act lost ground. I considered a change in tactic.

"Not gonna lie, Hattie Smith. I've done some bad things."

"That wasn't my question."

"I wouldn't do anything bad to you. I would never hurt you, not on purpose, anyway. I promise you that."

It seemed early for promises, but I was happy to hear it. With a gentle hold on his jacket's zipper pull, I gave a light tug. "Not even if I asked you to?"

His swift grab of my wrist startled me. "We've been over this, Hattie. We're not—"

"I'm joking, Trey." I laughed off the snub and wrenched free of his tight grip, wondering who had put whom in the friend-zone. With a playful shove, I walked away worried reckless Harry had just blown vestal Hattie's cover.

To get my bearings, I stuck my head in a bouquet an aisle away from Trey. When I chanced a look at him, he focused on his phone and his frenetic thumbs typing. Not a good sign, nor was his scowl. I pretended to enjoy the field trip while searching for a way to flee. At the same time, something about the man drew me to him. The ridiculous fortune cookie pickup line about destiny echoed, but then my eyes did their best to roll out of my head. *Earth to Harry.*

The considerable market crowd on Saturday shouldn't have been a surprise, but when I remembered that for many people it was a holiday weekend, with July Fourth falling on Thursday, it made more sense. Grub trucks were often part of the weekly occasion, but they were out in force that Saturday. My stomach rumbled, and I shrugged at my eagerness to eat, even in harrowing circumstances. A mix of food smells overtook the floral aromas by the time I reached the fence at the far end of the market lot. A dead end. If I hadn't sported the long dress, I might have scaled the chain link to escape.

"Looking for an escape?"

I jerked around, the sun blinding me until Trey moved to, once again, provide me shade. He held a bundle of phlox, hydrangeas, and cabbage roses, wrapped in brown paper, tied with jute twine. The sweet smell intoxicated me, as the sizzle of a nearby grill took a backseat.

Ignoring his "escape" quip seemed wise, but I couldn't help but wonder if Trey Popov *did* read minds. "Are those for me?"

"What? These? Oh, no. They're for my mom."

"Shit," I mumbled, a flush of embarrassment burned my cheeks.

"I'm kidding, Hattie." That devilish grin shone again. "Yes, they're for you."

"Oh." Flummoxed, I reached for the gift. "What for?"

"For being a friend. For playing tour guide. For coming to my defense with the cops. Though I'm not sure you made the smart play. I'm not a maiden in need of defending."

"That makes two of us." A blunt silence punctuated my remark.

Trey gave an airy laugh. "I can see that. Let me guess. You were the only girl in a house full of rough-and-tumble boys. You learned to hold your own, huh?"

"Actually, an only child, but after foster care, so—" It wasn't a lie.

"So, the no mother thing?"

"The truth." I encouraged our travel toward the food trucks. Lunchtime. "How about you? I mean, I get you're close to your mom. Hell, she calls to check in on a Friday night."

"Yeah, she's—overprotective sometimes."

We stopped at the end of a queue, and the conversation carried on, the tension from earlier barely noticeable. But the man avoided sharing any of his own details with impressive skill. I recognized the tactic but let it ride, not wanting to appear too eager. Slow and steady, like all investigative work.

We paused a moment to order. "They have the best falafel if you like it." I held up two fingers when Trey nodded. Smiling at the three men hurrying around in the cramped quarters of the raised mobile kitchen, I let Trey pay.

We continued our easy exchange. He was funny and smart, but I shouldn't forget, too young for me—oh, and probably a felon.

"Maybe you should count yourself lucky. Living with a bunch of boys is loud. And smelly. And one dirty joke after another." Trey reached up to the window to take the food the Middle Eastern cook handed him.

"Oh, I do *love* a good dirty joke." I took the warm, foil-wrapped pita dripping with tahini dressing. "Mmm, thank you."

When Trey turned to claim his lunch, one of the cooks gestured to him but obviously spoke to his workmates.

حمر الشعر الذي يحب النكات القذرة؟ يجب أن يتزوجها.

Hearty laughs bellowed from inside the truck until Trey let out a snort, too. They eyed my companion as the frivolity simmered to a low chuckle, and the men all shared a deliberate look before Trey walked away. He never said a word.

I grinned at the trio in the truck, hoping I wasn't the butt of some joke, then jogged to catch up with Trey. "What was that?" I asked.

He took a big bite of his falafel, and I did the same.

With his mouth full, Trey garbled, "Arabic, if I had to guess." He shrugged.

"Yeah, I'd guess Arabic too." I lifted my wrapped pita toward Trey's face. "Just sort of seemed like maybe you underst—"

Trey cocked his head with a grin and casually wiped away a dribble of sauce from my chin. Loaded down with flowers in one hand and my lunch in the other, I had no choice but to watch it happen. The slow-motion exchange made the bustle of our surroundings fade in the intimacy of the tender act. When he brought his thumb to his mouth and licked it clean, the day got hotter.

"You're right. It's delicious." He nudged my chin again and left me speechless in a sea of canoodling coffee dates and small dogs, amid the dulcet tones of an acoustic guitar.

Ten

"And you licked it off his thumb?" Leo stopped to fan himself while packing up a garment bag.

I looked at him from my spot in the beanbag chair. "No, *he* licked it off his *own* thumb."

"Oooh." Leo's enthusiasm wavered. "Still hot, but the healthcare provider in me applauds the more hygienic move." He focused on a shoe rack, unsure which footwear to choose. "All right, what's the deal, Harry?"

"It's nothing."

"*Ha.* Don't be that way. I'm all for a little distraction, and *gurl,* you need one."

"Come on, Leo. He's not my type."

"What's that? Old?"

I scoffed at his teasing. "That and there's sort of a work connection that makes it—inappropriate, let's say." I picked at a string on the seam of my stuffed seat to avoid Leo's eye. I didn't want more questions—or reminders that Trey was a *job,* not a potential—anything else.

"Plus, there's the whole tracksuit situation," Leo added as he zipped his bag.

"Yes." I nodded with a firm scowl affixed, not following. "The *tracksuit* situation."

"I'm all for bad boys, but some evils I cannot overlook."

"And tracksuits are one such evil?" I asked.

"Right up there with—well, they're right up there. Let's leave it at that. Now, I've got to fly." He flung the long bag over his shoulder and looked around the living room with his hand at his hip. "Now, where's my broom?" He laughed and then helped me to my feet. "You should call him."

"But you just said—"

"Don't listen to me—except *call* him."

"I don't know how," I grumbled.

"What?"

"I don't have his number. Wait a second." Inspiration hit—the silly, I've-read-too-many-spy-novels, what-if kind of inspiration. "Come to my place."

"Now? I've gotta go. I'm schlepping on the train to get to my gig."

"Come with me for a sec, and I'll get you a car. Humor me. Auntie Leo will not *schlep* tonight," I hollered and skipped to my door.

Leo dropped his bag to follow me, but before we entered my flat, I stopped him. "When we go in, speak casually but say what you just said. The— I should call him— thing."

My neighbor narrowed his eyes with suspicion.

"Just do it." I shoved the immovable man.

He gestured for me to open my door.

"You should call him," Leo droned with a sneer.

I punched his arm, then said my line. "Ugh. I don't know how."

My neighbor looked at me with wide eyes and raised shoulders. "What?"

I flailed my hands, motioning for him to keep talking.

"I mean, what do you mean? You don't have his number?"

"Nope."

"Well, maybe he calls you?"

"I didn't give him my number, either."

"You're an idiot." Leo's comment had only half to do with phone numbers. "What are the chances he shows up out-of-the-blue again?"

I gave an enthusiastic thumbs up. "That's good," I mouthed, then spoke aloud, "Maybe."

"Whatever." Leo wanted to be done with the game he didn't understand we were playing. "I'll leave your ticket at the door. Get dolled up and get your perky ass to Astoria by nine o'clock. And bring your checkbook. It's for charity.

"*Um*, okay, but what's a checkbook?" I gave him my best serious look, only to have Leo return it with his own playful shove. "You know you don't have to comp my ticket. I can buy my own."

"I know." Leo touched his finger to the end of my nose. "That's what makes me so nice. And now I'm feeling *super* generous, so just in case the track star shows, I'll leave two. Now order my ride. I'm hitting the sidewalk in two minutes. Tops. By-eee."

Before I could reply, Leo flew out the door. I grabbed my phone to order his Uber to a gallery in Astoria, the venue for an art auction with a cabaret act, featuring my talented friend, all to support a local art school. There would be a cash bar and maybe some food, but honestly, the liquor would be all I needed.

I tiptoed around the first floor of my apartment, surveying every lampshade and fingering every picture and door frame in search of some improbable listening device. "You *are* an idiot, Harriet," I grumbled, then sniffed the fragrant bouquet my "friend" had given me earlier in the day. For good measure, I added, "Alvah Popov, the Third, would never just show up." I waited for a beat, then laughed at my absurd behavior. With a sigh, I took the stairs two at a time to pull together jeans, a t-shirt, and a jacket to wear to Astoria. Black strappy heels would make it my version of fancy.

The knock at my door startled me. "I ordered the car, Leo. Promise." Reaching the bottom of the stairs, I flung open the door. "It's Saturday night. Be patient—*Trey?*"

"Hi."

"Hi." I twisted around to see my living room again. *Was* it bugged? No. He'd have to be listening from some place pretty close by to— "How'd you get in here?"

"Leo let me in." His blink made me wonder if that was true. "Almost didn't recognize me at first—"

"Yeah, well, no tracksuit." I pointed from a casual lean in my doorway.

"What?"

"Nothing." We fidgeted for an awkward moment. "You look handsome."

He did, too, dressed in dark, tailored pants and a crisp white dress shirt with loosely rolled cuffs. Forearm porn for days.

"Thank you. It's Saturday night, so—"

"It is." I nodded and bit my top lip.

More fidgeting. "I didn't have your number, and I know better than to think you don't have plans, but I thought I'd take a shot and show up—out-of-the-blue to see if you were free."

"Oh." The phrase "out-of-the-blue" made the hair on my arms rise. "I do." I folded my limbs across my chest. "Have plans, that is."

"Right. Of course, you do."

"Yeah."

"Okay." He pointed over his shoulder, and his black leather loafers chirped on the tile floor. They looked expensive.

"You should ask again." I turned on some flirting—for Marty's sake, of course.

"Ask what?"

"For my phone number. Since this tour guide thing seems to be working out—it'd be easier to have my number. And I *could* make myself available—albeit unscheduled—for more sightseeing *tonight*—if a trip to Astoria appeals. Just don't go making it a habit, yeah?"

"Something tells me you might be habit-forming, Hattie." He may have been trying for witty banter, but his grave face said otherwise. Sometimes I thought there might be two Treys, and both of them appealed to me.

I winced. "I'm sure that's not something you meant to say to your *friend,* Trey." Talk like that needed to be quashed, didn't it? The thump in my chest said so. "Anyway, there will be art and booze, and my neighbor is performing, plus dancing."

My heart sank when he shook his head with a grimace. Disappointed—for Marty's sake, of course.

"No. No dancing. I haven't danced since Miriam Jagoda's bat mitzvah."

"Oh. I see. Well, I'm committed to seeing Auntie Leo so—"

"No, the rest all sounds great. I'm in; besides, I've met your aunt, and he's got five inches on me, easy. No way I'm getting in the middle of that."

I reached across my apartment threshold, taking hold of Trey's muscular arm. Heat radiated from it. "I should probably confess something."

"What's that?" He eyed my grasp of his limb.

"Leo's not really my aunt."

Trey threw back his head, allowing me another sample of his charming laugh, and the tension eased. "Good to know."

"So, yeah, I really lucked out with this place. It's like it's incognito," I shouted from the upstairs, having left my guest with a beer, to give me time to revisit my attire for the evening. Jeans and t-shirt wouldn't cut it next to the track star *sans* tracksuit. Damn, he cleaned up good. I pouted at the reflection of my bruised, scraped cheek, and dabbed on lip gloss before darting downstairs. "Well," I sighed, "if no one looks at me from the neck up, I'll do."

Trey held his beer mid-swig and choked on his swallow. "Mission accomplished," he coughed.

I curtsied in a sleeveless, black, wide-legged jumpsuit. The front draped low, showing just enough cleavage, and the back dipped twice as far. I twirled in a way I swear I have never done before. *Get a grip, Harry.*

"Whoa, coming *and* going." My admirer guzzled the rest of his drink.

"Come on. I ordered a ride. It's twenty minutes by car, and I'm not taking the train in these heels."

Trey followed me out the door.

Eleven

The car ride to Astoria included friendly chatter and lots of pointing to show off neighborhood hotspots. I took my tour guide responsibilities seriously. But a few blocks from the gallery, instinct kicked in, and with it an urge to walk the rest of the way. We were already late, but I guessed Leo would forgive and forget when I walked in with the track star.

"Pull over here, will you, Chip? I'd like a stroll." The rideshare driver veered to the curb, and I scooted from the car. Trey followed. I met the sidewalk with my phone vibrating. A glance showed Uncle Marty's name, but it was not the time, so I dismissed the call. My date, who wasn't a date, gave a curious squint.

"What?" I asked.

Trey pointed to the car nosing back into traffic.

"Yeah, I don't think his name is Chip, either." I crinkled my nose and slipped my phone back into my pocket that held everything I'd require for the night, half-wishing I didn't need the cumbersome device. It mucked up the silhouette. "I swear, lots of those drivers pick another name for their job—a *nom du conducteur* kinda thing." I snorted at my French play on words. "We're a couple blocks up. You don't mind a walk in the fading twilight, do you?" I smiled, hoping I had distracted him enough to move on without questions about phone calls or impromptu mid-trip drop-offs.

"You're an odd bird, Hattie Smith. You open your mouth, and I can never guess what's coming. And you were the one who said we were late, plus it's hot, but sure, I'm following you."

I jutted my hip. "'Cuz ya like the view?" I gave an exaggerated wink. But before wet-blanket-Trey replied with an astonished denial, I wagged my hand. "Kidding, Trey. Just kidding. You're so serious. Let's go." Maybe the time had come for me to admit Trey Popov just wasn't that into me.

The streets of Astoria sat oddly quiet. The hours between the close of daytime businesses and the rush of the nighttime variety made for a stillness you might not expect. In an hour, the avenues would pulse with electronic dance music and the raucous fun of bar patrons stumbling from one watering hole to another, or stepping out to smoke their vice of choice. For now, car traffic played in the background, accompanied by the beep and vocal countdown commands of crosswalk speakers at major intersections.

I dove in for some recon. "How's it you're off tonight, Trey? I'd think a guy in the Birkin bag security game would be on duty on a Saturday evening. Not that I'm complaining. The notion I have my very own Kevin Costner for a night makes me wanna do somethin' reckless. As long as you're twentieth-century Kevin, not the current version." With our leisurely pace, I watched the man's laid back gait with his hands in his pockets, pleased to notice that his broad shoulders and handsome profile with tanned skin, and just the right amount of stubble, didn't distract me in the slightest. Come on, a girl can look.

That's when it registered that his unhurried stride slowed further, and Trey clocked two male figures approaching us a long block away. Jaw clenched, he spoke inaudibly, but whatever he said, it wasn't in English.

He avoided eye contact when he spoke aloud. "Do you—trust me, Hattie?"

I only paused a moment. "Not even a little."

He exhaled out his nose and grinned, giving me a glimpse of his lighthearted version. "Good." His reply surprised me.

"If I ask you to duck into the alley, we'll reach in—ten meters, will you?"

I stopped. "That'd be a hard no."

"I'd rather not make you, and we've been alone in your apartment. Twice. If I was going to do something improper, wouldn't I try it there, not on a public street?"

He had a point, and I cursed the brazen improvisation that got me in the spot in the first place.

"Maybe, but I don't know your kink?" Officer Lina was always good for a line to steal.

"My kink?" He shook his head with a furrowed brow. His serious side took the lead. "If we don't make this move in the next five seconds, they'll notice us if they haven't already." His elbow squeeze sent a nervy *zing* down my arm, and that pain provided enough distraction, allowing him to nudge me into the alley and to the far side of a dumpster. For the second time in as many days, someone had shoved me against a warm brick building. Truth be told, aside from the elbow *zing* thing, I preferred this time over the first, but mild panic hit, and my go-to had always been to crack wise.

"Gee, Trey. Is that a gun in your pocket, or are you—*oh my God,* is that a gun in your pocket?" My panic spiked.

"It's a knife and it's not exactly in my pocket, but I'm going to need you to stop talking now." His hot breath burned directly in my ear to dizzying effect. Seconds ticked by, and I thought we stood in the shadows for too long.

"Where—"

"Shhh," he cut me off. "Wait for it."

Not far away, laughter sounded, followed by the scuff of hard soles on concrete and the hushed voices of amiable chit-chat. They chatted in Russian.

From our spot in the dark, Trey and I held our breaths as two well-dressed, middle-aged men crossed the alleyway's entrance. When one stopped and then the other, I thought they caught us. *Caught? By whom? For what?* The taller of the two pulled a slim box from his pocket and opened it. On tiptoes, I stretched for a better view, only to have Trey push his chest more firmly into mine. I gasped, but the unmistakable *clink* and *scratch* of an old-fashioned Zippo lighter obscured my yelp. Trey's hand clamped my mouth. Eyes shut tight, I held that gulped air, hoping to hear the foreign conversation fade away, telling me the men continued down the block.

When Trey gradually freed my mouth, I took another slow draw of air. My nostrils flared at the stench of garbage, and with a swift jerk, I landed my knee in Trey's groin. A fast knuckled jab to his stomach followed. I didn't intend to incapacitate the man, so I quit before landing my elbow on his shoulder blade as he stooped in pain. But I wanted to be sure I had his full attention. He groaned with my release and stayed bent, wide-eyed, with a pinched mouth while I adjusted my jumpsuit and tucked a wayward curl behind my ear. The humidity wreaked havoc on my hair.

Trey needed a minute before he could speak, so I forged ahead. "Don't you *ever* do that again. Is that clear?" I snarled. The game had escalated, and despite the ill-advised pitter-pats in my chest, the doe-eyed routine ended then and there.

Still crumpled, Trey nodded.

"And now, I want some answers."

He nodded again.

"Who were they? Why did you hide from them? And how does a knife that size stay in your pants? Because it felt pretty big. Impressive, actually." I kept my interrogation to a whisper.

Trey straightened and raised his index finger, straining for a breath.

"Oh, right. Whenever you're ready." I waved before my hands found my hips, and I surveyed the toe of one of my strappy heels I couldn't see in the dark.

He expelled a low grunt before opening his mouth to speak. "Associates of mine, colleagues, let's say."

"Bit excessive for avoiding some coworkers, Trey. I get not wanting to mix business with pleasure—not that I'm—pleasure, but—"

"You've never met my coworkers, and not gonna lie, Hattie. I've had better dates." He wheezed his words.

"Well, this isn't a date, and whatever it is, it's over."

I was onto something now, and no way did I plan to let this evening end there, but Trey needed to work for it. And the rush? Hiding in the dark? Without the safety of the van? His body pressed to—well, I digress. The opportunity to employ my self-defense training some place *other* than in the ring at the gym sealed it. Plus, if I could get even a smidgeon of intel to take back to Uncle Marty, I would feel satisfied and then make a quick finale of this crumbling charade.

"Goodnight, Trey." I walked away, relieved to feel a modicum of breeze as I approached the street.

"Hattie, hold up."

The back of the jumpsuit looked *good* and worked like a charm. I kept walking.

"Let me explain." He'd caught up, but I didn't dawdle.

"You can talk, it's a free country, but I'm headed to see Leo and some art."

"Okay. I'm new to this—organization I'm working for, and there's a probationary period. A trial hiring until I prove myself, I guess. I'm on my boss's wife's detail, and she is away for a while, but I didn't make the team that made the trip with her. Not sure why, and it's not like I'm in a position to ask, so I just have to wait it out. That's left me with some free time."

I may have slowed my pace. No sense getting to our destination now that the man started to talk.

"Anyway, I've noticed some odd behavior, and I don't think most of my coworkers are very nice people. Not one hundred percent sure my boss is either. Getting picked up by the police yesterday? Not the first time. But I don't know anything so they can keep cuffing me, I guess but—and there seems to be an awful lot of scrutiny into employees' lives, by 'management,' I guess you'd call them, including who we spend time with off the clock. I didn't want you to be seen with me and get caught up in any of that, which is why I shouldn't have pursued you in the first place. I know better. My gut told me better, and I'm sorry."

I stopped under a streetlamp, hoping my interest in his story would encourage him to keep sharing. It did.

"Sorry for the Fourth of July, too. I thought you were following me *for* my boss. Checking up on me. Dumb, I know. But I got paranoid and then the farmer's market made me doubt even more, but then the cops and cuffs thing happened, and I'm *really* sorry about that, and you were so nice to wait for me, but I didn't want the weirdly watchful eye of my fellow goons to catch us together or the cops to think you knew me. If I'd known—I mean, if I thought you were— I never would have come on so—I wouldn't have spoken to you like I did at the park or the market. That's not me."

The tale of two Treys was making sense.

"Look, I was right the first time. I'm not the guy for you, the *friend* for you. I've never had 'normal.' 'Normal' has never worked for me, and I know that, *have* known that all my life. And I came to New York fully resigned to that fact. But when— I met a girl at a park and again at a farmer's market, and she was funny and smart, tough, but kind and—pretty—for a moment, it all felt so *normal*. Possible even."

Many thoughts flooded my brain at that moment. I'd mull over most of those at another time, but first and foremost, I thought Marty sure knew how to pick them. If anyone could be a C.I., Alvah Popov, the Third qualified. A good guy with bad luck in a horrible and extremely pliable circumstance. Sucked to be him. And second, I pitied the poor bastard. Everything he said squared with what I knew to be true. And what I didn't *know*, I believed anyway.

"Let me tell you a few things, Trey, then I'm going inside to hear my fabulous friend sing while I plunk down too much money on some kid's finger-painting. One. I'd hardly call what you've done *pursuing* me. Particularly for a guy who came out of the gate like *Bam!* The sixty-to-zero whoa-up makes more sense now. Two. I don't know your coworkers, but if they're *goons*, I wouldn't count you among them, not even a little, and three. What the hell does normal look like? Seriously, and who'd want it, anyway?" I placed my hand on the door to the gallery. "I do have one question." I paused, unsure if my fascination might give me away.

Trey waited patiently in the fluorescent light of a building sconce, then raised his chin, reading my mind again. Spooky, but sort of cool. "It's a Cold Steel Leatherneck fixed blade, American Tanto, seven inches in a slim holster around my hips. The knife runs down my thigh. Not ideal because of access issues, but better than nothing. I'd feel naked without it."

I pressed my lips together in a tight line and jiggled my head. "Well, no one wants to think about that, Trey." I pulled open the door, and Leo's melodious voice wafted an ironic Etta James tune about trust. "And since Leo comped your ticket, you should come in and buy me a drink, at least."

Trey took a breath like a death-row inmate given a reprieve. "I'm following you." He held the door for me, just over my head.

"'Cuz you like the v—?"

"Yes, I do. Very much," he quickly interrupted, but a glimmer of sweetness snuck past his serious façade as he ushered me into the gallery.

Twelve

The large gallery featured worn, narrow, wood plank floors and bare mechanicals circuiting the high ceiling, with fairy lights hung from steam pipes and air returns. A well-stocked bar welcomed us, along with buffet tables of assorted finger foods only meant to slow alcohol absorption. As it turned out, drinks were free, but cash donations would be "greatly appreciated" and, my cynical guess, the big moneymaker for the night.

I walked toward the makeshift stage, catching a scowl from Leo as he pointed to a watch he didn't wear. The singer's frown turned upside down when Trey met me with a coupe glass filled to the brim, garnished with a lime.

He spoke in my ear to counter the music's noise and the attendees' rollicking time. "I'm a vodka man myself, but I've heard gin is for drinking in the summer heat, and lime always refreshes. It's a gimlet."

"If it's cold and wet, it's perfect. Thank you."

Bistro tables and chairs dotted the center of the hall, and a dance floor stood between those tables and a raised platform holding the band and my Auntie Leo. They relegated the evening's supposed spotlight, the art, to the edges, lining the walls and display canvases on casters, forming two aisleways on each side of the large room. Exposed brick held framed art, as did both faces of the moveable exhibits. Guests could sit, stand, browse, or dance, but the hope was for money to flow.

The musical number ended, and the band announced their break. I crossed to speak to Leo.

"You're late but forgiven, given your companion." He wiggled fingers at Trey. "No fraternizing, so I have to scoot, but thank you for coming. Eat, drink, be merry. Buy art. I'll catch ya later." He blew a kiss, not letting me get in a word.

"Wanna browse? I don't think I'm leaving here empty-handed, so I might as well get to shopping." I gestured to one side of the room, and Trey followed. Walking along the periphery, I slowed at each piece, giving the appearance I considered every display. I did not. On the plus side, unlike what I originally thought, talented artists created the works, not grade school children as I'd feared. I'm no connoisseur, but some of the examples held some appeal. When I happened upon one I appreciated, I looked to Trey for his opinion, but he paid the exhibit no attention. His dark eyes were everywhere else.

"What are you doing?"

"Huh?" Trey's eyes kept moving.

"What. Are. You. *Doing*?"

"I'm watching."

"Watching what?"

"People, work staff versus patrons. Counting exits, counting chairs, counting empty glasses."

"You're one hell of a date, Trey."

"Thought this wasn't a date." A grin flashed. Kinder Trey. I liked it.

"You can say that again." Streamed music played, and the dance floor filled. "I'll leave you to your—counting, *Mr. Costner*. Grab a seat. Even though you don't, *I'm* gonna dance." I handed him my empty glass and spun away to join the grooving masses.

Two songs later, I needed another gimlet. On my toes, I motioned to catch Trey's eye amid the bouncing heads and shoulders of the crush on the dance floor. He sat at a distant bistro table, but he wasn't alone. Two men stood between Trey's spot and mine. I bobbed and weaved my way through the crowd, only to see him shake me off, like a catcher to his pitcher. His eyes implored me to stay away, but that wasn't in the cards. And while I might be mixing *all* the metaphors, I had no intention of hitting the brakes when I saw an easy lob sailing across the plate. No offense to Trey, but I had a job to do and no sense wading in the kiddie pool if I could snag a bigger fish on my line.

"Another drink? Don't mind if I do. Thank you very much." I sidled past the two strangers, noticing they bore some resemblance to one another, though at least a generation apart. The younger man stood taller than his elderly cohort and had dark curls like Trey, but longer. They included some product that slicked back his hair in an unattractive style, and it had a funny smell. Musky with some spice. I didn't like the look or the aroma but offered my most captivating grin despite it.

The older man was gray and liver-spotted but still spry, from what I could tell. "Won't you introduce us to your friend, Alvah?" His accent more than hinted at Eastern Europe. No shock there.

Trey moved to stand.

"I told you to keep your seat, Alvah. You really need to learn to follow directions." The old man's tone sounded jovial, but something sinister shaded it.

"Mr. Trubetzkoy, this is a new acquaintance of mine." Trey nodded to me. His balled fists and offset jaw added to my mounting concerns.

"And her name, boy? Don't be impolite." Mr. Trubetzkoy's eerie smirk flaunted an obvious joy at putting Trey in his place.

Trey stretched his neck an inch and returned to his chair. "Hattie Smith, this is Gleb Trubetzkoy, the generous man I told you was my employer."

"Oh, yes," I smiled at all three men. "To be honest, I haven't heard much about you. Trey is pretty tight-lipped about work stuff. But he loves your wife's Bichon Frise, so he was a little bummed to get sidelined for her recent trip: her loss, my gain. Trey's a real go-getter. Eager to climb the ladder, but what do I know? We just met a couple days ago."

"Aren't you charming?" Gleb chuckled. "Didn't you say you wanted a drink?"

Trey shifted again.

"Vlad will get it. What can my nephew get for you, my dear?"

"A gimlet, extra gin, please." I caught another subtle head shake from Trey as Vlad lumbered to the bar.

"What brings you here, Mr. Trubetzkoy? Art lover?" I slathered on more of the aforementioned charm.

"My niece teaches at the school. Anya, Vlad's sister. My sister's children. Life didn't bless me with children of my own since I fell ill as a child and—well, I have my niece and nephew. Anya is quite talented, I think. Vlad is an idiot. How he has lived this long, I'll never know. удача, I guess." Context said he probably meant luck of some sort, but the disdain for his nephew was clear.

The disparaged Vlad returned with my drink. Apparently, I was the only one partaking in this round. Trey's discreet head jiggle as he shot daggers at the glass in my hand told me what I needed to know. Message received.

"Won't you let me show you Anya's contribution to this evening's event? I regret to inform you, I have already bought the piece, so unless you plan to up the price—" Gleb let the rest of the statement hang.

"I'd love to see your niece's work." I didn't imagine walking the room with the geezer would be a problem, and instinct told me I didn't want to be anywhere near the idiot nephew. I took the arm the old man offered. Trey tried to stand again.

"Vladislav, why don't you keep Alvah company while Ms. Smith and I tour the exhibit. Alvah, be a good little Bichon. Сиди и оставайся."

No, I don't speak Russian, but when a master tells his dog to *sit and stay,* the language hardly matters.

Before we wandered away, I deposited the drink on the table. The music volume died down, or it seemed to my ear, but a tinny hum bombarded me, and the overhead fairy lights smeared. I reminded myself where I was and what I knew how to do if anxiety didn't overtake my senses. Leo's return to the mic and Gleb's speaking brought me to focus.

"Here it is. Anya's painting. She calls it *A Girl, Stuck.* I don't understand her meaning. It's just a girl sitting in a chair. A self-portrait, actually, but she isn't stuck. No one is holding her captive. No one tied her to that seat. Perhaps she sat in glue?" Gleb laughed. "What do you think?"

The oil on canvas caught my breath, more so when Trubetzkoy spoke the artwork's title aloud. What can I say? It resonated. "I think it's— beautiful. I see sadness perhaps, but she's a pretty girl in a pretty room surrounded by pretty things. It's also as if she knows something the rest of us don't. It's—it's lovely." I meant every word I said.

"You're lovely." The old man's tone had a new flavor to it, and when he ran his crooked finger down the length of my bare arm with a hum, I threw up a little in my mouth, momentarily stunned—no doubt, the slimy pervert's intention. *Focus, Harry.*

"Mr. Trubetzkoy?"

"Yes, my dear?"

"I'm sorry you've gotten the wrong impression here."

"Oh, don't be silly, Ms. Smith. There's no need to feel embarrassed; to be bashful, though it is enchanting."

"Oh, you misunderstand. The wrong impression? I'm not lovely. I don't feel embarrassed, I'm not bashful, and I sure as hell am not enchanting. And if you touch me like that again, I will snap your wrist, and because you're so old, maybe your ulna in two other places— because that's just how easy geriatric bones break." It disappointed me to hear the man's chuckle again, and his simper sent a chill down my frame.

"I'll take feisty over enchanting any day. Good evening, Hattie Smith."

I spun on my heel, eager to get out of the darkened corner and back into the crowd. Rounding the canvas on casters, I collided into a wild-eyed Trey. He held a drink.

"Is that dosed?" I pointed to the glass.

"Not this one, no."

"You sure?"

"Hattie, of course."

Snatching the cocktail, I downed it in three big swallows, scanning the room for Gleb. He'd vanished.

"Where's Vlad?"

"*Uh*, he didn't feel so great after he drank from your other drink. He's a big boy, though. He'll be fine."

"Isn't he the one who drugged it?"

Trey shrugged. "Must have forgotten. He's a notorious idiot. Are you all right?"

"Shut up." My anger found a misplaced target.

"Hattie, are you—"

"I'd be better if we had never met. I'll *be* better when you go away and don't come around again. And you should get as far from Gleb Trubetzkoy and his goon squad as soon as you can, and I mean, now."

"Did he say something? Do something? Touch you?"

I shoved Trey. "I'm not your damsel, Trey. I'm no Whitney to your Kevin. Get away from me. If you care even the slightest bit—go away." I meant every word of that, too. I'd seen some crappy things in my time, heard crappier stories, but this was the first time I ever stood that close to decrepit evil. Way out of my depth, I came away unscathed. Next time, I guessed I wouldn't be so fortunate.

"Did someone say Whitney because if ya did, *I Will Always Love*— am I interrupting something?" Leo appeared out of nowhere, a feat for a man his size.

Trey and I stood face-to-face. A standoff, but I blinked first.

"Trey's hitting the road. Movin' along. Leaving the building, as it were. With the promise never to darken my doorstep again. Right, Trey?"

"Hattie," he practically whispered.

"*Right*, Trey?" My volume climbed.

"Har-Hattie? Honey?" Leo murmured that time, taking my hand in concern.

Trey cleared his throat. "You were terrific tonight, Leo. Great set. If you practice medicine half as well as you sing, Queens' healthcare system is beyond privileged."

"Well, aren't you the—"

My elbow met Leo's ribs.

"—the, um, *worst*?" My neighbor bumped my shoulder as he moved away.

"I'm coming home with you, Leo. I'll get a car," I shouted over my shoulder, keeping my eye-lock on Trey.

"Whatever, honey. I'll be another hour, at least." Leo sighed with his hands flapping at his ears.

"Goodbye, Trey." My dismissal left no room for doubt.

He didn't reply but slid his hands into his pockets, and I remembered the blade resting on his thigh. I hoped he never needed to use it. His gaze met the floor like he searched for something to say to make the scene end a different way. He couldn't find it. Instead, he twisted past me and left.

Thirteen

Leo gabbed the entire Uber ride home, knowing I wouldn't want to share details of my night's disaster. It took him more than an hour to wrap-up an impromptu song request, the stage strike, thanking band members, and glad-handing art school patrons. I also "bought" him a drink and myself a couple. Okay, three. In our ride with our driver "Bob," Leo let loose about every glitch and error made on stage that night. No one would have been the wiser.

"It does feel good to give back, though. Help some while doing something I love." He rested his head and stared at the city sliding by as we made the trip home.

Saturday night traffic slowed us, and what took twenty minutes for Trey and me timed in at almost forty-five on the return. The last image I wanted to dwell on pounded my temple, and I knew I needed to engage with Leo or get lost in the look of *someone's* sad eyes and dark lashes.

"Wait. That wasn't a paying gig?"

"It's for the *artists*, honey," Leo cooed, dismissing my concern.

"Some of whom have families who could buy the block, much less the building. You should get paid."

"Did you not hear the part about giving back?" He patted my thigh. "I'm going to forgive your lateness, empty hands, *and* grumpy mood because your week just keeps on giving. Though a little goodwill wouldn't hurt. With the ongoing karmic bitch-slap happening over there, well, let's just say I'm not feeling very comfortable sitting this close to you." Leo inched toward his side of the backseat in a dramatic cower.

We crawled out of the car, and I sucked in air that wasn't cool or fresh and would never be both of those things, ever. The booze had gone to my head, but I was sleepy more than drunk and almost smiled, knowing I'd fall into bed in two flights and three minutes, give or take.

My strappy heels encouraged me to lean on Leo's colossal frame as we climbed the concrete stairway. Stepping into the dim hall, I flinched with sudden sobriety. A few yards away, a package leaned, propped against my apartment door. I didn't speak.

"*Aw*, you *did* buy something. Organizers said they'd offer delivery for some of the larger pieces, but it's awfully late and how'd they get in here?" We stood, arm in arm, staring at the brown paper-wrapped square resting against the doorframe. "Harry," he chastised, "did you not pull the front door tight—*again*?"

"*Uh*, Trey followed me out, maybe he—? But I didn't buy anything. I tried to show Trey a piece I liked, but—"

"*Ooh*, a man who buys you art? That's sexy. But show me another time. I'm whooped and off to some tunes and a steamy bath. Tomorrow is my sleeping day." Leo raised his fist in triumph, kissed the top of my head, and entered his apartment.

Leo's door latched, and the bolt *clunked* while I stared at the mystery gift. Guilt for spurning Trey singed my insides. I bent to pick it up but stayed in the squat and peeled open the wrapping. The pretty girl's eyes gaped back at me: *A Girl, Stuck.* The fire in my belly froze as I fell back on my ass.

I wheezed, "Leo?" through a tight throat and rolled back onto my strappy heels, resting my chin on my knees. My trembling fingers reached to touch the black frame like I tried to convince myself it wasn't there. That the pretty girl sitting in a pretty room surrounded by pretty things was a mirage, a figment of my tipsy imagination, but my mind didn't work that way. My psyche never played with such cruel creativity. Grabbing the bundle, I wobbled to stand, ready to knock on Leo's door, begging for one of our sleepovers. But the hardworking man had just declared his exhaustion, elated at having a "sleeping day." I couldn't disrupt that simple pleasure. Big girl panties officially hitched; I was on my own. The artwork was a warning shot, and Mr. Trubetzkoy's message clear.

The cumbersome load balanced on a bent knee with one hand while I unlocked the bolt with my other. The hinges moaned open, horror film-style. I'd never noticed the sound effect but only paused a second, disappointed to find Trey must have flipped off the light switch when we left earlier. I hated walking into a darkened apartment. Arms full of art, I pushed through the doorway. Hunched, my elbow missed the light switch while I hooked the door with my ankle to close it, careful not to let it slam.

A distinct spicy musk hit my nose an instant before fingers gripped my throat and rammed me against my closed door. I dropped the painting, but it landed on my assailant's foot in a muffled thud.

"The *painting*, Vlad, the *painting*," Gleb Trubetzkoy scolded his nephew from across the dark room. "And don't hurt the girl. She has value. Redheads fetch top dollar. Second only to virgins. And a redheaded virgin? Any chance you're a virgin, Ms. Smith? Please, say *yes*."

"Need to be sure the carpet matches the drapes, Uncle Gleb. Pick me to find out." Learning Vlad could speak was a letdown, regardless of his first words. But his first words were—*gross*. It got worse. Vlad bent his head to my cheek, running the tip of his tongue along my jawline to my ear. If he hadn't held me by the throat, I would have introduced him to my patella, like I had Trey in the alley, but harder. Much, much harder.

A lamp clicked on, and like an awful stereotype, the mise-en-scène included the ominous Uncle Gleb relaxed in an armchair, his scowling face just out of the throw of the dim incandescent bulb. The missing bowl of walnuts to crush played like a prop guy's bungled cue.

"Vlad, you are so—what's the word? Crass. Like father, like son. Stands to reason, I suppose. Now, Ms. Hattie Smith, if I have my nephew let go of your throat, do you promise to behave? No, yelling or kicking or scratching, as women often do?" He spoke like a sweet grandfather, but his sinister words said otherwise.

I squeaked out an affirmative.

"Promise?" Gleb asked again.

I nodded best I could with Vlad's grip still firmly around my neck.

"Let go, Vlad. Let go and apologize for your rude behavior."

"But—"

"*Vladislav*, apologize." The icy demand reminded me of the evil in the room despite the reprieve.

Think, Harry.

Vlad did as he was told with the pout of an eight-year-old. My hands went straight to my throat with its release, and I gasped in the freedom. The men were despicable beings, but the dynamic between the two made the scene so much worse.

"Sit, Vlad."

I found some solace in knowing Gleb treated most people like dogs. Okay, not really, but I grasped for an upside. Vlad obeyed his uncle and sat on the sofa. My mind wandered to thoughts of Scotch-guard, but I snapped to when a timid knock sounded directly behind me.

It could only be Leo, probably looking for bubble bath or a few of those gossip rags I kept around for long stakeouts. I hoped he'd assume I'd fallen asleep in my tipsy state. Suffice it to say, Gleb and Vlad were the ultimate in buzzkills. The knock sounded again, followed by a hushed appeal. My stomach rose and fell, but it all ended in an abyss.

"Hattie, it's me. Trey. Please let me in. We need to talk."

"My my. I couldn't have planned this better if I tried. Answer the door, Ms. Smith. Let the boy in, because he's right. We absolutely need to talk."

"That's right—"

"Vladislav, do not speak again unless I address you. Is that clear? Now open the door, Ms. Smith. *Now.*"

I rotated and clutched the doorknob, wishing I had kicked off my heels. Maybe I could have made a run for it. Too late for that. Plan B. I inched open the door. A disheveled Trey leaned on the doorframe. A bead of sweat streaked his cheek, and he'd untucked his once-crisp white dress shirt with enough buttons undone that I could see his undershirt and a small Star of David on a length of gold chain.

"You're—" Trey's eyes perked up at seeing me.

"Run," I whispered.

"What?" He squinted in confusion.

"*Run, please,*" I gritted.

"Let the boy in, Ms. Smith," Gleb called from deep inside my apartment.

Trey pushed open the door and barged across the threshold, nearly knocking me down with his bulldozing entrance. My first instinct was to flee but leaving Trey behind didn't feel like an option. And what about Leo? *Who's* the idiot?

"Mr. Trubetzkoy, this is too much. Hattie is no concern of yours. She is just some girl I met. Unimportant. A schoolteacher, no one to worry about. Let's just leave her alone, forget about her. She's nobody."

Ouch.

Gleb *tut-tutted* from his shadowy spot in my armchair. "Have a seat, Alvah."

"I'm fine to stand, sir." Trey's civility dumbfounded me. What kind of brainwashed oaf continued to show respect to a monster instead of bolting for the nearest escape hatch? What power did the old man have over this young one?

"Oh, I think you'll want to sit for this next bit." Gleb indicated Trey should sit next to Vlad. "It's about to get interesting."

Those words sent another chill through me. I looked at the painting lying on the floor, mostly covered by its brown paper wrapping. With all but the pretty young woman's face hidden, and she ogled me. A Girl, Stuck. *Preach, Anya.*

"Tell me, Alvah. How did you two kids meet? You and Ms. Smith here?"

"We met at Gantry Plaza. Thursday. Fourth of July."

"Is that right?" Gleb leered at me.

I nodded.

"Fireworks, was it?" The letch smirked.

"Something like that. Yes, sir. Then the next day, we bumped into one another at a farmer's market," Trey continued.

"A farmer's market? How delightful. Would have been a great tale for the grandkids, no?" Gleb snickered at his own quip but stopped short. "Didn't strike you as odd, the coincidence of it all?"

"Honestly, it did. But I came to realize it happens. Coincidences, I mean. Like I said, sir, she's just a schoolteacher."

"She's not, are you, Ms. Smith?"

I didn't move.

"She is, sir. I'd stake my life on it."

"Oh, you have, Alvah. You know how I know she's not a schoolteacher? No, no. Don't guess. I want to tell you." Gleb only had eyes for me. His tale would be told for my benefit. "After the auction organizer so willingly gave me access to the guest list and each invitee's pertinent information, finding your home was simple. Upon our arrival, Vlad here did as I often have him do, when I enter a place I have never been but for some reason gives me the—*heebee geebees*. You know this feeling? Heebee geebees? Your building's locks are no challenge for a kindergartner, by the way, but I digress. Vlad has this little black box, and he moves it around the room, up and down, round and round. Know what he found?"

"Shit," I cursed under my breath. Any P.I. worth her salt knew what the handheld black box provided. "You stinking son-of-a-bitch, Trey. You *did* bug my apartment. What an asshole."

"What? Bug? I didn't bug—"

"Don't even try you mother-fu—"

"Ms. Smith, such language. That mouth will get you into trouble one of these days. *Oops.* Too late. As my niece Anya is fond of saying, what goes around comes around. Clever of you to pin this on poor, poor Alvah. The timid, broken boy, with such a sad, sad past." Gleb made that disapproving sound again—all teeth and tongue and even longer this time. "You are a smart one, Ms. Smith, I give you that. But it wasn't Alvah who wired your flat. Couldn't possibly be."

Trey looked back and forth between Gleb and me, a bewildered face.

"I hate to be the bearer of such unfortunate news, Alvah, but they have snared you in what they call a honeypot. A pretty, young woman catches your eye, and soon she has you in her home, her bed, baring your soul. Pillow talk, you know, and all the while she is recording it. Every single word."

"That's bullshit. Whatever. Trey, I don't know your game, but I'm not going down for this—this—whatever it is."

"Deny, deny, deny, Ms. Smith, but it will do you no good."

"Who is 'they'? And why, Mr. Trubetzkoy? What's her endgame? Why would Hattie do this?" Trey implored his boss.

"Well, if she can't tell you, I suppose you could go back to visit her employer."

"And who is that?" The serious Trey asked the question, and I felt a shift. If he had ever been my ally, he slipped from me now. "Who's your employer, Hattie?"

"Jesus." Puzzle pieces fell into place, and the picture wasn't good. Uncle Marty's words wormed through the anxiety-induced whir, assailing my ears. *I can't be listening in. This is high-wire-without-a-net time, and you are* not *a cop.* I remembered his earlier call, the unchecked message. Apparently, Uncle Marty *had* found a way to listen in, and the untimely gesture might get me killed.

"The good ol' NYPD. I believe Ms. Smith is a cop." Gleb's satisfaction at wielding that blow on Trey proved gag-worthy.

"Hattie?" Trey stood. His eyes begged me to tell him otherwise.

"I'm not, Trey. I'm not a cop. Promise. You have to believe me."

Gleb rose from his seat and motioned for Vlad to do the same. The old man confronted Trey with pitying condescension as he took his hand and placed a few pebble-sized items in it. "NYPD standard issue. The bugs don't lie, my boy." Gleb patted Trey's cheek, but in two quick strides, Trey flew across the room and grabbed me by the hair with a vicious yank. His fury caught my breath, and his rough pull on my curls made my eyes water. With a hard swallow, I forced myself to meet his glare, darker than I had ever seen it. *Feral creatures will pounce on a dime. You might not see him coming.*

"I'd like to be able to take care of this for you, Mr. Trubetzkoy. I know it isn't up to me, but I want to prove I can solve this problem." He tugged on my hair again, and I gasped.

"What was it you said earlier, Ms. Smith? Alvah was eager to climb the ladder? Looks like he might just make it up a couple of rungs tonight. On your back, of course, and maybe your front and then maybe your back again."

The old man's insinuation sickened and terrified me, but my focus needed to be on the man whose grip felt capable of snapping my neck.

"Trey? Trey, this is not you. This is not the kind of man you are." I hated the pleading sound in my voice, but the books say to appeal to your attacker as a human being, Hostage Negotiation 101.

With another violent wrench, he brought my face to his mouth. "Just hold on, Hattie. You're about to find out *exactly* what kind of man I am."

Gleb raised his hands. "Okay, I go now. I don't have the heart to stay and watch. It's true; my cardiologist says too much excitement can be problematic. I'll let you handle this your way, Alvah. My consolation prize for you. You boys have fun." Gleb walked to the door, collecting his niece's artwork along the way.

"Mr. Trubetzkoy, sir? I don't—need an audience. And to be honest, I'm not a big sharer. I like mine to be mine." Trey avoided my eye when he made his appeal with its vile implication.

"Think of Vladislav as a babysitter, then. You are still on probation; let's not forget. I could instruct him to keep his hands to himself, merely observe, but—boys will be boys. And you know his appetite."

"Yes, sir." Trey's bootlicking roiled in my gut. My misjudgment of the man baffled me. How did I miss the signs? How was I fooled? *Forget it, Harry.* I focused on everything Trey had ever said to me, searched for his pressure point, and readied myself to squeeze. As if he read my mind again, Trey tightened his brutal grip on my hair and I fought the cry that clawed its way from my throat. If I could just get out of my damn shoes.

Fourteen

With Anya's portrait under his arm, Gleb Trubetzkoy left with his unsympathetic signature *tut-tut* that made my skin crawl. Brief relief hit when Trey let go of my hair with a harsh shove, and I massaged the scalp at the back of my head. Vlad still stood near the sofa, but his lascivious grin brought on more ick. Talking to these two—goons—might be my only saving grace. Trey moved away, pacing with a stony face, like he considered some diabolical plan.

"Trey, I didn't lie. I am not a cop. Have never been a cop. I am a teacher. That's the truth."

"Shut up, Hattie."

"I just need you to know, foster care, no mother, all of that was true—*is* true."

For a colossal idiot, Vlad moved fast. My gasp sounded, and I hit the floor before I registered the searing impact of his backhand across my left cheek. Everything dimmed.

"Hattie!" Trey's voice came next, followed by a guttural roar, "*Vlad!*"

All hell broke loose as I lay sprawled. A thud shook the floor, and more muffled growls rumbled while I willed myself to get up.

Remember your training, Harry.

My face burned, ears rang, punctuated by furniture scraping across the wood-floors and thumping against the window wall. The *smack* of tight fists hitting softer flesh mixed with the muted grunts of two men trying to kill one another. When my vision returned, hazy as it was, a tangled human knot came into fuzzy view. Vlad had the upper-hand, and he pummeled Trey beneath him. The idiot's knees had his opponent pinned at the shoulders.

My turn to move fast. I didn't get to my feet, just sprang from my knees, lurching toward the two figures. Below Vlad's thick thigh, Trey's shirttail flapped open, and the black steel butt cap of his blade protruded from the waistband of his pants. The next moment blurred. I lunged for the knife's handle, hearing a yelp I'd swear belonged to Trey. Frantic, I finally scrambled to my feet, and with two hands and a flat blade, I drove the steel hard into the base of Vlad's skull. Certain of the deep puncture, I gave a quick jerk with a reverse grip toward his spine. A textbook "Rubicon Blow." That's what my instructor called it, anyway. If done right, it was a near bloodless, noiseless, instant kill. Vlad stiffened and dropped like a boulder atop Trey.

I did it right.

Falling on my backside, I struggled to breathe, staring at my quivering fingers. A crippling, shrill whine bombarded me, almost paralytic in the stillness. But Trey wrestled his way out from under Vlad's dead weight. With a gravelly moan, he wriggled free and rolled, sliding toward me.

Move, Harry.

The word "Hattie" cut through the high-pitch hum still assailing my senses. Trey wasn't done with me.

Get up, Harry.

Prone, his long arm extended, bloodied knuckles reached, seizing my ankle, jerking me hard. I slid a foot closer to him.

Fight, Harry.

I thrashed, kicking to get free of his bone-crushing hold. A desperate protest whimpered, "No," as I struggled for traction to stand again, but the smooth sandal sole of my unrestrained foot slipped on the hardwoods. Just when I could have used the heel, the strap on the shoe snapped. It barely hung on my toes and then fell to the floor.

Kick, Harry.

I got in one more strike. Missing Trey's face, my foot grazed his ear and smacked his shoulder. A pathetic hit. He coughed but then got his legs underneath him, able to get to his knees. He loomed over me.

"Stop, Hattie." His hands flew up, palms facing me like surrender.

I halted in a crab crawl position, my breath fast and rasping. *Think, Harry.*

"It's okay, Hattie. I've got you." He bent toward me with an outstretched hand. I recoiled with another feeble kick he caught and held my ankle.

"Let go of me," I snarled with another useless punt.

"Whoa, okay." He set my foot on the floor, assuming the surrender pose again. "I'm not going to hurt you." Tilting to all fours, he inched toward me with reassuring eyes. Past my splayed legs, Trey sat next to me, leaning on the sofa. He wrapped his arm around my shoulders, pulled me to his side while I struggled for a deep breath. Rocking, a gentle hush met my ear. "Shhh. It's okay, you're safe now."

The thud of my heart ousted the ringing in my ears. It pulsed down my limbs, and when I found air, I pulled from Trey's embrace to look at him. His hand brushed my wet cheek. I winced. Whether shock or the brutal wallop was to blame, my face tingled, numb. I didn't feel much. "Do they match now? My cheeks?" My tight throat squeezed my voice.

Trey, his dark brow creased with a softened frown, nodded. "Little bit. Yeah."

Warning: this next bit won't be pretty.

I grabbed Trey's collar, pulling his face to mine. As far as first kisses go, it couldn't have been much worse. Tears and snot smeared my face, and two and half seconds into the sloppy, desperate attack of Trey's mouth, I turned my head and vomited all over my sofa. Throw in the overturned chair and the dead body for ambiance, and it was one for the ages.

I scrambled to all fours, feeling faint.

"Hold on, Hattie." Trey lunged for a wastepaper basket stowed under a sofa side table, placing it under my floor-facing chin as another hurl gurgled out of me. "Let it out," he encouraged, sweeping up my hair to give me a clear shot at the small trash can.

"*Ow,*" I snapped. Shoving him away, I rubbed my scalp, stinging from his earlier roughness. "You pull hair hard, Trey. That house full of smelly boys teach you that?" Rolling upright, still on my knees, I dragged my forearm across my mouth. "Sorry." I blew out a long breath.

"It happens. A lot. Pretty normal, actually. Particularly if it was your first time."

"Oh no, I've kissed men before, and *that's* never happened, so—it must be you." I heaved another retch but got nothing to show for it. Trey sat behind me again, resting alongside the low sofa, legs outstretched. He rubbed my shoulder in an act of comfort, nothing else. I maintained my hover over the puke bucket.

His weak laugh faded into a sigh. "You're a pretty badass schoolteacher, cracking jokes while throwing up, having just severed a man's brain stem with paradigmatic skill."

I hunched my shoulders and spit, keeping my back to him. "Paradigmatic? Someone did well on his SATs."

"I thought the *teacher* would appreciate that." His repeat of the word 'teacher' shredded me like glass shards swallowed down a vomit-raw throat. The guilt accompanying it forced another nausea surge.

"Trey, *uh*—" I stalled, wondering if honesty was truly the best course.

"Hm?"

I still couldn't face him. "So, I'm not—well, I'm not *exactly* a schoolteacher." I winced, awaiting his reply.

"Nooooo." His low, slow delivery caught me off guard, and I spun to look at the man feigning shock, his head inches from the sofa cushion soaked in my sick.

"You knew?"

"I wouldn't be very good at my job if I didn't. And not all criminals are dumb, Hattie. I suggest you make that clear to your students. If they ever get real-world experience, they should go in knowing some of the bad guys are smart. They do their homework." He grimaced with raised brows and a condescending head tilt.

I didn't know how to respond. I tried to recalibrate, given the newfound information and the reminder I sat a foot away from a criminal. Though clearly, Trey's villain code differed from that of his face-down, dead colleague.

"What happens now? What do we do about Vlad?"

Trey coughed, looking at the body. "Yeah, that's a problem, but first things first." He squeezed his eyes tight and dropped his head back, just missing my barf puddle. "You still got that first aid goodie bag I brought last night?"

"Jesus, Trey. We'll take care of my face later. Seriously, dude. I'm not the first woman to get backhanded across the cheek." I wobbled, getting to my feet, finally prying off my other shoe. Trey didn't move from his spot.

"Yeah—seriously, *dude*," he mimicked, "not for you." Lifting the hand awkwardly positioned on his far side, his palm displayed bright red blood.

"Shit, Trey. How'd—" I fell to my knees again, noticing his pallor. Tearing open his loose dress shirt, I found the left-side of his body-hugging undershirt soaked in crimson. "Shit. Shit, shit, shit." Back to my feet, I ran to the bathroom to grab the bag of supplies I had stashed under the sink and pulled a hand towel off its chrome bar. "How'd he—?" I yanked the t-shirt over the wound. Swallowing hard, I looked straight at Trey, quelling my panic. So much blood. I covered the gash with the towel. "How'd he—?" I repeated.

"Oh, no, Top Chef. This filet job is your doing. When you pulled the blade, it ran up my torso. Got me good." He sucked air through gritted teeth as I pressed the towel harder to the three-inch vertical slice just below his ribcage. "Is there anything coming out of it?"

"Blood, lots of blood."

"But no—intestine, organs?" His casual delivery didn't help the bile climbing my stomach walls. "Hattie, I need you to look. Wipe it and pry apart the skin to see how deep it is."

"Won't that hurt?" My rigid hands hesitated.

"Yeah, it'll hurt, but I need to know what we're dealing with."

I did as he instructed. His muffled moan made every hair rise.

"Nothing poking out."

"Okay, I need you to poke your finger *in* to see if it goes clear into the abdominal cavity."

"What? No. Trey?"

"Come on, Hattie. I want you to."

"What?"

"Now you know my kink." The man bleeding out in my living room had the nerve to wink at me.

"Jokes? You're making jokes? Now?"

"Just until I pass out." His cough included faint laughter followed by a low grunty howl when my finger slipped inside the wound.

"*Sorry.* No, it's deep, but not all the way. I'm pretty sure. Your six-pack helped."

"That's an eight pack, thank you very much," he grumbled. "Now, got needle and thread?"

"I'm actually more of a knitter myself." I darted to get a clean towel and wet washcloths.

"Oh, I think I remember hearing my *Baba* knitted— or crocheted?" His head rolled back again. "Which one uses two—"

"I don't *knit*, Trey." My anxiety peaked. "I don't knit, I don't sew, I don't crochet. We have to call 9-1-1."

"That'd be a— hard no." Despite his grim condition, the man found the will to mock my earlier bluster—a trait I'd find a turn-on under different circumstances. "Dead body. Criminal." He pointed aimlessly in his woozy state.

I held another clean cloth to his slashed skin. "Stay there," I barked.

"Uh, ooo-kay."

I ran across the hall. My knock at Leo's door hammered like a woodpecker, fast and long. The door flew open, and my giant friend in the floral kimono gasped. My swollen cheek, bloody hands, and the whiff of retch that likely accompanied me spurred the medical man to action. He didn't say a word but whirled back into his apartment, only to reappear with a black leather satchel.

"Medical supplies. Old school. It was my Granddaddy's." He hardly made a sound and followed me back to Trey. "Sweet Jesus." Leo stripped off his kimono, down to boxer briefs and t-shirt and leapt to Trey's side. "How ya feeling, doll?"

"Meh. Not great." Trey's head flopped back onto the sofa.

"Grab a pillow, Harry. Prop his head. Wiggle your fingers for me, tough guy. Squeeze now. Whose vomit?" Leo had pulled on gloves.

"That's me. Mine. I did that. I puked." My confession tumbled out of me while I snatched a pillow for Trey.

"Friend of yours?" Leo's head pointed to Vlad and the knife protruding from the base of his skull. No one answered. He resumed caring for Trey's wound.

"Harry?"

Despite Leo's summons, I couldn't pry my eyes from Trey.

"Harry! I need you to listen to me. I'm in charge now. Go to the cupboard over my refrigerator. In the back, there is a nice big bottle of vodka—"

"Ooh, my favorite," Trey babbled, followed by a clenched, "*Gah*, that hurts."

"Harry, bring it and a shot glass here. Hurry."

I did as Leo ordered and returned with the bottle and two shot glasses. I poured, and Leo tipped both shots into Trey's eager mouth. I poured again. And again, Leo fed Trey. The third round, Leo downed one shot himself and gave Trey his fifth. I took a long swig straight from the bottle.

"We'll sit a minute. Let that kick in because the next part— is gonna suck harder than a mosquito at nightfall. I am plumb outta local, and I don't carry narcotics." Leo pulled a sealed, plastic-wrapped suture kit from his bag. "Harry? Harry, honey, are you all right?"

I appreciated Leo's calm but couldn't stop staring at Trey's ashen face and the glint of his necklace as his chest rose and fell with slow breaths. His eyes stayed closed, and those lashes lay fringe-like. It really wasn't fair.

"Harry?" Leo's sweet voice, laced with worry, drew my attention. "I know you don't want to talk about this, but I need to know some things so I can take care of you."

I touched my cheek, still numb, but it swelled. "I'm fine, Leo. It's fine. Just focus on Trey."

"Trey's going to be okay. But you—were you," Leo struggled, "—did—did this man—"

"No. No, he didn't— He didn't." I repeated. My chin moved in a vigorous shake.

"He didn't," Trey confirmed. "Would have been bad—"

"Stop— stop talking," I barked. "He didn't." I looked at each of the men, all three of them, one at a time. "He *didn't*." I reiterated and rolled over in time to throw up again in the waste bin. I'm not sure what made me sicker: thinking about what could have happened or recognizing my vulnerability despite a life spent ensuring the opposite, simply because I was a woman. That part infuriated me.

"Hattie," Trey whispered.

"Harry, go take a shower. Get the blood and vomit—"

"I'm not leaving him." I shook my head, wiping my mouth. Trembling overtook my body. "I'm staying."

"You can't help him, and no use watching this part. I'll take good care. You go get clean as long as—" Leo looked at the prostrate Vlad, the blade's handle at a right angle. "As long as he—"

"He didn't," I whispered. "And he's dead now, besides." Standing, I swayed a moment and took another long draw on the vodka bottle before handing it to Leo. "I'll be back."

"We'll be here." Leo nodded.

I trudged up the stairs to my bathroom and closed the door. The room filled with steam as I stepped into the shower. Shaky, discolored fingers reached for the bar soap, and I washed. The bubbles turned a brownish pink as the dried blood ran down the drain. Once my hands were clean, my face met the warm spray, and I hissed with the searing sting on my cheek. I hadn't stopped to check my reflection. Shampoo and conditioner came next, so I lathered, rinsed, and repeated for good measure. After I cranked the temperature control to full-hot, my legs gave way to the tiled floor. With my knees under my chin, arms wrapped tightly around my shins, I rocked as the scalding water rained over me, giving myself until the count of one hundred to stop crying.

Fifteen

I DESCENDED THE STAIRS, my hair wrapped in a towel. Leo and I wore matching kimonos again, now that he'd finished Trey's stitch job. I wished, more than anything, we could laugh about it, but out of the corner of my eye, I caught the bold black and gray stripe of a sheet I didn't recognize, covering a body I would never forget. I rattled my head in hopes, like an Etch-A-Sketch, I could shake my brain clean of the horrible image. My attention gravitated to Trey's new spot with better light, no corpse, or puddles of vomit in the way. He lay on the floor, shirtless, flat on his back, eyes closed. Some color had returned to his cheeks.

"I should put him in your bed in a bit. He needs to stay flat, but I don't want to move him until I'm sure the clotting is good," Leo whispered, taking his first close look at my face before placing a dishtowel-wrapped ice pack on it.

"Yes, of course. Whatever he—" I took hold of the cold compress. "He's—he's okay?"

"He'll even continue to breathe if you stop watching him," Leo teased, but I ignored it. "He's fortunate. Any deeper and—" The learned medical student didn't go any further with the guessing game. "Might not even need antibiotics if he stays down for twenty-four hours."

"Is that all?"

"If it stays clean, dry. That all goes out the window if he pops sutures. But it was a clean slice, not a stab wound."

I nodded. Evidently, Trey hadn't told Leo how the injury occurred.

"I'm hoping the pain does its job and slows him down, but the man has a hurt threshold like—" Leo waved away the rest of the thought.

"What's with—" I couldn't say any more about the body, simply pointed with my head.

"I grabbed a sheet from my place. I found yours but, honey, yours are too nice for this chore. And I know what I want for Hanukkah this year." Leo *hmphed* at his joke, then straightened when I didn't join him.

"What are you two hissing about over there?" Trey grumbled from his spot on the floor.

"Waste removal," I answered quickly.

"Like I told Leo, if you get it moved, I can get it picked up."

"Wait. What?" A new panic hit me. "Leo is not in this. Leo is *not* a part of this."

"I am now, Harry. I was in this the moment you knocked on my door."

"No, no, no, no, no. I needed medical help. You provided *first aid*. That's it. This—this—this is too much, and I can't let you." I pushed past my neighbor. "Trey, please let me call someone. Let me get someone here to help. I can't promise I can protect you, but I've got your back, and others have mine."

"Authorities? No. And do you really trust them? They bugged your home without telling you. Could have gotten you killed or—worse," he reminded us, pushing up on his elbows with a grimace. "I will be out of here before you finish dialing. I've got my own someone to call. Someone I trust with my life, and *yours* by the way. I just need the body moved, and Leo's plan sounds like a good one."

"Lie down, Trey," I barked, and to my surprise, he did. "Leo, doesn't this break some code? An oath or something?"

"One look at your face tells me everything I need to know about that animal. My conscience is clear."

"I don't know, Leo. I can be pretty mouthy."

He let out a small airy laugh. "That's a good sign. The return of wit. Dark, but I'll take it." He lifted the ice to my face again.

From the far side of the room, Trey chimed in, "She's not kidding, Leo. That mouth—"

"Can it, Trey. Now tell me the plan."

We raced the clock before *rigor mortis* could cause problems. After dressing in the jeans and t-shirt I wore earlier, I met Leo back in my living room.

"Why scrubs, Leo?"

"No one will look twice when I dump scrubs covered in bio-matter at the hospital laundry. And, obviously, I'll be doing the heavy lifting."

"Right. Smart."

Trey's "someone" knew his or her destination was our duplex, specifically the back alley. When I questioned suspicious movements, Trey waved off my concern. His "someone" would be fast and quiet, a model of stealth. The outlaw underworld has a host of talented ghosts, I guess.

Even in his pained state, kept slightly blunted with occasional vodka shots, Trey's criminal mind fascinated me. He thought of every contingency, including, it turned out, Leo's wardrobe choice. He also had us locate Vlad's phone. Trey planned to send a text or two from different locations to stall, if not completely throw off anyone looking for the owner. Unfortunately, being dead and face down for more than an hour made the face ID impossible. Which meant we couldn't access the phone. It had us longing for the old days when a thumbprint would do. *Thanks, technology.*

"It was worth a shot," Trey groused. "We'll get it far from here before disabling it for tracking purposes. This won't be the last place GPS puts him before we shut the phone down, not that anyone can pinpoint a location. But it might buy some time."

It wasn't anything I didn't already know, but I guess it qualified as good *criminal* craft too.

"Wait a sec. May I?" I beckoned for the phone.

Leo squatted at the body's head, still trying to get the phone to read the smooshed face. Earlier, he didn't hesitate to search the pockets for the device when he saw I couldn't do it. Getting near the man, as dead as he was, seemed more than I could handle. Auntie Leo did the job. He handed me the phone.

I typed six digits. "Here you go," I chirped. I love it when a hunch pays off.

"You got in?" Pleased, Trey tried to sit up again.

"Lie down, Trey." Leo and I spoke in unison.

I brought the phone to the cranky convalescent. It was the first time I'd registered the state of Trey's face. It had taken some hard hits, and I touched his cheek with the back of my hand. A jolt shot through me.

"You okay?" Trey kept his head on the sofa pillow.

"Shut up, Trey. Again, *not* your damsel," I snapped, handing him the phone, unable to temper how his concern infuriated me. "You want to charge it? I have the same—"

"No, not necessary. The sooner it dies, the better. How'd you know the password?"

"Not hard. I heard—more than once—Vlad was an idiot. One, two, three, four, five, six, seemed like a safe bet."

"The total package," Trey murmured with something like a grin, but he only had eyes for the phone screen.

I ignored his compliment. "What are you doing?"

Trey's thumbs worked overtime. "Sending some texts. Grabbing some data, copying his contacts, the usual." Trey had connected his phone to Vlad's with a piece of tech he'd pulled from his pocket, tech I didn't recognize. Then again, I didn't dabble in information theft. Well, not really.

The cavalier act didn't impress me. "Hey gang, we doing this? We need to get Trey to bed, and I need some sleep, too." I said it like sleeping was something I might actually do one day. A glance at the striped bed sheet flooded me with doubt.

Regardless, I had to find a way to get near the body. Summon my nerve. As soon as we got word that our "courier" arrived, ready to take delivery, we needed to act. But I couldn't get my feet to move.

"I've got this, honey. No need to get near him—*it*. I've got this." Leo jumped into action. The moment Trey said go, Leo returned the phone to the dead guy's pocket and pried the blade from the base of his skull.

I watched my giant friend drag the man-sized bundle out my door to the laundry room and the industrial trash chute with a silent thank you. Where it went from there, I couldn't muster the heart to care.

Sixteen

Leo continued with the heavy lifting by guiding Trey up the stairs. Above me, the two men spoke in low voices with a couple of grunts. My bedframe's squeak accompanied the muffled conversation. I didn't know the king-bed even made that noise. Unable to decipher their words, I focused on my task of cleaning vomit off my sofa. While I scrubbed, I composed a mental shopping list of items it seemed I should have at the ready: upholstery cleaner, needle and thread, a big bottle of liquor and maybe lidocaine. What every Millennial should keep on hand these days.

Leo's laugh timed perfectly with my mental quip, and I looked at the ceiling in surprise. Of course, Trey likely provoked Leo's outburst, and I tried not to want in on the joke. What was taking Leo so long up there, anyway?

My couch, with a seat-sized wet spot, air-dried as clean as it would get. Leo had scrubbed away what mess Trey's wound made before any damage set in, though my towels had seen better days. The sofa was the only indicator anything had gone awry in the room. I sniffed the bouquet that decorated my kitchen counter, wishing I could rid my nose of the odor stuck in it: vomit, blood, musky spice. A putrid combination I couldn't shake. Not even the fragrant phlox and cabbage rose could fight it.

"A stink stuck in your nose?" Leo returned from his upstairs nursing duties.

"Yeah," I shrugged. "Puke and something." I squinched my nose and smelled the flowers again.

"It's not, it's—death. It'll fade. It might take a bit, but you'll be better—*feel* better soon. You need some rest."

The laugh that honked out of me stunned us both, but ended abruptly. "Rest, huh?"

"Nurse Ratched's orders." The directive came with a firm scowl and an index finger pointed in my direction. "I'll be across the hall if you need me, but he should be fine. You both got lucky tonight."

I laughed again. What can I say? I had the sense of humor of a teenaged-boy, and it reared its head at inappropriate times.

"You know what I mean," Leo chastised.

"Why'd you laugh earlier? Upstairs, you laughed. A genuine laugh. What'd he say?"

"*Huh*? Oh, I don't know." Leo's obvious fib didn't include eye contact.

"Yes, you do. Leo?"

"Future physician's assistant/patient confidentiality, sorry." He winked. "I'll see you tomorrow or later today, I guess. If you're awake in an hour, check his bandage, then rest."

"Yes, Auntie Leo. And thank you for—everything."

He kissed my swollen cheek and left. I locked the bolt behind him, then surveyed the wet sofa and the spot on the floor where the striped sheet had lain the last couple of hours. My gaze landed on the stairs, looking steeper and higher than I'd ever noticed. Eyes back to the sofa, I only considered barricading the door with it for a moment. Instead, I grabbed a rocks glass of ice and the vodka bottle Leo had stowed in my freezer, then trudged the slow climb to my bedroom.

My still shaky hand sloshed some vodka over the ice, and I sat in the dark on the low sofa that would be my bed for the third time that week. A fuzzy Sherpa blanket decorated the settee, and I pulled it around my shoulders after a big swig of the harsh, clear liquor. My insides appreciated the heat of one, while my skin enjoyed the warmth of the other.

"You're gonna share, right?" Out of the darkness, Trey's voice had a warmth I appreciated too.

"You're awake?"

"I'm sure there's a joke to be made about my fantasies of being in your bed, but something tells me that punchline gets lost on a night like tonight."

"Ya think?" I took another swallow of vodka and blew out the burn. "Is it okay if I turn on the light?" I leaned to twist the lamp knob but paused.

"I'd rather you not."

"Why?"

"Not feeling particularly manly at the moment, if you must know."

"Trey. You took a beating and a knife to the abdomen. How could you—"

"Oh, no. That part's cool. I look *super* tough." I heard a smile in his quiet brag. "It's—"

I clicked the switch, and the lamp bulb eased into the room to full glow. My eyes adjusted as the room grew brighter. With another generous pour of drink, I left the bottle on the coffee table and took unhurried steps toward the bed on the dimmer side of the room. My smile spread, despite the pain that zinged across my cheekbone.

Trey scowled. "Go ahead, laugh it up." He lay flat, a single pillow under his head. Bed linens rested in neat folds at his hips.

From there up, the man wore a loose-fitting top portion of another set of scrubs Leo'd obviously lent the man. The oversized, boxy v-neck was Pepto-Bismol pink and dotted with various faces of *Hello Kitty*. "The least you could do is share the booze," he complained.

I offered him the glass, stifling my grin best I could manage. He lifted his head and drank more than I expected. Letting him keep the glass, I retrieved the bottle from the other side of the room. The short tumbler contained only ice cubes when I returned.

"Hurts, huh?" I pointed to the edge of the bed, asking permission to sit.

"*Nah.*" He patted the mattress and wordlessly indicated I should pour more vodka into the outstretched glass. The splash I gave didn't suffice. I poured again, but still, he silently asked for more. How could I say no?

Setting the bottle on my bedside chest, I watched him take a small sip, then extend the drink toward me. I reached to take it, but he withdrew, then offered again. Again, I tried to take the glass. He pulled it away. My quizzical look told him I didn't understand the game he played, and I wasn't interested in playing, anyway. When the vodka came at me the third time, I didn't move, done with his shenanigans. He pressed the chilled glass to my bruised cheek. I closed my eyes to hide the wince, but after the initial sting, welcomed relief. With his hand and drink in my grasp, I moved the rim to my lips to take a healthy gulp, then nudged the tumbler to rest on his Hello Kitty-clad chest.

My hand rested on his forearm while I marshaled the courage to find the words I needed to say. A hard swallow didn't help. Low light glinted off the pendant that hung around his neck. He didn't flinch when I took it in my fingers, but wrapped his fingers around mine. The abrasions on his knuckles would be a lasting reminder of the night's event—like we would ever forget. His scraped and swollen joints matched his face. Mine too. The phrase "two of a kind" crossed my mind when it registered he had brought my fingers to his lips. I pulled away with a jerk.

"I'm sorry. I shouldn't have—"

"No, Trey. I'm sorry."

"You?" He tried to sit up.

"Stay down, Trey." The hushed command stopped him, and his head flop punctuated the sudden quiet.

"It's the Hello Kitty, isn't it?" He covered his eyes with one hand, trying to joke his way past my rebuff.

I shoved his shoulder. "No. It's—I'm sorry if I gave you the wrong impression before when I—"

"Kissed me?"

"Yeah. I didn't—"

"Oh, sure. I get it. Heat of the moment. Death and danger. You'd have kissed anyone in that circumstance."

"Right. Exactly. Heat of the—"

"Just happened to be me there."

"Yes. Lucky you."

"Sure. If it had been Leo, your tongue would have been in his mouth. I get it."

"Um, no. I don't—uh, I mean, yeah? Probably?" I inched away; the air had grown more stagnant.

"Okay, Hattie."

"Yeah, and people don't call me Hattie."

"I heard."

"So, you don't have to keep calling me that anymore. If you don't want to."

"Okay," he said, then hitched with a pained grimace.

"You alright?"

"Yep." His clipped reply hinted otherwise.

"Are you— angry?"

"Angry? At you? No."

"Why not?"

"Huh?"

"Jesus, Trey." I sprang to my feet and paced. "How are you not furious? This is my fault. All of this is my fault. I inserted myself into a situation I had no business getting involved in, manipulated my way despite being ill-prepared. Shined a spotlight, and worse—worse, I provoked Trubetzkoy. I mean, I did. I opened my mouth, and well, it's my fault, and I am so sorry. So, so sorry."

"Yeah."

"What?" I stopped my back and forth.

"I agree with you."

Maybe the mix of pain and booze held the blame, but Trey's nonchalance didn't fit with the situation. Evidently, violence—up close and personal violence—was nothing new to Trey Popov. Life conditioned him to it, and when I recognized how calloused his psyche was, I felt even worse.

"You also saved my life—in spectacular fashion, I gotta say. So maybe that makes us square. Look. Vlad would have killed me. If not tonight, at some point. Gleb—likes me, so Vlad— hated me. It was only a matter of time."

Hearing the two men's names spoken so casually made my head spin. "Well, Gleb doesn't like you anymore." The gravity of the situation weighed on me.

"*Bah.* I wouldn't be so sure." Trey crept back up to his elbows with a self-assured grin. "I'm quite the likable guy once you get to know me."

"How? His nephew is dead."

"Yeah, you don't mind if I take *credit* for that, do you?"

"Seriously?"

"My guess is Gleb has been eager for someone to put down the idiot nephew for some time. Just no one had the—*nerve* to do it. Don't get me wrong. Going back won't be a picnic. I'll be disciplined, but no permanent damage. Gleb won't want that, but I'll need to be taught a lesson, made an example. But I'm also willing to bet that lesson comes with a nice reward, too."

"Whoa. Hold up. You're going back? You're going back for a sanctioned beat down and a payday. Who the—what the *hell* are you?"

He squinted with his head tilt. "Thought that got cleared up tonight. And don't tell me it's not exactly what you sized me up to be before you ever laid eyes on me."

"That's not fair—"

"Fair? Life is far from fair. And the sooner you wrap your head around that, the better." He stretched for the vodka on the nightstand, gasping at the motion.

"Trey!" In two quick strides, my hand met his chest, pushing him flat to his back.

Another low moan squeezed out of him as I emptied the last of the booze onto the remaining ice.

"That's the last of the medicine." I wiggled the bottle as I sat.

"There are other ways to numb the pain." He downed the drink while putting his hand on my thigh.

"Don't."

"Don't what?"

"Don't act like you're someone you aren't. Don't be like them. They're despicable. And you're—" My hesitation to fill in the blank wasn't because I didn't know how, but because too many words fit the space. I knew too many ways to describe the man, none of them bad. I couldn't pick just one.

"I'm what?"

"You're— *not*, and I'll never believe you are, so when it's just me, skip the toxic masculinity routine. Don't forget who you are." I took his hand, hoping to get him to look at me.

He did, but a flicker of surprise caught me off guard.

"Sorry. I didn't— Have you ever not recognized the voice in your own head?" He directed his question to the ceiling.

"Funny you should ask. For about a year, until a few days ago."

"What happened a few days ago?"

"Independence Day. And don't go thinking it had anything to do with you. Now lift your kitty shirt so I can get a look at this supposed eight-pack."

Despite his attempts to move, the wound looked in good shape. If there were awards for the best stitcher in the medical world, Leo would win first prize. Fifteen sutures lay neat and even and someday would provide a sexy souvenir of the night Trey spared me from the worst kind of ordeal, and I saved his life.

I tiptoed from my bathroom, dressed in a button-up set of pajamas with my hair pulled loosely on top of my head. Wrapping myself in the faux fur throw, both too warm for summertime and too small for sleep, I curled up on the settee. With each cheek bruised and my scalp still tender from the earlier tussle, I struggled to get comfortable.

An eerie calm blanketed the room with only the occasional thud of passing cars driving over the manhole cover in the street to interrupt it. The intensity of that sound swelled. *Thump-thump.* Stronger, and more frequent. *Thump-thump.* Louder too. *Thump-thump.* Each tire hit my chest. I was the bump in the road. The hollow *thuds* bombarded my ears, jarred down my limbs, stole my breath until I shot up, gasping. My own heart betrayed me. *Control yourself, Harry.*

"Plenty of room over here. It's a safe space, as the kids say."

Instinct said to trust Trey's offer, but I stalled a moment to consider it before finding my way to his side. Each on our backs, we lay motionless, inches apart. My mind's assault on my body subsided. "Trey?"

"Yes, Hattie?"

I paused. "I see we're sticking with that moniker."

"Do you mind?"

"No." It surprised me how quickly I replied.

"Good."

"Don't go back there, please. *Please,* don't go back." My clenched jaw could have broken teeth, and I'd never felt so frayed.

His battered hands rested in a mound on his chest, but one moved like he meant to touch me. He didn't. Instead, it rested at his side between us.

"So, a priest, a rabbi, and an atheist fall into a mud pit..." he began.

I took a gentle hold of his bruised fingers.

Seventeen

Turns out, an unhealthy amount of vodka after the bottoming-out of an adrenaline spike caused by a traumatic shock has the potential to induce some heavy sleep. Good to know. Daylight crept through the partially drawn blackout drapes I had neglected to close before crawling into my bed in the wee hours. I stretched my legs and closed my eyes, hoping to doze again but bolted upright when flashes from the night before rushed me.

Trey was gone. "Shit."

Elbows to knees, I cursed again when pain erupted in my cheek because of a poorly timed, aggressive face rub. I flopped to my back, chastising my carelessness and for thinking Trey would stick around for the morning-after. Sunday had arrived. The first Sunday in my post-Rubicon Blow life. My next move would take some consideration. But a joist on the stairway groaned an interruption, sending me upright again.

"I guessed the bed squeak meant you were awake." Trey topped the stairs carrying two coffee mugs.

"I didn't know it did that. Not until last night." The reply seemed silly, but I said it to mask my surprise at seeing Trey in my bedroom again, shirtless and with coffee like it was a very different kind of morning-after.

"Didn't know what did *what*?" He offered me a steaming cup with a curious, sweet smile.

"The bed. Squeaking." Heat crept up my already warm cheeks. Sipping my coffee, I hoped to move on from the topic. My gaze went immediately to the white rectangular bandage above the left side of the cinched drawstring of the borrowed, oversized scrub bottoms. '*Immediately*' might be an overstatement.

"I'm fine," he informed me before I could ask. "I checked it this morning. It's all good. I'm a big boy and take care of myself."

"I can see that." I disguised my smile with another mouthful of coffee.

"I figure if anyone asks, I'll say I had an appendectomy." He shrugged.

"Okay," I frowned. "Except it's a little big and a little high and on the *completely* wrong side, but—whatever."

"Don't tell me; you're a doctor, too." His teasing included the grin of that more relaxed Trey I caught glimpses of every now and again.

One side of my mouth curved up as I tilted back against the headboard. Pulling at the waistband of my pajamas revealed my appendectomy scar, barely two inches, on my lower right side.

Trey cleared his throat. "Must have been an emergency if they didn't do it laparoscopically." His focus darted away, like my brief show of typically concealed skin bothered him.

That flicker of shyness tickled me, and I couldn't help but pile-on. "It was. Don't tell me; you're a doctor, too." My mimic included his often-serious scowl.

He countered, hooking a thumb on his own waistband and inched the scrubs far enough to show me the result of his own significant appendectomy incision. "Mine too. I was sixteen."

"Twelve," I boasted, like I'd won some contest.

"Had to get mine stitched twice because I busted open the first job. Teenage boys." After an awkward pause, we each let go of our respective waistbands, and Trey jerked to set down his mug. "Well, while I'd love nothing more than to spend the day playing I'll-show-you-mine-if you-show-me-yours, I should get going."

"Wait, what?" I rolled to my knees, almost spilling my coffee. "Leo said twenty-four hours, plus I thought last night we decided—"

"We didn't decide anything last night, Hattie." Uptight Trey emerged.

"Then let's decide something now. Something *other* than you going back to whatever hell-hole you plan to return to for a beating you don't deserve. Not to mention might kill you." I pointed to his bandage.

"I have to go, Hattie. It's my job."

"Your job? Jesus. Get another freaking job." I slid to the other side of the bed to stand, facing away from him, somehow knowing I wouldn't win the argument.

"Don't forget about the reward. The reward is a big deal. It's important. And I have to make sure I get it."

I made a slow turn. "Wow. Are you kidding me? How much, Trey?" My volume climbed. "What's the dollar figure Trubetzkoy pays for you offing his idiot nephew? I mean, right after he has you beaten for doing it. No, I mean it. How much?" I couldn't comprehend the smile on his face.

"Why? You gonna top it? Make me some indecent proposal? Like some reverse Pretty Women plot?"

"Maybe. I don't know. I could."

"That's quite an offer," he put his hand over his heart, but his condescension mocked me. "You can't give me what Gleb Trubetzkoy will give me."

"Try me." I didn't know what road I headed down, but my stubborn streak pushed back at the smug man. "How much?"

"I don't recall anyone mentioning money other than you." Trey chose that moment to make my bed. "*I* never said anything about money." He tossed a pillow to my side and pulled the end of the top sheet tight to the head of the mattress. The blanket edge came next, followed by the bedspread.

My frustration exploded. I grabbed the pillow and chucked it at his head with a grunt. "God, why are you such an asshole?"

That outburst made him laugh, making me angrier.

"That mouth," he scolded. "I've been called worse but not by anyone so *adorably* excitable." He walked toward me, wearing a cheeky grin.

"Gleb called me lovely."

"What?"

"Gleb said I was lovely. Before he put his hand on me."

Trey's smile vanished, and his jaw tightened.

"That's when I threatened to snap his wrist. Could have, too."

Trey stepped around me to pull together the other side of the bed. "I don't doubt it. Which is why I'm going." Any signs of fun had disappeared.

"I don't understand."

Trey's attention to pillow placement took an abnormally precise turn. He couldn't have been more exacting if he'd had a ruler.

"What the hell, Trey?" I crowded him, cornering him by the bed and the nightstand.

The closeness didn't faze him. He lifted my chin, and I braced myself for whatever came next. It wasn't what I thought.

"*You're* the reward, Hattie." His words were quiet, and his stare bore through me while the explanation landed a massive weight. "My—compensation—will be the opportunity to ask for one thing, and that one thing will be you. Your life. Your get-out-of-Trubetzkoy-jail-free card. I go back, take a beating, and you get safety. And there is nothing you can say or do to keep me from doing that. You saved my life. Now I save yours. And no Trubetzkoy ever touches you again. End of discussion." Trey released my chin, walked around me and into my bathroom, sliding the pocket door shut.

The slider closed before I could stammer out a word. "Excuse me? End of discussion?" I shouted at the door. "A discussion isn't over just because you say so, Trey." I waited for a reply but got nothing. "I don't know who you think you're talking to, but let me assure you, we are not done with this discussion." I almost sat on the immaculately made bed. "That's fine. I'll wait."

His responded with nothing but the rush of shower water.

"Fine. *After* your shower, then. I set out towels and a new toothbrush. Help yourself to whatever." I pressed my ear to the door, but got no reply. I threw on joggers and a tank top and placed a clean men's t-shirt—a remnant of another era—on the bed for Trey to wear. Hello Kitty wouldn't suit in the daylight hours. I headed downstairs to make breakfast.

Ten minutes later, the creaky stairs alerted me to my infuriating antagonist's arrival, but I kept busy in the kitchen. Trey entered, his hair damp and wearing his dark pants from the night before, the dried blood invisible unless you knew to look. He carried the t-shirt and his coffee mug.

"I'll need another round of ointment and a bandage. In a bit. I didn't get it wet."

I whisked eggs, avoiding eye contact. Beckoning for his mug, I refilled it and slid it to him, biting my tongue to keep from taking another verbal swing in a fight I recognized I'd already lost.

"Who went to Northwestern?" Trey ended the short-lived stalemate, holding up the heather gray t-shirt I left for him. "I've seen your CV. I know it wasn't you."

"I assume whoever owned that shirt." I didn't want to talk about it, and I certainly didn't want Asher Cray's name on my lips.

"If you're implying you don't know who it belongs to, I don't buy that."

It hadn't been my intention to suggest I entertained a revolving door of men leaving their clothes in my home, so many I couldn't keep track. The truth didn't come close to that scenario. I simply shrugged.

"If it's special, I don't need to take it—if it means something to you."

Was he fishing?

"I wouldn't have offered it if I wasn't willing to let it go." I gave him a sincere nod.

"But you don't want to say whose it is?"

"*Nah*, it would sound like bragging, and you'd feel uncomfortable and probably jealous, and it would turn into a whole thing so—"

"Ignorance is bliss, huh?"

"Well, I've got no *personal* experience with ignorance, but yeah, that's what I've heard."

"God, you're a smug handful." He slipped the shirt over his shaking head.

"Two, really—sorry." I immediately regretted the suggestive quip and looked away when the faded purple letters stretched across his chest. My indelicate mouth and penchant for playing with fire were trouble. "Eggs? Toast? Peaches? My purchases from the market yesterday. Jeez, that seems like a lifetime ago."

"You don't have to cook for me, you know."

"Kinda feels like I should. Sending you off to endure something horrible for me, because of me. The least I can do is—just eat the goddamn breakfast, Trey. Please?" My jaw clenched.

"Hattie," he paused a beat, allowing a flicker of sad eyes. "Breakfast sounds great." His kind face relieved and worried me at the same time. Relieved because I knew he'd be safe at least another hour or longer if I could devise a plan, but worried because his sweet sincerity made me feel something I didn't want to feel. *Jesus, it's just the damn t-shirt, Harry.*

Eighteen

I CANNOT OVERSTATE THE absurdity of the situation. There I sat, delicately swabbing a stitched knife wound with the Neosporin my once-again shirtless "patient" BYO'd. It was an injury I had inflicted, trying to save the man I now nursed, only so he could volunteer for more harm in the hopes he might garner enough favor to ask for my safety from further reprisals. All because I'd insulted a depraved old man with a twisted mind and gnarled hands he needed to learn to keep to himself. The criminal world was bananas, and I straddled a line with law enforcement on one side and a decent man, who thought himself too far down the lawless path to turn back, on the other. *Breathe, Harry.*

A fresh bandage firmly affixed, I kept my palm pressed to the wound, willing it to heal with imaginary powers I desperately wanted to believe I possessed.

"What are you thinking?" Trey put his bruised hand atop mine.

"See, and here I thought maybe you could read my mind."

"Oh, the trouble I'd find myself in if I tried to do that. Worse than anything I might encounter later today."

"Flatterer." My doe-eyes were in jest that time.

"Tell me." He kept a heavy hand on mine, like maybe he believed in my magical healing abilities, too.

"Just wondering if the Mets might have a shot this year. I mean, they've been strong off the bench this season and—"

"Hattie." He took hold of my fingers and squeezed.

"I wish I had become a cop. That I had taken one of the many opportunities made available to me, opportunities I shunned to hide in a van and a classroom. Opportunities I wasted because I was young—and grieving—and—a coward. And more the last thing than anything."

He offered me a thoughtful look, but it didn't hold an ounce of pity. Lucky for him. "Grief can make a person do—or *not* do lots of things, but while I could describe you in many ways, Hattie Smith, 'coward' is one label that would never stick. Not ever. Oh, and you're still young, by the way."

My mile-a-minute brain couldn't conjure a response. Just as well, because my throat tightened too much to speak it, anyway. Making matters worse, Trey's words weren't the reason for my momentary mute state. My own confession had struck me dumb, and that I admitted it to him surprised me even more.

Trey released my hand and stood to pull on the t-shirt again. I think we both needed air in the weighty moment. "And if you were a cop? What then?"

The answer to that question took no thought. "I'd cuff you where you stand." Anything to keep him from walking out the door.

His head pushed through the shirt neck with the biggest grin I'd seen him make yet. "Now you're just being a tease." Weighty moment over. "It's a shame, you and me. That we couldn't—work. I mean, my being too *young* for you and—"

"A rising star in a rapidly growing criminal empire? Yeah. Shame. It could have been—"

"Great. Sure wish we'd met under different circumstances."

"If wishes were horses."

"Fishes," he corrected without skipping a beat.

I focused on packing up the first aid supplies to keep me in my seat and from doing something foolish that would make the next part harder.

"On that note, I'm gonna go." He had to feel the tension, too.

"Yeah." I bounded to my feet, rocking the table in my hasty move.

"I'm in no position to make demands, but can I offer some advice?"

"Hm?" Words wouldn't form.

"Keep your head up and definitely keep up with the self-defense stuff. You got skills, kid." He shadow-boxed with silly jabs, landing a nudge to my chin. But his serious face returned, telling me to be careful.

I nodded with a tight jaw as he walked to the door.

"And you should change your locks. You need better security. It really is a joke how easily I got in last night. I know someone—"

I shook my head, waving off his suggestion to call *his* someone.

"Right." His eyes lit up when he must have recognized the irony. "Last, and this part is important. Remember, you said it yourself. I'm an *asshole*, so whatever I got coming, I probably deserve."

With a huff, I stepped to stand toe to toe with the man, mustering all my nerve. "Really? Come on. Like I'll ever forget what an asshole you are." My hand to his chest, the tip of my finger touched the gold star before I tucked it inside the well-worn Northwestern t-shirt. It was tacit consent. If Trey Popov wanted to kiss me, nothing stood in his way.

He took one step back, reaching for the doorknob. Disbelief may have shown on my face. "Goodbye, Hattie." Trey's hobbled jog carried him down the hall and out the front of the building. The heavy industrial door banged shut in his wake.

Leo's apartment door opened a slow inch at a time until he leaned in the frame. I kept my eyes to the exit; confident Trey would come back. Any second, he'd return because leaving was the stupid move. And going like that? Well, talk about cowardice.

"You tell the man twenty-four hours, and he can't even give it twelve. Shocker," Leo sighed. "You okay?" He followed me into my flat, where I just missed the still damp spot on my sofa as I sat to lace up my sneakers.

"Not really, Leo. But I will be." I bounced to standing and grabbed my bag. "Thought today was your sleeping day?"

"Where are you going?"

I brushed past him, headed for escape. The crash of the metal push bar echoed in the vestibule before I called over my shoulder. "I'm going to go hit something. Hard."

Sweat *already* dripped from my—everywhere when I yanked open the door to my gym. The place never got cool in the summer or warm in the winter, but I felt relief from the day's heat when I got out of the sun. I pulled my bag off my back and bent, hands to knees, slowing my ragged breath after my sprint to get there.

"Harry, what can I do for you today?" Nate, one of the gym owners, shuffled toward me. He reminded me of a bowling pin, bald and wobbly, but never falling, particularly in the boxing ring.

I barely looked at him. "I need a four-foot, sixty-five-pound bag hung, and fast, please."

"Feel the need to pound on something, do ya?" Nate's usual smile flattened when I stood.

"You've got no idea." Suddenly self-conscious of my bruised face, I dipped my chin, knotting my hair atop my head. My scalp still smarted.

"You want twelve-ounce mitts or fourteen?" Nate rotated and veered to the far left of the echoey concrete space. The facility stood vacant, but Sunday mornings had never been a high traffic time.

"Twelve, thanks."

"I'll grab the tape and get you prepped. Hydrate, kid." He tossed me a chilled squeeze-bottle of water before teetering off to get my gloves.

Nate had just locked in the heavy bag to my height on the pulley system and stepped away when my right leg sent the bag swinging with a powerful body shot.

"Whoa, somebody's been eating her Wheaties." Martin O'Shea, out of nowhere, grabbed at the bag to steady it. "I got this, Nate. Thanks for the call."

"Really? Et tu, Nate?" Who needed family when the entire neighborhood had their nose in your business? Three punches hit the hanging black Everlast™ sack. Marty caught it again, then ducked out of the way when I didn't hesitate to attack with another series of strikes.

"What's going on, Harry?"

"Just working through some stuff but ran out of vodka. So, here I am."

He steadied the bag from my continued assault. "Wanna tell me what happened to your face?"

"You wanna tell me what happened to *yours*?" My witty snark lacked its usual intellect.

"If you don't want me to treat you like a twelve-year-old, you might wanna try not acting like one, Harriet. Now what the hell happened to your face?" Marty using profanity was a rarity. Doing it on a Sunday? Unheard of.

"You don't want to know, Uncle Marty, but I blame you." I punctuated the statement with another power kick and a quick round of jabs.

"Me? How's that?"

"Bugging my apartment without telling me first?"

"Hey, I called from your front stoop. I left a message to say I planned to enter the premises, left a detailed explanation of what I was doing, where each unit was hidden, and how to deactivate and reactivate them for your own privacy. Was that not clear? I assumed that's exactly what you did."

"Assumed, huh? Well, you might have considered someone else finding them before I got your message." Another barrage of blows sent the bag swaying.

Marty showed actual alarm. "Is that what happened? Did Popov find them and take it out on your left cheek? Because if that son of—"

My next impact was *almost* a vicious, two-gloved shove on Uncle Marty's chest. I checked up just short of making contact. Marty never flinched. An inch from his face, I snarled, "Trey Popov wouldn't hit a woman to save his own life. And if he *ever* shows up in your precinct again or any other station you know of, I need you to do two things. Protect him and call me, day or night. Is *that* clear?" I rounded the bag again, sending it flying with a brutal push kick.

My teeth met the Velcro binding of one of the gloves as panic hit me. I couldn't get out of the mitts fast enough. Marty hurried to step in to assist.

"Let me help. Breathe, kid." His nimble fingers untied the knots and ripped apart the mesh straps.

As soon as my taped hands were free of the gloves, they gripped the water bottle to squirt the lukewarm liquid into my mouth and onto my face. I tossed the bottle, and with two more punches, landed each ungloved fist on the bag while a strangled, "Shit!" wailed out of me. My scream reverberated in the cavernous concrete space as I clung to the bag and then, at his insistence, to Marty. It was the second time we'd shared a moment like that.

After the scene settled, Marty and I sat on rickety metal folding chairs. Nate had brought me another water but left us alone. Knowing me for thirty years, Marty understood pushing me to talk would never work. From the terrible twos to the tumultuous teens and beyond, he'd learned to wait with patience. Once I organized my thoughts and feelings, I'd share if the situation called for it. My dad had set the example.

"Shouldn't you be at mass?" I asked after another long slurp.

"I went early, but thanks for asking. You worried about my soul, Harry?"

I snorted. "Just as soon as I'm done worrying about my own, Uncle Marty."

"Why? What'd *you* do? Kill somebody?" He gave my shoulder a playful shove.

"Yeah, but it was totally justified, I swear." One of the perks of being an incessant smart-ass included telling the truth and no one taking you seriously.

Marty chuckled. "Come on. Come to the house for lunch. Bess would love to see you."

"Looking like this? She'll flip her wig."

"No, but she'll probably have some make-up tips to help cover up some of that."

Elizabeth and Martin O'Shea had been married since before I was born. And while taking care of me unfairly fell to her in my earliest days, a different plan settled into place when my dad, Martin's partner, got his bearings around solo-parenthood. The divide with Bess grew wider when she and Marty struggled to have a child of their own. They never succeeded. That chasm never affected Marty and Dad as far as I knew. As I got older and Bess grew resigned to her lot, she tried to reinsert herself into my life as the female figure I so desperately needed, at least in her mind. As Queens' *Ms. Jolie: Beauty Products for the Modern Woman* salesperson of the year, six years in a row, Bess thought it would thrill me to be her personal Barbie doll for experiments and product demonstrations during my teen years. It didn't.

We were all past that now, mostly. And though Bess and I would never be close, she had been a real comfort to me in the days and weeks after my father died. In fact, she was instrumental in making the teaching gig at St. John's possible. She knew someone who knew someone. I'd always been grateful to her for that.

Going back to my apartment held little appeal, and I could always eat. "Throw in a beer, and you got a deal."

"It's a deal then."

I might not have filled Bess's beauty-queen-daughter void, but I held my own, filling Marty's rougher-around-the-edges version.

We spent the afternoon on the O'Shea's beautiful backyard deck, overlooking their small but lush urban oasis. Bess had the same discerning eye and artistic touch on their home as she did for faces. Room by room, they had remodeled the house they owned outright, and like my building, the bland outward appearance hid a modern, high-end, skillfully designed renovation inside it.

Bess played the merry hostess and fed us fried chicken, collards, and potato salad with peach cobbler for dessert. Like Leo, she had transplanted her southern roots decades ago, but you'd never know it to hear her speak.

It was the peaches that brought the visit to an end. A flashed image of Trey sniffing fresh produce at the farmer's market turned to the horrifying thoughts of the ordeal he'd endure getting back in Gleb Trubetzkoy's good graces. And even if Trey's boss said he'd let me be, who would trust him to keep his word?

I asked Marty to take me home.

Nineteen

On the ride home from Sunday dinner at the O'Shea's, I wondered if getting dropped off by an unmarked police car helped or hurt my chances in the aftermath of my lethal assault, but I didn't much care. We rolled past a dark blue sedan I didn't recognize with a person I didn't know in the driver's seat. My healthy paranoia gave me an itch. Did I know every car on my block? No, don't be silly. That would be impossible, but I *did* know every resident's car in my neighborhood and those that frequently visited. *This* was not one of those cars. I would also like it noted for the record that, less than twenty-four hours earlier, I performed a textbook Rubicon Blow, killing the nephew of a crime boss. Everyone should excuse me for being a tad twitchy.

"Hey, take another lap, yeah? I meant to ask you about something."

Marty kept driving, but his eyes were in the rearview. "What's that, kiddo?"

"You got a good security firm? Locks and such? It's time this building owner made some improvements. I'm thinking of beefing up the place a bit. Nothing major. No barbed electrical or anything, just an upgrade."

"Sure. I'll send you somebody. Be here tomorrow," Marty kept his tone breezy. "And while we're chatting—there's no reason you shouldn't sleep at your place tonight, is there? If you need a bed, you could—"

We drove by the blue sedan again. It sat empty, but a stick-straight woman, with dark hair graying at her temples, had just closed the trunk and carried a box to the row house just behind it. I expelled a breath and thought Marty did also.

"I'm good, Marty. You know I love my home. Just want some peace-of-mind."

"Yeah, why don't I meet you and the security guy? Maybe I could make some suggestions. Be sure he gives you a good deal."

I wanted to say no, but a quick glimpse at Marty told me I wasn't the only one in need of some peace-of-mind. "Sounds great. Let me know the time. I'll be here." I hopped out of the car and gave a gentle hip check to close the door. "And—now, don't be thinking one has anything to do with the other, but if you're headed to the range anytime soon, I wouldn't mind blowing the dust off my nine-millimeter. I mean, if you're going." I leaned in the open window, aiming for nonchalance.

Marty frowned with one eye closed like he flipped through his mental calendar. "Let's do locks tomorrow, Glocks on Tuesday." He smiled at his rhyme.

"You just come up with that, or have you been holding on to it on the off chance this day would come?"

"I'll never tell. Good night, kid. See you tomorrow. And I'm in no rush so, I'm gonna sit here and watch you walk inside. Not for any reason. Just because."

"Good night, Marty." I didn't have the heart to tell him how little safety that exercise offered or how I knew that now, but I smiled and waved as I stepped into the easy-to-breach vestibule that in another twenty-four hours would be a fortress. Marty would see to it.

Instead of unlocking my door, I knocked on Leo's. Apologies were in order, and they came with a heaping portion of peach cobbler.

"Like my Mee-maw used to make." Leo made grabby hands for the dessert.

"So, I'm forgiven?"

"For being pissy earlier? Shut-up." He fetched a spoon and dove into the summertime treat. "Mmm, it's still warm. But would some vanilla ice cream have killed ya?" A grin followed another bite, then he pointed at my other bundle with the utensil. "What's in the bag?"

"*Ms. Jolie.* Bess thought I should cover this." I gestured to my entire face. "Guaranteed to match my skin tone," I chirped.

"Well, thank goodness. You'll never snag a man looking like that. Speaking of a man..."

"I wasn't, and I don't want to." I hadn't meant to snap. "Sorry."

Leo waved off the second apology.

"No, Leo, really. Are *you* okay? I mean, I've always known you were a force, but you were incredible—"

"Hush. Growing up a queer Jew in the rural south, at a time nowhere near as accepting as today, I have experienced my share of shit. And while I always had my sister—and Sadie Jane is a real hellcat to be reckoned with— eventually, I had size on my side. But my work in an emergency department gives me a front-row seat to the effects of violence perpetrated by brutes, far too often. The opportunity to *take out the trash* was some of the best therapy I've had in years. And hear me when I say, I have had myself some therapy. Don't think me cold, but I *have* not and *will* not lose any sleep over my part in this brouhaha. I'm just glad it wasn't worse—for you and that our new friend saved the day."

"Oh, he didn't—I mean, if he hadn't shown up, it would have been bad, but he didn't—I'm the one who—"

Leo put up his hand, saving me from a confession. "And just when I thought I couldn't love you more. Sorry I assumed wrong. Should have known you were the real deal. My little ginger badass."

I appreciated the compliment and was only slightly stunned by Leo's ability to brush off the *brouhaha*, to use his euphemism. "I'm having the locks changed, upgraded, tomorrow. Maybe some extras? Nothing real obvious. It's all my treat, of course. And for the record, you have *zero* knowledge of anything happening across the hall the last twenty-four hours."

"You have my key. If you need in here, you do what you gotta do. And as for the last twenty-four hours, I don't have a clue what you're prattling on about."

My phone buzzed, my personal line, but it wasn't a number I knew. I dismissed the call.

"I won't make too much mess. Promise."

"I'm not worried—"

My phone buzzed again. Same number. I declined it— again.

"Sorry. I don't know the number, and it's not my business line, so I'm not answering." I slipped the phone back in my pocket, then caught Leo's wide-eyed look. "What?"

"Don't you reckon you should? Could be—?"

"Shit!" I scrambled to retrieve it. "Shit, Leo. Shit, shit, shit. No, he wouldn't—he wouldn't call." I glared at the screen, willing it to ring again. Nothing. I sighed, "I'm going to bed." But when confronted with my apartment door, I stopped short, not eager to enter.

"Honey, want me to come with?" Another man with another breezy tone asking another question with heavy subtext.

"Nope. I'm good. Ginger badass, remember? Thanks though. Night, Auntie Leo."

The place loomed ghostly quiet, but with everything exactly as I'd left it. I hung my knapsack and carried my *Ms. Jolie* upstairs. Across the room, my bed with its meticulously placed pillows struck me as odd. The tight bed linens could have passed a barracks inspection. Hard to imagine Trey in the military... or was it? *Hm.* Nope. There should be no thinking of Trey, in any way, shape, or military branch. Effective immediately. I approached a window and only paused a second before pulling the drapes closed. No light pollution would disturb me in the morning. I could sleep until noon if I dared. Nothing to keep me—my phone chirped, and I couldn't move fast enough to get to it.

Marty: *Locksmith at 9am tomorrow*

I replied.

Me: *Great! See you then.*

I slipped the phone back into my pocket. So much for sleeping until noon. Who was I kidding? I'd be up, anyway. Kicking off my shoes, I shimmied out of my joggers while fetching the top of my pajama set. The laundry mound reminded me the next day was wash day, but the idea of a visit to that room made my skin prickle. As if on cue, my phone rang again, the buzz coming from the basket of dirty clothes. I rummaged through the pile and accepted the call as soon as I got my hand on the device.

"Hello?"

Silence.

"Is it—you?" Somehow, saying Trey's name seemed risky. "Jesus, are you okay? Because if you mean to ease my mind, I—I appreciate it, but you're doing it wrong." I waited, finally hearing an exhale on the other end. "Please—say something."

A cleared throat sounded, followed by, "Hattie?"

Imagine my surprise when a woman's voice spoke my name—that wasn't my name. No woman had called me Hattie since Ms. McDermott, the first day of eighth grade. I had become Harry that summer and from then on would only answer to that, with the rare exception for Harriet. Until Friday. Seventeen years and a Friday later, I became Hattie again.

The woman repeated the name, nudging me from my stupor. "Hattie Smith?"

"Who's calling?"

"It's—Trey's—*Mom*."

My legs gave way. I skimmed the edge of the bed, sliding to the floor. While I tried to swallow and focus on breathing, the room tilted as light flashes in my periphery disoriented me.

"He's—Trey is—okay," the woman finally said.

"Jesus, Mrs. Popov. You really should have led with that." My head rested back on my mattress; the feeling slowly tingled back into my limbs.

"What? Uh, no. Don't call me that, please."

"Oh, sorry. What should I—"

"Mom. Just call me Mom."

"Not sure I—"

"What you call me is irrelevant. We won't ever speak again. But he asked me to pass along a message."

"And he's— okay?" I needed to hear it again.

"He's alive. He will heal."

"Thank you. Thank you for letting me know. I've—"

"There's more, and I can't talk long."

"Oh—"

"I don't know what these next two items mean, so don't waste time asking me questions." "Mom" sounded a bit perturbed, if not overtly civil. And frankly, I had a difficult time believing the woman was old enough to be Trey's mother. She didn't sound it, but it was hard to judge over the phone. I forced myself to focus on any background noise and whether I detected an accent. I heard neither.

"Okay."

"First, he said he got his reward."

I didn't make a sound but closed my eyes, hoping to slow the spinning room this new information propelled.

"Does that make sense to you? Do you know what he means?" Mom's tone included concern now, but I had lost my initial warm fuzzies and had no intention of divulging any intel to the nameless, faceless woman who may or may not be a true ally.

"What's the second thing?" I let Mom know two could play the stoicism game.

Her frustration read plainly with another cleared throat. "He said, and this is a quote, Hattie, if I had, I wouldn't have left, end quote."

I let the words sink in and nodded to no one. "Uh, Mom?" I didn't like the way that word felt coming out of my mouth.

"This is a burner, so don't bother with the number. Goodbye." The line went dead.

Twenty

SLEEP DIDN'T COME EASY. "Mom's" words echoed, *Trey is—okay, He's alive. He will heal.* And while the relief at hearing those words lifted the suffocating weight of *not* knowing from my chest, the heft of the guilt that replaced it smothered me in my bed. And how did I know any of it was true? Was "Mom" someone to be trusted? Trey had obviously confided some personal information to the woman. Then again, she admitted she didn't know the meaning of two of the messages, and I was only certain of one. I couldn't be sure of the last part. *...if I had, I wouldn't have left.* If it meant what I guessed, it was more reason not to sleep and definitely not something I wanted to hear by proxy. Maybe not at all.

Every time I closed my eyes, the *smack* of hard fists hitting softer flesh assailed me, followed by the grunty whisper of my name, *Hattie*. Each jerk awake, I grew angrier, realizing I found myself in the one role I never wanted to be cast, the damn damsel, the maiden in need of saving. I thrashed out of my sheets in a sweat and a grunt of my own, equal parts furious at myself for causing the predicament and outraged at Trey for stepping up to rescue me, as it were. How *dare* he?

Laundry day kicked off early. Sunlight before five-thirty seemed as good a reason as any to get on with the scheduled task. I took solace in the start of a new week, back to my humdrum existence, the routine I longed for and prided myself for keeping. Last week had been an outlier, an aberration, but it was over, and life would settle into its usual rhythm beginning with two loads of wash, one for lights, one for darks. Banality at its best.

My return to the tedium I sought hit a momentary hiccup when I pushed through the laundry room door and remembered what Leo had done there Saturday night. A light and funny podcast would need to accompany the morning's chore. I'd be skipping the true-crime options until further notice.

By seven-thirty, my second pot of coffee brewed while I put away the last of the towels I failed to free from the bloodstains. So no, my mood had yet to improve. A timid knock on the door could only be one person, and Leo and I rarely interacted so early in the day.

"Heard you up and about. Headed for an ED shift at Westrock, but I thought I'd drop these by." Leo filled my apartment door frame dressed in lavender scrubs and Nikes. He held a white bundle in one hand and a crisply pressed, white dress shirt on a hanger in the other.

I stared.

He paused with an *ahem* before offering the garments again. "Cold water and ammonia get out the blood."

"Now you tell me." I grimaced, thinking of my stained towels.

"This one has a slice through it—from the—"

"Yeah, I remember." I took the folded men's undershirt.

"Glad I could salvage this. No damage done. Just wish it fit me." The dress shirt swung side to side on the index finger, balancing the hanger hook. "Tom Ford. It's a $600 shirt."

"Seriously?" More math I couldn't figure.

"Yeah, your track star has expensive taste."

"He's not my—"

"Yeah, yeah. Just saying you might overlook the Adidas. Tom Ford washes away any number of sins." Leo's bright eyes were more than I had the stomach for at the early hour, and he wasn't helping me get on with my mundane way of life.

"Maybe, but not all the sins." I stalled before reluctantly taking the hanger.

"Ain't nothing wrong with a little sin, honey." He held up his index finger and thumb, measuring an inch in front of a wicked grin and a wink.

I didn't know how to reply, so I moved on to the day's business. "Security company coming today, don't forget."

Leo sighed with a disappointed look. "Fine. We won't dish." He waved his hand as he walked away.

"Wait. What am I supposed to do with this?" I called to Leo, who made his escape for the day.

"Return it to its owner." Though he faced away from me, his sigh told me of his exasperation, and I could imagine the eye roll accompanying it.

"Pretty sure he's not coming around again, Leo. Scene of the crime and all that."

"*Ha.* Oh, he'll be back. But he won't be comin' for the shirt, honey. That's for *damn* sure." Leo never looked back as he cackled his way out the front door.

Marty arrived shortly before our nine o'clock appointment with his security guy. Top Security was a local outfit with close ties to law enforcement. They provided personalized service without requiring cameras or speaker panels I had no interest in installing.

Between their expert, Marty, and me, we devised a plan that satisfied everyone, and I didn't feel like I'd turned my home into a fishbowl.

"Coffee?"

"No, thank you. Trying to cut back. Hey, you okay, kiddo?"

"Lack of sleep." I shrugged.

"*Hm.* Well, hopefully today's upgrades will be a help."

Marty had the remarkable ability to let me know he had a pretty clear understanding of what I *wasn't* saying, and it relieved me to know he noted my concern but still respected my not wanting to admit to any of it. My dad had often been supportive in a similar way. Why wallow in the details when a *humph* and coffee would do?

After a twelve-hour shift, my poor neighbor listed blurry-eyed as I ran through the additions to our new bastion. We reset access codes and safety phrases with Top Security, the firm responsible for all the latest bells and safety whistles. We got a bit silly in our shared exhaustion and it was almost fun.

Despite the rush job of Marty's guy tightening up the duplex security, sleep remained a stranger. Lying in bed, I should have been a study in serenity, a paradigm of peace, but it all made me more paranoid. I convinced myself the only way I would ever rest easy again was if I set eyes on an alive-and-well Trey Popov. *Dream on, Harry.*

Twenty-One

"Hey, kiddo. Slight change-up in our gun range field trip." Marty sounded remarkably chipper for the Tuesday morning phone call.

"What's that?"

"We'll still go, but I'm held up a bit at the M.E.'s office. Was hoping you could holster up and meet me here. Is that a problem?"

"No, no problem. Already holstered even. I can be there in twenty if I leave now. Can't help but notice a certain smile in your voice for a veteran detective meeting with the Medical Examiner. Care to—"

"I'll tell you about it later. Meet you at the south lot. See you soon." Marty ended the call.

No, an outing to target shoot wasn't a regular excursion, so routine eluded me for yet another day. But monotony would be back in force any minute, and I would spend the rest of the summer eager to return to the classroom. As a matter of fact, I could already feel normalcy creeping its way into my life. *What does normal look like? And who'd want it, anyway? Not cool, Harry.*

The heat of the day in full swing, I kept to the street's shady side on the mile trek to the hospital campus that included the Medical Examiner's office.

"There you are. I was thinking of calling again. Thought you might have gotten lost or chickened out." Marty sweated on the street corner, forced to wear a jacket and tie while on the job.

"Sorry. Trouble getting the lead out these days. But chicken out? I don't think so. Best shot wins lunch. And I *love* lunch."

We rode to a local indoor range. The owners appreciated a police presence on the grounds, and we didn't need to jump through any NYPD approval hoops to get me in the door. My dad taught me to handle a weapon and regularly tested my abilities. Since he died, Marty had taken me to practice a handful of times, but he never pushed the issue. I appreciated that.

As it turns out, I lost the friendly competition, but not by much. Considering how long it had been since I'd fired the handgun, it gratified me to see I still had the goods. Likewise, my challenger was a phenomenal shot. Even broaching his mid-fifties, I rested easier knowing Marty had my back. He also bought me lunch. I only fought him for a moment, but since Sunday, when we made the plan, I figured Martin O'Shea would insist on buying me a burger and fries after he put me through my paces. We sat at a graffitied picnic table, appreciating the shade of an out-of-place maple tree in the urban setting. I sprinkled malt vinegar and dove into the salty tang of the best hand-cut fries in Queens.

"So, what brought you to ol' Dr. Dom's today?"

Dr. Dombrowski reigned as the local M.E. for years, dating back to when my dad was on the job. But since moving out of Major Crimes Homicide Division and onto Special Enforcement, Marty didn't need to frequent the tiny woman's crypt often. I don't believe he missed her, either. He never said, but I imagined memories of his partner on a cold slab still haunted him. I never had to endure that particular nightmare because Marty stood in for the identification. In truth, I never saw the dead body, or *anyone's* dead body, until Saturday.

"A buddy from Major Crimes wants some insight on a case he caught. A cadaver dump. A strange circumstance that gets stranger, the more Dr. Dom looks into it." Marty's cheerful air mystified me.

"What gives? Not like you to be so cavalier when speaking of the dead."

"Couldn't have happened to a more wretched individual. One less bottom-feeder for us to deal with if I can be so blunt. Wouldn't mind shaking the deadly hand of the perpetrator, though. That's what makes it an interesting one. Someone tried to disguise the cause of death, probably hoping no one would go looking too deep into the matter—the Scum of the Earth and all."

The first warning bell sounded in my head. My mouthful of burger grew, and I forced myself to chew, hoping I could swallow it.

"Of course, that's also the downside of the situation. The creep got off easy. Sure, a few hard blows prior. More than a few, to be sure. He must have made someone good and angry and that someone landed some doozies to confirm just how raging mad he was about it."

I'd been in such a haze, lying on the floor in my apartment while Trey fought a losing battle against the bigger Vlad who had gotten the upper hand. To hear that, even in the weaker position, Trey had fought hard, done some damage in my defense, served as an awful reminder of how badly the night could have ended.

"But then he took a blade to the base of the skull." Marty jerked me out of the terrifying flashback, confirming my fear. "Probably never knew what hit him. A shame, really. Thing is, whoever did the deed was trained—*well*-trained. This was no backroom brawl gone amok. Someone put *Vlad the Bad* down." As the detective told his tale, he continued to gobble up his burger and scarf down fries while I lost my appetite. "You okay, Harry? Sorry, was that inappropriate mealtime conversation? Probably."

"No, it's fine." I picked at the sesame seeds on my bun. Despite the summer heat, my hands had gone cold and clammy, my stomach tightened. "*Vlad the Bad*, huh?"

Marty chuckled. "Yeah, and while the name certainly suited, it was even more fitting because 'bad' was the extent of the miscreant's spelling ability. Long on the propensity to knock around women, short on IQ points. You sure you're all right? You look pale. Green, almost."

I nodded.

He paused. "You gonna eat those fries?"

I pushed the grease-splotched cardboard container toward the man, officially done with my meal.

"Anyway, my buddy caught the case and heard I'd been looking at suspected crime boss Gleb Trubetzkoy. He thought I might have some insight, seeing as Vlad is—*was* Trubetzkoy's nephew. Another fun fact—your new pal? Popov? These are the people he's spending time with these days. Well, not lately, actually. Popov seems to have fallen off the radar."

Eye contact, Harry, and keep eating.

I shrugged. "Told you he wouldn't stick around with the dowdy schoolteacher beyond the weekend." I forced myself to choke down another bite of the burger. It lodged midway.

"So, Popov—"

"What's to come of poor ol' Vladislav now? I mean, what'll be your involvement?" I bulldozed the good detective, hoping he'd take the hint and back away from my personal life, at least long enough for me to figure out how to handle the situation. It was ham-fisted at best.

Marty tidied up the remnants of lunch, but his tone hardened from his earlier light-heartedness. "Not my case, not my problem. I'm months away from retirement, and I've kicked over enough rocks in my thirty years. I'm tired. I'd like to ease on out, if possible."

I strained for a deep breath and slurped on my straw to force down that last morsel.

"You sure you're okay? Typically, you'd be all over a thing like this. Drilling for details. Where was the body found? When? Did he have a phone? Boxers or briefs? Not like you to be so—indifferent."

"It's like you said, just one more bad guy off the street, right?"

"Yeah, interesting though. Whoever dumped the body must have wanted it found. And while all signs point to it being a *domestic* dispute— let's call it—if it had been an in-house job, there's no way they'd want that body recovered. Curious, right?"

"I guess." We plodded to the car. I slid into the hot vehicle, resting my eyes and head, but my stomach churned more with every word Marty spoke. "Crank that A/C, yeah?"

"Sure. Sure." He turned up the blower and let us ride in quiet for a block. The respite didn't last long. "So, if I could pick your Ivy League brain for a sec—what kind of professional offing looks decidedly *unprofessional*, followed by a double-down on the amateur angle, making sure local LEOs find the body? Unless, maybe, it's a message, letting us know a regime change is on the horizon. Someone new on the rise. Quietly making a name for himself while clearing the way of competition. Of course, that'd probably be somebody fresh on the scene, out of nowhere, someone that nobody saw coming. Smart, though. Patient."

Trey flashed in my mind. I fought it, but things only got worse from there.

Marty wouldn't let up, and I recognized the tactic, but it was too late. The flow through the vent wasn't cool, much less cold, and suspicion told me the air "malfunction" was by design. I may have inadvertently pulled the pin on a grenade I hadn't even realized I held. The questions remaining: was it a dud, and if not, could I get the handheld bomb re-pinned?

I doubled-down too. "I really couldn't say, Uncle Marty." When in doubt, ingratiate yourself.

"Right. Well, someone else's pickle to get out of, I guess." He pulled to the curb in front of my duplex.

"Thanks for to—"

"Something else I find funny?" Marty pushed further. "Not funny, ha-ha, but funny, peculiar, and it's just this last thing, and then I'll let you go do whatever it is you seem to be in such a hurry to go do."

In total opposition to his words, Marty seemed to slow his prattling. A tortuous rambling layer added to his ploy. The heat blasted. Sweat soaked through my shirt and carried the telltale acrid whiff of stress. If I'd just...opened... the door— but that would mean admitting defeat. *Dig deeper, Harry.*

"The thing is, most people hear the name Vlad—and I don't know if it's twenty-first-century politics or what have you, but most people—I dare say, *anyone* who isn't of Russian descent anyway, most *anyone* who hears the name Vlad would assume the person called that—*Vlad*, I mean—*most everyone* would think his name was Vladimir. Funny, though, and again, not funny ha-ha, but more—*funny*-isn't-this-interesting—*you* went with the far less common Vladislav, which, as luck would have it, *is*—or *was* Vlad's real first name."

As the metaphorical grenade exploded, I pushed open the passenger side door, and for the second time in three days, depending on how you want to count it, I vomited. This time directly into the sewer grate, where the calculating Marty probably had the forethought to park.

Twenty-Two

"WHAT DO YOU SAY we get out of this heat, let you wash up, and then have a chat? An honest one. And that goes for both of us." Whatever pleasantries may have remained fell to the wayside, and Marty didn't wait for a reply. He reached the sidewalk before my brain coordinated with my legs to exit the pressure cooker of the unmarked police car.

My body continued its betrayal as I struggled to decipher Marty's expression. Disappointment? Hurt? Anger? Maybe some fear? All of it, I guessed, plus something else. I'd seen the mystery look before, if only for a flicker, but its significance eluded me. My guess was it involved my dad.

I left Marty downstairs and took my time washing up in the privacy of my bedroom. The impending "chat" would be an uncomfortable interrogation, and I wasn't eager for the grilling. Stalling further, I stopped to touch the well-pressed and apparently expensive dress shirt draped on a hanger that dangled from a dresser drawer pull. My imagination fancied it a sort of guardian angel since Leo had given it to me. A white seraph that kept watch as an ethereal addition to the more high-tech security installed for my safety. Now, my trust in the garment had waned. I almost laughed when that silly notion skittered across my brain.

Such faith in a shirt? Even Tom Ford? My humor fizzled, and more doubt flooded in to take its place. Was Trey Popov some diabolical mastermind intent on usurping the power of a major player in a criminal organization? Had I inadvertently paved the way for his speedy rise? I suspected Marty had plans to make the case for this very thing, but instinct told me the veteran police detective had it all wrong.

Of course, I had no evidence to the contrary. And who the hell was I to think I knew better than the trained professional with decades of experience? Sure, my alma mater would claim they'd prepared me for this moment. But along with the fancy degree, I also had implicit bias—a big no-no in my field, but at least I recognized it. Historically, my gut had proved reliable. But in this scenario, a part of me wondered if I mistook that intuition for something else—something less logical, less trustworthy, more quixotic. *Shit, Harry.*

"I'd offer you a beer, but it's two o'clock on a Tuesday. Then again, the adage 'it's five o'clock somewhere' never felt truer than it does right now. Actually, going on a week, if I'm honest." I returned to the living room but didn't stop on my way to the kitchen.

Marty sat next to my sofa's now undetectable vomit spot I could never unsee. I added *new couch* to my growing shopping list.

"Just water, thanks," he replied.

I bided my time, pouring two full glasses. The wall clock's tick *clunked* louder, the only sound as I delivered the beverage, then settled into the armchair adjacent to my guest's perch. It required significant resolve to stay in that seat when I remembered Gleb Trubetzkoy had been the last person to use it. A visible shiver racked my frame at the same moment the air conditioner hummed to life. Irony and tension hung around my shoulders like weights, keeping me pinned to the chair forever soiled by that most recent occupant. *Add new chairs, too.*

Marty sipped his water but raised a finger to signal he meant to speak first. After placing the glass on a coaster, he sat back in the low-profile divan—his effort to look relaxed apparent, but unsuccessful.

"I'll ask the annoying question first, so we can get the touchy-feely part done, since neither of us cares for such—stuff." The mere mention of such *stuff* propelled him forward again to take another swallow of water. This kind of agitation from Marty was new to me.

"Are you—okay? I mean, physically? Your face looks better than at the gym. Much better. Sometimes it doesn't go that way. Sometimes it's a few days later, and it looks worse even, but yours looks—better. And obviously, I don't mean just your face, I mean are you—" Marty's voice hitched, "Were you—"

"Whoa, Uncle Marty, I'm okay," I rushed to relieve the typically composed man. "Whatever nightmare you've concocted—it didn't happen."

The back of Marty's head hit the wall as a chest full of air exploded toward the ceiling. His hands had a subtle quake as he rubbed his face before his fingers tugged at his hair. If I didn't know better, it looked grayer than yesterday. Grayer than an hour ago. His cheeks glowed pink, shades darker than a few minutes earlier when I entered the room, too preoccupied to notice the man's pallor. In hindsight, the difference registered.

"Are *you* okay?" I'd never seen the man so haggard or so flustered.

He sighed, "Better now. Yes. Better now. It's just Vlad has—*had* a nasty M.O. and—"

"Didn't happen. Could have, but—" Revisiting the nightmare served no purpose. I moved on. "How did you know? How'd you connect it to me?"

"I didn't. Not until you stopped eating and even then I—"

"Outed by my love for French fries? Thwarted by carbs, again." My attempt to lighten the mood fell flat.

"You need to tell me what happened. Where? Witnesses? Everything."

"Am I talking to Uncle Marty or NYPD Detective Martin O'Shea?" I flexed and squeezed my fingers and hands together, trying to regain feeling in their cold numbness.

"I'm both, and it doesn't matter with you. You will always be on the right side as far as I'm concerned. Always."

I wished I believed Marty's sentiment. I'm sure *he* believed it, but I had lost trust in everything for the moment, and I treaded lightly through this minefield. I told no outright lies. My dishonesty came in the form of omission, and I had no qualms about the information I left out of my story, plus some details that had no bearing on the night. Leo's name never crossed my lips.

"It wasn't until Trubetzkoy left that things really turned violent," I continued with the vague play-by-play. "Aside from Tr—Popov's rough handling of me, but that was— a ruse."

"A ruse?"

"He only meant to buy time and hoped to get both Gleb and Vlad out of here. Of course, I didn't know that. Even after Vlad was down, I didn't know."

"How did you—"

"Vlad backhanded me," I pointed to my cheek, "and in the initial shock of that, I admit, things went hazy for a bit. I didn't lose consciousness, but I got my bell rung pretty good. When my vision cleared some, Popov and Vlad were going at it, hard. I don't know why I didn't just run, but I saw the blade—it belonged to Trey—and it was automatic. I acted without thinking and pulled the knife. Exactly as my training taught me."

We both took a moment to breathe.

"But just Vlad?"

"Yes, I only *stabbed* Vlad. Then Trey made it clear he wasn't there to hurt me. I believed him. He took care of getting rid of the body. I can't tell you anything about that. I mean, I don't *know* anything about that."

"So, Popov was alive last you saw?"

The question knocked the wind out of me. It had been two days since I heard Trey was okay. *He's alive. He will heal.* But even that held no guarantee. I cleared my tight throat and stretched my neck to speak, hoping it looked like a casual nod. "Is he— dead now?"

"Don't know. Just MIA, let's say."

Marty's answer provided little relief, but I knew I needed to get okay with the idea I might never find out if Trey Popov lived. I wanted to be done with the conversation.

"And he just left? No discussion of his plan to explain his boss's nephew's untimely death? Popov took the body and left?"

"Uncle Marty, the last time I saw the body, it was being dragged from this apartment. Hand to—"

"Let's not bring God into this, okay, Harry?"

I omitted Trey's plan to take credit for the killing and his intention to ask for my freedom from any retribution. I didn't even know if any of that was true anymore, so I kept those nuggets to myself and hoped I satisfied Marty enough to let the whole ordeal drop—at least for the time being. "Can we be done? Can we let this go now?"

"Not just yet. I owe you an apology, Harry."

"Okay."

"Friday, when I called, and Gantry Plaza hadn't gone down the way I hoped, I said I knew better than to get you involved. I did, but sometimes, as a cop, you get desperate. And as an almost *retired* cop, I'm feeling some serious desperation. My clock is running out, and I've got a cold case that I want more than anything to close, and the brass won't let me have it. So, I called you."

"Uncle Marty, it's—"

"Let me get this out, kid."

I eased back into the sullied chair to allow Marty to clear his conscience for inviting me into a mess I had twisted into an unmitigated shambles.

"I wanted a way into Trubetzkoy's world. I've been eyeing him a long time, and some weeks back this new guy showed up out of nowhere. Low level, periphery stuff but a new rock to kick over, nonetheless. So, with a couple of rookies joining the squad, it took little urging for them to be on the hunt. To drag him in if they got the opportunity. *Any* opportunity. I know. Not my most scrupulous career move, but like I said—desperate. After my first interview, like you, I saw more to the man, but I missed something. Missed the sociopath signs. I didn't see the drive or initiative to climb the criminal ladder."

"Sociopath?"

Marty kept talking. "Blinded by the frustration of going out without finishing the job, I guess. I saw a sad guy who didn't like what he'd gotten himself into, and I figured I could use that to get inside and clear my case—the last case before I put my shield in a drawer for good. I got tunnel vision, duped by the rare smart felon, and it put you in a bad spot."

My brain spun at Marty's determination to paint Trey as some puppet-master villain. My instincts said otherwise, but then I doubted I could trust those instincts. The theory versus practicum debate replayed, and I wondered if the talented Mr. Popov had duped me, too. I wished it was my gut that said no, but I feared the intuition lived somewhere north of there, but south of my brain. And I'd rarely known my heart to be trustworthy.

"The irony being I wanted to close the case for you. Prove law enforcement is a righteous path, a noble way to go, good wins, even if some good guys get lost along the way. I've seen you're stuck, and I wanted to pry you free. Get you back on track. Do you know what the average age of a recruit at Quantico is?"

"Thirty," I mumbled.

"Of course, you know. So, you've been considering it? Again, I mean."

I shrugged.

"And how old are you?"

"Thirty," I sighed.

"And you're in fitter shape, a surer shot, and smarter than any of them."

Truthfully, I'd been considering it for a while, and never more so than the last few days. I had initiated the process once before but quit. Getting anyone's hopes up—including mine—with the prospect of taking another run at it didn't seem fair or wise.

"What's the case?" I opted to switch gears.

"*Hm*?"

"The case you want to clear before you and Bess begin living your best Caribbean cruise life?"

The wounded look took over Marty's face again, but I also thought I detected shame. Only one thing shamed Martin O'Shea, disgraced him in his mind.

"Dad's? Trubetzkoy killed my dad?" The shock kept my question to a near-whisper.

"Not the old man, but yes, his people were responsible. I'm sure of it."

And that was the moment the plan to take down Gleb Trubetzkoy took root—my mundane life, Marty, and *everyone* else be damned.

Twenty-Three

As the week went on, I hit pay-dirt. Not with my plans for the Trubetzkoy takedown. That would take time, patience, planning. All that happened too, but I couldn't rush the scheme. My immediate success came in the form of my routine—old habits made new again. I went to the gym and upped my workout, including running a little farther each day. Scheduled chores got done on their assigned days, and ultimately I sent that *final* whopping invoice to the writer-client that shan't be named. By Friday, I looked and felt more like myself again, except better, stronger, with a clearer head and new goals in mind.

Marty conducted a daily check-in, which isn't something he'd done in the past, but I concluded it might continue for a while. A quick phone call didn't infringe too much, so I allowed it. If I could provide the man some peace-of-mind, why not? And seeing the strain I'd caused earlier in the week, a regular *Hello. How's it going?* seemed the least I could do.

"Marty. Hello. How's it going?" I stopped at a bus bench to insert my earbuds for my phone.

"Made it through another work week, so I can't complain."

"Yeah, you're such a nine-to-five, Monday through Friday kinda guy, but whatever."

"Sounds like you're outside."

"Yep. Doing my Friday thing. But feeling a little *extra* today because Nate set me up with a new sparring partner, and I just kicked his ass—uh, *butt* in the ring. Good stuff. Got a little weird when the dude asked for my number afterward, but we agreed our time together would be best spent in the square circle."

Marty chuckled. "You both agreed to that, huh? Right after he asked for your number, and you shot him down? What was wrong with this one? Too short? Too young? Too dumb?"

"Take your pick." I continued walking. "I sure hope you're not implying I'm finicky or urging me to lower some too-high standards I've arbitrarily set."

"Who me? Never crossed my mind, and if it did, I'd never be fool enough to speak the words aloud."

"That's what I thought. Don't let anyone ever tell you that you aren't a wise man, Martin O'Shea." Finding our witty repartee again made me happy.

"Ok, kiddo. Glad to hear you're like your old self. If you have nothing *new* to report, I'll let you get on with your day."

"Right. Bye, Marty."

Hmm. Detective O'Shea's daily dialing had morphed from friendly chit-chat to more of an info dig. But surely the old man knew I'd detect the tactic. Don't get me wrong. I knew he cared about me, but it seemed he was nosing around, unable to let the Trubetzkoy thing go, like a dog with a bone. Too bad for him, really, because now that bone belonged to me.

The day grew overcast, but it didn't help with the heat. The humidity and workout sweat had my clothes clinging to me, and tendrils sprung from my messy bun stuck to my neck. To avoid the would-be suitor, I'd bolted from the gym without topping off my water bottle. Draining the last of it, I picked up my pace to get to my next stop before the skies opened and thrashed down rain. My Friday market visit would be a quick one.

Rounding the corner to the farmer's market gate, I found many of those earnest Friday shoppers shared my weather concerns. The lot teemed with customers trying to beat the downpour, and sellers scurried to erect pop-up canopies to encourage buyers to stick around if the rain came. But a little precipitation wouldn't keep me from my produce. Let's not forget, I had a schedule to stick to.

I completed my first pass, taking a mental inventory of the day's options, then grabbed a basket to make my selections. Vegetables and fruit made my list, also farm-fresh eggs and a crusty loaf of artisan bread. As usual, the leafy greens came first.

"Again with the picky lettuce inspection?"

A bundle of romaine rolled out of my grasp as I froze, stunned to hear his voice behind me.

"Don't turn around, please. Best not to be noticed talking to one another." Trey reached around me; his arm clad in the familiar navy-blue edition of his tracksuit collection. He placed my dropped lettuce bunch into my basket.

"Your—hand looks better." Those were the first words I could push from my lips, and I felt foolish when I heard them. Of all the things I had to say, all the things I swore I *would* say if we ever crossed paths, all the things I *had* said to his stupid dress shirt still keeping watch while I slept, and those were the four words to win out? *Jesus, Harry.*

"Your face looks better." He huffed and cleared his throat. "Sorry, that sounded—I just—I just wanted to see you. See that you were okay, and you said you came here most Fridays, so I took a chance."

Trey's heat radiated on my back, and I leaned into the basket wedged between my hip and the veggie display in an effort not to spin around to see him.

"Is that all?" I asked. The two of us stood still under a Day-Glo awning in front of shallow plastic crates full of lettuce varieties while rushed patrons jostled about the long aisle of produce. It struck me how differently the Saturday market crowd browsed while the Friday version bustled in a more business-like way. That afternoon's frenzy ran at an even higher gear than usual. Maybe the weather was to blame, or my stunned state was distorting my perception.

"What?"

"Is that all? Because if you just wanted to see me, you could have done that from across the street. Or near my apartment. But no, you had to come to speak to me, tell me I can't see you. I can't turn around to see if *you're* okay? I have to take your word for it, your—*Mom's* word for it? This may come as a shock to you, but I'm not a big fan of being told what I can and cannot do or getting left in the dark, or ghosted, or *stalked,* for that matter."

His breath swept my neck when he chuckled. "*God,* I missed you."

That blow stiffened me again, but I juddered out of it quickly.

"You *can't* say that. You can't *say* that." My anger ratcheted. "You are the most con*founding*—" I clenched my jaw and my fists, unleashing on the leafy greens just above a whisper. "Why are you—you said—I don't know what you want from me, and while I hate to admit it, you— got under my skin. Not sure why. Could be the whole bad-boy-mystery thing, which has never *been* my thing but you *did,* you *have*—but I've had a few days to—you know—get over it, because you and I are just an *awful* idea on *so* many levels. And while I appreciate you coming around to check on me, which, by the way, is also *not* my thing, you need to stop. You go your way, and I'll go mine because let's remember who and what you are, and I am the *absolute* opposite of that—or could be. Unless you're planning a major career change, which I highly recommend because—you *should*. I'm a pretty good reader of people, and you're a good person. Leo thinks so, and you're smart and funny if not a tad serious and not bad to look at—at least five days ago—full of potential—which is probably why I like you—*NO*, I dislike you, and you need to stay away."

Jeez, Harry. If that wasn't the most ridiculous rant—so absurd. I didn't even *want* to turn to face the man. But his silence, his lack of response, was—

He wasn't there. Vanished in a sea of hooded rain jackets and umbrellas, as the gray skies did what gray skies tended to do.

"Seriously?"

A harried woman nudged in beside me.

"Did you see a man? Standing there? Navy Adidas? Tall. Dark curly hair?"

"Was he wearing sunglasses?" She placed bunches of lettuce into her basket indiscriminately—like a *monster*.

"I don't know. I didn't turn to—oh, never mind." I went in search of the other items on my mental shopping list.

The rain didn't bother me, and I took my time filling the plastic tote, distracted by the run-in with my favorite felon. When I stood at the cashier canopy, I stared, dazed like an idiot, for too long before I finally stuffed the items into my backpack.

"Whoops, you're gonna want this." The cashier held up a phone she'd pulled from the bottom of the basket I'd used.

"*Uh*, I don't think so."

"Hattie?" The young woman looked at me, askance.

"*Um*, sort of. How did you—"

"Says *'Hattie's phone'* on a piece of tape—on the back here. Are you all right?"

"Yeah." I took the device from her. "It's—new. I forgot. Thanks. See you next week." I waved over my shoulder, brushing off my idiocy. I couldn't get home fast enough, and the rain was picking up steam.

Twenty-Four

"Wʜᴀᴛ's ᴜᴘ, Bᴜᴛᴛᴇʀᴄᴜᴘ? *Oof*, I see you're going for the drowned rat look—*again*." Leo glided into the hall, likely summoned by my squeaking wet sneakers. He also glided past his joking criticism with an enthusiastic, "Yay, market day. What'd we get?"

"The usual. Salad fixings, fruit, bread, eggs, a new phone. You know." I unlocked my door, and Leo followed me into my refuge.

"Really? A phone? I guess it was only a matter of time before some little tech biz loop-holed their way into a farmer's market. Just as long as you can port your old number because you'd..." Leo rambled on while I unloaded my purchases in the kitchen. The man's lung capacity had to be substantial, and his ability to natter on about anything and nothing might be one of his most charming attributes. *Might* be. Depends on the day.

I still reeled from my unexpected market encounter and uncharacteristic confessions to the leafy greens section. How much had Trey heard before going poof?

"...or a brolly—which is a term we all should use more, but you know they've been around since ancient times, Egypt, Greece, China, all had them."

"Phones?" I tuned in to Leo again, confused.

"What? No. *Umbrellas.* Sometimes I think you aren't even listening to me, Harry. Anyway, get one, Miss Watership Down."

"Those were bunnies, not rats."

"Yeah, yeah. Got plans tonight?"

"I do, actually." I exited to the hall to get my mail. Leo kept close at my heels.

"*Gasp.* What? Good lord, is it the end times?"

"Shut up. I'm doing some research, the online variety. Sort of got a new project I'm looking at. Something to keep me busy these last weeks before the fall semester."

"Snore. That's not Friday night plans, honey. For the record? That's lame and sad and totally not worthy of you."

"Sticks and stones, Leo. I'm getting in the shower, shoo." I ushered him to the door.

"Fine. Hey, if you saw you-know-who, you'd tell me, right? *Will* they? *Won't* they? I'm still *shipping* you two."

"Well, I'm not sure *shipping* is something people still do, but yeah, if I ever saw his *face* again, I'd tell you. Probably." I smirked, then wondered if I *would* ever see that face again. "Bye, Leo."

I'd climbed halfway up the stairs when the Tom Ford guardian, still hung on a dresser knob, came into view, causing a swift about-face to grab the new phone I'd left in the kitchen. After a long shower that ended on a prophylactic cold note, I examined the device. Every trick I had learned to find trackers and old messages, including texts, email, and voicemail, reaped nothing. It appeared to be a spotless device, and while I still had Trey's number from our exchange the weekend before, *and* the one "Mom" told me I shouldn't bother to keep, dialing either seemed like the wrong move. Nothing to do but wait. And waiting—this kind of waiting— was one more *thing* that wasn't my thing.

Back downstairs, I sat on the floor and opened my laptop to dig into my new project.

A rainy Friday night. It seemed we'd had our fair share this summer. Then again, maybe I was projecting. The stormy skies brought an earlier nightfall, and lightning did its best to up the creep factor. My neighborhood had the occasional flash flooding, and the whoosh of water as cars drove by my building accompanied the downpour and the storm's rumble. A bluish-white zig-zag lit up the sky, with a crack of thunder following too soon after it. At the same moment, there was a knock at my door, and the confluence of the three spiked my heart rate.

"You okay, hon?" Leo wore a surprised expression and scrubs when I flung open my door.

"Yes, big boom, that's all. I thought you had plans, like fun plans, tonight."

"Got a call for help at Westrock. They're actually sending transport. Dark and stormy nights tend to wreak havoc." Leo eyed over my head to the coffee table. "Is that Twitter— I mean *X* on your computer?"

"Huh?" I folded my arms and leaned, a model of nonchalance.

"You don't strike me as a big Tweeter. Don't imagine *he* is either, but you do what you gotta do, sweetheart." Another thunderous crash shook the sturdy concrete building, and lights flickered.

"That's what Mother Nature thinks of you teasing me, and I'm not doing anything that has to do with *him*, thank you very much. It's research, I told you. Hey, be safe out there."

"You be safe in here." Leo's phone chirped. "That's my ride. I don't know how late I'll be. Keep everything charging in case the power goes, okay?"

"Yes, Auntie Leo. Go save some lives." I smiled as my hulking friend hurried out the door. Another nearly simultaneous flash and bang erupted. With a jolt, I slammed my door and went in search of chargers for all my devices. With a beer in hand, I settled back on the floor to resume my work. None of my furniture seating appealed to me these days.

Twitter. Or X or whatever app trended at the moment—I didn't get it. Social media might appear to be an ideal invention for an introvert like me—a mouthy, opinionated loner who likes her solitude. But my sort of reclusiveness is not merely a physical choice. I don't need anyone knowing my business: who I'm with and where or what we're eating, drinking, or watching. All that said— God *bless* it. It makes the investigative game easier to play from the comfort of my own home with a wealth of data to discover. And if a subject falls in the teens to fifty range, older even, good odds they're out in the ether, unwittingly aiding your case. Ones and zeroes paved the information highway, and with a little time, patience, and intuition, those single digits painted a picture worth far more than a thousand words. And my artsy metaphor was intentional.

Halfway through my second beer, a pleasant buzz spread through me, and dinner took priority. I clicked on some music only to be mocked by Chet Baker, but I smiled at the joke and let it play. *I fall in love too easily...* When I opened the freezer to retrieve pine nuts to toast for my salad (yeah, I'm a bit of a foodie), the liter bottle of vodka I bought earlier in the week winked at me. The adage that began *beer before liquor* ran through my mind, and I grabbed a handful of the precious nuts and closed the freezer door.

Rain fell harder, but while the squall's crackle and spark part had subsided, another line of storms moved in behind it. A bottle to my lips, I watched the downpour from a living room window. A blinding flash split the sky, and a thunderous boom exploded less than *one Mississippi* later. Lights blinked inside. On the other side of the street, the streetlamp and residences remained lit while mine guttered to dark with sudden silence. No more Chet.

"Really? Just *my* side of the street?" My knowledge of the electrical grid lacked, but I breathed relief when another flicker brought my lights back to life. I leaned my head on the windowpane after another swig and exhaled an airy laugh at my jumpiness. When my phone rang seconds later, it didn't help matters.

"*Hello?*" I half-shouted.

"Ms. Smith?"

"This is." I steadied my clipped reply.

"My name is Felix. I'm an on-call safety specialist from Top Security."

"Yes, what can I do for you on a dark and stormy Friday night, Felix?" I channeled Leo.

"I'll need you to give me your safety phrase, Ms. Smith." Felix's tone exuded all business.

"I'm sorry. Is there a problem?" The hair on the back of my neck prickled, and I wished I'd skipped the dark and stormy quip.

"Ma'am, I'll need the safety phrase before we can continue. It's for your protection. It lets me know you are safe and authorized to speak to me about your property's security situation."

"Yes, of course. It's—*uh*," I regretted Leo's and my punchy mood that sleep-deprived evening we set up the pass phrases and replies with the new home security firm. "It's: *Know any dirty jokes?*"

Felix's demeanor relaxed. "That's correct, ma'am."

"And your reply, Felix?"

"Right." The security specialist gave a nervous laugh. "Um, a priest, a rabbi, and a—"

"That's good enough," I interrupted. "What the hell's going on, Felix?"

"Stormy weather, ma'am." Felix's "ma'am" thing irked me. "It seems your security has gone offline. Chances are it just needs a reboot, but it's not working from our side. I'm going to need you to go to the unit on your end to do it manually. I'll walk you through it. You remember where the box is?"

"Gee, the install was Monday, so yeah, I remember, Felix."

"Yes, ma'am."

"The lights are back on here, but the system isn't on? Is that what you're saying?"

"Yes, if you'll take me along with you, I can tell you which button to push, and we'll have you up and running again in no time."

Another loud boom rattled the windows. That's when I smelled the burning.

"Shit. Shit, shit, shit." I ran to the kitchen.

"Is everything all right, Ms. Smith?"

"Well, Felix, I just burned $57 worth of pine nuts, and you're giving me a creepy *the call is coming from inside the house* vibe, but other than that, yeah."

"I get that a lot," Felix dared to laugh again.

I dumped the scorched nuts in the sink and dropped the sauté pan with a bang.

"Okay, Felix. Let's do this."

I jogged to the laundry room—still not my favorite haunt these days. But since I had the entire building wired for safety, easy access for Leo *and* me necessitated the communal spot. The task didn't take long.

"That should do it, Ms. Smith. We apologize for the inconvenience and hope you know you are a valued Top Security client. Have a good evening." Felix ended the call.

I forced a deep breath and returned down the dim hall back to my apartment. Kneeling on my sofa, my forehead pressed to the window gave me a better view up and down the block. The porch light was out, but I'd have sworn it glowed when Leo left. Nowadays, my imagination seemed to run wild, and I chided myself for my skittish behavior. The universe replied with another lightning strike that illuminated the figure of a man standing on my front stoop. I jerked backward and kicked the coffee table, nearly sending my laptop to the floor.

"Shit." Scrambling to my feet, I flew up the stairs to the locked gun case on my nightstand. It took too long to get the nine-millimeter into my grip. Why did I leave it locked in my room? *Because rules, Harry.*

Without a door to my bedroom, my bathroom provided the only place to lock myself in, or any intruder out, while I called security or 9-1-1, or Marty. "Shit, no phone." I'd dropped my phone in the panic at seeing the dark figure on my front steps. "Breathe, Harry," I spoke aloud.

Music. Music played again, quietly, but not from my living room speakers. I recognized the song with its sad, muted trumpets, but in my petrified state, I couldn't recall the lyrics. The melody stopped. I held my breath. Weapon at my side, I crept to the doorway at the top of the stairs. The music began again. Longer this time, with a crying clarinet joining the tune. More thunder rumbled, low and distant, as the line of storms moved east. My heart thudded, and my icy fingers gripped the gun. Again, the music cut out, then played again just as quickly. It was a ringtone.

Hattie's phone—*Trey's* phone—rang with a familiar refrain. An old song, a French one.

I slunk down the steps, careful not to make a sound, not that anyone on the small front porch could hear. Did training exist for situations like this? When I reached the first floor, the music stopped for the third time. I blew out a long, slow breath. The phone didn't "ring" again.

"Shit. Please show a number, please show a *number*," I pleaded as I crept to the plugged-in device, avoiding the window just a few feet from the outside stairs. Crouched by the sofa, pressed to the window frame, I placed the screen against my chest when it lit up, afraid someone would detect any movement through the glass. Sneaking a glance, the unfortunate message, *'unknown caller,'* appeared. Another curse whispered out of me, followed by a startled gasp when the trumpet wailed again. "Trey?" I murmured, but immediately regretted saying his name. I swallowed hard.

"Hattie? Are you okay?"

"No." I stopped speaking when firm soles scraped on the nearby concrete steps.

"What's—what's wrong?" Trey's panic seeped through the phone.

"Somebody's—here." I squeezed the words out as the hollow *clunk* of the heavy industrial metal door echoed in the front vestibule. "They're trying to—"

"Hattie, it's me. I'm at the front door. Let me in."

"What?" I slumped, my ass hitting the rug while my stomach rose and fell at that welcomed news. "Jesus, Trey." I dropped the phone in a rush to stand and ran out of my apartment to get to him. The patter of bare feet *smacked* on the hall floor tiles in my hurry to open the door.

Twenty-Five

"Whoa." Trey seized my arm with one hand and snatched my gun with his other before I ever knew what happened. "I'll take this." He clicked the thumb safety.

I pounced, grabbing him at the waist but let go at his sharp gasp and grunt. My hands flexed at shoulder height. "Sorry, I shouldn't have—"

"No, it's—" Trey grumbled with his hands raised too.

"No, I just panicked and then—relief. I wasn't—I mean, it didn't—" We stuttered over one another in the commotion.

"I'm still bruised, is all." He twisted into a small stretch and grimaced.

I shook my arms and brushed down the front of my shirt. "And wet."

"Yeah, didn't know if you noticed. It's raining." He gestured with my weapon over his shoulder.

I exhaled a laugh. "I did. Yes. Wanna come in? Can you?"

"Sure, I think it's safe enough. I see you upped the security. That's good. Real good. Glad to see it. Glad to— see you, Hattie."

I reached for his face, finally able to focus on the battered state of it. Wounds from the weekend had faded some, but new ones marred it. A butterflied cut over his right eye and a notable bruise near his mouth highlighted a split lip. I winced as my fingertips grazed both injuries.

"They're fine. I'm fine." He wrenched away from my touch, and I lost eye contact, but just as quickly, he clutched my wrist. "Looks worse than it is. Sorry."

"No. Tough guy. I get it." I pulled from his grip and beckoned for my firearm. "Come on, if you're coming in." I headed down the hall, glad to hear his chirping footsteps behind me. Inside, I motioned for his dripping windbreaker to hang and bolted the lock. Mildly dazed by Trey's latest look, I stalled a second when his jeans and fitted black t-shirt threw me. "Let me go secure my piece." I took the stairs two at a time.

"Something to drink? I'm having a beer. I've got vodka, American-made, though. From Texas, I think. But hey—" I darted to the kitchen and continued my rambling. "There's a French one I like, but vodka isn't something I keep on hand ordinarily—Oh my God. *La Vie En Rose.* It's French. You chose that song for the phone. French, because when we met— my t-shirt..." Yep, that's how my brain works.

He nodded with a smile, but he flinched when it tugged his split lip. "I'll just take a beer. No need for the hard stuff tonight. Did you—burn something?" He scrunched his nose at the acrid smell.

I sighed. "Yes. Pine nuts."

"Ouch."

"Right?" I handed him the beer, and we clinked bottles before each taking a super-sized slug. "Hungry? I was making dinner. Pine nuts for a salad, greens with some gorgonzola, and the last of the raspberries for the season. Some crusty bread."

"You cook?"

"I make—salad." I grinned as the tenor of my voice ended oddly high, sounding more like a question than the statement I intended. *Nerves much, Harry?* I took another swig before an actual question came to mind. The obvious one. "Wait, why are you here?"

Trey walked away, roughing up his wet curls and studying the framed black and white photographs hung around the room. The Arc de Triomphe de l'Étoile. The Eiffel Tower. Sacré-Cœur Basilica. "Did you take these photos?" He evaded my question by asking his own.

"I did. Nothing original, but cameras aren't just for catching cheating spouses. *Why* are you here, Trey?"

"When were you there?"

"Five years ago, after my dad died. *Trey*? Why are you—"

"I don't know, Hattie," he barked, then settled into a low growl. "I sure as hell shouldn't be."

"Shouldn't be like, it's not a great idea or shouldn't be like it's gonna get us killed? I'm all for the occasional rule-breaking, I mean, damn, I'll buck the status quo with the best of 'em, but—"

He still faced away, but his chin hit his chest.

"What?"

"Because of *that*. Because, for some reason, I can breathe around you. I can breathe, and everything slows a bit, and I can hear myself think again, my own voice, despite your unrelenting chatter. And I wasn't sure if it *was* you that made all that happen, but when I heard you at the market today—" Trey didn't finish his sentence but sipped his beer, still focused on my wall art.

"Wow. That's quite a talent I didn't know I possessed. Harry Smith: *criminal* whisperer."

"*Hattie* Smith. And I'm pretty sure it's not the criminal in me you—" He swallowed his words.

"That I whisper to? *Relentlessly*?" The entire scene felt surreal. "Are you okay, Trey? Is something going on I should—"

"No. No, I'm sorry. Should I go? I should—I should go." He finally rotated to see me, but I retreated to the kitchen.

"Up to you, of course. If you've done all the breathing and hearing yourself think you wanted to do— but I'm gonna make a salad and warm some bread. You're welcome to join me. Dinner is the least I could do. And we can talk. Or— *not* talk. I've got no place to be."

Quiet hung too heavy, with only the distant splash of tires in puddles interrupting it. I regretted the *not talking* option. When the thump of opening and closing drawers and the clang of silverware grew tedious, I hit the button on a sound speaker. Saved by Chet Baker.

"This music. How old are you, again?" Trey loomed in my kitchen, bigger than I'd sized him up to be before we first met. "Sorry. Did I scare you?"

"Yeah. No. Just a little jumpy, I guess." I grabbed a kitchen towel to keep my hands busy before anxiety had them flailing. "My dad was a jazz fan. Chet Baker. Miles Davis. Coltrane. He's to blame."

"No, I like it. Soothing."

"That's what he'd say. It soothed him. He'd pour a taste of good Scotch and spin old, crackling vinyl after a twelve-hour shift chasing bad guys. *Oh,* no offense." I enjoyed the memory and the not-so-subtle dig, not hiding my grin.

"No. None taken." He waved me off with a fake frown that quickly turned upside-down with a sweetness that set me on fire. But that flame got doused just as fast. "So—your dad was a cop?"

My grin vanished, and I let the question dangle as I pried the top off another bottle of beer and set it in front of Trey with enough force it foamed up and dribbled down the neck. "Let's not do *that,* okay?"

"What? Talk? Thought you said we could—"

"Talking is fine. Asking questions like you don't already know the answer? Not okay. I don't know what's going on here—what you want, but whatever it is, I need it to begin and end with honesty, and while that might not be your default mode, and I get that, I do, I'm gonna need you to at least try not to play me for a fool. Respect me enough to be truthful when you speak, and if you can't, then don't say anything at all. Omission is one thing, I guess. But lying? I can't—I can't *do* lying. Not with you, not now—not after—not anymore." We stared a long beat, but he blinked first.

"Okay, Hattie."

"Okay?"

"Okay. I promise." He walked around the small butcher-block island to stand in front of me. Heat flushed my chest, and I forced myself not to move when his hand came close. Plucking a raspberry from the salad bowl at my elbow, he popped it in his mouth with a raised brow. "Supper ready? I'm suddenly starving." The kitchen shrank.

"Uh, yeah. And I didn't burn this round of pine nuts."

Stepping aside, he took the pan from the stovetop and sprinkled the warm nuts on top of the greens, berries, and crumbled cheese. Their toasted aroma met my nose, calming me. Trey carried the bowl to the bistro table I had set for us. Sliding the towel off my shoulder, he used it to remove the foil-wrapped bread from the oven and place it on a cutting board. It could have been his own kitchen, the way he maneuvered around the small space. He slid a serrated knife from its woodblock and expertly sliced the rustic round of bread. The warm, yeasty tang of sourdough further soothed my angst, and I remained perched in front of the sink, out of the way of the culinary takeover. It took him two drawers to find the salad tongs. He rested them across the greens, then surveyed the table and around the cramped kitchen, finally deciding everything was ready. He pulled one of the dining chairs out from the table with a jesting formality and motioned for me to sit.

No sooner had he pushed in my seat, I remembered the vinaigrette I had whisked. "Oh, the dressing. It's by the fridge."

He squeezed my shoulder. "Stay seated, I've got it."

"You are full of surprises, Mr. Popov." I relaxed in my seat, placing a linen napkin on my lap, but caught a hitch in his frame.

"Well, I wouldn't want to wear out my welcome—"

"Never gonna happen," I interjected too quickly, with too much honesty.

"And I'm trying to dispel the whole—what was it? Bad-boy-mystery thing?" He joined me at the table.

"Oh, jeez. I wondered how much of that you heard before your vanishing act." I snatched my drink to avert my eyes and appease my suddenly dry mouth. "Don't suppose I could unsay some of that?"

He raised his beer bottle and waited for me to do the same. "To things unsaid. And прекрасным женщинам, которые приносят нам радость и беды." He tapped the neck of his bottle to mine.

"Dude, I can't toast to words I don't know."

"Oh, it's a customary toast. Nothing special. Basically, just means—*cheers.*" He failed to hide his smirk while taking a drink.

"Seemed like an awful lot of words just to say, *cheers.*"

"What can I say? It's a funny language."

I eyed him warily as he placed his napkin in his lap. Over his shoulder, the light from my computer caught my attention. "You're not on Twitter, are you?"

"You mean X? *Uh, no.*" He delivered a side-eye look with a head shake.

"Yeah, I didn't think so."

He forked a bite of salad. "But my Insta is *huge*."

"What? Really?"

"No, Hattie."

I let out a genuinely joyful laugh.

He stifled his own and focused on his plate. "It's getting late. You should eat."

The moment of fun faded. "Are you—in a hurry to go?"

"Not if staying means I get to hear more of that laugh."

Twenty-Six

I BIDED MY TIME, finished my salad, then picked at a chunk of bread in a relaxed silence. A hundred questions wrestled in my brain, but I knew better than to bombard my stoic guest with all of them.

"This is nice."

"Is it?" He looked at me from under his dark lashes. *Have mercy.*

"Yes. A quiet dinner for two, nothing but the gentle shush of rain."

"*Huh*. I know we've only known each other a short while, but I don't think I've seen you stay silent for this long a stretch. Sorta thought it might be kind of agonizing for you, chatterbox that you are." He winked with his teasing.

I slumped with a clenched jaw, showing my teeth. "It is. It *really* is."

Trey chuckled. "Go on. What do you want to know?"

"You. I want to know you." Permission granted, I leaned in, eager to learn.

At the same time, he sat back in his seat with a resigned sigh and wiped his mouth with the napkin. Trey's reticence to share read clearly, but I watched his desire to do it anyway win. I took it as a compliment.

"Raised by a single mom in Virginia, a single mom *and* the rabbis at the temple where she worked. Secretarial and housekeeping sort of stuff. We had a tiny apartment in the basement. She's Russian, her first language, so she raised me to speak it. The rabbis tutored me in Hebrew, *Sesame Street* and public school taught me English, and all of a sudden, I had a knack for languages."

"She sounds like a native English speaker, not a hint of accent. Your Mom."

He stiffened and didn't reply. I surmised he meant to keep our deal of omissions over lies. A deal I made, so I had to make peace with it.

"So, *I* had a dad, and *you* had a mom." Something rang poetic in that.

He simply nodded.

"Ooh, do you speak French?"

He shook his head, "No, I—no, I don't."

"*Hm.*" Disappointing, but I moved on. "And the house full of boys you mentioned? The rabbis were smelly and told dirty jokes?"

He grinned with his explanation. "No, that came later. Military school."

The tightly made bed skill explained.

"Military school? Sounds like you've been a *bad* boy most of your life, then. Hard to ask you to break the habit now, I guess."

He only offered a raised shoulder, then said, "My turn. Quid pro quo."

I rested my chin in my hands, enjoying more Latin and eager to play his game.

"If you had a dad, why foster care?"

"That's how he got me. My birth parents dropped me at his precinct when they realized *this* wasn't something they were ready to handle." I indicated myself, then folded my hands to keep from further flapping. Cursed with excitable limbs. "Those crazy kids took a cab from their lush life on Central Park West all the way to Queens. As far as their allowances would carry them, I guess." I jutted my chin, then tried not to flinch when Trey lay his hands on mine. "Still, I'm thankful they did the right thing."

"Me too."

The clunk of the outside door jerked me from Trey's hand-holding, and I had that panicked feeling like the time my dad caught Pauly Moretti and me rounding first base in tenth grade. "No way you get out of here tonight without my warden catching you."

"Who's that?"

"Auntie Leo." I couldn't decipher Trey's look, and not understanding forced me to stand to get some distance. The evening's calm vanished. "Unless you meant to see him. Maybe get your wounds checked?" I pointed to his face and torso.

"No. That won't be necessary. I've been seen by my—boss's physician." He had the decency to sound something like embarrassed by that, at least.

"Oh, that's nice." I leaped from sincerity to snark in point-two seconds. "The man has you beaten but then provides medical care? Any thoughts on finding *new* employment?" I took a beat—long enough for Trey to intervene, but he didn't. "Never mind." And just like that, our night took a wrong turn.

"Hattie," he spoke the name in a sweet whisper.

"No, forget it." I gave one of my exaggerated hand waves, then crossed my arms to mitigate more fluttering and definitely *not* forgetting it. "I'm just trying to wrap my head around why you would choose—choose *that* when you have other options. But, I'm in no position to—"

"Other options?" He stood as I walked to the living room. "I don't regret my choice. I don't believe I *have* options."

The reality of our situation crash-landed, and two factions, my head and—some other organ, went to war. "Yes, you do. You have—options."

"What would you have me choose, Hattie?"

"Fine. I'll say it. I'll just—say it. *Me.* You could choose *me* because I can't—" I wagged my finger between us. "I can't—if you're—you get that, right? I can't—we can't—there is a line we can *never* cross if you are—what you are. I might not *be* a cop, I *know* I'm not a cop, but I bleed blue, so— I can't— this is all we get." I twirled my index fingers overhead and around the room, full-on whirling dervish. "One thousand square feet, two floors, and no touching. That's it."

In contrast, Trey stood unflappable, wordless.

"Oh, my God. I did it again, didn't I? I misread the situation. Dammit. I *thought*—but then—*Wow.*" I seemed incapable of finishing a sentence. "How did I—? It's not like I don't have a master's degree in *reading* people, basically. Years of study to learn how to observe and detect motive and intention, and yet, here I go—"

"Hattie. God, you *really* never stop talking, do you? Yes, you read it wrong, but not how you think. I *did* choose you. I chose to keep you safe—"

"*Jesus*, Trey—" I snapped with clenched fists.

"I know, Hattie." He pressed his palms to his eyes as his volume climbed. "I know. *Not* my damsel. You've said. But we got in a jam, and now I'm taking care of it. Call it what you will, but I made a choice, and that choice means I stay, and I'll take a thousand square feet and not touching you over not having you at all, *any* day."

We took a collective breath, but I held mine.

"I get there's a line we can't cross, believe me, *more* than you know, and I have pushed that line further than I have the right to, so say the word, and I'm gone, because I *do* respect you and who you are and who you want to be, and I don't want to mess with any of that. Still, at the same time, I—feel other things too, and the truth is you showed up at a moment in my life when things were spiraling, *worse* really, but now things are better. I'm better, despite the shit week we found ourselves in, *you* make me better so—so maybe I'm *your* damsel."

My head spun and not only for lack of oxygen. "And—I'm just supposed to worry about you all the time? Wondering where you are? If it's dangerous?"

His split lip quirked, like the question amused him.

"That's funny?"

"Kinda. I worried about *you* all week. Got very little sleep, concentrated even less, and as you might imagine, that's an occupational hazard. And tell me, Hattie—now we're riding this truth train—would it be any different—would it be easier for you— if I—carried a badge? Would you worry about me any less?"

I sniffed at the man's logic. But my own secret concerns reared their ugly heads. "Fine. But what if the *badges* come busting down Trubetzkoy's door, and you get scooped up? Then what?"

"I'm not worried. And you shouldn't either." His lack of concern should have caused me plenty, but those two emphatic statements got lost in the next newsflash. "But I should tell you—I'm leaving town Monday."

"Wait, where?"

"I'll be traveling with the boss's wife."

"How long?"

"I don't know."

"Birkin bags and Bichons on holiday?" My lame wisecracks landed on cue, hoping to obscure the recent baring of souls. "It might be nice. Seaside, perhaps? Work on your tan?" In my mind the burgeoning plan to bust up the local cabal with Trey out of harm's way started to take shape.

"Look, you have that phone. If you need anything, call. I'll give you a number. If I can't get to you, someone you can trust will." Trey made his way to his windbreaker and the door.

"Who?"

His steely look said *omission over lies*.

"Where are you going now?"

"I'm leaving."

"Thought you had until Monday."

"I have a job to do."

"Tonight?"

He paused. "No."

"Then stay." We both jerked at the unexpected invitation, but I stumbled headlong with more of that promised honesty. "One thousand square feet and no touching, but I like having you here. I don't have many friends, and well— I could use one and this—"

"Feels good, right?" His earnest face made me smile and goaded me to tease his sincerity.

"You know what else feels good?" I gasped in jest, shaking my head like I couldn't believe I'd said the words aloud.

"*Hattie* Smith. That mouth." Trey chided with reddened cheeks. "One thousand square feet and no touching—"

"I know, but you like my mouth. Pretty sure you just said—" My tension-induced jokes continued. Oh, how I enjoy playing with fire.

Twenty-Seven

We planned to Netflix and chill, except with Netflix and *actual* chilling. Pauly Moretti got more action from me in the tenth grade, and that's saying something. But truthfully, I looked forward to sleeping unencumbered by worry, thanks to the man who rested at a respectable distance on the left side of my bed dressed in the gigantic scrub bottoms he wore on his last visit.

Before we settled in with my laptop, keeping a clear line of demarcation between us, I offered the washed drawstring pants I hadn't returned to Leo, and with them, Trey's own sliced-through undershirt saved from the bloodstains.

He eyed what he mistook for my handiwork. "Ammonia and cold water? Works like a charm, doesn't it?"

"Apparently, that's something everyone knows but me. Leo washed it and your dress shirt," I confessed and gestured to the Tom Ford still hanging from a dresser drawer knob. "You should take it when you go. In case you need something fancy while you're away." I may have given the shirt a wistful look. I'd miss Tom, the unimaginative name I'd given my French cuffed sentinel. But something about the button-down seemed lucky, so it would be best if Trey had it with him, wherever Mrs. Trubetzkoy and her envoy headed. "I'll get changed in the bathroom. Make yourself comfortable." I grabbed my most modest pajamas and scurried to the privacy behind the pocket door to get ready for bed.

In my defense, one doesn't typically think to knock on the door as they *exit* a bathroom. I regretted not doing it that night, except not really. Trey faced away from me, on the far side of the room. He'd put on the scrub pants and removed his black t-shirt. His head and arms had slid through the appropriate holes of his clean sleeveless undershirt, but he hadn't pulled the ribbed, white cotton down his torso. His body's condition provoked an audible gasp from me, and he rushed to cover his bare skin. Colorful bruises, albeit fading, spread wide across his back. But it was the contusion still boasting the unmistakable tread of a combat boot that made my stomach lurch.

"Sorry." I spun away, intent on pretending I hadn't seen it, for his sake as much as mine. I faced the wall and squeezed my eyes tight, willing the image scrubbed from my memory. It didn't work.

"Hattie?" His voice seemed closer than it should have been.

"Don't come over here." I kept my back to him.

"But—"

"No, buts. I'm sorry, I should have given you a heads up before coming in. I apologize."

"It's okay, *I'm* okay." Again, he sounded closer. Too close.

"Good. Glad to hear it. Then why are you coming over—"

"That's my side."

"Huh?" With a slight jolt, I turned.

"That's my side of the bed. Or it was the last time. Do *you* want that side?" He pointed to the bedside closest to me, the side he slept on that last visit. His raised brows asked permission to move again.

I breathed an airy laugh. "No. Please." I gestured to "his" side of the bed. "It's good to get these things out early. Note to self: *Trey is territorial*, got it." I winked and gave the A-OK sign, eliciting a small chuckle from my guest. The unfortunate bruises were in the rearview, and we moved forward.

He took slow steps toward me, and my eyes moved from his lashes to the gold star at his chest, to the three phones in his hands. A wisecrack about his number of devices jammed in my throat when it occurred to me that I also possessed three phones I kept at the ready. Two people. Six phones. *What kind of world...*

I kept a desk drawer full of charging cords and adapters for all my investigative equipment needs and had plenty to offer for each unit. A power strip kept them all together on the workspace in my bedroom's office area.

In keeping with the night's surreal and slightly awkward theme, we bumbled our way through our decidedly platonic existence, hunkered down with Rod Serling and the original Twilight Zone television show. We sat propped up with pillows against the headboard and the laptop between us. It offered the only light as it played decades-old episodes in black and white. We swapped childhood stories and shared memories of our parents, and I couldn't recall a more enjoyable Friday night, despite our circumstances.

Trey's exhaustion showed, and part of me hoped he would fall asleep fast—for many reasons. I took it as a good sign when he did. If he felt comfortable enough to sleep, I could relax, too. Both of us needed to catch up on the rest we'd lost the past week. And while evidence plainly indicated his week had been harsher than mine, relief washed over me as I closed the computer and set it across the room with the other charging electronics. The storm had moved through, but the splash of puddles and slowing metered drips from gutters lingered. I drew the blackout curtains closed in hopes the light of day wouldn't disturb us come sunrise.

With one knee on the mattress, I stopped short of slipping into the covers when a phone lit up and vibrated. On autopilot, I bolted to answer it, hoping the man in bed didn't wake. The phone belonged to Trey.

"Hello?" I whispered with a grimace, knowing I should have simply dismissed the call when the letters MOM appeared on the screen. But I assumed she would only continue to ring back until she got an answer. I'd witnessed the woman's persistent dialing before, after all. More than once. Talk about relentless.

No reply came to my hushed greeting, but I simply waited. Finally, the woman spoke. "Hattie?"

I took some immediate comfort in her guessing my name first. Jealousy wasn't something I dabbled in, not romantic jealousy, anyway. *Whoa*, romantic? I suppose I could ruminate on that another time. I'm just saying of all the names she could have guessed, she guessed mine—first. *Whatever.*

"Yes?" I murmured my reply as I unplugged to hurry into the bathroom, where I could speak more freely.

"Is he—" In two syllables, her angst flooded my ear.

"He's okay—good, well, I mean. Just sleeping. He's exhausted." Did that betray some confidence? I made sure to measure my speech in the future. I didn't know if I could trust the woman, no matter what she said to call her. "Mom?"

"Is—he with you, or are you with him?" The riddle-like question hung in the air.

"We're together, and where is not for me to say, but we're not—I mean, it's not what you might think. Not that I need to explain myself to you, but he needed—"

"I know what Trey needs." Her curtness didn't sit well with me, but I tempered my defense of the man who apparently embodied our shared concern. "When Trey wakes, you need to be sure he calls home."

"I don't need to do anything you say. But because Trey and I are honest with one another, I will tell him you called, that you and I spoke, and make your request known. I can't promise you more than that."

Condescension tinged her voice. "If you and Trey were *honest* with one another, I imagine you and I would be having a *very* different conversation right now." Her words stung, but I surmised she intended to inflict pain.

"You won't make me doubt him. I'm not a fool, and I recognize the inherent danger, but you will not manipulate me into distrusting him. I don't know who or what you are, what part you play, but if it's helping Trey, save your energy for that endeavor. He'll need it. And the distrust thing? It's never gonna happen, so don't waste the effort."

"*Hm*," the woman emitted a short, introspective sigh. "Perhaps we will speak again, Ms. Smith. Best get some rest and allow—my son the same. Until next time." She ended the call.

Demon butterflies ricocheted, and I pressed against the bathroom sink to settle my breath after the nerve-racking phone conversation. I tiptoed from the bathroom and plugged in Trey's device, then eased into the covers to lie on my back, hoping I didn't disturb the man beside me. My long, slow exhale of relief came to a quick end when Trey's hand took a gentle hold of mine.

He whispered, barely awake, "So, two pigs sit in their sty, and one turns to the other and oinks..."

I snorted and gave a firm squeeze of Trey's fingers and didn't let go.

Twenty-Eight

Sun snuck through the overlapped drapes, but not enough to light the room. A fine line of a bright glow was the only thing to see as I lay still on my side, afraid of disrupting the calm. If Trey still slept beside me, he rested far enough away I couldn't feel him. Not his heat, not his presence, and certainly not his body. I listened, hoping to hear him breathe, but only the whoosh of traffic sounded. By the regularity of it, the hour had made it well-beyond sunrise. *Roll over, Harry.*

I eased to my back, trying not to disturb the bed and risk waking Trey if he slept. A grin jerked at my lips when his profile emerged in the dark. He lay exactly as he had the night before, on his back, one hand on his chest, the other rested where I held it before drifting off to sleep. Had he not moved in the night? How was that possible? What kind of life provoked the need for that kind of discipline?

Straightening my arm, I gently placed it on the swath of mattress between us, our fingers not an inch apart. One thousand square feet and no touching. It surprised me how willingly I accepted that existence—all twelve-ish hours of it. Laughable. Of course, I knew it would be a short-lived way of life. I planned to see to it. Trubetzkoy would go down, and Trey would be free of his obligation. My safety, no longer at risk, would liberate this sleeping man from any "reward" debt and the dark side, as Uncle Marty called it. From there, we would see. We had options after that. Until then, one thousand square feet and...

As my eyes adjusted to the dark, I stared at our hands positioned so close to one another, wishing I hadn't let go in the night. Then again, we'd held hands for some length of time, and the world kept spinning. No one got hurt. Nothing bad happened at all. So, what would be the harm in letting it happen again? One thousand square feet and a tender handhold. An innocent line. Harmless to cross. My pinky barely moved. It stretched that inch, and my ring finger went with it. Little by little, my hand edged its way over Trey's, hovering with only the heat of his sleep between his skin and mine until I allowed the two to meet. My fingers wrapped around his. The gentlest embrace. And yet, a wave of fear or pleasure or relief rose and crashed inside me.

"You came back," Trey whispered and tightened the hold.

Any air I possessed stuck in my throat. I pushed to reply, "Did you sleep?"

"I did. Too well." He kept his eyes closed, and his voice hushed.

"Is that a thing? Sleeping *too* well?"

"It is in my world. A big no-no."

"Speaking of no-nos—" I reluctantly pulled from his grasp. His hand balled, then flexed with my release, and my adjusting eyes read pain or frustration on his face. I didn't know which, but it seemed I caused it. Nevertheless, I couldn't apologize for following the rules, even though I broke them in the first place. Best to move on. "You must be starving. I barely fed you last night."

He rubbed his eyes and pinched the bridge of his nose while I heard my words take on a meaning I hadn't intended. I scrambled out of bed, paying no heed to the bounce and squeak of the box spring or the tug of the linens. When I drew the drapes wide, warm sunshine hit me, and clear skies shone the brightest blue over the peaks of the row houses across the street. The summer day enticed me to enjoy the outdoors until I turned to the man still lying in my bed.

"What are you thinking?"

Trey rolled to his side, holding his head in one hand while the other stretched across the bed's middle, feeling the sunlight that didn't reach his half. "Just admiring—your sheets."

"Well, you are welcome to them as long as you like. I'll go rustle up some breakfast?"

"Rustle up?" He gave a too-rare grin.

"I'm guessing an excursion to my favorite greasy spoon or to the Saturday market is out of the question?" I don't know why I bothered to ask. I knew the answer, and the inquiry wiped away his contented smile and brought back the face of thoughtful stoicism. He retracted his limb to his side of the bed.

"I'm sorry, Hattie. We can't."

"Oh, good," I lied. "I didn't want to go anywhere, anyway." I slipped on a short robe. "I got some early blueberries at the market yesterday, and you're gonna love my blueberry pancakes. They are typically a Sunday thing, and you know I'm a big believer in keeping a schedule, but I'll allow the change-up. For you. Of course, we run the risk you'll never want to leave, but that may or may not be part of my dastardly plan. Oops, but there I go, giving away my sinister scheme. Guess that's why I'll never make a very good bad guy." I held my laptop to my chest and chanced a look at my guest.

My *Trey-whispering* succeeded. His grin reappeared, and I returned the expression. With a deep breath, I encouraged him to take one too; a wordless reminder breath came easier in this space. His chest rose and fell, then did it again for good measure.

"Shower. Shave. Don't shave. Do whatever you want." I meant the last bit more than I cared to admit but turned to descend the stairs. "Oh, and your mom called last night. We had a pleasant chat. She asked that you call home."

"Hattie," he yelped as he sprang from the bed. "What did you—"

"I didn't tell her anything. Your mom, your business. I only said you were sleeping."

His fingers pulled at his hair. Concern flashed.

"And that us being together, late at night, didn't necessarily mean what one might assume it meant. Anyway, you should call her." I kept my tone light but bolted down the stairs, leaving him to his phone call, hoping I hadn't broken anything that couldn't be fixed.

I made coffee and rinsed blueberries, wishing I could hear the conversation taking place upstairs. Damn the solid concrete structure I called home.

The pancake recipe, perfected over my adolescent years, didn't exist on paper. It hid, locked away in my brain with myriad other secrets. The ingredients mixed, I let the batter rest while I waited for my guest to join me downstairs. The kitchen sink window allowed a sliver view of street traffic, more pedestrians than cars. It was much later than I'd first thought, or time ticked by faster than it should, faster than I wanted. The sun, mid-sky, radiated heat. Waves of it blurred from the blacktop. Even the pigeons waddling the sidewalks appeared too put-out to make any effort to fly. Very few made the quick trip to the power line overhead, where I imagined they might find a breeze. I sipped coffee while I counted the seconds between lift-offs.

When firm hands grasped my hips, I jarred out of my haze as heat ran up my back. The roughness of a days-old beard brushed my cheek, and I leaned into the sturdy frame pinning me to the counter. Tilting my head, I enjoyed the tickle of warm breath on my neck, in my ear, then my hair. The grip at my hips slid down my thighs, then up again to my waist with a tighter, needier squeeze.

"Hattie?"

"Hmm?" The reply hummed in my throat as sweat prickled along my breastbone.

"Hattie? Are you all right?" Trey's voice sounded far away, and I no longer felt his hold.

I jerked around to face him, the fantasy interrupted. Trey, wet-headed and dressed in his black t-shirt and jeans, stood in the living room, several feet away. He hadn't shaved, and his dark scruff of beard looked darker still in the bright light of day.

"Huh?" The strangled, high-pitched sound did its best to give me away, but I fought the exposure. "Ready for those pancakes?" I spun back to the task, regretting the extra layer of a bathrobe, my face reddening.

"Not sure that's a good idea, Hattie."

My chin hit my chest. He needed to leave. His mom had called him home, and our vexing game of playing house had to end. For the best, really. I rotated back but kept my gaze to the floor, my mouth shut.

"I mean, I'm a disciplined guy. But I'm only human. And while there isn't much that will turn my head when I have a job to do, very little that I'd consider a *true* distraction, but the siren song of—blueberry pancakes might just—"

"*Shut* up." I flung a dishtowel in his direction. "Pour yourself some coffee and sit your ass down for some breakfast." I ladled out messy splats of batter, then thrashed out of the bathrobe, tossing it onto the back of a bistro chair. On my return to the pancake station, we did a hesitant, side-step, hands-up dance-around after he filled his coffee mug. I caught his raised brow and smirk. "What? It's hot standing over that griddle," I scoffed. "And thank you." I flipped the flapjacks.

"Thank you? For what?" A snicker alive and well in his voice.

"For reminding me what an asshole you are. I *almost* forgot."

Our good-natured ribbing eased my fantasy-induced angst and the mom-provoked stress, and we enjoyed our meal. *Huh*. Brunch with an age-appropriate friend? It wasn't Sunday and didn't quite qualify as "normal," but I could see it from there. My inner thoughts caused an outer grin, and my brunch-mate caught it.

"What was that?" With a fork in one hand and a butter knife in the other, Trey leaned in with his question.

"What was what?" I'll admit my poker face needed some practice.

He didn't ask again, but his expression read as a reminder. It said to share, or omit, but don't lie.

"I was thinking back to a lifetime ago when you and I had an exchange about 'normalcy.'" I flexed the air-quotes. "You said you never had normal, didn't think you could, and I asked the rhetorical questions, 'What does normal even look like? And who would want it, anyway?'"

"I remember." His watchful eye looked for more, but he tilted further with a hesitant verbal nudge when I kept quiet. "And?"

"And? And— I think you can, and I think it looks a lot like this and turns out, *I* want it." I grabbed my plate and headed for the sink before I continued. "Don't panic. I'm just saying it's nice to wake up next to someone I can make blueberry pancakes for on the weekend. And the kicker is *none* of that has anything to do with that line we can't and *won't* be crossing, so yeah—okay, maybe—*not*—*normal*." The panic, which I'd mistakenly assured Trey was unnecessary, hit me. "Excuse me." I exited the kitchen and beelined to the upstairs, scolding myself for speaking without thinking through the consequences of sharing these new, unanalyzed thoughts and feelings. *Dumb move, Harry.*

It didn't surprise me to find my bed made, covers pulled tight, and pillows arranged just so. Trey's neatly-folded sleeping clothes rested on the settee, and "Tom" still kept watch from his hanger. I headed straight to the shower for a quick rinse to wash off the stink of shame and embarrassment. It also shouldn't have surprised me to find Trey gone when I returned downstairs.

"Shit. Shit, shit—well, this seems about right. So much for providing a relaxed place where breath and thought comes *easily*, Harry. Nope. You had to open your mouth and say the most ridiculous things to the poor guy. Wait. Poor guy? He's a felon climbing the criminal ladder. A sociopath, so Uncle Marty would have you believe. So, maybe this isn't as lamentable as you're making it out to be. And let's not forget, come Monday you begin the—"

Leo's gregarious laugh interrupted my out-loud reprimand, howling as his apartment door opened to our shared hallway. My neighbor's distinct cadence continued, but the concrete building didn't allow me to understand his words. By the time I reached my door and squinted through the new fisheye security lens, the knob turned in my hand, and the metal door inched open. I sucked in a gulp.

"Sorry. I should have knocked. Thought you might still be upstairs."

I stared as Trey closed the door behind him.

"I went to get the medical professional to take a look at his handiwork. He says it all looks good. I'm an excellent patient, minus the more recent bruising, but what are you gonna do? Another week tops, and the stitches can come out. He offered to do the job, but since I don't know my schedule in the near-term, he gave me a primer on how to do it myself." Trey carried his coffee mug to the kitchen to pour another cup. "Snip and pull. Pretty self-explanatory. More coffee? I brewed another pot." Trey held up the stainless carafe.

I declined with a head shake, baffled by his casual attitude.

"So, I think you're right." He spoke like our conversation had never ended. "Not about all of it. The last part is debatable, but also probably better left for another time. But I just took my coffee mug—well, *your* coffee mug—to the neighbor's flat to say hello. What's more normal than that? Sure, he looked at sutures he'd stitched in me a week ago under unusual circumstances, but if we just focus on the coffee and the neighbor and the hello bits—pretty normal, right? And who's to say my normal, *our* normal, has to look like anyone else's and that our normal can't evolve over time?"

Somehow we'd each found justification for an existence we both wanted but knew would never work. I had to admit our ability to make the absurd sound rational, possible even, was nothing short of impressive.

"Trey."

He fought the inevitable. "Look, Hattie, I know it isn't ideal, that it has its obstacles, but—"

"*Trey.*"

His slow steps traveled in time with the wall clock's tick, while his gaze never parted from mine. I stopped him an arm's length away, but only just. Splaying my fingers across his chest, they noted the medal hidden under his t-shirt. He placed his hands over mine.

"We made a mistake, huh?" Our hands pressed against his frame, and his heartbeat thumped against my palm, faster than it should.

I shook my head again and gave a sad smile. "Not yet, no. But—it's only a matter of time. Not proud of it, but I don't have nearly the self-discipline you possess, Mr. Popov."

He flinched; a full-body shudder I'd seen before but couldn't explain. It seemed a response to how I said his name. A painful one.

"I have to go, don't I?"

"You do. But if leaving now is—unsafe—in the daylight, I mean. I can go, and you can stay until—"

"No. I'll be careful."

"Will you?"

He nodded as his free hand reached to tuck one of my damp, wayward curls behind my ear. His finger traced my jawline, then lifted my chin. Somehow, the protection of the arm's length distance had disappeared, and we stood too close.

"Last time—*after* I'd gone, I sent word saying if I— *had*, I wouldn't have left." His hand slid to my cheek, and I closed my eyes and tilted into his palm.

"I remember," I echoed his earlier reply to revisiting a past conversation.

"It feels worse this time. I mean, if I do, if I—"

"Don't say it."

"If I *kiss* you, I'm afraid I won't leave."

Just the thought of it overwhelmed me. Hearing him say it nearly broke me.

"It *is* worse this time," I assured him.

His knitted brow asked why.

I dropped my gaze, ashamed by my wilting resolve. "If you *do* kiss me, I *know* I won't let you go."

Trey released me, dropping the hand that cradled my face. He grabbed his jacket from the hat rack and tore out of my apartment before either of us could say goodbye.

Twenty-Nine

Not gonna lie. I took the next day and a half to myself—a self-imposed and completely necessary *time-out*. No destructive behavior, no broken dishes, or burned clothing. Just thirty-six hours to get my head straight and refocused. July was speeding along, with less than six weeks before the fall term at St. John's commenced. The coming semester had me taking part in a guest lecture series, a once-a-week seminar for grad students. With my material long since prepared, I had the time to pursue other endeavors and decided to ease into one of those as of Monday. A welcome distraction and a noble one, too.

As far as the *What's next?* question, a fair bit of it rested outside my control, as was often the story with investigative work. I had to roll with it—take my time and use *all* the patience.

On Monday, after my usual workout and completing my daily chore list, I slipped on a cute sundress and grabbed my messenger bag. It carried a well-worn sketch pad I liked to doodle in and the necessary supplies for such activities. I headed out in a roundabout way to a popular (or so social media said) sandwich spot in Astoria, a neighborhood I'd visited not so long ago.

I beat the lunch rush, which was my intention, and grabbed a table by the front window. My prime spot sat near the door with a clear view of the coming and going foot traffic. So far, things couldn't have gone any better. With just the right amount of pungent feta, the buttery spanakopita provided the delicious time-filler I needed to keep watch while looking like I belonged.

The small Mediterranean café filled quickly, and as I guessed, many of the patrons were regulars. Jovial greetings, back slaps, and many kissed cheeks said as much. Their hum of friendly chatter bounced around the linoleum floor and rough plastered walls decorated with beautifully hand-painted plates and platters in the vibrant cornflower blue traditionally seen throughout Greek culture. Fans spun on long pendants hanging from the high pressed-tin ceiling, and the haunting strum of the bouzouki wafted cheerful tunes laced with a sadness I had to remind myself I didn't relate to. The savory pastry helped, but timing played a vital role in my scheme, so I slowed my dining to a nibble and looked busy sketching on my pad. I also reminded investigator Harry of the virtues of patience, and if today didn't yield results, there would always be tomorrow.

As it turns out, the P.I. gods were on my side. The brass bell that ting-a-linged whenever a patron came or went chimed again. A tall brunette with tight but soft curls skimming her fair-skinned shoulders stood in the doorway, surveying the crowded restaurant. Not a seat to be found. She gave a weak wave to an employee behind the counter, then a disappointed shrug to no one in particular.

Closing my spiraled sketchbook and stowing it in my bag, I made my move. "Here, take my seat."

The woman I'd guesstimated at my age smiled. "Are you sure?"

"Absolutely, I've gotta fly. I recommend the spanakopita. Delish." Ducking my head under my bag strap, I pushed in my chair to squeeze through the jam-packed lunch crowd.

"Yes, I agree. I'm a regular, so..." She eased her way toward the table, signaling the counter attendant again and pointing to her destination.

"My first time, but I'll definitely be back. Enjoy." I avoided eye contact with the woman throughout our quick exchange, but smiled and sprinted out the door, brushing past a bystander just outside the café. In half a block, I rounded the corner and slowed my speedy gait, taking a deep breath. "Well done, Harry." I looked skyward with a bit of pride and headed home by a different route from earlier.

With a spring still in my step, I bounded into my building, snagged my mail, but then stopped short, seeing Leo's open door. More than the air conditioning chill hit me. The clink of glasses made its way to the hall as I crept to his apartment. Shouldn't Leo be in class at this hour?

"Leo?" I called in a whisper before I peeked inside and heard the louder clank of dishes coming from his kitchen on the far side from where I stood. I repeated his name louder.

"In here," he answered. "Hey, you. Didn't want to miss you, so I left the door open. You've been mighty absent. Everything okay?" Leo unloaded his dishwasher while I reminded myself the days of skittish behavior were behind me, and I best act like it.

"Yeah, why do you ask?"

That garnered a side-eye look from my colossal friend. Disappointing Leo was never high on my to-do list, but *I* needed to make it clear *he* needed to give up on the notion of the *not-so-nice* Jewish fella and me.

"Are you sure?" He pouted when I finished explaining what could never be. "What's with the sassy dress and espadrilles, then? You mean to tell me this isn't about a man?" His finger pointed up and down at me.

"Uh, no. A *woman*, actually." I grinned at Leo's double take. "Never mind. It's work." I brushed off Leo's questioning look. "Didn't school start up again?"

"I'm officially a third-year. All clinicals, all the time. So, my shifts will be all over the place. Hard to believe I graduate in a year. And your Jedi mind tricks don't work on me anymore, but if you don't want to talk about it—"

"I don't want to talk about it." My interjection came fast.

"Harry." Leo shook his head and tried to avoid letting me see his glassy eyes.

"Leo, I get you jumped on the Team Trey bandwagon early, but he's hell-bent on sticking to his path, and you know I can't be a part of that. Look, I've obviously got issues with picking the wrong men. This one just got nipped in the bud quickly, before any lines got crossed, any damage got done, any hearts got—well, this is actual progress, Auntie Leo. You should be pleased."

Leo kept up the sad look. "I think you're wrong. And I think you know it. I've seen you two, and there is something there, something real."

"I think you're sweet to care so much. But I'm not the one in need of saving. Trey is, and I have no authority; I don't have the *tools* to do the job."

"That's not how I heard it, honey. I heard you could—"

"Well, Leo," I cut him off, knowing to dwell on it any longer would do more harm than good. "I don't know what to say. You heard wrong." With a shrug, I left him to wallow since I couldn't allow myself to, determined to focus on *Day Two* of my new project.

I buried myself in work. Multiple rabbit holes enticed me to explore, and I dipped my toe in each of them. It wasn't until my stomach gurgled with impressive noise that I realized I was sitting in the dark, well-beyond my bedtime and definitely past the dinner hour. I stumbled to standing. Hours of hunched shoulders and twisted legs, sitting on my living room floor left some body parts aching while others were merely numb. Why didn't I use the desk and comfy leather high-back chair in my bedroom's office space? Too adult, I guessed. Popping the top off a beer bottle constituted making supper, and I trudged upstairs with my messenger bag, ready to call it a night.

"Tom" still hung at my bedside, left behind when Trey bolted Saturday. Keeping the shirt made little sense, yet I couldn't even make the move to put it in my coveted closet, much less dispose of it.

I plugged all my electronics in for recharging, save one. The burner, still labeled *Hattie's phone,* came to bed with me, where I contemplated irresponsible behavior like texting a certain number. I simply wanted to hear he was safe, sunning it up in Tahiti or on a Birkin bag buying binge in Hermès' hometown. That notion led to fantasies of Trey's long lashes and his devilish grin on the Champs-Élysées and the realization it was going be another long night.

When the clock numbers turned from two-fifty-nine to three o'clock in the morning, I threw rational thought and caution to the wind and typed:

Burner one: *Tell me u r ok*

My thumb hovered over the "send" arrow for what felt like a lifetime. I remembered how Trey's discipline and self-control impressed me, even if it didn't necessarily suit me. The irony. I hit *send*.

Despite the late hour and the man's restraint, he was also merciful. A few seconds later, my phone chirped.

Burner two: *It's Tuesday, bathroom cleaning day, and the mop turns to the bucket and says...*

With a smile and wistful look at Tom, I fell asleep.

Thirty

Tuesday's workout proved grueling, by design, and not *my* design. On little sleep, I headed to the gym earlier than I would typically, because *Day Two* of my oh-so-righteous plot took on urgency after *Day One's* success. The sooner I made serious headway, the sooner I could gain actionable intel to avenge my dad, assuage his soon-to-be-retired partner, and rescue my own damsel trapped in the horrible circumstance of my making. Three birds. One gigantic stone.

Nate hovered near the door, and an undeniable twinkle sparked in his eyes when I moseyed into the concrete facility. A few stragglers from the daybreak coffee klatch crowd finished their early fitness sessions. The trainer's teetering seemed on full tilt, his smile indicating he knew something I didn't, though he looked eager to let me in on the joke. The joke came in the form of a new exercise regimen, compliments of Uncle Marty. Apparently, my mentor got the idea I'd been getting soft in recent weeks. I assured Nate that Detective O'Shea had it all wrong, and I had actually upped my workout-game of late. The bowling pin's reply?

"I guess we'll see, won't we, Harry?"

On my third round of burpees—a version that included a twenty-five-pound medicine ball slam—it occurred to me Marty may have taken my knowledge of the Quantico question as proof positive of some intention on my part. It was all the evidence he needed to pursue his own new project: me. But clearly Uncle Marty meant to keep a degree of separation from his latest scheme. It also meant me losing my ill-advised morning bagel and herb cream cheese schmear in a ringside spit bucket. I think Nate felt terrible about that.

"See you tomorrow, Harry?" Nate offered me a sports drink, but I declined in favor of plain water.

"Not if I see you first, Nate." I grimaced with my joke, sipping water as I limped to the door, surprised I could raise my arm to wave goodbye. I'd earned my shower and some *vitamin I* but had no time to rest on any laurels—or ice packs. Besides, another serving of spanakopita called to me, and after the morning's rough workout, maybe some baklava too. Sketchpad tucked in my bag, and dressed in a short romper, I returned to Astoria, using a new combination of subway, Uber, and walked side streets, hoping I'd have *another* accidental run-in with a curly-haired brunette.

Tuesday's crowd differed from the day before, but I had done my research, and the odds for a "chance" meeting were in my favor. I took the same seat and ordered the same savory pastry, taking advantage of the window's view to sketch the streetscape in the bright noontime sun. Drawing the straight lines of architecture and lettering of signage wasn't my strong suit, but I did my best to look competent.

Growing up in a police station, I'd spent more than a few hours with a freelance sketch artist who, on occasion, worked at the precinct. An elderly woman, she had the time and sought companionship on her lonelier days. Sharing tips and techniques on how to render accurate facial features and detailed tattoo art became a regular occurrence, and it seemed I had a knack for it. My dad would have been the first to admit any artistic talent had to be in my DNA because it hadn't rubbed off from him.

The brass bell yanked me back to the task at hand. I chided myself for getting lost in thought when I should have been keeping track of my surroundings. Startled, my abrupt movement to vacate the premises might have been too obvious. I also didn't have the benefit of a fully packed café to help in my ruse. Quick thinking launched an impromptu Plan B.

The young woman entered the restaurant alone as she had on *Day One* and walked to the counter, I presumed, to order lunch. Steadied, I bided my time a few feet from her, perusing the overhead chalkboard that advertised the daily offerings. On closer inspection, my old sketch artist tutor in mind, I realized the brunette wasn't so young. My initial thought that we were the same age wavered the closer I stood to the attractive woman with alabaster skin. That pale complexion gave away some blemishes up close. Dark circles and fine lines edged her tired eyes, and taut skin at her jawline indicated angst, stress, or sadness. Probably all three. And for a moment, guilt seeped into my gut for the game-playing. Then I reminded myself it wasn't a game.

Whether she was lost in her own thoughts or just not observant in her usual routine, she didn't acknowledge my presence until I spoke to the café employee.

"Yes, I'd like a piece of the baklava, please. But I'll take it to-go." I glanced at my watch to iterate my rush, with cash ready to make a speedy transaction.

"Good choice." The woman stepped aside but appeared to wait for the order she'd placed. "The Bougatsa is great too, but to go, baklava is the right pick." She kept her eyes on her phone screen and scrolled, not making any real effort to engage me. "You came back."

Her phraseology stunned me as she spoke the exact words Trey used the last time he woke in my bed, but the legitimate head jerk worked to my advantage. "Oh, hi," I chirped as if I had only just realized we were familiar with one another. "Yes, I did. It's a nice spot at the window to sketch. You're welcome to it now, though." I took the white paper sack the cashier handed me with a cheerful, "Thanks, until next time." I spun on my heel and beelined for the door, less confident in *Day Two's* success.

Reaching the sidewalk, I nearly slammed into a man, dressed head to toe in black, standing at attention near the café door. He had an athletic build with impressive biceps bound by the short-sleeved cuffs of a dry-fit polo shirt. A surly scowl and something about his flattened nose screamed, "goon." In retrospect, I had brushed by him the day before, too. I hadn't considered the possibility, but it seemed my new soon-to-be friend kept hired company. Fresh data to add to the equation, but I had more than a day to recalculate. With some feigned distraction, I hurried past the brutish bystander on yet another meandering route home.

I've mentioned it, but before sharing this next bit, I want to reiterate, and say it loudly for the folks in the back: I am *not* some mushy romantic. That sketchpad I'd been carrying would *never* include doodles of hearts and flowers unless, of course, they framed some badass skeletal demon ink design on some perp's body art. But it was Tuesday, and as I crouched on all-fours with an old toothbrush to scrub the caulk around my toilet base, I couldn't help but think about a certain quick-witted man at the ready with a "dirty" joke. Somehow, in all the chaos of his criminal lifestyle, he found the bandwidth to remember I had mentioned Tuesday was bathroom cleaning day. Sweet, right? *Shut up, Harry.*

Wednesday was a day of rest, but not from Nate. I endured the workout from hell, glad to have the distraction. And I skipped the heavy breakfast, so my wobbly coach appreciated the vomit-free fitness session. *Rest* meant no visit to Astoria. Three days in a row of chance meetings threatened to be overkill.

"Got time for an ad hoc lunch?" I breathed a little relief when Marty answered on the first ring. We hadn't spoken since Friday, and while in the past, I would go a week, sometimes longer, without hearing from him, my less-than-forthright behavior of late left me uneasy and a bit guilt-ridden.

"Does that mean you're buying?"

"If you'll let me," I offered.

"I won't. Let's meet. The rookies are in the house, so—"

"Yeah, I get it. Rico's?"

"One hour?"

"See you then."

Uncle Marty ended the call, not a syllable wasted.

Rico's was a favorite neighborhood eatery. The diner stood only a quarter mile from my home, with chrome stools at a stainless-steel counter featuring a view of the miraculous short-order cooks. Booths lined the slanted, windowed walls of what used to be a gas station mid-last century. It was also the last place I ate with the old writer guy, and I'd been eager to replace that memory with another. Weeks had passed, so it was time. No matter the hour, the greasy spoon smelled of sautéed onions and maple syrup, and with all that description, if I ever sat at a *clean* table, I'd have to check twice to be sure where I was. A laminated menu sticking to the Formica constituted charm, and I loved it. I also knew Marty had an ongoing love affair with Rico's tuna melt with Swiss cheese on seedless rye, so his accepting the invite was a foregone conclusion. What I didn't expect was his beating me to the joint.

"Slow day at the salt mine, Uncle Marty?" I joined him, sitting on the opposite side of the booth he'd chosen.

"Slow enough." The man's bagged eyes squinted to study the menu, like maybe the tuna melt on seedless rye *wasn't* the sure-bet I'd thought. Then again, maybe the detective merely avoided my eye.

"What's up, Marty?"

"Up? You called me, kiddo."

"I did. Hadn't heard from you in a few, not directly anyhow. Nate sends his best, by the way."

Marty started to chuckle but had the good sense to stifle it.

"Anyway, I had a free day, so I reached out. Now you beat me here—which never happens, and you won't look me in the eye, so—again, what's up, Marty?" My mind reeled. Was Marty sick? Bess? Or maybe there had been some *Vlad the Bad* blow-back? Had the seven-inch Cold Steel Leatherneck American Tanto fixed blade—I swear I still felt it in my grip some nights—resurfaced? With my fingerprints on it? Trey's? Trust me. I had run the scenarios. Thanks to the Fourth Amendment, I imagined Trey Popov's prints weren't in the system, and he had a knack for keeping his hands in his Adidas pockets when he wasn't cuffed. On the other hand, I had a concealed carry permit, and in New York City, that privilege came with a souvenir card showing my unique prints, plus a digital version the great state would hold in perpetuity.

A young waitress skipped to our booth with a notepad, pencil, and an inquisitive eye. Thoughts of Trey conjured a hankering for bacon—the "forbidden meat" jokes wrote themselves.

"I'll take a BLT on toasted wheat. Add a slice of cheddar and a side of fries, please." I nodded to my lunch companion.

Marty sighed, "Tuna melt on seedless rye with Swiss and a side of slaw."

I smiled as we both tucked our menus in the chrome holder in front of the window.

"What?" Marty caught my smirk.

"Huh? Nothing. You were saying—"

"Was I?"

I only stared.

"Okay, kid. Can't say I appreciate your voodoo mind-meld psychic powers when used on me but—heard from our friend lately?" His boss-like posture, hands folded in front of him, meant to set a strictly-business mood. I didn't feel like playing along.

I steadied myself. "Our friend? You hanging with my millennial peeps again, Uncle Marty? Didn't realize you and I had been missing each other at the Gen Y Club meetings." I sipped my iced tea through a soggy paper straw.

"You know your nervous tell is cracking lame jokes, right?"

He wasn't wrong.

"When did you last see him, Harry?"

I sat ramrod straight and cleared my throat. My eyeballs rolled up like I scanned some sci-fi futuristic mid-air projection of my personal calendar. "Uh, Sa-tur-day?" It sounded more like a well-contemplated question, but it was the truth.

"You mean— Saturday a week ago."

"Do I? Sounds like you're the one keeping track." I straightened the salt and pepper shakers. "Why do you ask, anyway?" I asked, hurrying past the detail. "I meant what I said at the gym that day, Marty. If Popov shows up, if you hear he's been picked up, I want him protected, and I want a call. Day or night. We're clear on that, right? I mean, I haven't asked for much; I don't pull strings or hound you for favors, but this one? I need it." The slight quiver in my voice and my trembling hands threatened my cool guise. I placed the shaky limbs in my lap, but the damage was done.

Marty nodded. "Word of advice? You're just starting out, haven't even started really, but I know you'll be a heck of an asset, and whatever you decide to do, whichever direction you choose, you go knowing Harlan Smith would be the proudest Pop there ever was."

It seemed Uncle Marty *had* pinned some hopes on the Quantico idea. Still, I didn't need the added pressure, so telling him I had recently inquired about restarting my application process felt premature.

"But here's the thing, kiddo—you can*not* save a man who doesn't want saving, no matter what he's drowning in. You hear? There comes the point when you have to let go. Might be the hardest part of the job."

I tried to reply, but he didn't want to hear it.

"I don't know what happened, not all of it, anyway. Not sure why you're holding a candle for this one, but I can't help but feel some responsibility. You have my word. My ear is to the ground, and if I hear something, I will let you know."

"Thank you," I squeezed the two syllables through my tight throat then leaned in for reassurance. "So—"

"It's like Popov's a ghost. And with *Vlad the Bad* dead, you might need to get yourself prepared to find Popov is too. Or get your head around the fact we may never know. Sometimes people just disappear."

The food arrived, and Marty and I both stared at our respective plates. My *newest* Rico's memory felt worse than the old one. And that was saying something.

Thirty-One

Thursday had a make-or-break kind of feel, and while Nate fed me through another day of his torture workout machine, breaking seemed a *real* possibility. I'm not sure what he and Marty thought I might encounter in the fitness portion of any application process that I may or may not be mulling over, but whatever it was, it must be fast, strong, and maybe inhuman.

Pinned to the mat by a sweaty, tank-top-wearing behemoth who had nearly a foot and a buck-twenty-five on my size, I tapped out with an ironic *uncle*. Rocco, another new sparring partner, quickly hopped off my sprawled frame, but I refused the hand he offered to help me to my feet when I rolled to my back with a groan.

"Sorry, Harry." The hapless forced volunteer pouted with his hands on his hips as he stood too close for the view his FDNY shorts provided.

"Jesus, Rocco." I draped my arm over my eyes. "Don't beat me *and* pity me. What are you trying to do? Make a girl cry?"

"No, Harry. Jeez. Nate said—"

"Just bustin' your balls, Roc. We're good—uh, but speaking of, how about you take a step back, yeah?"

The firefighter extended his hand again. When I took it, my stomach rose and fell at being briefly airborne. The kind brute had utility poles for biceps.

"We should do this again," I offered while toweling off both Rocco's and my sweat from my back.

"Yeah?" His eyes brightened a little too much.

"I mean, not anytime soon, but…" I grinned and winked in hopes he could keep up with my joking, but I had little faith in his ability. His head-scratching confirmed as much. But what he lacked in gray matter he more than made up for in his humanity and life-saving skills. "I'll see you around, big guy. Stay safe out there." I climbed out of the ring and headed for home to get ready for a different sparring match.

My next planned "chance" meeting was less of a sure thing. Plus, it had the potential to be weather-dependent, so while I dressed and made my way back to Astoria, I reissued the "patience in investigation" lecture to remind myself tomorrow was another day. Of course, the next day was also Friday, and I had some unrealistically-high farmer's market expectations for another *sort* of chance encounter with another *sort* of person who provoked all *sorts* of inappropriate thoughts and feelings. *Focus, Harry.*

I ambled my way to a new locale in the neighborhood I'd been frequenting lately. Athens Square offered a small amphitheater space with Doric columns and statues dotting a fenced green-space in an urban setting. Playground equipment to one side of the small park attracted children, of course, but benches and tables tucked under trees and surrounded by lush shrubbery enticed picnic lunches, chess games, readers, and, on Thursdays, artists. Well, one artist, if you believed her social media.

After Nate had Rocco grind me into the mat that last round, the clock was working against me. Time forced a more direct route to the city park, but I stopped at a charming bakery to grab an iced coffee and a croissant that sparked bittersweet memories of my days of mourning in France. The café's aromas brought a barrage of recollections, including a day spent with nothing but a sketchpad and the sights and sounds of Paris to inspire me to explore. Now, settled into a verdant nook near a bronze bust of Aristotle, I reminded myself that my days of *exploring* were done. Now, I hunted.

With a sip of creamy coffee, I pinched off a flaky, buttery morsel, letting it melt in my mouth while I surveyed barely-there shadows the overcast skies and oak leaves cast across Aristotle's wavy beard and the long bridge of his slightly upturned nose. The dark bronze emphasized the high cheekbones and vacant eyes that held little detail compared to the sculpted hair's texture, neck muscles, and deep wrinkles in the chiseled rendition of the Greek philosopher. The empty eyes drew me in, and my pencil went to work on the thick, toothy drawing paper in my lap. Long-ago lessons in comparative human anatomy and facial expression echoed. I remembered how I enjoy the feel of graphite in my grip and its scratch on the roughness of quality paper. I got lost in the sensations of it.

"You're not bad." The woman's comment came from behind my bench seat. "I'm guessing you haven't been traditionally taught, but someone who gave you some tutorials along the way had training. And there's an intensity in your stroke that is telling."

Not going to lie, the woman startled me, and whatever intensity she *thought* she saw in my stroke, I *knew* I heard in her voice. In hindsight, I should have paid closer attention.

I didn't take my gaze from my bronzed pal Ari. "I'm just doodling, really. But you're right. When I was younger, a woman who watched me after school some days was an artist, and she tried to teach me things. I'm a little surprised how much of it stuck."

"Well, surely one of your parents, grandparents, maybe, imparted some talented genes your way. May I?" She made slow strides around the far end of my bench and asked if she could take a seat. As focused as she remained on my sketchpad, I kept centered on the subject of my drawing, save the uninvested nod I offered her request to sit.

"Sure. And I really couldn't say. I don't know much about any family DNA. Certainly not anything about talent, artistic or otherwise."

"What other kind of talent is there? Other than artistic?" Despite her efforts to engage me, my concentration remained unchallenged, or so I had it seem.

"I think some people have a talent for figures or talent for persuasion," I paused with a flicker of thought. "Or a talent for discipline." I nodded to myself with the idea of that particular skill set.

"But it's all art, isn't it? Math? Coaxing? And discipline could be self-restraint or punishment, but still artful. I think so, anyway. Then again, I see art in everything." She spoke with a hint of sadness that I thought I understood, if not one I found wholly relatable.

"That must make you an artist."

"*Ah-ha*, I am. And what are you?" A joyful tone overtook the sorrowful one, and while I still didn't look at her, an audible smile sprang from her direction.

"Not an artist, that's for sure. Just an observer," I chuckled.

"But that's exactly what an artist is. An observer, first and foremost."

"An artist, huh? Don't say that too loud. My uncle would *hate* that." I imagined Uncle Marty jeering at the notion. "Of course, he's not really my uncle."

"My uncle is a big supporter of me and—my art. How lucky am I?" She sounded like she didn't feel lucky at all. Pity for her panged in my chest. "Well, since I have discovered you, this new artist who has always been, you *must* tell me your name."

"Sorry." For the first time, I put down my pencil and looked the woman directly in the eye, but not before a subtle but feigned double take. "Harriet." I offered a handshake with my head cocked. "But haven't we met? Twice now?"

"Well, not formally. Nice to meet you, Harriet. I'm Anya." The pretty girl who had a pretty room full of pretty things took my hand and smiled.

Thirty-Two

It's not news that *this* kind of work is unfamiliar to me. When I'm not presenting a kickass lecture, I sit in front of a computer screen or in a van, safely behind a camera lens. With luck, I eavesdrop with a well-placed listening device. Personally engaging with a subject under less than scrupulous circumstances was a tact I had only attempted once before... a few weeks ago... and we saw how well that went. In my defense, I learned a lot from that debacle, and this particular mark wasn't some street punk, some criminal on the rise. She was an artist, a sad, lonely, *stuck* artist. I offered her friendship, and while friendship belonged on my not-really-my-thing list, someone could make the argument that I was being nice. Well, they *could*.

The run-up to Anya and me getting to know each other happened gradually, or as slowly as I had the patience. It required subtlety. I couldn't have her picking up any pushy vibe. Just a stranger she bumped into a few times, always some place *she* found me—an indifferent nobody who happened to share a pastime. A young woman who turned up in the artist's radius on occasion, as if the universe meant for them to know one another.

Unfortunately, in a different matter entirely, an accidental run-in with my likable lawbreaker didn't happen on my Friday farmers' market visit. I hadn't banked on it, but I'd hoped, and the extent of my disappointment pissed me off to no end. I'd put on lip gloss after my Nate-supervised thrashing, for Christ's sake. And after I grumbled about it on my walk home and stewed further as I unpacked my fresh food purchases, I showered off the sweat of the workout and hot afternoon shopping trip, not to mention the stink of my Trey-induced frustration. Okay, sue me. I mentioned it.

I blame all that annoyance for my next hasty move.

Hours of cyberstalking told me Anya had a reliable habit of visiting her own kind of market on Friday evenings. Not always, but often, and since I had no other engagements and craved distraction, venturing out to provoke another chance encounter seemed like a *fantastic* idea. Anything would be better than wallowing in the letdown of a rendezvous not realized. I grabbed my emptied knapsack and headed for the door.

"Hey, Leo. You okay?"

Leo stood in a slumped, lumpy stature in our shared hall. Glazed eyes barely acknowledged me.

"Leo?"

"Huh?"

"Are you okay?" I took him by the arm, hoping he wouldn't release all his weight onto me. As strong as my new exercise regimen made me, my muscles ached, and I could never carry all of him.

"So tired. So, so, tired. I forgot what I'm supposed to do next." Leo's weary tone sighed out of him as he swayed dangerously far.

"How about we get you inside? Give me your keys." I pried the jangling ring from his fingers and helped him into his apartment. "Want to get to your bed?"

"No. Sofa will do. I just need a nap. They don't call the first week of a third year's schedule Hell Week for giggles. It seems a bit of hazing comes with the launch of our final push." My neighbor's head clunked the wall when he collapsed onto his couch. The way his eyes closed and his mouth hung open, I thought he'd fallen asleep that fast. But when a snort jerked out of him, he spoke again. "Are you cute? I thought I saw you looked cute, but I can't open my eyes again. Do you have a date?"

"Sort of." I untied and wrestled off my drained friend's Nikes.

"*Yaaay*." Sweet Leo mustered all the enthusiasm his exhaustion allowed.

"Well, it's work, really."

"*Boooo*." Dissatisfaction grumped out of him, then he sighed.

"You sleep. I'll check on you tomorrow. Oh. Quick question. Your friend that lives in Astoria near Mt Sinai Queens? Steven, is it?"

"Ste*PHAN*. Heavy accent on the second syl*LA*ble," Leo laughed, getting punchier the longer he stayed conscious. "Yes. What about him?"

"What's his address? Somewhere off 30th Ave? On 35th Street?"

"34th Street. Why?"

"Just looking for a point of reference. I'll know it when I see it. Not important. I'm locking you in using my key. See you tomorrow, Auntie Leo. Sweet dreams," I whispered, but the gentle giant emitted a low, buzzy snore before I reached the hall.

For the second time this month, I found myself in Astoria during those quiet hours between daytime and nighttime business activities. Per usual, I took a roundabout route, this time to a five-story dark brick walk-up on 34th Street—for a point of reference. It was a terrific block, and the building was only a few years old. Gentrification was alive and well in Astoria. I took in the surroundings, noting a "for rent" sign in the first-floor apartment's front window. From there, I took a chance, strolling up 30th Ave, then left on 31st Street to a little Euro-market.

Research told me the store not only sold a wide range of Mediterranean fare but also a host of Eastern European deli favorites, plus an excellent wine selection. A wine purchase would be my subterfuge on the warm Friday evening. Imagine my delight when I approached the single-story grocery mart and found a burly man dressed in black, keeping guard outside the glass doors. His face wasn't familiar, but I knew his uniform, and congratulated myself on research well-done and for acting on a hunch. It almost provided a bit of consolation for the earlier letdown in my neck of the woods. *Focus, Harry.*

I caught the back of another athletic figure wearing the requisite black polo and dress pants like the man outside. This one turned down the second to last aisle furthest from me, presumably following his charge. The last lane housed the wine I wanted, and I hurried, hoping to beat the woman perusing the previous aisle. Success. I held a bottle of pinot grigio in one hand and a chardonnay in the other while exploring the options in front of me when my new friend rounded the other end of the wine section.

"Yes, I know rosé is so trendy right now, but on a hot summer night, I am not above pouring a glass of this over a few ice cubes and enjoying it with a book on the rooftop of my building," Anya spoke as if we were mid-conversation and thrust a bottle of pink wine toward my already full hands. "But if it's a more formal summertime affair, this sauvignon blanc can't be outdone for the price point." She held up another option.

"Huh," I played along, pleased at the easy rapport we had with one another. "Gotta go-to for a girl who's new to town, looking to get a little tipsy on a Friday night while sitting alone on her fire escape? Wow. That sounded *really* pathetic." I placed my two bottles back on the shelf, trying to look sheepish.

Anya laughed in a tight-throated way, like laughing wasn't something she did very often. I smiled when I reached for the wines she offered, but she didn't let go. Instead, she placed her recommendations back on the shelf too, and she lifted her chin. "You—wouldn't want to grab a drink somewhere, would you?"

That's when I decided to notice her escort, who pushed a cart a few feet behind her.

"Yes, we'll have a bit of a—babysitter." Anya leaned toward me with an annoyed frown. "Not him, another one, but he'll be inconspicuous."

"Hell, he can sit in my lap if he wants. Anything would be better than spending another Friday night alone in a practical stranger's apartment. There's a little wine bar up past my street—34th. It's a bit of a hike, but if you don't mind."

"I have a car, so if you point the way—"

"Absolutely."

Anya spoke into her cart-pushing shadow's ear. There was something beautiful about the quiet cadence of her foreign words despite her harsh glare at the bulky man. He made no reply.

"Not a big talker, is he?" I mused.

"Oh, not unless I give him permission to speak." Anya's face offered a stony, wide-eyed stare, but then it collapsed into a grin. "I'm kidding, of course." She giggled unlike I'd have expected and linked her arm with mine, practically dragging me to the store's exit.

I don't know what became of the inside-the-store goon or Anya's cart of groceries, but she barked at ruffian number two, who stood at attention outside automatic doors as we hit the sidewalk. He closed in at our heels, and we practically skipped to an illegally parked black sedan idling in the store's delivery alleyway.

"Where to?" A giddiness belied everything else about her, but it vanished in an instant, like she didn't want to give away how excited the prospect of a new friend made her feel.

"Uh, it's on 30th Ave, at 37th Street, I think."

Though her stare unnerved me, I returned the thoughtful scrutiny in case she perceived any dishonesty. She embodied the notion of an artist being an observer above all else, but her watchful eye felt more like calculating science than art. But then, a cool kindness swept away the almost callous dissection. Before long, we sat reading menus in a charming neighborhood wine bar without either of Anya's men-in-black. Her driver took his perch at the main entrance, as he had at the market. Without looking up, I spoke, "So, I gotta ask. What's with—"

"Hans and Franz?" Anya interjected.

I peered over the paper carte du jour, "Oh, my God, *please* tell me those are really their names."

"Sadly, no," she snickered. "But would you believe they are *both* named Sergei?"

"That might be even better," I whispered. "I feel like such a rube, but are you—famous? Important, somehow?"

She ignored my question, waving it away with her long, fair fingers. "I am sorry about them. My uncle insists on the escort, and he's probably not going to be too pleased about this little side trip. But I've been cooped up, not that I am ever the girl-about-town, but my brother died not too long ago, and I've been meaning to get out to celebrate."

I choked on my sip of water. "Celebrate?"

"Life, I mean. It's short, and we should enjoy it, right? Why squander what precious little time we have?"

I let her dodge what sounded like a clumsy save in the low din of the wine bar. My on-the-job brain went to work. Awkwardness shrouded Anya, and I couldn't quite pinpoint the cause. She was obviously smart and artsy, but social ineptitude bubbled around her despite her intellect and physical beauty, like she didn't get out much, and I guessed that was likely the case.

"I'm sorry about—your brother." This wasn't entirely true. I had no regrets about Vlad the Bad being dead. He was a horrible waste of space, but I wished I hadn't been the one to sever his brainstem. I definitely regretted that part. "We don't need to talk about it if you don't want to."

"Thank you. Truth is, my brother had some serious demons, so—but you're right, I don't want to dwell on it. How about a charcuterie board?"

And it appeared to be the beginning of a beautiful friendship.

Thirty-Three

To be honest, I hadn't thought much beyond this point in my plan. To connive my way into Anya's universe seemed like a tall order. Conspiring any further would only buoy my hopes of finding some damning evidence to bring down the criminal empire responsible for my dad's murder. My scheming would help others, too. Success would also free Uncle Marty from his cold-case burden and Trey from the yoke of a reward he believed kept me safe. But when I factored in my concerns about the fallout that would impact my new "friend" Anya, I couldn't move fast—or slow enough to be sure I got the whole deal done without any unforgivable missteps. My early victory encouraged me to press on, but I also had to prepare myself for the moment I'd inevitably hit a snag. I'd proven a knack for clandestine work, in my own mind anyway, but my Wallendas routine didn't include a clear outline, or an exit strategy, or a net.

Anya and I planned our next meeting. A legit one, scheduled with her knowledge. No longer having to "bump into" her relieved a big headache. Still, my approach remained cautious and coincided with what I knew her typical calendar entailed, thanks to her social media broadcasts. Something her overprotective uncle must not have followed. Our next gal pal get-together would be lunch on Tuesday, at our favorite neighborhood Greek café.

To date, Anya knew I had recently moved from Philadelphia to 34th Street in Queens. I'd been camped out on the sofa of a friend of a friend while I figured out what came next after a lousy break-up (with an older guy) that made staying in Pennsylvania a no-go. I definitely didn't want to talk about it.

The story contained a fair bit of truth. I went to undergrad and grad school in Philly, so I knew the area well if I got quizzed. There was an older guy I definitely didn't want to talk about, and a friend (Ste*phan*) of a friend (Leo) lived on 34th Street, and the "fact" I didn't have a place of my own explained why I could never invite Anya over for "girls' night in." Frankly, it surprised me how uninquisitive my new friend had been. I shared very little, and she asked for even less, so I kept it simple for the time being.

Anya rolled Kalamata olives around her plate of Greek salad she'd barely touched. "If you're looking for an evening escape, I'm teaching a sketch class at the Astoria Art Alliance Thursday night. Seven o'clock. It's a two-hour session, and the class includes a wide-range of talent, so you'd be—"

"I'd be what? Not completely embarrassed by my deficiencies?"

"No. I didn't mean—"

"I'm just kidding, Anya. I'm the first to admit I'm no artist."

"But you are, Harriet. And besides, we're focusing on faces night after next, and your Aristotle at the park that day showed promise."

I appreciated her compliment and, even more, the opportunity to turn down her invitation. I didn't want to appear too eager to become her constant companion.

"Well, thank you, but I'm really not in the position to be paying for art classes. I need to be saving up to get my own place, and the sooner, the better." I gave an uncomfortable eye roll.

"You don't have to pay. It's *my* class. No one at the school would ever question me about your being there. Not if I make it clear that you're my guest. Come. It'll be fun. You might even learn something."

Anya had a point. I might learn something, and opportunities to enter other spheres of Anya's influence probably wouldn't happen every day. And the more often I appeared, the more relaxed others in those circles would become. That's when things might get said or done. A lead to a discovery that might mean the death knell of the Trubetzkoy kingdom.

"Okay. I'll take you up on your generous offer. But, I owe you. If only for giving me a couple hours to have some place to be."

"Don't be silly. What goes around, comes around." Her smile conveyed satisfaction in my acceptance of her invitation, but something in her words struck me with a bolt of cold. I heard the lilt of her Uncle Gleb using the same phrase, and my spanakopita tried to make its way back up my gullet. I swallowed hard and forced a smile.

If I've said it once... investigation, at times, includes a long con, and my Trubetzkoy endeavor certainly fell into the drawn-out category. With my foot in the door, the next step meant taking advantage of the opportunity to listen to everything said while I hoped that those talking ignored me. But while I couldn't force those opportunities, I needed to focus on other things, and by *things*, I did not mean tall, dark, and long-eye-lashed things.

My daily workouts got easier, which dared Nate to make them harder. And dammit, if he didn't rise to the challenge. I also had to study—actual book-learning. As a research junkie, hunkering down to read didn't amount to much hardship, but major tests waited on the horizon if I took that leap. And with each passing day, my head, heart, and gut told me I *would* pursue Quantico again.

The initial hurdle had more to do with what I brought to the FBI's table: my aptitude for the work duties that FBI special agents performed. Having enrolled in the process five years ago put me ahead of the game. After my recent inquiry, I received an invitation to move forward, which meant the clock had started. I had twenty-one days to schedule my Phase 1 assessment test, leveling up in the Quantico application process.

Life had gone from humdrum to hectic in a matter of a month, and I didn't even have the time to stop and think about what it could all mean for the future. Would I have to choose between the academy and my father? Again? Different circumstance, but the same result. Giving up on either didn't sit well with me. And while I had no control over the FBI's schedule, I sure as hell could ramrod my way into the Trubetzkoy den of thieves.

While I enjoyed my time in the Thursday art class and earnestly sketched the various model faces, lit at odd angles to accentuate shadows and manipulate perspective, I intended to do a little exploring and make myself seen by those who interacted with Anya. Late in the session, I excused myself to no one in particular, under the guise of searching for a restroom.

I nodded to the man standing guard outside the classroom. The men-in-black were commonplace to me now, but I still checked-up at their size and hostile demeanor. Quietly closing the door, it surprised me that, in addition to this "Sergei," another stood at the end of the hall. A chanced look behind me revealed yet another man-in-black held a post at the opposite end of the corridor. Why so much security for one little artist? I supposed Uncle Gleb might be on high alert in the wake of his nephew's death. Then again, hadn't he known (and appreciated) the supposed perpetrator of the notorious idiot's demise? No, something more necessitated this protection detail. Some after-hours activity took place somewhere in the vicinity, and maybe, just *maybe*, poor Anya and her sketch class provided cover for the increased traffic in and out of the old building.

The gallery where the art auction took place weeks ago made up the entire first floor of the Astoria Art Alliance. Four stories above housed classrooms, offices, and who knew what else. Formerly a neighborhood elementary school, upstairs neither needed nor saw much renovation. Wide halls of vintage asbestos tiles alternated squares of speckled minty green and gray, separating tall, solid-wood doors with leaded-glass transoms. The architectural details provided a sensorial time portal with the colors and echoes of bygone days. The whiffed combination of paste, musty books, and rectangular pizza made with government cheese still clung to the plastered walls and sped me to another era.

I crossed the hall to the arcanely labeled *girls' lavatory*. Inside, a large window hung over a long radiator in the three-stall, three-sink restroom that switched to a pastel pink and gray color scheme. The window glass allowed light to pass through, but a frosted texture obscured the view, and the once-operational sash had long since been sealed shut, making it impossible to note any abnormal street-traffic for a Thursday night.

Muted talk outside the bathroom drew my attention. I toyed with the idea of opening the working transom but thought it might make noise, even if the movement got missed. But with my ear pressed to the door, I realized nothing intelligible would come from my eavesdropping, likely because the muffled words were Russian. I rolled my eyes at the impediment. *Foiled again, Harry.*

The figurative gut-punch hit when I inched open the heavy door. I swore I recognized a voice. The first time I heard Trey speak Russian, it, too, was through a bathroom door. The second time, we sat face to face, toasting "to things unsaid." Neither of those instances included much to go on, but it seemed, day or night, no matter the language, when Alvah Popov the Third spoke, I knew it. Why was he at some apparent ground zero of activity when he ought to be sunning it up with the boss's missus and her damn Bichon fur-babies?

Thirty-Four

I REWASHED MY HANDS at one of the kiddy-sized porcelain sinks, hoping to steady myself, then held a damp paper towel to my throat while I formulated a plan. If I encountered Trey, I would act like a stranger unless he behaved otherwise. This was his world, and I would follow his lead. I steeled myself for whatever came next. Of course, if Gleb appeared, all bets were off.

When I exited the restroom, people trickled out of the sketch session, and Anya stood at the classroom door bidding goodbye to her students. My eyes wanted to believe I caught a glimpse of Trey exiting through the wide double doors at the far end of the hall, but my gut couldn't be sure.

"You okay, Harriet? You look pale." Anya had seen me exit the bathroom and smiled through words one might assume were of concern.

"Not feeling so great, actually. I think I'm gonna head home."

"Oh, let me get you a ride. I can't go. I have another meeting to attend, but—" Anya beckoned the closest man-in-black.

"No. That's not necessary. Some fresh air is probably all I need."

"Fresh air? In Queens? In July?" She looked at me askance. "I'm getting you a ride."

An actual Sergei stood at attention, waiting for instructions Anya kindly gave in English.

"Take a car and see Harriet home. And no dropping her at the corner. Walk her inside, see her to her apartment. I want a full account of the carpet and drapes. You understand? See her *safely* home."

A new panic washed over me and my usual litany of expletives rattled off in my head. Not only because of Anya's bizarre mention of my carpet and drapes, which I hoped didn't constitute a metaphor *this* time. Her insistence that Sergei accompany me safely inside the building and to my apartment meant I had a problem. I didn't have access to the dark brick walk-up that supposedly housed my friend-of-friend's one-bedroom one-bath. How the hell could I let a member of the goon squad take me there when I couldn't enter it, much less acquaint him with my home décor? And if Anya hadn't said "see her *safely* home," what might have been the alternative?

"Would you believe no carpet or drapes? Men? *Amirite*?" I pressed my hand to my abdomen, and Sergei cleared his throat.

"Speak, Sergei." Anya's earlier quip about "the help" speaking only when given permission might have been more fact than fiction.

"Мне нужно будет—"

"*English*, Sergei. Don't be rude." Anya's snap eerily mimicked her uncle.

"Sorry, ma'am. I'll need to inform Command. New security measures since—"

"Yes. Well, then *call* him," Anya interrupted her minion again, then offered me an apologetic look. "What's the address, Harriet?"

I stuttered out the location and then excused myself to the restroom again. Truth be told, if I had had the time to empty my stomach, I probably would have, but I could only delay so long, and I needed a plan. Phone at the ready, I slammed into a small toilet stall and dialed Leo, hoping I could get him to get *Stephan* to meet me at "our" apartment building and play along with my ruse. Leo didn't answer. I texted him to call me ASAP and seriously considered a call to Marty or Lina Fuego. But how could I possibly admit my unsanctioned undercover work to Detective O'Shea or risk even a trace of police presence around me when everything else had been going so well? Until now, anyway. That snag I mentioned earlier? I really wished I hadn't.

After a toilet flush and another round of hand-washing, I poked my head out to the hall. Anya and Sergei were the only people there. I did my best impression of meek while I took another stab at slowing our departure. "Don't suppose you have any bottled water, by chance?" I half covered my mouth, implying it could use a rinse.

"Yes, in the classroom mini-fridge." Anya raised her chin to Sergei, and he hurried to retrieve the refreshment. His swift obedience impressed me.

"I don't mean to hold you up, Anya. If you need to go—"

She had returned attention to her phone. "Don't be silly. They can't start without me, so I'm not missing anything." She spoke with something like sweetness in what seemed an attempt to ease my worry. But her apparent lack of respect for anyone else's time left her privilege showing, and I couldn't help but wonder what life was like for the closest thing to a mafia princess I could imagine. Then I remembered the beauty of *A Girl, Stuck,* and the solitude and sadness that permeated it.

Sergei reappeared with a bottle of water and his phone to his ear. The last time a person looking like him proffered me a beverage, I was silently warned not to drink it. I cracked the seal on the unopened bottle and hoped for the best. With three quick slugs, some relief flowed through me. The respite was short-lived.

"Thank you, Sergei." I grimaced with another swallow and caught his stumped expression. Had he never heard the words thank you? "And thank you, Anya, for lending me your man here. I appreciate it."

"Well, I have others, so..."

Being 'sick' freed me from having to fake a laugh at her glibness that lacked any real humor. "Hope you don't mind a slow stroll to the car." I rested my palm to my middle again.

Sergei *ahem*-ed, again.

"Yes, Sergei," Anya sighed.

"Command asks that we hold at our location until he can—"

"*Ugh.*" I expelled a groan as my insides cramped for real. "Anya, I really need to get going." The last thing I wanted was a confrontation with the Head Goon in Command, much less Gleb Trubetzkoy himself.

Anya stopped texting and looked from Sergei to me and back before she spoke. "I've asked you to take my ailing friend home, Sergei, and you'd do well to remember where your allegiance lies."

"Yes, ma'am."

"Call me when you're better, Harriet. I hope it passes quickly." Anya smiled, then resumed typing on her phone when she spoke to the chastened and apparently surplus member of her security team again. "Я хочу, чтобы ты отвез девушку домой, Сергей. Сейчас." Clearly, it was only rude when others didn't speak English. She walked in one direction while my loaned driver gestured for me to go the opposite way.

Despite my eagerness to exit the building, I took slow steps in hopes Leo would reach out and save me from myself. *Think, Harry.* I'd be damned if my cover got blown by some hapless lackey. Despite our snail-like pace, by the time we reached the car, I still had no word from Leo, and my guts truly churned.

Sergei opened the rear passenger door. His uniform shirt sleeve inched up, showing a tattoo—the bottom-half of what I guessed was an octagram. This Sergei wasn't the first of the Trubetzkoy crew I'd seen sporting this inked starburst design. Trey didn't have one—at least not the last time I saw him shirtless.

"You know, I really don't mind walking if you'd like to take a little 'me' time. I'll never tell."

A flicker of a grin might have shone for an instant, but evidently Sergei knew who buttered his beets, and he had no intention of crossing Anya. His loyalty was clear. Resigned, I ducked into the backseat of the black sedan. Just my bad luck. Traffic moved remarkably fast, and before long, we pulled up to my pretend home. It was after ten o'clock, with no parking to be found.

"You can just drop me. Cops will ticket you in a heartbeat around here. Tow you even. A neighbor will call in an illegally parked car faster than you can—"

Sergei ignored me and exited the vehicle, letting the engine run. He opened my door, and I slid to the sidewalk, afraid I might upchuck for real. With my new tail close at my heels, I forced my feet to move down the brick-edged footpath. My steps slowed as I dug into my knapsack for keys I'd never find, keys I never possessed. At the base of the short stoop, I stopped and looked back at the idling car. "Huh. I can't seem to find my—"

"I'm here. I'm here." A woman's voice came out of nowhere. A shadow stretched across the neighboring walkway as the owner of a shrill Queens accent appeared in the harsh streetlamp glare, arms full of two overloaded paper grocery bags. "Sorry, I didn't return your text, dear, and sorry to hear you don't feel too good. But have I had a day from H E double hockey sticks, if you know what I mean. First, the computers go down at the office, and well— I can tell you all about that over the tea I'll make ya. I gotcha some *sawltines* too. Well, don't just stand there. Take one of these bags, at least."

I did as the nagging stranger directed, then watched her pull keys from her pocket to unlock the main entrance to "our" building. The mix of relief and confusion on top of my nausea made me a convincing scene partner, despite not knowing what to say.

"So, who's your friend?" She pointed with her head as we gained access to the communal foyer.

"Oh, he's not a friend. He's my ride. His name is Sergei. But I don't really know him." Or you, I thought. My voice wavered, echoing in the small but high-ceilinged lobby.

"Oh, well, hello, Sergei." She barely looked at the man or me while adjusting her heavy load and fiddling with her keyring. "I'm Edna, and my friends call me Eddy, but if you ain't a friend of hers, you ain't a friend of mine, which means you don't step another foot deeper into the building than where you stand right now. I'll be taking over the nursemaid duties, and that won't include making the poor girl climb all the way upstairs when she can sip tea and nibble some crackers while keeping an old lady company right here on the ground floor." My apparent savior shuffled to the first door on the right and inserted a key, but where I stood, I thought it was the same one she used on the front door, and it had an odd shape. She made a well-practiced effort to disguise her actions using the grocery bag and her chit-chat as a distraction.

The apartment door opened a few inches when she turned toward Sergei and me with wide eyes and a raised brow. "Come on, *dawll*. We'll get you feelin' right as rain in no time. And no offense to you, ya big lug, but we girls can't be too careful these days. Shoo now." Her fingers flicked as you'd imagine.

I stepped nearer Edna's apartment before speaking to the stalwart man staring us down from his spot just inside the front door. "Uh, yes, thank you, Sergei. I'm gonna hang with Eddy for a bit. I promise an A-plus report back to Anya on your behalf." I gave a reassuring nod and breathed some relief when the man's broad shoulders dropped, resigned to leaving despite not following Anya's instructions to the letter. He dipped his chin and exited at the same time my fairy godmother pulled me by my free arm into her home. I nearly tripped over my own feet with all my attention on Sergei, making sure the auto-lock security door closed decisively behind him, so I knew he couldn't reenter if he had a sudden change of heart.

Half a breath caught in my throat, and my blood ran cold when Edna's door came to a swift but quiet close, and I rotated to find I stood a few feet from the completely empty living room of an obviously uninhabited apartment. In my mind's eye, I flashed to the "for rent" sign I noted the first time I scouted out the place for a point of reference. Someone had haphazardly tossed that sign onto the breakfast bar, dimly lit by pendant lights. Fresh paint smell wafted, and plastic sheeting covered much of the hardwood floor. The raspy *crinkle* sound reverberated around the vacant space as Edna walked across it. I'd seen this creepy scene in a movie, and it did *not* end well. Gripping the grocery sack with both hands, I watched the old woman deposit her bag on the kitchen counter and hurry to peek out the front window draped in sheer, floor-to-ceiling panels.

A phone appeared. "He's pulling away now. She's here. She's fine." The woman delivered the succinct message without even a hint of the strident Queen's inflection, and the elderly woman gained some height and sudden youthfulness when she straightened her posture and drew back her shoulders as she walked toward me. "Give me that." She reached for the bag I clung to like it would protect me from whatever weapon the seventy-year-old turned fifty-something might brandish.

Something about the upright middle-aged woman carrying a heavy load rang familiar, but I lost that train of thought when she spoke again. "There's a bathroom around the corner there. You look like you could use it," she scoffed as she relieved me of the market tote, never meeting my eye.

I had yet to say a word and planned to keep mum until I could assess the situation. The bathroom seemed as good a place as any to do that. My bag with my phone came with me—no new messages. "Think, Harry," I spoke to my reflection, then opened the mirrored medicine cabinet and the sink cupboard. Empty. While the toilet flushed, I paced a quick back-and-forth in the small powder room, reminding the mirror image I knew how to handle myself, and Edna didn't look like much of a threat—as long as she didn't carry a gun. Not quite cold water wetted my parched throat as I cupped it from the small spigot into shaky hands and gulped. With nothing to dry them, I wiped my palms down my thighs before grabbing my backpack to leave.

As it usually does, it happened very fast. I rounded the corner, and the tall figure loomed. I dropped my bag, tucked my chin, and barreled into the man's body. My right foot planted between his size twelves, I pressed my knee to the inside of his, skewing his balance. One raised, bent arm protected my head while my other elbow swung around, stunning him with a hard hit to his temple. A knuckled jab to his throat, exposed by the head blow, *should* have followed, before the heel of my hand slammed his nose, crushing it through his nasal cavity. But I didn't get beyond the strike to the side of his skull.

"*Hattie!*" My name yelped out of him, and I immediately dropped my fighting stance. *Too* soon, it turned out. His arm wind-milled around, and he grabbed my wrist, twisting my limb behind me, wrenching it, so the back of my hand pressed between my shoulder blades. A rough shove had me chest-first against the newly painted wall. Another sharp jerk of my captured arm drove me harder into the plaster, and I swallowed the bulk of a cry.

"Don't *ever* let down your guard. I don't care who your opponent is. You don't stop fighting until he's unconscious. Do you understand me?"

I nodded with an audible exhale, my head constrained to the wall.

"Say yes," he hissed over my shoulder with another punishing tweak of my pinned wrist.

"Jesus, Trey. *Yes.*" The pain and the fumes made me dizzy, and I sucked air through clenched teeth to mitigate vertigo.

He loosened his grip but still held firm. "Now, I know you're pissed, and your adrenaline has spiked, so I want you to count to five before you go off and do something we'll probably both regret." He slowly eased his grasp of my arm.

"First of all, and I know you might be a little fuzzy on the *law*, but counting to five only makes what happens next premeditated. And second, if *this* is an extracurricular you'd like to pursue, I'm here for it, one hundred percent, but we *definitely* need to establish a safe word."

Trey released me, but not before his muted laugh blew in my ear. I pushed off the wall and spun, landing a stout two-handed shove to his chest. He skidded on the plastic drop cloth before he steadied his balance. I wiped away angry tears that I refused to let fall. Apparently, the chemical rush made my eyes leak, and *that*— pissed me off.

"Hey." He reached for me, but I slapped his hand away with a vicious swipe. Repeating the gesture, he whispered my name and caught my wrist when I took another feeble swing. He gently squeezed and pulled, and I staggered into his chest while his arms held me tight. Safe.

Thirty-Five

I COULD HAVE STOOD there for a long time, my relief palpable. Despite the heat of the un-air-conditioned apartment and the biting aroma of VOCs lingering in the recently painted room, Trey's powerful arms and citrusy scent surrounded me, and, given the chance, I'd have taken up residence in that spot. But when I remembered who he was, the plummet to Earth came fast, and I pulled from the embrace enough to see his handsome face. I'll admit, my moral compass wobbled a bit.

"Where's Edna?" I looked over my shoulder.

"Who?" He squinted.

"The woman with the groceries and adaptable accent?"

"Oh, Eddy, was it?" He nodded with insight he had no plans to share, clearly disinterested in that line of questioning. A relaxed grin flickered.

"Don't look at me like that." My demand included a scowl.

Trey's eyes widened, and he strengthened his hold, like holding me was something he should do—as if it wasn't against the rules. "Like what?"

"Like *that*. Kinda—gooey."

"Gooey?" His smile broadened, and I entertained the notion the man keeping me near might be some Alvah doppelgänger.

"Yeah, gooey, like you're gooey for me."

The corners of his mouth curved down as he looked to the ceiling like he considered the descriptor.

"Wait. What the hell are you doing here?"

He wrenched his neck. "What am I doing here?"

"Okay, Trey. This is gonna take a while if you just keep repeating everything I say. Now, what are you doing here?"

"Looks like I was saving your ass. You're welcome."

"Excuse me?"

"Oh, sorry. Your *fantastic* ass."

His continued admiration for my rearview and his bawdier way of expressing it pleased me, but I gathered myself quickly and broke the embrace I longed to make my own private and permanent zip code. As my hands skimmed his sides, he felt slimmer than I recalled. He gripped me tighter, fighting our split but then let it happen when he must have remembered the "rules" and that he had his own questions.

"What the heck are you doing, Hattie? Why were you at the art school tonight? Why are you suddenly palling around with Anya Trubetzkoy?"

"Hey, why is her name Trubetzkoy? She's Gleb's niece, from his *sister*. Did Anya's mother marry *another* Trubetzkoy?"

"When Anya and Vlad's father died—suspiciously, I should add—Anya took her mother's maiden name."

"Huh." I pondered the artist's reasoning. "To avoid any notoriety after her dad's death, I guess."

"Well, if *I* had to guess, I'd say just the opposite of that. But don't change the subject. What's going on, Hattie?"

"I'm not changing the subject." I put more distance between us. "You asked about Anya. I asked about Anya. No change in the subject. Anya this, Anya that." An uptick in the heat hit me.

"Hattie?"

"What? I can't make a new friend? Jeez, Trey. Taking your territorial proclivities a bit far, don't you think? Don't be jealous. We braid each other's hair; do Cosmo quizzes together. Nothing you'd be into—I don't think. Of course, I shouldn't assume. You know what they say. Assuming makes an—"

"*Hattie?*" The echoing bark signaled the end of playtime.

"Don't suppose me telling you to *mind your business* would work, would it?"

"Anya *is* my business."

I didn't like the way he sneered.

"What's that mean?"

"It means Anya has a security detail, and I am part of the security detail."

"I thought you were on *Mrs.* Trubetzkoy's detail."

"I was, but things changed."

"So, now you're what?" I stared at him.

He stretched his neck with a short cough, all while avoiding my eye. "Now— I'm in charge of security."

My eyes flew wide. "In charge? *Command*, I think it's called? Wow. That's quite the meteoric rise, Alvah. To what do you owe such stunning success? I mean, that's some spectacular rung climbing there, *fella*."

"I'm very good at what I do, Hattie." A glimmer of condescension and pride showed on a face that grew difficult to recognize.

"And what exactly *do* you do again?" My fake sickness roared back for real when Trey turned from me. No one spoke, and the scraping sound of the clear tarp under our feet bounced around the otherwise silent room. I was losing him. Despite my efforts to secure the opposite, Trey fell further down the hell hole, but I had no plans to give up yet. "I'm sorry." I stretched to take his hand, the rule breaker that I am.

He didn't allow it, and the rejection crushed me more than it should have. His hands found his hips while his gaze kept to the floor.

I apologized again. It wasn't exactly a hostage negotiation, but it was a mediation of sorts and I employed my know-how. "I know you're only doing what you need to do to keep your head above water. I get that. And having some power might mean you can make some positive change in some way."

"Oh, come on. I know you don't believe that, Hattie. Don't use the playbook on me." Hostility snarled out of him. I didn't understand his harsh reaction or the swings in his demeanor, like Jekyll and Hyde battled in front of me, but I refused to let him see any fear.

"I know you aren't so naïve, so blissfully unaware to think that's possible. But I don't get who you're trying to fool. Yourself? Because if it's me, save yourself the bother."

I forced myself to close the distance he'd put between us, wondering how Trey had earned his new power position. What had he done to deserve it? "What happened? What's changed? I haven't seen you in two weeks, and now you seem—sound—even look different—hardened."

He wrenched away, twisting with a startling raised arm. "Shit, Hattie. You just accused me of being *gooey*. Make up your goddamn mind, woman." The outburst and abrupt movement made me flinch. His volume and unfamiliar vocabulary frightened me, and the shock must have shown on my face. Trey rushed to apologize, to calm the cruelty of the out-of-character eruption, and he did it while moving toward me.

Shrinking from him was a reflex, involuntary, and I'm not sure which of us was more stunned by my reaction.

"Hattie, I—"

"No. It's okay." My voice pitched higher than I wanted it to, but my professional brain reminded me to deescalate the situation. "You know me. I push, and I push. My mouth gets me in—"

"Я люблю твой рот." He winced at the words I didn't understand. His palms pressed his temples like he throbbed in pain, spiraling further.

"Come home with me. Come home with me and breathe." I threw the only lifeline I had to offer. "Take a timeout, and find *your* voice, and listen to it. Remember who you are. Come home with me for one night, and you can tell me more about your mom, and I'll talk about my dad, and you'll tell me a dirty joke before we fall asleep. One thousand square feet and no touching, but in the morning I'll make pancakes, even though it's not Sunday, and—"

"I can't," he murmured, rubbing his face. "I can't go home with you. I can't be *here* with you. It's not safe."

"Safe for who?"

"Either of us. I gotta go." He pulled out his phone. "I'm ordering you a ride. When you get there, I'd appreciate it if you'd text me on *our* phone to let me know you're home safe. That's—not a demand, but I'd feel better, so if you would do that—"

"Of course. Yes. Done."

A small groan came out of him as he pinched the bridge of his nose. "One more thing. And this is *really* important, Hattie. I can't impress upon you just how much I need this next thing."

"Name it. Anything." I took hold of his biceps, still tattoo-free, protruding from the cuffs of his black uniform polo shirt.

Trey *had* lost weight, and that, coupled with the near groveling, scared me more than anything.

His gaze drifted over my head while he wrapped his arms around me, stalling like he couldn't find the words or he needed to double check to be sure he got them right. His high cheekbones were more noticeable in his thinner face. All of it troubled me. I did the unexpected thing and kept quiet but led by example in taking a deep breath.

He followed my tacit instruction before he spoke. "Never," he paused, "and I mean *never*, under any circumstances, lie for me. Don't lie about me. Don't lie to protect me. *Never* lie. Not even a little. No matter who asks the questions, you answer them honestly. I don't care if it hurts me. I don't care if you think you are betraying me. My deeds are my own. Is that clear? If the truth scares you, if it makes you feel sick, embarrasses you? I don't care. Take a breath, and tell it anyway. Do you understand what I'm saying? Trey. Alvah. Popov, the Third. Whether I'm part of the question or I'm the answer, you speak the truth. Always."

"What are you—?"

"Promise me. Swear on your father's honor that you will tell the truth."

"Trey, I—"

"*Promise* me, Hattie." His phone chirped, signaling the arrival of my Uber.

"I promise. I swear on my father's honor that I will only speak the truth when it comes to you."

"And stay away from the Trubetzkoys. All of them."

I shook my head. "That I can't promise. Just telling you the truth."

Trey's jaw clenched, and his phone chirped again.

"My turn. Quid pro quo."

His face softened, and he indicated I should get on with *my* request.

"Don't ever, and I mean *ever*, forget where to find me. Day. Night. I've got a thousand square feet, and it's yours whenever you need it. No reservation required. Lifetime offer." Our eyes bore into one another. "Promise me, Trey."

"I promise, Hattie."

Thirty-Six

As requested, I checked in with a text when I arrived home. Trey offered no reply, making it a fitful night for one riled redhead. "Tom" still guarded and taunted me through the night, but when my phone rang at eight-thirty in the morning, it woke me from a deep sleep.

"Harriet Smith?"

"Who's calling?"

"This is Special Agent Michael McQuade. I'm calling from the New York field office. Is now a good time?"

Oh, I was awake now. "Yes, yes, of course. How may I help you, Special Agent McQuade?"

"Mike's fine. Fine for now. I knew your dad. Harlan and I came out of the Police Academy together. I moved on to the Bureau after some time, but we kept in touch. I was at his funeral—"

"Yes, of course. Thank you." I chided myself for the unintentional abruptness. "What can I do for you, Mr. McQuade? Mike?"

"Right. It's really a matter of what I can do for you. Your application landed on my desk. I know it's not your first application, but I read the dates and get the picture."

"Yes, I withdrew after beginning the process. It's been five years. I can see how that might hurt my chances. But I'm—"

"No harm, no foul, Ms. Smith. Under the circumstances."

"Oh, that's good to hear."

"You were recruited pretty heavily."

"Yes, sir."

"After grad school."

"Yes, sir."

"By more than one agency."

I paused. "Yes, sir."

"Anyone ever accuse you of having the gift for gab, Ms. Smith?"

"You'd be surprised, sir."

"All right. Moving on. You will need to retake the Phase 1 test, but last time you sailed through it. Logic-based and figural reasoning, your personality assessment, preferences and interests, and situational judgment. All good. And records show you had already submitted your PFT self-evaluation, critical skills, and self-reported language sections. All will need to be resubmitted, of course. You were ready for your *meet and greet*."

I didn't have a reply for Special Agent McQuade. He hadn't asked a question.

"Are you ready, Ms. Smith?"

There it was.

"I am, sir. More so than last time, by a mile."

Special Agent McQuade let out a brief chuckle. "A mile's a lot, Ms. Smith."

"Yes, sir."

"Well then, interested in heading over to Federal Plaza for a day? I'd be happy to buy you lunch. Harlan told me once you *loved* lunch."

I only checked up a moment hearing Michael McQuade's personal anecdote with my dad. It certainly sounded like something my old man would share. "It's one of my top three favorite meals, sir. And name the day. I'm there."

"Great. Noon today, then. Check your email." Mr. McQuade didn't strike me as much of a kidder, but the quick timetable caught me by surprise.

"Today?"

"Is that a problem?"

"No, it's just it's a Friday in late July, so I figured by two p.m. the office would be a ghost town. Everyone hitting the Jitney out to The Hamptons. That'll make it nice and quiet, though. Perfect for buzzing through a three-hour exam. Of course, with the late hour, it'll mean dinner, not lunch."

"Dinner sounds great, Ms. Smith."

"Who knew the Bureau could be so flexible. You know that two p.m. Jitney thing was—"

"A joke? Yes. Good one, too. You are *definitely* Harlan Smith's kid. See you at noon? Federal Plaza?"

"You bet your a— yes, sir— noon, Federal Plaza." I was relieved that earned another chuckle.

"Looking forward to it, Ms. Smith."

"*Harry*, please."

"See you soon, Harry."

An hour later, I downed the last of my coffee and grabbed my leather messenger bag before hurrying out the door. I had plenty of time, but I'm a firm believer if you aren't early, you're late, plus I didn't want to dwell on the night before and someone else's erratic temper or his puzzling requests.

"Hey, you." Leo floated down the hall, a laundry basket to his hip with a grace that contradicted his stature.

"Well, look at you all upright and conscious," I teased. "Things settle out on the job?"

"Hardly. It's called *assimilation*, and whatever doesn't kill us makes us stronger." Leo sighed with a wistful smile.

"I'm not so sure that's how—" I stopped mid-sentence.

"What?" Leo squinted, cock-eyed.

"Assimilation?"

"The complete adoption of another's practices. Sometimes by choice, other times for occupational survival. I'm the latter."

"Right." Something itched the back of my brain, but for the moment, it needed to stay there. "I'm headed into Manhattan. Be there 'til nightfall."

"That explains the grown-up costume. When was the last time I saw you in heels and slacks and—? You look very—wait a minute. Are you—?"

"Don't jinx me, Auntie Leo," I interjected. "Let's just say—I'm going to see a man about some *tools*." That was the moment I realized how much I wanted this. How hungry I'd been for it despite all the years I hid in the van and the classroom.

I think Leo saw it too because his eyes lit up, and his kind smile grew broad as he clutched at pearls he didn't wear. He beamed pride, and it served as a lovely reminder that everyone should have an Auntie Leo in her corner. I telepathed my thanks for his well-wishes, then raced out the door before the lump in my throat grew into anything more troublesome.

Twenty-six Federal Plaza was not a pretty structure. It stood forty-one floors of bland, but for all that the staid rectangle lacked in architectural panache, it tried to make up for with its surrounding fountains, public squat spots, and landscape. Understandably a stress-inducing destination, it countered the angsty vibe with magnificent pink granite and amoeba-shaped gardens that edged smooth, round, marble seating and curvy chartreuse benches snaked atop swirls of purple paint. I took advantage of some shade from area Saucer Magnolias and sipped my water bottle with thirty minutes to spare before my scheduled meeting with Special Agent Michael McQuade.

I found little information regarding Mr. McQuade, but confirmed he graduated from the Police Academy the same year as my dad and headed to Quantico three years later. The short notice didn't allow for a deep dive, and further Googling halted when my phone rang.

"Marty. To what do I owe the pleasure?"

"Hey, kiddo. Got to checking up on you, and Nate said you were a no-show this morning."

"Yeah? Well, my arrangement with Nate is kinda fluid. If I show up, he makes me regret it. If I don't, well—"

"Okay. Just wanted you to know you crossed my mind. I figure whatever took precedence must be important, and you can tell me about it later. Maybe Sunday? Bess will make her dry rub you like so much. What do you say?"

"Not sure what all the benevolence is about, but I'll take it, Uncle Marty."

"No, I'm sure you don't. Sunday?"

"You bet."

"And give my regards to Special Agent McQuade." Marty ended the call before I could respond.

I shook my head. Law enforcement's old boys' network proved faster than any I knew, and I only hoped that despite the nomenclature, it didn't require a Y chromosome to join. Then I quickly reminded myself of the order of carts and horses.

"Ms. Smith?" A tall, trim man with salt and pepper hair, straight out of central casting, approached my shaded spot.

I stood. "What gave me away? Because I have seen at least a dozen of this exact outfit enter or exit the building in the last twenty minutes."

"Most people would take solace in fitting in, Ms. Smith."

"*Hm*. I tend to miss the silver linings, Special Agent McQuade. Thank you for the reminder."

"I'm about to lose that Special Agent title, so you can drop it now."

"Retirement, I hope?"

FBI bylaws mandate a special agent's departure at age fifty-seven. I guessed Mr. McQuade's day had come.

"Done my twenty, and then some, but I'm just trading one windbreaker for another. Now, let's talk about you." He ushered me toward the intimidating building, and hopefully, the start of my next career.

Thirty-Seven

"How about we grab that dinner, Harry?" Michael McQuade met me at the proctored computer lab door, where I'd ground out the Phase 1 aptitude test. It would be the easiest part of the application process, but it still took a toll. At four forty-five in the afternoon, it felt early for dinner. Then again, I could always eat, and I had skipped lunch.

"Thought it only took about an hour for the results of this round." I rocked my head back and forth, feeling the acute stress of the day.

"Oh, well, government work, you know, and it's a Friday—late in the day, so we're looking at Monday, earliest."

"Wait. What? Really? Wow. I didn't think—"

"Just yanking your chain, NAT. We've got time for a drink. And they'll email us. You're not concerned, are you?"

"Well, *NAT* is premature, don't you think? Not a *new academy trainee* yet. But I'll take that drink, if only to put up with your sad excuse for a sense of humor there, Mike."

The man's laugh rumbled hearty and real, and I heard whispers of my dad in it. "I'd been told you're a force to be reckoned with, Harry Smith. Then I thought maybe I'd heard wrong after the start of our phone chat. I see you just take a minute to warm up."

"Guess I'm not a morning person, but who's been talking about me?"

He held his grin. "Your dad. Back in the day. There's a bar across the plaza. Got a go-to drink?" Mr. McQuade stepped toward a bank of elevators.

"I prefer the cold, wet kind, but just wet will do in a pinch." I sped up to keep stride. "I can sip chardonnay with the best of them, slug some Scotch too if need be, but I'll reach for an ice-cold beer any day. Particularly on a hot summer Friday."

"A real cop's kid, huh? Well, it's on me."

"Lead on." I followed the stiff gentleman, fatigued by the day's brain drain and mildly distracted by the recent, constant reminders of Harlan Smith.

So, I passed. Not a big surprise. Seventy percent typically make it through round one, and I had done it five years ago. I thanked Mr. McQuade for the opportunity to jump in and get the process going because it *was* a long process. He assured me Bureau Recruitment had tagged me as a quality candidate, and as a quality candidate of the female persuasion, I drew some attention. When I assured him I had no interest in filling some quota just for quota's sake, he quickly informed me the qualifications were steadfast. I had to pass on my own merit, and it was a tall order.

At the same time, he planned to fast-track the meetings, interviews, and pending test requirements to get me through the deep background check so I could head to Virginia in the early spring and graduate that summer. While that part of the procedure involved my Personnel Security Interview (PSI), polygraph, drug test, fingerprinting, and medical examination, the real onus was on personnel like Mike. They had to dig through my garbage, sift through my internet search history, and interview my third-grade teacher and poor Pauly Moretti.

It neared dark when we said our goodbyes, and I grabbed an Uber home instead of the hour-long train. I'd earned it. Sleep would come hard and fast, and I craved the oblivion.

I'm not a big dreamer, in any sense of the word. If there is something I want— to do, to have, or some place to go, then I do it, get it, go there, or—I don't. But sitting around wondering what if seems like a big ol' waste of time to me. Vacant stares picturing another existence had never been my regular practice. That said, the recent Saturday morning kitchen incident still pinked my cheeks when I thought about it. The nighttime version rarely invaded my sleep either, at least not any scenarios I woke remembering. Again, if that's nature or nurture, I don't know. Maybe a part of me appreciated I was *living* the dream, considering my police precinct start that could have easily been a Central Park trash can. It was a sobering reflection that kept my feet on the ground, my head in the here and now.

Of course, never say never.

Miles Davis's Blue in Green *played from nowhere. Fairy lights glowed, suspended from invisible supports in an otherwise black void. I wore a simple dress I didn't own in real life, but it reminded me of a lacy shift I wore to a dance with Pauly Moretti when I was sixteen. My dad appeared, offering me a glass of champagne.*

"I hear congratulations are in order?" He puffed up with pride, looking fit and strong, as handsome as I'd ever seen him.

"For what?" The champagne flute morphed into a vodka shot when I took it, then to a bottle of beer when I brought it to my lips.

"That's good. Keep it close to the vest, Harry. No one needs to know your business. No one needs to know what you know, and when you know it, and certainly not how it makes you feel."

"The Smith Slogan," I mumbled.

"What's that?"

"Why share it when you can suppress it? Right, Dad?"

"Is that what I taught you?"

"Among other things, yes. Look, I haven't seen you in five years. I don't wanna fight."

"Who's fighting? Why don't you tell me why I'm here?"

"Gee, Dad. Maybe it's because I've got some serious change happening in my life. Because I'm thinking of taking an enormous leap, and I'm unsure."

"Unsure of what?"

"Unsure I can do this. Unsure I'm capable, and it all sure seems awful fast."

"Are you ready?" Special Agent McQuade appeared, repeating his question from our phone call, then faded away just as fast.

"What's the deal, Harry?" Leo popped in with a wink and vanished, too.

"Do you want it, Harry? I mean feel it in your bones, want it?" Dad spoke again.

"I do, but Jesus, it scares the crap out of me, but at the same time, I have never felt so certain about a thing, so sure of it, even when everything says I shouldn't. And I wish you were around to help me through. And see it happen."

"Well, as long as he makes you happy. That's all I want."

The music stopped—no more Miles Davis.

"What? He? Happy?" I didn't understand.

"You're right, Harry. Happy is a bit simplistic. You should feel satisfied, worthwhile, his equal, safe, but strong. Of course, these are

your words because—" My ethereal dad pointed behind me with his chin raised. "You should go—"

I twisted to look. Trey stood in the shimmering fairy lights dressed in Tom Ford. A quick glance back, Dad disappeared. The muted trumpets of La Vie en Rose floated out of the dark.

Trey walked toward me with arms outstretched. The clarinet sashayed in to join the muffled brass, and the beautiful man smiled the affable grin that, too often, he seemed to hide. The music skipped but started again. "Care to dance?" He wrapped me in a proper dance pose.

I leaned in, and we swayed, but when the music quit only to restart, I stiffened and pulled from his strong but gentle hold. "Wait. But you don't dance."

He held tighter in our intimate stance. I heard his smile as he breathed into my hair, pressed his mouth to my ear, and whispered, "Trey Popov doesn't dance."

I relaxed like his response satisfied me, but when the old French tune cut short for a third time, I went rigid, yanking from his embrace. Trey evaporated.

I bolted upright in my bed and *La Vie en Rose* played again.

Scrambling out of my tangled sheets, I tripped across my pitch-dark bedroom, the lit-up phone a beacon, charged on the faraway desk.

"Yes?" I squawked, flustered. Half asleep and entirely discombobulated by the unknown hour, the baffling dream, and the startling musical ringtone. I had no idea how many times the phone "rang" or how long it had been ringing.

Silence met me on the other end.

"Shit." I figured I missed the call, but when I pulled the phone from my ear, the digital seconds ticked on. The call had *not* ended. I hit the speaker icon. "Trey? Are you there?" More nothing.

"Trey? If you can't say anything, well, that sucks, but I'm here. I'm here, and I can just talk to you if that helps. But if you're hurt or in trouble, I don't—I don't know how to help, but I'll just keep on the line and rambling, cause that's what I do, right? —except now I'm freaking out because *now* I'm afraid you're hurt or in trouble, and— shit, shit, shit—Okay. Maybe you could cough or—Jesus, Trey, if this is some poorly timed butt dial, I'm gonna kick your ass the next time I see you, and don't think I can't because—"

"Hattie—"

"Oh, thank God. Are you okay? Where are you? Can you—"

"I—I'm here."

"I'm here, too. I'm here. What can I—"

"No. I mean, I'm *here*. At your door."

I'd raced down most of my bedroom stairs before the words "I'm on my way" spilled from my mouth.

Flying from my apartment, I pattered down the hall to the vestibule and quietly pushed open the heavy door. Trey stood partway down the cement stairs in the glow of the recently replaced porch light. He wore jeans and a hooded sweatshirt, an odd choice given the heat. Gripping the railing on both sides, his back was to me as he stared out into the night.

"If you're gonna make a habit of these middle of the night visits, we might consider a key and an access code for you." I was half-serious but got no reply. "Trey?"

Steps below me, Trey's slow turn revealed dark, wide eyes. The sweatshirt zipper undone allowed a full view of his gray t-shirted torso soaked and stained in a dark burgundy. More blood streaked his chest, splattered the skin of his neck, and smeared across one cheek.

"*Leo!*" I screamed for my neighbor over my shoulder as I lunged for Trey. "Leo, hurry!"

"Hattie. No. It's fine. It's not mine. None of it is mine." Trey bounded up the rest of the stairs and pushed me inside. The door slammed shut, and he cupped my face. "I'm not bleeding. Anywhere."

I pulled at the jacket, lifted his shirt to see if it was true. Grabbing his face, I moved his chin and ran my fingers through his hair, yanking his head down to look for any head or neck wounds. He gave into my harried inspection, assuring me he had no injuries.

Leo flew out of his apartment, wide awake and alert, ready to handle whatever calamity he met in our hallway.

"Leo, I'm fine. Sorry for the—" Trey tried to dispel our worries with a quiet calm I couldn't rationalize.

Wordless at first, Leo joined in the examination, focusing on the would-be patient's eyes and extremities. I moved to give the professional room to work.

"Follow my finger. Not with your head, just your eyes." The nursing tone soothed, gentle and caring, while Leo moved his index finger side to side, up and down, then patted Trey's cheek. "You need me?"

"I'm fine. Sorry to—"

Leo interrupted, speaking to me, "Do you need me?"

I gave a quick head jiggle and watched my friend return to his flat and close the door. The clunk of his bolt lock made me flinch, and Trey reached for me.

"Whose blood—" I tried to ask the obvious question.

Trey shook his head with a barely perceptible "no."

I didn't finish my question, but pulled him down the hall and into my apartment.

Thirty-Eight

"UPSTAIRS. CLOTHES OFF. SHOWER." I'd found terra firma, gained control of the situation, and set to work. Steadied, I hung his zip-up sweatshirt and focused on helping the bedraggled man up the steps to my bedroom and bath.

"Hattie, I—"

"You wanna talk now, or get clean? Your call, but I think you'd feel better if—"

"Yeah, a shower would be good." He stood in my bathroom with a dazed look, like he had more to say, but couldn't remember his next line.

I moved to my dresser to take out his sliced-through undershirt and the too-big scrub pants. "Here. Give me your shirt. It's got the worst of it. I can wash it—or burn it."

His huffed exhale included the briefest smile before he reached behind his head to pull at his shirt. He hesitated, a new show of inhibition.

"Oh, sorry. I'll give you some privacy—"

"No, it's not that." He yanked the t-shirt over his head.

You'd think my gaze would have lingered on his shapely chest or rippled midsection, the debated eight-pack that was noticeably slimmer, maybe his constant Star of David or the fresh scar, now suture-free, on his left side, but no. While he faced me, his back reflected in the large-framed mirror hung over the sink vanity.

Bruises hardly shaded his skin anymore, but a recent addition provided new color. Red scratch marks, evenly spaced, etched Trey's back. Lines crossed just below his left shoulder, and another batch streaked the midsection of the other side, curving under his scapula. No blood had been drawn, but the redness was fresh and significant, with little question as to their origin.

Trey swiveled to see the cause of my stunned expression. The thin stripes blazed in the bright lights flanking the mirror. His chin landed on his chest.

"It's not what it looks like, Hattie." He spoke no louder than a whisper.

I swallowed hard. "Oh, good. Because it looks like—" My mouth wouldn't form the words, but my eyes couldn't stop staring.

"Hattie—"

I shuddered to attention, back in control. "You should shower. You don't owe me an explanation." When I reached for the bloody t-shirt, he grabbed my forearm.

He repeated my name as I wrenched out of his grip and snatched the garment.

"No touching, remember? And thank goodness, or this would be awkward. You know where the towels live, yeah?" I spun on my bare heel and slid the door closed between us before heading to the kitchen for ammonia and cold water, the combination I knew would remedy the new mess. The bloody t-shirt mess, anyway.

Remaining calm, I focused on the laundry task, thankful to have something to keep my hands busy. *Calm* might not have been an accurate word choice. *Numb* was the better descriptor.

Either my guest hurried through his shower, or time sped quickly, but movement on the stairs soon alerted me to his approach, and I dried my hands, leaving the stained cotton to soak in the stainless sink basin.

"First, I don't want you to think I—hurt anyone," Trey jumped into what I imagine was a hastily rehearsed justification as he stood firm in his baggy "sleepover" ensemble.

I didn't respond to his opening statement, not verbally, anyway. Instead, I pulled two short glasses from a cabinet by his head, leaving the shaker door open as I yanked the vodka from the freezer. Generous pours followed.

I considered his claim that he hadn't hurt anyone. Still, I thought the devastating ache clawing through my chest told a *very* different story before I realized the implication of his remark. It may have been an incredibly clever ploy, but somehow I felt culpable despite knowing I'd done nothing wrong. Guilty for a thought I never had.

"Jesus, Trey. I *never* thought *that*. Did you think I would? Do you think I would willingly spend time with someone I imagined didn't understand no means no? God, I don't doubt whoever—branded you—did so willingly. Those are not the result of—a struggle. They're a product of—of something else." I slid a glass to him across the kitchen island and raised mine in a shaky hand. "To things unsaid—and let's leave it at that." I downed the icy liquor and spasmed with the alcohol's burn.

"I don't want to leave it at that." He hadn't made a move for the drink, and I considered consuming it for him, but the pain in my chest traveled lower, and throwing more vodka on the fiery hurt seemed unwise.

"Why? Why do you want to tell me? Why do you want me to hear how someone got what I can't have? What good does that do?" The hurt had crept its way into my voice.

"That's not what happened. That *didn't* happen, Hattie."

"Well, something happened. The marks are pretty distinct. And you're well within your rights to—"

"*Stop!*" He roared, slamming the cabinet door. The loud *thwack* echoed like a starter pistol, followed by a short rattling *clink* of glasses, then silence. "I'm sorry, Hattie. Sorry. I would *never*—"

"I know, Trey." I had no fear, just sadness.

"How do you know?"

"Because you promised you'd never hurt me, not on purpose, and because— I know you."

"No, you don't." He shook his head, unwilling to look at me.

"I do. I know enough."

"How? How do you—"

"Because, like you, I'm good at what I do. Something I got reminded of today. And it's about goddamn time."

I led him back upstairs and encouraged him to relax on "his" side of the bed. I could have done without seeing the ends of the scratches peeking out from one armhole of the man's tank-cut undershirt, but once he faced me, propped against the padded headboard, the offending marks were out of sight, out of mind. *You lie, Harry.*

I squeezed his hand, but per the rules, I let go. "I'm gonna sit over there for now." I pointed to my settee. "Talk whenever you're ready." I wished Trey had been more interested in keeping the booze flowing, if only to have some other activity to accompany the next grueling bit. But if he wouldn't drink, I wouldn't drink anymore. There was equity in that, somewhere. I crisscrossed my legs and pulled the little Sherpa blanket around me, feeling an unexpected chill I imagined would be short-lived.

"Before I go into this, the blood and the scratches are unrelated. It was two different—" Trey rested his head against the upholstery, and while I never took my eyes off him, he couldn't find his way to look at me.

"Trey, we don't have to—*you* don't have to— If it helps you, then yes, but I don't need you to explain."

"We get tested," he forged ahead. "Tested all the time. Different organizations have varying rules and systems for reward or punishment, but it's word of mouth and often inconsistent, coupled with in-fighting, deceit, and an unhealthy dose of competition. It's a nightmarish minefield, and like I said, each faction is different, so if you move from one to another, it's like starting all over again. You learn things along the way, though, and if you don't fuck it up—sorry—" He took a breath. "If you don't mess it up, you can rise quickly."

"And you're good at what you do. So, you rose quickly?"

"Yeah. I can read a room. Usually."

"So, someone tested you? Tonight?"

"But I failed."

"Failed who?" I wished I hadn't asked.

Trey's eyes found mine, and I steeled myself not to react, no matter his answer.

"Trubetzkoy." He stopped there.

"Temptation is an unfair test. There is something primal about *want*."

"What? No, I didn't—I couldn't."

"Oh. Well, I hear that happens, too."

That earned a sad chuckle. "How old do you think I am, Hattie? Oh, that's right, you prefer an older man. I almost forgot. Tried to, actually. No, it wasn't an equipment issue. That's just biology. I don't know if—*want*, as you say, is primal. Maybe if someone is—starving, but if he's not—starving, I mean—if a man's hungry, but would rather eat steak when he's offered chicken, he can wait for the steak. He'll wait. If the steak means enough to him, he'll wait."

I had a feeling the man in my bed painted his metaphor with a broad brush. My guess was most men would partake of any meat put in front of them. Then again, it wasn't that long ago another man, a certain famous writer, turned down the offer to—dine—in this very room. I opted to push ahead. "Even if it means flunking a test? The double standard aside, what are the consequences of failure?"

"Again, it varies. Sometimes it's the loss of privileges, sometimes the infliction of some painful punishment, some worse than others. You saw an example of that. Crueler yet is when they decide to exact your punishment on a co-worker. Great way to seed doubt and distrust in the ranks. Worst-case is dismissal, and that comes with a body bag."

By that point, I could only take in the information and do my best to digest it. Uncle Marty crossed my mind, but I pushed him away. He'd get a full report someday, but for now, I needed to focus on the drowning man in front of me.

"That's not true," Trey drew me back. "The worst-case is if they choose to punish you by going after someone you care about."

I may have blanched at that news.

"Which is why I didn't want you anywhere near this. Which is why I shouldn't have—"

I tried to loosen my constricted throat. "That's on me, Trey. I put myself in that spot. You warned me off, and I jumped feet first into those shark-infested waters. Not your fault."

"Still—"

"Back to the test. First, and I don't mean to doubt you, I don't doubt you—but are you certain the— other party wasn't conscripted?" I struggled to get a clearer understanding of the situation I wished I had no knowledge of at all. We tip-toed, avoiding the hard words, the terms that would make it all too real. I didn't want the gory details but seeing the big picture could prove crucial. It was a weird headspace.

"I am." He didn't hesitate with his reply.

"But how—uh, if she—or he was young or— are you sure—"

"Yes, and it was a woman. And if you're under the impression women can't be a party to coercion, think again. You're gonna have to take my word on that. And again, I would *never*—"

I raised a hand to stop his denial. I knew he told the truth. "So, again, with the double standard, but would it have been so bad?" As the question left my lips, somewhere in my mind, the ominous creak of a heavy door juddering open to a new existence echoed. No more black and white, but rather a whole spectrum of dismal gray appeared in front of me. Life outside a classroom or a windowless van insisted such absolutes go to the wayside. Lines would get crossed I never conceived of. Lines I wouldn't know existed until I looked down and found I already stood on the other side. At what point would a look back not even cross my mind?

And while I might have preferred an iceberg to romaine lettuce analogy, I stuck with the one Trey used. "I mean, if the steak said, 'go ahead, nibble some chicken' to save everyone some grief, could you get a do-over? Lie back and think of England, as they say— or think of steak?" And the deep end got deeper.

"Hattie." His shocked expression lit up across the room.

"I'm sorry. I am trying to be helpful here."

"Full disclosure, I did—try. How do you think I got the marks? But all I could—"

I stood. Rolled might be a more apt picture, but fortunately, my feet got under me in time to make it *look* like my brain controlled my body. I wasn't so sure. An agonized groan grumbled out of me as my head rocked with vehemence, and I squeezed my eyes tight to stop the image from forming in my mind's eye. I didn't want to hear any more about Trey's efforts to—comply. "Can we talk about the blood? I'd really love to hear about the blood. Now."

The story of when the cat's away, the mice will play summed up the second half of the night's failings. Except in the *Criminal Underbelly* version of the fable, Trey played the cat, the new Command in charge. Some of the mice tore into one another, incited by the aforementioned seeds of doubt and unhealthy competition. The new Command had been running a tight ship, but at the first opportunity, while Command faced a twisted loyalty test, some inmates ran roughshod over the asylum. The incident ended when a well-meaning comrade of Trey tried to ease the tension. Those mice mutinied against the interceder with brutal swiftness, and Command, fresh off one disaster, happened upon another. He arrived just in time to hold the young man while he bled out on the floor of some unmentioned location—a tragic mess.

"Two failures, one night. For what? What the hell am I doing there? And Mischa? Hell, the kid's name wasn't even Mischa, but he was so damn desperate to fit in that he wanted a name that sounded more—whatever. What a waste. He was my responsibility, and I—how did I—?"

I didn't know how to answer his questions, and they weren't for me, anyway. My role meant letting him bark out his frustration and hopefully glean some usable intel that might somehow end this chapter. As I mentioned, it was a weird headspace, but I knew I needed to find my way back to my *criminal*—or *Trey-whispering* ways.

"I'm sorry about your friend. I can tell you the incident isn't your fault, that it's an unfortunate but *predictable* consequence of the environment, but you already know that, more than I do, in fact. On a different note, it's nice to learn about some of your boundaries. Downright charming in a twisted-God-I wish-this-episode-of-Black-Mirror-was-over kind of way. And while your protein diet analogy has my head spinning a bit, I hope I'm not wrong in thinking I'm the steak. I am, right? The steak? That's me?"

"I didn't mean to offend you, Hattie. You know that, right? God, I *am* an asshole." His hands rubbed his face as he knocked his skull against the headboard.

"Funny, I'm just coming around to the idea that maybe you aren't. An asshole, I mean. Just wanted to double-check. Because I gotta say, when it comes to you, I'm feeling more like a pork chop or a slab of bacon, which of course means I'm not even on the menu, not your menu anyway, not an option. But if I were, I'd be some grade A prime, right? A filet mignon?"

Trey's head hung as it went side to side in his serious way, and I feared my attempt at Trey-whispering marked one more failure on the night. "While we're baring souls, I should probably tell you I'm a Delmonico guy myself, so if it's all the same to you—"

"Men and their meat," I sighed, relieved the rough sea had settled some. I realigned the blanket on the sofa, taking a moment to collect myself with Trey out of my field of view. "Can I get you anything? You can stay, can't you? To sleep? Will you sleep?"

"Always with so many questions." He said it like he enjoyed my inquisitive nature but couldn't quite find his way to a smile. "I don't need anything. But I do sleep best with you at my side. I did the math, forty-two square feet, and no touching, of course."

"What?" I squinted with a grin.

"A king bed. It's forty-two square feet." It wasn't the first time I had seen him bashful, but it made me lightheaded.

"I should see to your shirt."

"Forget the damn shirt. I'll wear the sweatshirt out of here. It'll be fine. Come to bed."

The words were right, but the reality? Not so much.

Thirty-Nine

THE NEXT MORNING DIDN'T include pancakes. There was coffee, too many lingering looks, and very little talking, but when Trey asked, "So, how are you? How are things? Anything new?" he met silence—omission over lies.

How could I tell him what the last twenty-four hours entailed? How could I talk to him about my life's trajectory taking a major turn, sending me into a whole new direction? Except, an itch in my brain told me the haggard, shirtless man leaning against my kitchen island could provide some insight and support if I'd find the nerve to confide in him. No, too risky. If that leap ever got made, Trey had to do the jumping. I didn't see any way around that.

While I didn't want him to go, I *did* want the leaving part to be over. It was inevitable. I trailed him as he walked to the hat rack at my apartment door to collect his sweatshirt. Faint lines barely streaked his back. *I* could see them, but maybe the vision had merely been etched into my retinas. The closer he got to the exit, the more my frustration bubbled with my need to make the scene go a different way.

"Trey?"

"Yes, Hattie." His sighed reply echoed my exasperation, coupled with his fatalistic acceptance that I had to make that one last-ditch effort to change our fate, no matter how futile.

"All things being equal—"

"That never happens," he interjected.

"I know. But for argument's sake—all things being equal, if it weren't for me, for the mess I made—if you didn't feel the need to stay where you are to—protect me, would you leave? Trubetzkoy, I mean. Would you leave that life?"

Trey lifted my chin to look me in the eye, but he didn't speak.

"Is that your answer?"

"I have made you exactly three promises, Hattie. Three. What were they?"

"You promised not to hurt me, not on purpose, you promised not to lie, you promised never to forget where to find me, ever."

"Seems to me you have me in a catch-22. If I say I'd leave, you'd be plagued with guilt for inadvertently keeping me—stuck. That would hurt you. If I say I'd stay regardless, you'd assume that means I'd choose this life over you, and I *think* that might hurt you too. Plus, I can't lie—because—I promised. But atop all that, as foolish and ill-advised as it is, know I will find you. I will always find you. Promise."

Perched in my doorframe, I watched him back down the hall to the building's exit. This departure played differently than the others. This time, he didn't hurry or turn away but instead kept his gaze locked on mine, and I knew if I didn't do something, if I didn't make a serious move, regardless of his intentions, his promises, I would never see the man again. What should my last words to him be?

Trey must have read the flicker of panic on my face. "Hey, Hattie? Knock, knock."

I smiled. "Who's there?"

"Just some."

"Just some who?"

"Just some asshole telling a lame, dirty knock, knock joke."

I grimaced with a mock-disappointed head shake, then grinned, appreciating his corny attempt to make me feel better. "Trey?"

He raised his chin in reply.

"Find me."

He nodded. "Promise."

Even after he left, out of my line of sight, I stayed in my spot. Arms crossed, I contemplated that next action, fighting the inertia that urged me to crawl back into bed, back to where his sleep smell lingered, and I could wallow in all I had left of him. Instead, I pulled my phone from my pocket and dialed. The call went straight to voicemail.

"Hey, it's me. Wanna get together sometime soon? Lunch? Dinner? Name it. Call or text, I'm footloose and fancy-free, so—okay, later. Bye, Anya."

A visit to the gym for a much-needed thrashing would be just the thing to clear my head or provide some distraction. Either would do, and Nate didn't disappoint.

"Are you limping?"

I moved slow enough that when Leo heard me enter the building, he made it *out* his door long before I reached mine.

"Not sure," I groaned. "Limping implies the favoring of one leg over the other because of a one-sided injury, right? I hurt *everywhere*. I think maybe I'm hobbling." I winced as my backpack slipped off my shoulders before I unlocked my door.

Leo snickered. "Is this Nate induced?"

"You know it." The chit-chat served as a warm-up for Leo to hear more about the recent late-night antics. "If you want to pester me with questions, Auntie Leo, follow me in because I *have* to get off my feet."

The slap of Leo's palms *smacked* behind me. "Yesssss. I'm grabbing wine. Be there in two shakes." He sang a made-up tune.

The afternoon was a long overdue catch up on life. Leo drank his wine, and I sipped a beer while we gorged ourselves on Indian takeout. We laughed a lot and mostly enjoyed a rollicking good time, but he took a moment to get serious with me.

"Not to make light, but I should apologize for being so adamant about the two of you."

"Who's that now?" I asked with a mouth full of tikka masala.

"Ha. For real, Harry. When two dates include clothes with significant blood splatter, you might want to rethink your relationship goals. And considering your recent incredibly exciting day in Manhattan, I can see how fraternizing with a suspected felon might be problematic."

"You think?" I took a bite of naan, knowing I couldn't share my growing suspicions regarding Trey's actual criminality.

Leo sighed. "Whatever is going on should probably stop."

I shrugged. "That's the thing, Leo. Nothing is going on. Nothing has gone on. Not like you'd think. It's not like that."

"Huh? You expect me to believe when he looks like him, and you look like you and he looks at you like—"

"Like I'm steak?"

"*Gurl,* and he's *hungry* for it—"

"What can I say, Leo? If I'm steak, Trey's gone vegan. And I've taken on a life of celibacy." I cleared dinner from the coffee table to avoid Leo's gobsmacked look.

"Wait. You mean, on purpose?"

I chose a change in topic. "How's about a little online shopping. I foresee blouses and slacks and comfortable but cute chunky heeled shoes."

The sharper edges of the evening rounded out and we found *our* normal—a normal I had missed and knew better than to take for granted.

Forty

I MADE QUICK WORK of getting my next round of documents submitted in the Quantico process, including my first physical fitness self-evaluation. Nate helped. As soon as I hit send, my next email went to Michael McQuade. I didn't know what sway he had on his end, or if sway existed at all in those circles, but the tall order of joining the following spring's recruitment class held all sorts of appeal, so I readied myself to move heaven and earth to make it happen.

Since Uncle Marty outed himself as being in the know, I kept him up-to-date on my progress.

"As things wind down for me, it's nice to know how you're spending your days, kiddo. Peace of mind is a wonderful thing. I suppose, even with the application bear, you are preparing to head back to the classroom?"

"Yeah, it's sort of ideal that I only have a once-a-week seminar this semester. Lots of flexibility if the Bureau calls for another hoop to jump through. Sorta took time off from the P.I. gig, but I'll be open to taking on a case or two after my Phase II exam—if there is a Phase II exam."

"Prepare yourself, Harry. It's happening. In the meantime, take it easy, except on the workout and the studying."

"Yeah, yeah. I'm wearing out my *FBI for Dummies* book. Don't worry, Uncle Marty."

Before I answered the phone, I took a cleansing breath. "Anya. Glad to hear from you. I feared my unfortunate G.I. issues marked the end of our—friendship."

"Harriet. What's a little vomit between—friends?"

I caught a hint of disdain in the artist's tone but ignored it. Add it to my list of poor choices.

"All better, now. Sorry about that. And thanks again for the ride home. I'm just glad I didn't spew all over the back of Sergei's sedan. Thank him again for me, won't you?"

"No, I don't imagine I will, but your appreciation is noted. What's new with you?"

"I got a job." I had a story prepared.

"Super." Anya's perky single-word response sounded unnatural. Her lack of interest beyond her periphery puzzled me. Then again, she was an odd duck in a weird world.

"Wanna celebrate with me? Life is short, and all that."

"I've got another sketch class Thursday evening. Afterward?"

"See you at the school, then?"

"Perfect, Harriet. See you then."

I gawked at my phone like it would tell me more than I already knew, then shrugged off the strangely stilted conversation. Some people just aren't *phone* people.

That blissful banality struck again with continued workouts and chores completed on their assigned days. Nighttime was the hardest—that quiet time when things got too still. But I only let my mile-a-minute brain ride off the rails so far before I wrangled it with regular reminders of what kind of man my gut told me Trey was. Putting a label on it—on him, even in my head, wasn't something I dared, but I clung to the hope. Worry wasted time and energy. Besides, he made me promises. Somehow, he'd keep them.

When Thursday came, my eagerness to get away from my studies had me buzzing. After the close call with Sergei, I decided this last-ditch effort to find some weakness in the Trubetzkoy armor would be just that—the last. A professional position that would afford me all sorts of access to take down a criminal organization hovered on the horizon. More of that investigative patience was required. My selfish motive to free Trey from seeing to my safety conflicted with his greater duty, or so I guessed, but if I could open a door, crack a window, I wanted to give it one more shot. In a sundress and espadrilles, I made my way to the art school to meet my new friend with the dreadful phone skills.

The evening's sketch session included the clichéd fruit bowl—six varieties, one heaping pile of produce after another—a little slice of hell on Earth, if I'm honest.

"*Great* class," I chirped as I strolled to the door at the end of the two hours. I'd lingered at my seat while Anya said her goodbyes to the other students, then collected my things to join her for our girls' night out.

"I thought you looked rather bored." Anya dumped all six mounds of perfectly good fruit into a large garbage bin on wheels, including the decorative bowls, but her face showed no signs of anger or irritation.

"No, I never really noticed the distinct differences in the shape of a Golden Delicious and a Macintosh." I nudged the tall brunette, grinning.

"I think you're pulling my leg. Who hasn't noticed that difference? It's pretty plain to see."

I didn't know if Anya meant to joke or not, but I realized I wouldn't miss her much when my ruse came to an end. "Ready to hit a wine bar?"

"Oh," she wrinkled her nose and frowned. "I'm kinda tired. Mind just heading upstairs for a drink?"

"What's upstairs?" Oh, sure. *Now* things get interesting.

"Directly above us, there are offices, a conference room, a couple more classrooms, and a smaller gallery space. For solo shows, that sort of thing. Above that is—well, for employees only." She shooed that phrase away with her long, fair fingers. "And on the top floor is—me. I live here. You didn't know?"

"No, how would I?" I had to give it to her. She asked a good question, and why didn't I know?

"Totally gutted and renovated with a rooftop garden you are going to love. I've got a bottle of that rosé on ice waiting for us."

"Sounds good."

"Doesn't it? This way, Harriet."

We encountered a couple of men-in-black on our way to a cargo elevator and bypassed two floors before exiting. The top two stops required a key for access, but that security measure didn't surprise me. When the doors glided open on the penthouse floor, high ceilings and large windows were all that remained of the old elementary school. Everything had been ripped to the studs: plaster walls, asbestos floors, and any signs of academia, and replaced with an exquisite living space—pretty rooms full of pretty things for a pretty girl. A real-life ivory tower. Anya Trubetzkoy's version of *stuck* didn't look so bad.

"Anya. When I get my place, you *must* give me the name of your decorator," I quipped in obvious jest. No one would ever think otherwise.

"Oh, that'd be me," she replied in earnest. "Just toss your bag there and follow me to the rooftop." She snaked her way through the immense space, and I had to hurry to keep pace while taking mental notes on the scene.

The gilded living room overflowed with books and art, a grand piano, and three different seating areas configured for socializing that I imagined rarely happened there, if ever. Sumptuous draperies puddled, and baroque fabrics adorned oversized furniture, the antithesis of my apartment's sleeker style with its mid-century vibe. Still, put together, everything in its place, Anya's home was gorgeous. Something out of a magazine.

One of the giant original windows provided the quirky access to the roof. Two steps opened to a fire escape, and we traveled the steep stairs to an open-air botanical paradise, a secret garden artfully hidden from the ground. Globe lights hung in enormous potted trees. Fragrant blooms perfumed the air, aided by beautiful fans that blew a subtle breeze, keeping it comfortably cool despite the humid night.

"What'd I tell you?"

"Holy *crap*, Anya. This is freaking amazing," I sputtered with genuine enthusiasm.

She sighed. "Your vocabulary is—crass, but you sure pull it off. I like it. I like *you*, Harriet."

I forced a smile to hide my sudden unease. Not only for being called out for my turn of phrase but also for Anya's own word choice. Her uncle's creepy lilt invaded my brain when I couldn't help but compare the supposed compliment given in such an unpleasant way.

"Have a look around. I'll pour the wine. But don't get too near the edge. Hate to have you go splat."

I wished away my apprehension. My Spidey senses told me to keep on high alert—I am an academic profiler, lest we forget. But part of me thought my imagination had to be in overdrive. *Note to future self:* heed your Spidey senses.

"Come. Have a seat." She held up two glasses containing plentiful servings of pale pink liquid. "You're my first guest to visit, my first company—aside from some personnel. But personnel is *not* company. Even if you want it to be. Not really, is it, Harriet?"

I sipped the cold, dry wine, pleasantly surprised it didn't taste like Kool-Aid. "Don't suppose so, no, Anya. But I don't have much experience with the ins-and-outs of *personnel*." I drank again.

"You like it?" She raised her glass.

I nodded and returned the gesture before taking another swallow.

"Harriet. That's an interesting name. How'd that come about?" My hostess sat in a fan-backed rattan chair painted peacock blue that creaked when she moved. With her rigid but graceful posture and alabaster skin, dressed in a black v-neck maxi-dress, if it weren't for her curly hair, I might have mistaken her for Morticia Addams. I sat on a matching sofa. Both pieces included plush cushions, and I sank, stifling a laugh at my Morticia Addams inside joke.

"Harriet? My dad named me. Well, he wasn't my dad at the time, but he adopted me. Fostered first, then adopted." *Gee, Harry, what's with the over-share?* I sipped more wine to busy my loose lips, curious about Anya's sudden and unusual inquisitiveness. Maybe in her own environment she could relax, open up, and show more interest in things outside herself.

"Is there some significance to the name? A family thing or something quaint like that?"

"Harlan—that's my dad—he's dead now—" *Jesus, Harry.* "He was a big history buff. American history, specifically. The Civil War fascinated him. Wow, that's more than you asked to know." I found myself with an abnormally relaxed tongue that I couldn't seem to stiffen. I tried to whoa-up on the personal revelations with another taste of rosé. "He appreciated Harriet Beecher Stowe. Debunked legend has it, President Lincoln quipped something about Stowe being the little woman who brought on the *big* Civil War. Dad thought I'd be a little woman who'd make a big impact on the world, too—his world anyway." I'd never shared that story with anyone and wondered why I had now. The empty glass in my hand likely played a role. "*Mmm*, that tastes like 'more,'" I joked inappropriately, failing to recognize the sensation of careening down a hill with failing brakes.

"By all means." Playing the generous hostess, Anya refilled my glass. "Have you always gone by Harriet? Nothing wrong with it. It's just such an old-fashioned name for such a hip, modern— *chick*." Her emphasis on that last word sounded out of place, and my laugh erupted.

The unseemly guffaw ended as abruptly as it exploded from me when I noticed the tree lights danced and the fans swayed on their stands. I couldn't feel the glass in my hand when I clearly still held it.

"I go by—Harry in day-to-day life. I have since before— high school." My speech slowed. "What did you give me, Anya?"

"Give you?"

"In the drink? You— dosed it. What was it? What's— your plan?" Now my tongue felt thick as I licked my numbing lips.

Anya *tut-tutted* just like her uncle, and it brought on the queasiness his presence provoked. I wished I could vomit, maybe rid myself of the poison in me, but I knew the damage had been done. At her bidding, I had left my bag with my phone at the penthouse door, not that I could operate it any longer. I reminded myself not to panic. A raised heart rate would only force the drug through my system faster. Resting my head against the raspy scratch of the broad rattan seatback, I hoped to stay conscious long enough to talk with my hostess-turned-hostage-taker.

"I don't know what it is—something my brother liked to use. So, if I had to guess, whatever happens, you'll be aware for most of it, pliable but unable to defend yourself. Vile, isn't it?"

"Ya think?" The words tumbled out, the last for a while.

"I told you the man had some demons, Harriet."

The glass fell from my hand, spilling on the jute rug without breaking.

"Oops." The curly-haired Morticia let slip a giggle I had heard once before, but giggling didn't suit the Anya I knew.

My loss of motor-control precipitated, including speech, and sleepiness washed over me. *Don't fall asleep, Harry.*

"I heard somewhere that Harriets are sometimes called Hattie."

My heart sank while my brain swirled, and my worlds collided.

"Not sure why that is. Hattie, Harriet. Harriet, Hattie. I think it's a cute nickname, but it certainly doesn't suit *you*. Not like Harry suits you. No, you are definitely a—"

"*An-ya.*" Her name roared from a distance, an angry bark that came from downstairs, but as I've mentioned when Trey spoke, I knew it. Unfortunately, nothing was to be done about it. I faded fast but willed myself to take in all the information I could. "Anya," Trey growled the name again, nearby this time, steps behind me, but I couldn't turn to see him.

"Alvah. So hostile. *Hostile.* Quietly, but decidedly *un*friendly. Even when I make such an effort to be nice to you. I could be *very* nice to you. Or not. You pick first. Then me." Another giggle. "Don't suppose you've changed your mind since last week? Hmm? Please, say yes." She had a sickening pout somehow laced with hope, all while echoing her creepy uncle again.

My head spun as I realized who had tested Trey last week, what woman had been a party to coercion, who had left her mark on his back. I vibrated with the scream I couldn't get free. A memory of Vlad pouting like an eight-year-old boy flashed. Now, Anya chattered in a twisted eight-year-old girl version of Gleb Trubetzkoy. *Focus, Harry.*

"Anya, we've talked about this. And if you'll pardon the expression, I don't shit where I eat. It's bad business."

Anya gasped in a fake huff. "Did you hear that, Harriet? Such talk in front of a lady. Two, if we count you." She smirked, then looked at Trey. "She can't talk now, but I'm pretty sure she can hear us." Her ear bent nearly to her shoulder, contorted as she squinted at me. "I wonder what she's thinking. Don't you, Alvah?"

"I wonder what *you're* thinking, Anya. We had a deal. Gleb and I had a deal, and you ought to abide by it."

"That was before I knew the tramp you thirsted for and my new bestie were one and the same. And don't talk to me about Uncle Gleb." Anya's resentment flared, her first sign of real rage.

Trey took a breath and his tone changed, too. "Why, Anya? What's he done now?" He immediately quelled the woman like some bizarre version of a mentoring figure, a life coach, a not-so-Oprah-Oprah.

The power shifted as Anya's anger subsided and her child-like demeanor returned. "I'm just sick of it all. The mess, the violence."

"Surely you see the irony in that, Anya. Look at what you're doing. Right this moment."

"This isn't violence. It's not messy. Well, Harriet spilled her wine," she tattled with a curled lip, eyeing the puddle at my feet as if my spilled wine was the evening's biggest problem.

"And how do you suppose I'm going to have to clean this up?" A hint of accusation colored his question.

"It's not my fault, you know." More pouting. "I was fine with her nosing around. Awed by her tactics in retrospect. She did fool me. *You* have no one to blame but yourself, Alvah. Or perhaps if her history-loving papa hadn't cursed her with such a wretchedly unique name." Anya tsked again. "But when I relayed the details of yours and my *highly* unsatisfying liaison to Uncle Gleb—"

"Почему ты сказал ему—" Trey's interjection thundered.

"*English*, Alvah." She met his frightening volume. "Our guest doesn't speak Russian, so neither will we. And when a man says another woman's name in the throes of—well, whatever that sad display was that night—it—"

Another scream erupted, this one inside my head.

"What? I did what?" Trey paced. Panic took hold, and the power swung the other way.

"You said *Hattie*. Turns out, my uncle is familiar with the name. I wouldn't have made the connection otherwise. Now, don't worry. He'd been enjoying one of my special nighttime cocktails I like to make for him occasionally, so I can learn things—like I gave Harriet—uh—Harry—no, *Hattie*. His are less strong, obviously. It makes him very chatty, for a bit, anyway. Then he sleeps. He really is clueless." She gave a pointed look. "For *now*."

"What do you want, Anya? I am doing my best to make changes in the organization for you. Weed out the more troublesome elements, pressing harder to toughen the more compliant. Right the wayward ship in your favor. It's going to take some time, but I'm on it. A mutually beneficial *business* arrangement. It will be an outwardly kinder, gentler criminal empire with you pulling strings for everyone to know. I got rid of Vlad, and you thought that was impossible. I am clearing the way, just as you asked."

"Yes. Free at last, free at last, but you *know* what I want."

"But we're not mixing business with pleasure, are we, Anya? We see the wisdom in that, right?" Trey's coaxing reeked of condescension, but Anya lapped it up like a kitten with a saucer of milk. She nearly purred, and my fury burned as she mewed.

"No. *Yes*. But that's not *all* I want. Clear the rest of the way, and potty-mouth Harry gets to live. And if you need inspiration, other than this silly crush you clearly have on her, which is so, so sad, really. You must know she would never put up with the likes of you. She might be crass, but she's principled, and her precious daddy was a *cop*. I shouldn't tell you this, but Uncle Gleb had him killed. *Oops*, I told you." She held her hand over her O-shaped mouth while her eyes gaped wide in feigned shock. "It's a small world after all." As she sang the tune, the more child-like she got, like her grown-up meds were wearing off, and she was due another dose. Her need for a security detail was less of a mystery. When her expression went vacant in a long pause, the image terrified me. "Fix it, Alvah. *Fix* it, or else."

Afraid Anya had won, I fought to keep my eyes open half-mast because the latest development was too much to risk missing.

After a drawn-out stare, her impishness snapped back. "Have a drink with me, Alvah. Have a drink, and let's toast our *new* deal. Yours and mine."

Trey stalled in his reply, then spoke with quiet firmness once he considered his response after a new read on the room. "With *pink* wine? I don't think so, Anya." And like that, the power shifted again.

Anya hung her head.

"Don't mope, Anya. Just go get me some goddamn vodka. Chilled, *extra* cold, in a short glass. I've got work to do. And I don't want even a sliver of ice, so no shaking it. Understood?"

"Yay." At once smiling, Anya hiked up her long dress and scurried off, leaving me alone with the scariest Trey I'd ever known.

"Hattie. You're gonna be okay. Blink if you can understand me." *My* version of Trey reappeared.

I closed and opened my leaden lids.

"Good. I'm sorry about this, about all of it. I really am. But we don't have much time." On his knees, Trey held my face in his hands, and those impossibly long lashes fringed his dark eyes that glistened in the blurring round lights. He let go of my cheeks, and my head rolled to the side. He righted it. "Dammit," he whispered. "Я задолбался. Это заканчивается сейчас."

Stay awake, Harry.

Trey spoke again, but not to me. "Я не собираюсь быть дома на ужин в воскресенье." I strained to hear his words, but they meant nothing. He paced, speaking on his phone. When he stopped, he looked directly at me. "Mom, I'm not going to make it home for dinner on Sunday." He returned the phone to his pocket and sat next to me, wrapping an arm around my shoulders. "Let yourself fall asleep, Hattie. It shouldn't be hard." He gently rocked me as he whispered in my ear, "I swear you'll wake-up in your bed, unharmed, safe—with a *hell* of a headache. God, I'm sorry. Go to sleep now." He kissed my temple. "Wait, Hattie. I—"

Everything went black.

Still wearing the dress from my nightmarish girls' night out, I woke in my own bed, safe, unharmed, and with a *hell* of a headache. On my bedside, two tall glasses of water propped a note I could barely focus on to read. *I'm sorry. Please believe me. You're safe. Now drink the water. Sleep. Then drink some more.*

I fell asleep again.

"Honey? Harry? Open your eyes for me. Harry?" Leo patted my cheek with one hand while he gripped my wrist with the other. "There you are. How's about sitting up and drinking some water." He eyed his watch.

"What? Why are you—"

"Someone slipped a note under my door telling me to check on you and to get you to drink lots of water. But this is no ordinary hangover, honey. What's going on?"

"Huh? Oh my God, my head hurts."

"Drink."

I did.

"What day is it?"

"Oh lord, Harry. It's Friday, late afternoon."

My scrambled brain took its time to *clear*, but I did my best to sober up, speak cogently, and relieve Leo of his worried look. I couldn't tell him the truth and needed him to leave me alone to figure my next steps.

"Let's just say that pink wine should be called *rosé Rohypnol*. On an empty stomach anyway. I'm fine, Leo. Overdid it is all."

"I'm gonna go, just to stop the lies coming out of your mouth. If you need me—" Leo didn't finish the statement. He simply waved over his head as he took the stairs out of my bedroom. "Drink more water," he shouted from the first floor.

I did.

Forty-One

I COULD NOT GET my body to agree to a workout. A meager run was a monumental hill to climb, so I laid low to avoid any damage. I hoped a quiet weekend would cure me and bring me some intel on the Trubetzkoys and, more importantly, Trey. I got nothing on the latter.

With my focus on that book-learning and my daily chores, time went by in a murky blur. The only bright spot was the notification of my scheduled *meet and greet.* One or more evaluators would conduct an in-person review of my application and validate the information submitted. They'd assess that material to gauge my competitiveness for Phase II. The meeting would take place in ten days at the New York field office, where I'd taken the proctored Phase I test. It also marked the point at which I pulled my application five years ago. I quit, withdrew from consideration, and slunk off to Paris in a cloud of despair because my father had died.

I wrestled with the fact my plan to right the wrong of my father's death had failed. Holding Trubetzkoy responsible in the eyes of the law had been an impossible pipe dream. I recognized that now. But knowing the reason for his murder was a more personal vendetta stoked the burning in my belly. Seeking justice when Harlan Smith had gone down as a byproduct of Trubetzkoy "business" felt noble, if not pie-in-the-sky. Now that I knew

Trubetzkoy's goons assassinated my dad, fulfilling a kill order, I hungered for revenge. The professional in me looked down the road to a day when I might have the full force of the law at my back. Vengeance or no, Trubetzkoy would remain in my crosshairs.

Anya was a clusterfuck all unto herself and a fascinating lesson in psychopathy. Theory versus practicum bit me in the ass again. And where the hell was Trey?

More than a week had passed since the bizarre night on that rooftop in Astoria. It was the hottest week of the summer. Not a drop of rain fell. Clouds were non-existent, and the sun beat down on the city, unencumbered in a relentless assault.

After a long Saturday of more studying, I changed my clothes and ran a hard sprint to the gym despite the heat.

"Hey, stranger. Nice to see you again," Nate chortled as he wobbled toward me. "Thought maybe you'd moved on to the YMCA, traded us in for a Jazzercize class, Zumba, maybe."

"Jazzercize. That's a good one, Nate. But don't knock the franchise. More than fifty years can't be all wrong."

"Okay. What can I do for you this evening? Hang a bag?"

"Yeah. I've been recovering from a bit of a bug, but I could hit something."

"You got it."

I pictured Gleb Trubetzkoy's face on the sixty-five-pound heavy bag, and it felt good to beat on it. Not proud, but I wore myself out, wishing I could make it bleed. When that face morphed into Trey's, I continued to pummel it until I clung to the swinging *Everlast*™ sack to stay upright.

"Hydrate, kid." Nate offered me a water I gladly accepted with two boxing-gloved hands. "Then scoot. It's after nine o'clock, and I need my beauty rest."

"Is that your secret?" I winked at the man as he untied the laces on my mitts and freed my taped fingers.

"Now, don't go telling everyone," he snickered. "Hey, it's dark. You need a lift?"

"Nah. It's not far. I'm good. Thanks though. Good night, Nate."

Out in the night air, the dog days of summer did their best to suffocate. In a few short weeks, sooner even, cooler air would blow through without warning; autumn would drop its leaves and usher in snow. And after the scorcher of the past week, I looked forward to it. But just as the notion of cold flitted through my mind, a chill hit me, and my pace on the sidewalk stuttered a step, then picked up speed. I remembered a note to self: *heed your Spidey senses.* I shored up my backpack and made a sudden spin to look behind me. Nothing. No one to see. I kept digging on my route home but sensed someone's eyes on me. The buzz of streetlamps and distance traffic noise filled my ears when I stopped again on the vacant side street.

"Are you here?" I hollered into the dark. No reply. I shook my head, half-embarrassed, half-certain I had company. "Trey? You son-of-a—" I waited. Hands to my hips, I refused to move, certain I'd coax him out from his hiding place. No one emerged from the shadows. My stomach hurt, and I wanted to scream. Instead, I dropped my head and took a deep breath of garbage, sun-soaked in the week's searing heat—the summertime version of Queens' signature scent. Straightening up, I pushed back my shoulders and cleared my throat. "Okay. I know you have a job to do. One I even respect. I get it. But— *God,* I miss you."

A short honk sounded, and a car door slammed. Tires squealed. A sedan peeled out of an alleyway, yards ahead of my spot. High-beams blinded me, and the vehicle screeched by before I could discern any detail. The commotion stopped my heart, but I rallied and hurried home through the lingering fumes of a gunned engine and burnt rubber.

I'm not an over-indulger. At least not when it comes to drinking. I like good booze and a cold beer, but only to relax, and rarely to obliterate a moment in time. No joke, the matching silk kimonos Leo and I purchased one rowdy Rosh Hashanah fueled by Manischewitz wine was the most outrageous drinking tale I had to share. On the sidewalk, in the wake of the random crazy driver and my overactive imagination, I felt the sting of tears and the tight throat of a burgeoning cry, but I was determined not to succumb to it. Once I reached my apartment, an ache stretched its way from my center and slithered through each limb. It throbbed in a way that felt out of control, and I begged it to stop. The sprint home helped. The vodka I drank once I got there helped more. God bless Texas.

If that sounds badass, this ginger would be happy to hear it, but it didn't take much to find my way to unconsciousness after a long, hot shower.

While I couldn't have told you at the time, after the mental replay of the next several hours—moments I'd run on a loop for months to come—it was precisely seventeen minutes after two on a Sunday morning in August the last time *La Vie en Rose* cried its sad strain from my phone.

"Trey. I knew you were *there*. God. I *knew* it. Why didn't you come out? Are you here now? I'm on my way to the door. I just need—"

"Jesus, Mary, and Joseph. Harry?"

A thud stopped time at *eighteen* minutes after two o'clock on a Sunday morning in August.

"Uncle Marty?"

"Oh, kid," a despondent Detective O'Shea practically whimpered into the phone. "Harry. I'm going to need you to sit tight. I'll call you as soon as I can. Don't call me. I'm hip-deep. Sit tight, kiddo. I'll call *you*."

"*Marty*?!" I wailed.

"Tag it and bag it with the rest. I'll call her back on my line." Marty spoke those words to an unseen stranger, a stranger to me anyway. Three pulses told me the call had come to a definitive end. None of my phones rang for another two hours and fifty-six minutes. I sat without moving and watched each second of that time tick by.

The sun broke the horizon, reflecting off every shiny surface I walked toward. I chose a path through the St. John's Campus until I hit the quiet residential street that ended at the Queens hospital. Single-family dwellings mixed with attached townhomes and small apartment buildings. Likely, a combination of college students and forever-residents lived there, but none of them were awake at that time of day. I imagined if people knew the beauty of the morning glow at that hour, they would make more effort to see it. If only I had been in a better frame of mind to enjoy the dazzling glint of cars and street signs and the more subdued purple hue that lightened the western sky as the sun made a flashier show, rising out of the east. The dichotomy brandished a poetic moment to no one but me, but like I said, my frame of mind couldn't appreciate it, not like the gods of *whatever* would have wanted. A waste is what it was—a fucking waste.

Once I crossed 164th Street and schlepped onto the Queens Healthcare campus, time sped up or slowed down; I'm not sure which, but it all came to a frenzied halt when Uncle Marty met me outside the double-wide doors of Dr. Dom's crypt. And like the former Mets coach (that's how I like to remember him) Yogi Berra apparently said, it was "like déjà vu all over again." Martin O'Shea and I needed to stop meeting like this.

Forty-Two

"I WISH YOU HADN'T come down here, kiddo."

I sniffed with my eyes to the sky. An early morning birdsong volleyed in some campus trees, and I hoped Marty wouldn't interrupt the repetitive melody. The phenomenon would be commonplace to most folk, but I wanted to relish every chirped note, the last moments of *The Before*. Five years ago, I'd gone from having a father to not having one without taking time to enjoy that final moment of *Before*. I sped into *The After*, and once there, things took on a life of their own. Decisions had to be reached, calls needed to be made, hands to shake, cheeks to kiss, and casseroles to eat. I knew *this* impending *After* would be different. Less to do, quieter, lonelier. So, I took in the morning glow and the avian refrain with a whiff of the dewy grass, enjoying one last moment of *Before*.

The crash of metal on metal as an orderly plowed a gurney through the swinging doors in the ambulance bay marked the end of the tranquil daybreak, but I still couldn't find my voice.

"Sorry I didn't call sooner, but it turned into a bit of a sticky wicket. Dr. Dom trying to collect as much—well, and with two bodies—"

"Two?" My first word.

"Harry, Popov is dead."

I knew it was coming. I knew when I heard Marty's voice after I answered *La Vie en Rose*, even so, as I tumbled into *The After*, the sensation wasn't what I thought it would be. Turns out, not all heartbreak feels the same, and this new-to-me version ripped wider and deeper than I thought possible. I shook my head.

"Harry." Marty held my arm, steadied me upright as the chasm tore through me in a way that said I would never be whole again.

"He promised," I whispered.

"Who promised? Popov?"

"He *promised*," I repeated louder, and the fury took hold. I yanked from Marty's grip, spinning in the momentum of it before I took quick, stomping strides down a walkway to the security door into the M.E.'s wing.

"Harry? Where are you going?"

"I'm going to remind him. I'm gonna look him in his dead face and remind him how he promised he wouldn't hurt me. He promised, so he doesn't get to die. He doesn't get to *go gentle* into that good night and leave me here to rage, leave me before we had our time. Nope. This is not the time to die, and I'm going to tell him. Because he promised."

"You can't, Harry," Marty shouted. "You can't."

"Oh, the *hell* I can't, Marty. Watch me."

"He's not there."

I'd pulled the door handle but stalled in the rush of cold air. An appropriate special effect for a crypt, I thought. I waited for an explanation.

"You'd think that Trubetzkoy would have been the more political quagmire, being the noteworthy stiff—"

I flinched at the detective's vocabulary.

"Sorry."

"Trubetzkoy's dead too? *Gleb* Trubetzkoy is dead?"

"Dead as a—yes. Gleb Trubetzkoy is dead. And him, you can see, though I don't know why you'd want to."

"Jesus Christ, Marty. What the hell is going on?" I ignored all concerns for Marty's sensitivities.

"Best we can figure, as I surmised, Popov made a power grab and succeeded in taking out Gleb. But then got toppled himself shortly after that. Someone dumped the bodies together."

"No. You're wrong, Marty. You're wrong. You got it all wrong. And what do you mean he's not here? Where the hell is he? Who claimed him? So fast? In a few hours? Isn't there a crime to investigate here? That's—"

"They'd been dead for days, Harry. Days. Out in the elements, in this week's blazing heat." Marty's disgusted face contracted like he could see and smell the aftermath. "Who knows who knew what on that end, but it had been days."

"But who—"

"Turns out your guy—Trey Popov—was Jewish."

"I'm aware, Marty. But he wasn't exactly lighting the candles on Friday nights, so—?"

"So, somebody made a call to the local Chabad—"

"Seriously? I didn't realize he was so orthodox. Who called? Maybe Mo—" I didn't understand. I meant the questions for me, and Marty pushed past them, anyway.

"Doesn't matter. Chabad acts as a sort of catch-all for unaffiliated Jews— and a *very* adamant Lubavitcher rabbi demanded the body. No embalming, no autopsy—not that the remains were conducive to any of that—and to release them to Sinai Chapels *immediately*. By the time Dr. Dom got here, it was all she could do to get down some basic details. But no one is looking too hard at it."

"Well, why the hell would they? I mean, who cares, right? He's just some lowlife goon. Why risk your seat at the donut shop getting cold for a—"

"Hey. Now I know this stings, so I'm going to give you a pass, but let's simmer down the rhetoric. There's a backlog of unsolved, unexplained deaths of far better men than the likes of—"

"Better men? *Better* men? Says you, Marty!" I spun and shoved through the door. The shuffle of feet told me the detective followed.

"Kid, where are you going?" Marty chased me down a long hall bathed in the harsh glare of bare fluorescent tube lights that hummed and *tinked* overhead.

Ignoring him, I slid to a stop and rapped my knuckles on the open office door conveniently labeled Medical Examiner. "Dr. Dom, I'm Harry—Harriet Smith, and I—"

"Yes, Harry. We've met." Dr. Dombrowski looked up from her desk, her eyeglasses barely perched on her nose.

"Yes, we have. I have questions about the recent body brought in."

"Which? There were two."

"Yes, the one that got poached."

"Well, they both got pretty well baked out there." Her head wobbled with her joke.

"Not *cooked*, Dr. Dom, plundered, stolen, pilfered."

The doctor's gallows' humor might have been requisite for the job, but it evaporated. "Religious communities are well within their rights to see remains cared for according to tradition, Harry. We take those rituals, whatever they may be, seriously and do it by the book. And as a Jew myself—"

"That's great, Dr. Dom. What can you tell me about the remains?" My patience for a lecture on cultural and religious post-mortem practices didn't exist.

"They were a mess, and I had little time." She directed her frank reply to her notes. "Male, Caucasoid, mid-thirties, maybe. Appeared fit but hard to tell in that condition. Seventy-two to seventy-four inches—like I said, he was a *mess*—dark hair, curly, dark eyes."

I took in the information like she read a grocery list. Everything fit Trey's description *and* most of the men-in-black I'd encountered in the last month and a half. The Trubetzkoys had a type. I stretched to get air to speak. "Identifying marks?"

"You mean like tattoos?" She read her file. "No, nothing like that. Then again, Jews tend to avoid tatting their skin. That tenet is relaxing some, but no, he didn't have any ink."

I had inhaled half a cleansing breath when she cut it short.

"He did have a fairly recent wound. Mid left side. Sutures had been removed, but the perpetrator, probably more than one, gave it a good working over. All of him, really. Blunt trauma—everywhere. Repeated. Even if we had dental records, it wouldn't have mattered. Again, I didn't have much time, and the body had been out in the blistering sun, plus some subsequent scavenging—hard to tell what caused what or when without more time with the remains, and I just didn't have it. He was basically a sack of bones. Catastrophic injury. Someone was sending a message."

"Okay, Doc," Marty made himself known again. "I think we've heard enough. Harry? Let's get out of here."

"Hey, the Sinai guys took off out of here in a rush. A late-night crew I'd never worked with before. They left this, but the vic wouldn't be buried with it, anyway." Dr. Dom pulled at a small manila envelope paper-clipped to the file. She squeezed its creases, spilling the contents into her palm: a simple Star of David on a length of gold chain.

My knees gave way, but Marty caught me.

"Oh," Dr. Dom stood, suddenly stunned. "Harry. I didn't realize— I didn't realize this was someone you—"

"May I have it? The necklace? Is it evidence or—"

"Uh?" The M.E. looked to Marty. Out of the corner of my eye, he nodded.

My quivering fingers reached toward the petite woman in her oversized lab coat. She placed the pendant in my shaking hand and closed my fingers around it. "I am sorry, Harry." The doctor returned to her seat and leafed through the folder with very few pages to it. "Interesting."

I cleared my throat, desperate for water—or vodka. I wrapped the chain around my fingers; my thumb stroked the charm. "What's interesting?" I squeaked.

"No tattoos despite his—more criminal vocation. The well-worn pendant. The adherence to burial ritual, quite strict adherence at someone's behest. All signs of a devout Jew—at least to the *traditions* of the faith."

I stared as she closed the folder on the body diagram that included some cursory notes. I kept my eyes on the folder when I spoke. "And? Your point?"

"His name. Popov."

"What about it?"

"It's not Jewish."

"It's not?"

"Just the opposite, actually. Means son of a *priest*. So, *very* not Jewish. Maybe Russian Orthodox. Definitely Christian. Curious, huh? Of course, tradition also states one gets his Jewishness from one's mother. So maybe his mother married a gentile."

"Thank you for your time, Dr. Dombrowski." I turned into Marty and nodded my readiness to leave, then stuttered to a stop. "One more thing, Dr. Dom. Any other—scars? Anywhere?"

She moved to open the file, but she didn't need to look. "Not that I cataloged, sorry. Something specific or just—"

"Just wondering." I shook my head. I imagined Trey tugging on his drawstring pants to show me the puckered scar of the twice-stitched appendectomy incision. Would Dr. Dom have noticed it in the body's beaten, baked, and gnawed-on state? "Do you have the contact info for the mortuary, by chance?"

She passed me a card, and I took it in the hand wrapped in the gold jewelry.

"Thank you, Dr. Dom." Marty ushered me to the hall.

Back outside, the sun shone, and life beyond the birds hummed. I looked around, unsure of what should happen next.

"Harry? Let me give you a lift."

I didn't respond to his offer for a ride, too distracted by the pain in my dark purple fingers bound by the familiar chain.

"*Harry.* Give me that." Marty grabbed my hand, unwinding the necklace.

"I should take that to his mom."

"You know his mom? Harriet, how deep did you get with this—how did you not tell me? Never mind. For another day. Let me get you home."

"No, I think I'll walk. I need to call Sinai, find out about the burial." I flipped the business card in my hand. "It's gonna happen fast. Those are the rules, but I don't know if—I don't know—What about the Trubetzkoy family business?"

"A path got cleared. Someone's happy."

Clear the rest of the way, and potty-mouth Harry gets to live. Is that what happened? Trey saved me—again and got beaten—again? To death this time?

"Harry? What are you thinking? What's going on in there?" The cop tried to make eye contact, but I couldn't let it happen.

"Run with this. Pass it on. Pass it off as your own. I don't give a shit. Someone needs to look at Anya Trubetzkoy. Gleb's niece, *Vlad the Bad*'s sister. Tear apart the Art Alliance in Astoria. The third floor, in particular, I'd guess. There's something there. Probably a lot. A paper-trail, maybe blood even." I thought about a young man whose name wasn't really Mischa. "But you should move fast."

"Harry?"

"It's like déjà vu." I didn't want Marty's questions about what I knew and how I knew it. "Days out from my *meet and greet,* and the rug gets yanked. Just like last time—"

"Look, I get this is a blow. I get that I dropped the ball here. Let you get sucked into something. And I'm sorry. Take a beat, take a breath. But don't let this opportunity pass. Don't make any rash decisions. I'll put a call into McQuade. Explain. I bet we can buy some time. Take some, Harry, but then—"

"No, Marty." I shook my head, waved off the veteran detective's offer for help. "Time isn't gonna fix this. There aren't enough beats, enough breaths. You calling McQuade won't be necessary. Thank you, though. I'll handle it."

"What's that mean?"

I looked skyward. "It means Quantico better buckle up. Next spring, there's a ginger badass headed to Virginia."

Forty-Three

I grabbed the umbrella hanging on the teak coat rack. Leo's and my recent night of online shopping included every stitch I wore. My outfit screamed young female federal-agent for the twenty-first century. But Leo swore I could fit within the Bureau's dress code and still feel fabulous. He wasn't wrong. Throwing the umbrella into the virtual shopping cart was a giggle-worthy afterthought.

A cold front blew through the Mid Atlantic. A sudden and likely short-lived reprieve from the past week's heat, but also a preview of weather soon-to-come. It came with dampness, and the whole scene had a "Screw you, Harry Smith. Sincerely, Karma" kind of vibe.

"You ready, honey?" Leo, dressed in a dark suit and tie, waited patiently for me in our shared hall. With red-rimmed eyes, he forced a smile and offered me a gentlemanly arm. "You're taking— the umbrella?"

"Don't you mean the *brolly*? See? I listen. And it's raining, isn't it?"

He looked at me, askance.

"Trust me. If anyone would approve of me carrying a Hello Kitty umbrella to his funeral, it would be Trey." I hiccupped to stifle an unexpected sob that *almost* escaped from me. A subtle head shake accompanied the slow breath I used to steady myself, securing my emotions.

My phone chirped.

Clutching the crook of his arm, I lifted my chin and squeezed out a toothless grin. "Car's here. Let's go."

"Hey guys, I'm Chaz."

Leo and I slid into the backseat of the ubiquitous silver Honda Accord.

"Let's see. Where are we headed on this rainy Monday? Don't rainy Mondays suck? Let's see. Linden Hill. Okay. Wait, isn't Linden Hill a—"

"Cemetery? Yes. What do you say we make this a silent trip? You'll get your five stars. Thanks, Chaz." Leo spoke to the rearview while he patted my knee. I thanked him with a nod.

I didn't think I had it in me to sit through any sort of service. I didn't know what to expect under the circumstances, so I'd contacted the mortuary for the details. With them came an education in the Jewish death tradition.

Members of Chevra Kadisha, the Jewish Burial Society, would be on hand to say Tehillim or psalms, over the body, which is never left unattended until it's moved to Linden Hill for burial. The dead are wrapped in nothing but a hand-sewn linen shroud and placed in a plain pine box. No clothing, no jewelry. You go out the way you come in. I appreciated the simplicity. And learning the specifics of the ritual gave me something to think about other than a dead Trey. If I drowned in the minutiae, then how could I drown in grief?

The gathering would be graveside and short, and they hadn't announced plans for anyone to sit shiva—good news as far as I was concerned. I had no need for socializing, but if I didn't see the mound of dirt, I'd never get on with the rest of the *getting on*.

Once Chaz dropped us at Grand View and Metropolitan Ave, finding the gravesite was simple. The cemetery had erected a canopy with empty seating for a dozen mourners.

"No one is here, Harry," Leo whispered the obvious. "Why is no one here?"

I took the gentle giant's hand, wishing I could ease his hurt, placate his ire at what he deemed an injustice of some sort. "We're here. So, let's just take a few minutes, say our goodbyes, and move forward because I, for one, can't get stuck again."

We sat on squishy grass in wobbly plastic chairs not made for the likes of Leo's size. I don't know how long we sat in the cool dampness. Wrapped in a silent fog, away from city noise, I waited for the big reveal, waited for Trey to wake me from the nightmare, but Leo nudged me from my stupor when he murmured, "Take all the time you need, honey. No rush at all." Pushing himself out of his seat, he sighed and walked away.

"I sure hope you can hear me," I growled, to clear a cry from my aching throat. "You broke a promise. And I know it wasn't a fair one—and this isn't what you meant, but—I *hurt*, Trey. I hurt, and you are the cause, and you promised." The first tear fell, but I rushed to wipe it away, afraid someone might see, and that wasn't something I could allow. I inhaled and smiled, breathing in the wet air that held more chill than seemed appropriate. "The solution, of course, is simple," I continued. "Don't be dead. Don't be dead and come back, and I'll forgive everything. *I* promise. Now's the time." I sucked in another gulped breath. "Come back and tell me a dirty joke, and we'll go home. One thousand square feet and—screw it—there *will* be touching. And pancakes. And I'll teach you to dance—"

"Now that I would have liked to see," a woman's voice interrupted me.

I bolted upright in my chair. My palms did their best to blot away the wet on my cheeks. I tried to make myself presentable, sniffed, and wiped my nose with the back of my hand, avoiding the woman's gaze. *Jeez, Harry.*

"I'm sorry. Please excuse me. I—wait. Aren't you—"

"I knew Trey Popov, yes." She handed me a handkerchief and indicated I should clean-up my face. Her apparent impatience for an untidied appearance reminded me of a brunette version of Bess O'Shea. Her impudent manner was familiar in other ways, too. She stood tall in a black suit, hair graying at her temples, with tired, dark eyes that dared me to keep looking at her.

I dropped my stare and wiped my nose on the fine linen with an embroidered *AR* in tight black stitching at one corner. When the mini *thump, thump, thump* of a single drip spot on the canopy marked too much time, I scrambled for my pocket. "I have something for you. You should take this." I offered her my closed fist but hesitated with second thoughts about relinquishing the only thing I had left of him. Knowing it belonged with her, I opened my hand, bidding her to take Trey's necklace.

She reached for it but pulled back without it. "You keep it."

My mouth opened to protest, but no sound came. I closed my fingers around the gold and placed it back in my pocket.

"He cared for you; you know?" She only had eyes for the mound of dirt over my shoulder, so I took the opportunity to examine her. She had a tightly set and off-center jaw. The deep crow's feet were likely well-earned if her rigidly dignified posture provided any clue. I knew I had seen her before. This chameleon had offered me tea and *sawltines.* I also believed, long before that night, the day after I killed Vlad, she'd pulled a box from the trunk of a dark blue sedan parked on my street.

"Did *he* tell you that?" I wondered if this person provided a place for Trey to share things, his thoughts, feelings. Because it seemed, until he found me on a July Fourth, he lived a life on guard and unto himself, no home base to return to, where he could relax, breathe easily, and hear his own voice. I provided that sanctuary, and he came back for it time and time again. I allowed it, and it got him killed.

"He did, and then some. But he didn't need to—a *mom* knows."

"*Huh*," I scoffed. "Well, I wouldn't know anything about that—what moms know." I offered her the monogrammed handkerchief.

She grimaced and waved her hand for me to keep it. Considering its damp, snotty state, it was probably best.

I didn't want to continue this aloof heart-to-heart, and I moved to make my getaway. "My condolences, Mrs.—Mo—Ma'am."

Leo watched from under a brick archway, and I had to walk past the woman to join him.

She took my wrist. "Don't let this stop you. Remember him. And *everything* he said. If he got in the way of your success, it would kill him—all over again."

I wrenched my arm from her tight grasp. Anger lived in her voice. It seemed misplaced, but she was grieving, so I let it go. Of course, I didn't know what I didn't know.

I closed and bolted my door, then hung my wet Hello Kitty umbrella. After toeing off my new chunky heels, I padded to the kitchen for a tall glass I filled with too little ice and too much vodka before heading upstairs.

With my shirttail pulled free, I undid the buttons one-handed on the slow climb to my bedroom. Emptying my pockets, I lay the handkerchief and Trey's necklace on my bed and sipped my drink, the elixir to help me through the next part. Every stitch of the new stylish-but-sanctioned clothing fell in a heap on the floor. "Tom," finally relieved of his hanger post, slipped over my shoulders, and I slid my arms through the crisp cotton sleeves. One button done would do. With the hankie and pendant clutched in my grip, I crawled into my smooth sheets, curled into a ball on *his* side of the bed, and gave myself until the count of one hundred to stop crying.

Forty-Four

"I DON'T WANT YOU to be unnerved when you walk in the room, Harry. Let's chalk up the extra interest to you being an intriguing, quality candidate with some watchful eyes looking to speed the process. More eyes mean more scrutiny and fewer questions about rushing the matter later. This is a good thing." Michael McQuade attempted to assure me the upcoming interview wouldn't be a difficult one, and, until then, the thought hadn't occurred to me. It was the process, a means to an end, and I planned to see it through with success.

That said, I heard Uncle Marty in my ear. *You realize telling me to relax has the opposite effect.* If I didn't know it before, I sure as hell knew it now.

"No worries, Mike. Not the first time I've provoked a little *extra,* if you know what I mean." I winked at the uptight federal agent.

"Uh, I don't, no." He squinted with the cocked head of confusion.

While it wasn't standing room only, they'd squeezed more chairs than usual around a long table. Each observer was introduced, name and division. I hoped there wouldn't be a quiz.

Nearly three hours later, my butt sore from sitting so long, it felt like the inquisition might wind down. It was a lot of information to get through, and I had—feelings about some things. I'd planned to go in with an open mind, very little filter, and total honesty about anything asked of me. It's what Trey would have wanted. And if it isn't what the Bureau wanted, this *meet and greet* was the time for them to say.

"Last item, Ms. Smith." Magic words. Lots of paper around the room got shuffled. Glasses of water finally got drunk, and phones appeared, messages checked.

"What's that, Special Agent Chen?"

"A bit off-topic, but maybe something you'd have an interest in hearing."

I simply raised a questioning brow from my side of the conference table.

"Were you aware a team served a warrant at the Astoria Art Alliance in Queens last night?"

I played cool. "No, I was not, Special Agent Chen." It was the truth.

"Of course, I'm not at liberty to discuss an ongoing investigation, particularly with someone not attached to the Bureau. And it is very early days, but the findings were major, and some of my fellow agents and I thought you might like to know things are moving. A Detective Martin O'Shea with NYPD said you and your private investigation work were instrumental in providing some direction for an ongoing Major Crimes and Special Enforcement dual investigation. Feds are taking over the case."

"Oh. Well, I merely loosened the lid on that pickle jar. I hope they can clean up whatever mess gets uncovered. For the sake of the artists." I offered a tight grin and a solemn nod. "And— for anyone else taken out in the wake."

The agent closed the file in front of her—a symbolic gesture that read like she wanted me to do the same.

I received my invitation to take part in the Phase II test. The ball kept rolling down the field. I had two weeks to schedule the exam which, like the other segments of the process, took place at the lackluster rectangle standing on the Seussical-like grounds in lower Manhattan. The first portion entailed a written assessment involving fictional scenarios. It took two hours and thirty minutes. The second section comprised a one-hour sit-down interview with three Special Agents—just a simple chat. *Your mileage may vary.*

Two weeks later, I learned I'd advance further by submitting to the official physical fitness test. You never saw a more disappointed Marty and Nate when they learned they couldn't be onsite to cheer me on, but for the record, I kicked ass. Next came the Conditional Appointment Offer. Reaching this level meant the launch of my official background investigation—a months-long deep dive into my life, all thirty years of it.

"Maybe not so much with the caffeine this morning, honey." Leo yanked my half-full Grande coffee from my grip and dropped it in a trashcan. "Let's not give the needle any more reasons to jump around, 'kay?" My neighbor had been excited to join me in Manhattan as a source of comfort and camaraderie for the next fiery hoop Uncle Sam required me to jump through as the cataloging of my deeds, good, bad, or indifferent, commenced. When the day had come and Leo realized the kick-off consisted of a polygraph, his enthusiasm morphed into panic. He fretted, far more angsty than the one about to be tied to a chair while her personal history got raked over the coals one yes-or-no question at a time.

"Way to be a calming force in my time of need, Auntie Leo," I joked. Fall had arrived, and we walked arm in arm across the windy garden spot at twenty-six Federal Plaza.

"Dammit. I'm sorry, Harry."

"I'm kidding, Leo. I'm cool. There is nothing to be afraid of here. I have only one thing to do today. Just *one* thing." I left him in the lobby and headed off to meet with the Personnel Security Adjudication Section.

"Are you aware of what this next part will entail?" The middle-aged woman never looked me in the eye as she prepared me for my next "interview."

"Well, I've seen *'Meet the Parents'* like a dozen times so—uh, yeah. I've got it." Tough crowd. I raised my arms so the administrator could attach the two rubber tubes of the pneumographs around my chest and abdomen. They measured my respiration. A blood pressure cuff also took readings, while galvanometers slipped onto two fingers, took note of how sweaty they'd get during the strictly yes-or-no question session. When I looked at the obvious two-way mirror, hairs on the back of my neck sprang to attention. I hadn't been nervous until then, but I imagined father-figure Michael McQuade on the other side of the glass. He wasn't, of course. This wasn't a spectator sport, but somehow I felt unseen eyes on me. I chided my paranoia, took a deep breath, and readied myself for whatever came next.

The questions included the basics: name, place of birth, education—information available to the interrogator on the many pages of my application materials. Items traveled down more detailed and personal avenues, too. For example, have you ever:

Used or had unauthorized dealings in controlled substances?

Committed theft, fraud, or misused government property or funds?

Intentionally and without authorization destroyed, altered, misplaced, taken, falsified legal documents or evidence?

All were easy enough to answer. Then came:

Have you ever had a relationship with or allegiance to a known or suspected felon?

I eyed the two-way mirror, took a subtle, deep breath, and answered the question.

The administrator detached all the tubes and wires, shook my hand and told me I'd be hearing from the someone one way or another, depending on the results. When I stepped outside, I welcomed the fresh air, gulping a couple servings as Leo walked toward me across the purple swirls of painted concrete.

"So?" His brows nearly met his hairline.

I shrugged. "I did the one thing. I told the truth. Now let's go home." I linked my arm in his and headed for the subway.

Lest there be any concerns, I am proud to say I got to Quantico, a feat in itself. But that was where the real work began.

On a warm day in late June, giddy recruits watched hundreds of friends and family fill an auditorium to commemorate the last five months of hard work and sacrifice. We were well-aware there would be more to come. Each academy trainee waited in the wings to cross the stage and finish what we'd all fought so hard to start. We raised our hands, repeated the oath, and received our credentials and the coveted gold badge. Applause thundered at length. The formal fanfare made for some misty eyes. Not *mine*, but some.

The ceremony didn't end in the auditorium. Before we loaded our cars to head home and then onto our new field office assignments, we each stopped at the armory. We received our own FBI-issued sidearm and ammunition with the reminder of our oath to protect lives and safeguard the nation. Or, as Harlan Smith would have said, "locking up the bad guys."

"If I didn't know better, I'd think you were wearing Ms. Jolie's long lash plumper. It's nice to know that even though you are a federal agent, you can still look pretty, Harry. And that mascara really is a miracle in a tube considering what you have to work with, dear." Bess had my chin in the grip of her thumb and index finger; her smile beamed.

"It is, Bess. Thank you for seeing to my cosmetic needs." I grinned at the woman and rolled my eyes at her husband.

"Looking tan, Marty. Fit. Retirement looks good on you."

"It's these green shakes Bess feeds me. Every time I want a donut, she makes me drink a green shake. You'd be surprised how quickly I stopped wanting a donut."

I laughed.

"What's next, kiddo?"

"I gotta get home. I've got another graduation to attend tomorrow. 'Tis the season. Then I'm going to sleep for a week before I get myself ready to head to Boston."

"Why'd you pick Boston?"

"It's not like they give us a choice, but I'm happy about it. I'm a northeast girl, but I need to get out of New York. A change of scene, a fresh start away from some ghosts. But it's close enough, I'm keeping my home. For now, anyway. Just a train ride away, don't you worry."

"Worry?" He shook his head with a frown. "I don't do that anymore, kid."

Forty-Five

Two graduations in two days in two different states, after five months of the hardest mental and physical challenge of my life, proved—exhausting. But nothing would keep me from cheering on St. John's latest Red Storm alum. Leo graduated, officially a physician's assistant, and I flew to New York to see him cross that finish line despite having just crawled across my own.

"Well, who do we have here? No, wait. She looks familiar. Red hair, great rack, an ass that just won't quit. What was her name?" Leo waited outside a neighborhood bar with his hand on his hip and pursed lips with faux disapproval.

"Hello. Mr. Leopold Klein, P.A. extraordinaire. Did you get taller?"

Leo wrapped me in his long arms, lifted me off the ground, spinning us in a circle. My bare legs swung like a rag doll. "Ya don't *call*, ya don't *wriiite*, ya don't *Faycetiime*." His exaggerated *twang* made me laugh, but his tight, muscular squeeze muted my sound.

"You didn't think I'd miss this, did you?" My feet found the sidewalk.

"I'm sorry I missed your *kinda* big day."

"I'll give you a pass. You had— stuff. Marty and Bess were there. It was kind of them to make the trip. Easy now that they're living the unencumbered life. They deserve it."

"Let me look at you." He twirled me under his arm, and I curtsied, pulling out the skirt of my short dress. "A dress? Strappy heels? You got a date?"

"Have I got a date? Yes, I do. With my pillow. I expect it'll be a hot and heavy week-long affair. The only breaks will be for junk food and beer while I catch up on my shows."

"Hmmm. Kinda sounds amazing, minus the beer. Ooh, maybe consider keeping Friday night free? My kid sis Sadie is in town, and I got a gig for the Fourth of July. Now that I've got a job with a regular schedule, I can get back to booking the occasional singing engagement." Leo's buoyant face suddenly fell flat, likely because mine did.

I didn't want the reminder it had been nearly a year since a tall, dark, and handsome man made my tail in the nighttime shadows of Gantry Plaza State Park.

"I'm sorry, honey." Leo held my hand; sad eyes of concern threatened what should have been a celebration.

I waved him off and pried out a smile. "It is so good to see you, Leo. But I don't want to bring you down or get in the way of your good time tonight. Go celebrate with your fellow grads and Sadie, and you and I will catch up for real before I head to Boston." I rose on my tiptoes to kiss his cheek.

The door to the bar swung open, and the raucous crowd thundered inside as music blared. A voice on a microphone boomed over the noise, "Did someone say karaoke?"

"That sounds like your cue, Auntie Leo." I spun and shoved him toward the party.

"You sure?" He asked over his shoulder. "Walking home alone?"

"You kidding? I'm an official G.I. Government issue, Special Agent Smith. Go have fun." I pirouetted away from him and took off for our home a few blocks south.

The summer heat had arrived in Queens, but I'd spent the last five months in Virginia, so my winter body had thawed long before June. The distinct *parfum de city* smelled different after so much time living in the rural confines on the Potomac River at Quantico Station. It felt good to be home, even if only for a little while.

Fresh from such an intense learning environment, I should have been more aware, kept myself tuned-in to my surroundings. A young woman walking alone in a city at night should always take precautions. We all know that. Hell, Dad had drilled it in me from the age of six. In my defense, I was *super* tired and thinking of the next big adventure waiting for me in Beantown—yeah, if I called it that again, I might lose my badge. The Hub is what Bostonians called it—short for 'the hub of the universe.' No joke. Those *Massholes* were going to take some getting used to.

Anyway, tired and distracted, when I turned onto the walkway to my building's stairs, my brain didn't make the jump. *Couldn't* make it. I stopped, frozen in the June heat of the Queens' nighttime.

The man sat halfway up the concrete steps but pulled himself to standing, a hand on each pipe-rail. Jeans and a snug, dark t-shirt showed his surprising size with a frame that carried more than a few new pounds, most of it muscle. Unexpected, considering he'd been dead for the last ten months. When he opened his mouth to speak but then didn't, I had a moment of panic, thinking I had finally broken with reality. Then again, the white coats at Quantico surely would have caught it. They never would have let me pass the psych evaluation. That's when I figured some fatigue-induced fantasy was at play. But for the record, he looked *very* real.

I took slow steps toward the stairs as he descended them, eyes locked on one another. When we stood toe-to-toe, I glanced around to be sure no one witnessed me reaching out to touch the likely delusion. *Huh*, felt real too.

I lay my hand flat on his chest, and he placed his hand atop mine. My knees buckled at the feel of him, but I righted myself quickly. His firm grasp of my elbows helped. A mini tug-of-war commenced when he tried to draw me close, while I wrenched away with an ardent head shake. He let me win.

"Say something," I whispered to the ground, wondering what the sound of his voice would do to me.

"Hi." He shoved balled fists into his pockets and rocked back on his sneakered heels.

My chin rose as my head cocked, and I squinted. "Say more than that," I demanded, voice still low.

It appeared his hands in his pockets meant to keep him from touching me, and for those first baffling moments, I appreciated him sticking to the old rules.

"Hattie, I love you."

My eyes gaped wide. "Jesus, Trey. Don't say *that*."

"Sorry." He pinched the bridge of his nose. "Jeez, you'd think with ten months to rehearse this, I'd be doing better—"

"Why? Why are you here? Why now? Why— why did you wait so long?"

"Because—I needed time to get better. Reprogrammed sort of, and you had a huge challenge ahead of you just to get to Virginia, and I didn't want to distract from that and once you got in, you needed to focus on that job, getting through it. It's grueling, I remember." He let me take one hand while my free one indicated it was all I had to give at that moment. "You look great. You *did* great.

I knew you would, but I was so proud, Hattie. Watching you rise in the ranks—"

"Watching? When?"

"All through it. Every step. You were amazing and under the circumstances—"

"You were around?" I yanked free.

He hung his head. "I've been around some, yeah." His thrown-away hand found a pocket again.

"Some?"

"I was around," he confessed.

"On my walk home from the gym that night?"

He cleared his throat. "Yes."

I drew a ragged breath. "Did you know? Did you know you were going to be found that night?"

"*Popov* got found that night," he corrected me.

"Don't. Don't do that," I growled. "It was the same to me, and you goddamn well know it," I seethed.

"I came to tell you. To spare you. I wanted to, but—"

"At the cemetery? Were you there?" I pushed for more information.

He hesitated, then nodded.

"Where else?"

He didn't answer.

"Where *else*, Trey?"

"Yesterday. Graduation. I couldn't miss that. And I almost came to you then but—"

"But, you chickened out?"

He exhaled a joyless chuckle. "Maybe. It was a big day, *your* day, I didn't want—"

"When else?"

"Huh?"

"When else were you—*around*?"

"Hattie."

"When else? The poly? Were you behind the glass at the poly?"

He looked skyward with a deep breath. "Yes."

"Because you thought I'd lie?"

He reached for me. "*No*. No, I did *not*," Trey answered emphatically. "I *never* thought you'd lie. I knew you wouldn't, but others were less sure, and I wanted to see to it you weren't strong-armed into some—technicality."

"Oh, my *hero*." Disdain seeped out of me, and I couldn't quell it. I wasn't sure I wanted to. The night's humidity had my dress clinging to me, and my curls tightened at the base of my neck, but I barely registered any of it. "Now what?"

"Now what?"

"We've discussed how you repeating what I say just slows us down, right?"

"Look, Hattie, I know it was a terrible thing. I did a terrible thing—a few terrible things, but once I pulled the ripcord on Trubetzkoy, it got crazy. Things happened fast. Implementing an extraction plan with no warning. It could have been too fast. It got dicey. My team was scrambling, pissed. The brass. I mean, the paperwork alone—"

I snorted, and it was the first sign things might be all right.

"I know I broke a promise, but I also promised I'd find you, and I seem to remember you made a promise, too."

"Me? What was that?"

"Don't be dead. Don't be dead and come back, and I'll forgive everything—"

"Wow," I interrupted. "That's some seriously good recall there, dude." I couldn't keep my snark in check.

"We wired the canopy—in case any Trubetzkoy crew showed. But there was more, the good stuff came after—"

"Yeah, I remember." Images flashed of a sterile government vault somewhere, storing a record of me blathering about dirty jokes and touching, pancakes, and dancing. *Fantastic, Special Agent Smith.* "That was a long time ago."

"Ten months, two weeks, five days, and going on eleven hours." Trey looked at his watch, a watch I'd never seen him wear.

Somehow hearing the countdown hurt my—*everything*, and I squeezed my eyes. Once I assured myself, I could do it without falling, I stepped to Trey. Motionless, his discipline remained intact.

Close enough, I caught his citrusy scent I'd missed for so long. I wanted to get closer. "I have a question. Maybe two."

"Only two? Why do I find that hard to believe?"

I nodded. "Still an asshole, I see. Good to know."

He laughed out loud, his head thrown back with a toothy grin. It was beautiful. He was beautiful. I smiled wider than any I had eked out in the last ten months, two weeks, five days, and going on...

"Question number one?" Standing close, he had to look down to meet my eye.

"What's your name?"

His sweet grin faded, and I lost his gaze for a moment. "Trey."

"No one names their kid Trey," I reminded him and fingered his chin, so he looked at me again. The new contact sparked electric and gave permission for him to touch me too.

He tucked a wisp of curl behind my ear and raised a shoulder. "I've been called Trey all my life."

My brow asked for more, no longer interested in omissions or lies.

"Alvah with an h, Rabinovich, the third."

My eyes lit up. "Rabinovich. The *Jewish* Popov. You son of a rabbi."

His head had a subtle shake. "The total package."

"If I was the total package, I'd have figured it out long before—" My hands grabbed for his, but I didn't finish my remark. I didn't know if it would have changed anything. Saved us some time, some pain. I stared into his dark eyes. The lashes, still impossibly long, decorated a more relaxed face. Less tension riddled his brow, his jaw. The corners of his mouth curved up naturally with a calm I had only caught glimpses of before he—died.

"When did you know?"

"I was never one hundred percent. But one thing on top of another and by the time you left with that lame knock-knock joke, I knew you had to be law enforcement. No one else could get away with such a crime." Yep, humor would be a must if we were going to get through this. Humor and—

His thumbs stroked my fingers and brought me out of my daze. "Hattie? Your second, but surely not your last, question?"

"Oh. Sorry. Yeah. Uh, why the hell haven't you kissed me yet?"

"What?" Even in the nighttime light, backlit by the dim porch fixture, his cheeks grew rosy. "I, uh, was trying to be a gentlem—"

My mouth collided with his. I held him around his neck, and his hands gripped my waist before he lifted me from the ground and turned, setting my feet on the first step of the stairway. Face-to face, I leaned into the kiss, taking note of every touch, every movement, every sensation I had imagined for far longer than ten months, two weeks, five days... His hands cupped my face, and his lips got softer, slower, more tender at the same time, exposing a deeper hunger. It stole my breath, made me dizzy. I grabbed the railing to my right.

My hand pressed to his broader chest, I pulled from him with the gentlest nip of his bottom lip and looked away.

"You okay?" He tilted his head, trying to meet my eye in the shadowy scene.

"Me? Yep, just wanted to be sure we didn't have a repeat of our first kiss. But nope, must have been a one-time thing." I grabbed for his smiling face and devoured his mouth again.

I'm not one to kiss and tell, but good *lord*, this son of a rabbi knew what to do with his lips and his tongue and his teeth. Talk about the total package. Not interested in surrendering his lips, I held him by his cheeks while I tried to navigate the concrete steps to go inside, backward and in heels. Trey followed, but forward momentum halted when I found myself pressed hard to the door. But where progress in geography stopped, hands and mouths picked up the slack. Our grip on one another grew more possessive, ardent, and our year-long craving escalated from mere hunger to starvation.

I released his mouth to speak but lost my words when his kisses seared my neck. Tugging at his curls, our tongues swirled their way together again, but the sudden pinch of the door handle at my back reminded me what I wanted to say.

"Trey?" I managed one word before his eager and welcomed mouth consumed mine again. "Trey?" Another gasped attempt to get his attention slowed him, us. His hands landed on the door, boxing me in. I clung to his forearms that caged me as another gentle peck feathered my lips, then my cheek. We both swallowed hard, breathless.

"Yes, Hattie," he whispered the name I'd missed hearing.

Hidden in his shadow, my fingers caressed his neck, sliding from his Adam's apple to the hollow of his throat, the stubble of his end of day beard rough to the touch. I gave a light tug on the collar cuff of his t-shirt. "I—I should unlock the door, yeah?"

"Oh. Yes. Sure." A note of relief might have lived in those three syllables like he feared I would send him away. He gave me room to turn around so I could enter the code into the lockbox. He kissed the back of my head, his palms slid along my sides, his chin hovered over my shoulder before he realized the potential intrusion. "Sorry." He twisted away to give me privacy.

I grabbed at him to keep close. "You can know the code. Zero. Seven. Zero. Four. Three."

He wrapped himself around me. "*Aww*. That's kinda—gooey."

I elbowed his ribs as I crossed into the vestibule. "Hey, don't ruin this."

He snickered with a playful grab at my dress as I spun away from him to unlock my apartment door.

"Wait a minute." My hands landed on his shapely chest. Another shock registered, and I stopped us in the dim hallway. "Did you say you *love* me?"

"Wow. Way to play catch up there, Special Agent Smith. Yes. I did."

"Holy shit." I backed into my apartment.

Trey remained in the hall with a stunned expression. "That mouth."

I covered *that* mouth. "Sorry, but you like my mouth."

"I *love* your mouth—even more than before." His head wobbled toward the front entrance, wide-eyed, with his cheeky grin.

I beckoned him with my index fingers. "We should probably talk about all that. Because I—"

"Wait." He didn't let me finish. His mischievous smile evaporated, and he spoke with a seriousness I remembered with mixed emotions. "We should talk about lots of things." He entered my home and closed the door behind him.

Forty-Six

THE AIR-CONDITIONING BLASTED, AND my sweat and humidity-soaked dress stuck to me, magnifying the chill. Gooseflesh sprang up on my biceps, as did a couple of other indicators of the sudden cold. I crossed my arms when I noticed, but my guest had already seen what my thin cotton dress couldn't hide.

"A/C works," Trey piped up, looking everywhere but at me.

"Darn right nippy?" I bit my lip, trying not to laugh like a twelve-year-old boy.

Trey stifled his amusement best he could but didn't have much luck. He opted for a change of subject. "You bought new furniture."

I looked at the sofa and chairs I purchased last fall. Part of the *getting on* I fought so hard to do. I could only nod as an awkwardness permeated the scene. Those weeks had been some of the hardest of my life, and like the other most trying times, I'd faced them alone. My choice.

"Hattie?"

"Hold on, Trey." The reality crashed around me, and with it, a mix of feelings and contradictions. Should I jump into the man's arms or knee him in the crotch? The desire to do both ran high. I rubbed my forehead with the back of my hand, afraid the hail of questions ricocheting in my skull might break loose.

He waited patiently but then finally spoke; his soothing tone calmed me. "I know I've had the benefit of knowing this would happen someday. Not the specifics, obviously, but I knew I'd do my best to come and apologize and explain, and if I found some luck along the way, maybe you'd trust me again. And, not gonna lie, it's gone pretty damn well so far, but I understand if now the shock is wearing off, you feel differently—if you need time. I'm not fool enough to think this is just gonna happen, you and me. It'll take some work. I know that, but I'm up for it. I'm in. One hundred percent. No more secrets, no more omissions, no more undercover work, ever."

"I don't even know if I like Trey Rabinovich. I mean, I agree, so far so good— like *really* good but—"

"You know Trey Rabinovich more than you think you do. That was part of the problem. Rabinovich met you, and Popov didn't stand a chance."

To hear Trey speak about the two men like they were two *different* men made sense. Professionally, I understood it, and yet my head spun when I considered it. More theory versus practicum. I recalled moments we shared where I caught glimpses of two personas—grins, flinches, expressions that showed pain, all more understandable now. My morphing expression must have broadcasted some of that.

"Yeah, there has been and will continue to be a lot of therapy. But I'm good, and I want you to be part of that too, and *wow*, I'm moving too fast. I see that, but standing here with you and thinking about how much time we've lost, all I have to make up for—I...Like I said, I've had a good bit more time to contemplate this—not to mention some of Uncle Sam's best head-shrinkers to sound off to. Oh, no offense."

I *hmphed.* "No. None taken. Can I get you a beer or, believe it or not, I still have that vodka. Are you really a vodka guy?" I made my way to the refrigerator, needing some distance, not eager to dwell on being the topic of someone's therapy session. "Leo was sweet and stocked me up before my return today."

"If you're inviting me to stay awhile, I'll have a beer. How is Leo?" We took a break from the headier topics.

"Seems good. Real good." I popped the tops off two bottles and brought them to where Trey stood. When he took his, I raised mine in a toast. "To health."

"На здоровье." He tapped his long-neck to mine.

I hesitated but then drank, knowing a stupid grin smeared across my face. Trey returned the look, and shyness blanketed the room. Leo flickered across my mind again. Could I tell Leo? How could I not? Marty? More questions to add to the fast-growing pile. Ignoring them wouldn't make them easier to tackle later.

"Have a seat. I'll be right back." I kicked off my high-heeled sandals and hurried to the stairs, taking them two at a time. Rummaging through the luggage that I hadn't unpacked, I found what I wanted and returned to my guest. He bounded to his feet when I reentered the room. Nervous energy bounced, his and mine.

"Sit with me, yeah?" I asked permission to join him on the sofa.

"Yes, please. It's nice. The sofa."

"Thank you."

"I just bought furniture too. It's in storage but—"

Trey's reticence to share grappled with his desire to do it anyway, a contest I'd witnessed in the past. In retrospect, that war had raged in him from the very beginning. I would let him talk and try not to pelt him with too many questions out of the gate. *Patience, Harry.*

"I bought a car, also."

"A car in New York City?"

"Oh, I don't live in New York."

"Oh. Where—" I stopped, knowing I should let the man tell me in his time.

"I've been in D.C. and Virginia, working on Mom's little farm while on leave. My *actual* mom. Fresh air, manual labor. The best medicine."

"I see." I squeezed his brawnier shoulder, realizing the marked difference in his appearance. Seeing him healthy and at ease, aside from the moment's understandable tension, reminded me how he spiraled those last few times I'd seen him. Then, to hear we'd been so close to one another these past months made me grieve the lost time he mentioned.

"It's surprising how things change when you're not living in fear twenty-four/seven, and you sleep regular hours and eat when you want to, what you want to, and have a state-of-the-art exercise facility at your disposal."

I pressed my palm to his cheek, and he leaned into it. I had to touch him. "I'm sorry." It was a blanket apology for so many things I wished had been different.

"Don't be. It was the job I signed on for, and I was good at it— until I wasn't." He sipped his beer, and I stroked his stubble with my thumb. He continued. "I was in D.C., Chicago, moved to Miami, then here. Popov moved in and out of these very mid-level, connected families, rose the ranks, because I knew things about the competition, and then disappeared. Shortly after I—*Popov* moved on, those organizations took some serious legal hits. Feds swooped in to bust stuff up after my exit. But the last move raised some questions. I got a little cocky. Someone with Trubetzkoy got nervous, curious. They welcomed me in, but then hamstrung me. I couldn't get any traction, so I took more risks trying to prove myself. When my handler wanted to pull me out, I refused. I knew Gleb liked me—in his way—so I thought success was close and figured if I could take this last group down, wound them anyway, I'd get out, be done. But it took longer than it should have because there was some sloppiness in Miami. All on me. So, I had double to make up for."

"How long were you in? Undercover?"

"Six years. Five were deep. Too long. Too long for me."

"But you succeeded."

"It worked out, but I bailed. Sent up a flare. After months of digging in my heels, I quit with no warning. And my team had very little time to implement our extraction plan. On the fly like that is dangerous, certainly not ideal, and I had little. Nothing actionable. Man, I'd never seen them so pissed. It got ugly."

"Why? Why did you pull the plug?"

He looked at me with an incredulous grin I thought hid some shame, maybe some regret. Obviously, he had no easy answer.

"I'd been teetering for months. I should have let them pull me out, but I was determined to finish this *last* job despite the obstacles. Then, for better or worse, you provided a respite, a hotly argued reprieve, but you also helped me gain that traction I needed with Gleb. With paradigmatic skill. And I'd gone rogue by then. Between missed check-ins, some unsanctioned gambles, and you— MOM was fit to be tied."

"Mom?"

"MOM. What we lovingly called my handler. Maintenance On Mobile."

"Mom," I repeated the clever, albeit misleading, acronym. It proved remarkably apt.

"But when I got in deep enough and found Anya was the real shot-caller or was about to be, and then discovered you, drugged on the rooftop with that driven, completely unpredictable, ego-maniacal, and dangerous—woman, I called MOM and said—"

"You wouldn't be making it home for dinner on Sunday," I interjected. "Some of the last words I ever heard you say."

Trey frowned and pulled me to him, stopping with our faces an inch apart. He let go with a murmured apology.

I closed the distance, brushing my lips against his for a too-brief kiss, then sat back. "I have something for you, two things now. I believe they both belong to you." I opened my clenched fist to reveal his star pendant and the fine linen handkerchief embroidered with AR in tight, black stitching. "Alvah Rabinovich?" My thumb stroked the monogram before handing it to him.

"I hated doing that to you." His eyes focused on the hanky. "God, the hardest thing I've ever done, and I've done some stuff. But that—I made Mom go speak to you, take you this *stupid* piece of fabric that was supposed to—to what? It took three agents to keep me in my chair. I swear, Hattie. I fought it, but you'll learn sometimes you have to follow orders. And I was already in the doghouse, but you saved the day when you gave Special Enforcement and Major Crimes a reason to bust down the door and where to look once they did it. Federally, our hands were tied until they blew it open. That was all you. You saved my ass and not for the first time."

I interrupted his praise. "You sent Mom more than once. The apartment in Astoria? A spot down the block here?" I motioned to a long-gone dark blue sedan that moved onto my street the day after I killed Vlad the Bad.

When Trey shook off my attempt to return some gratitude, I pounced. Crawled onto his lap, straddled his hips, and kissed him hard, but it wasn't long before a laugh bubbled out of me. I continued my amorous charge, trying to control my silly giggle. Trey laughed too, finally halting the ridiculous make-out session.

"What is going on inside that head of yours?" He looked up at me, hands everywhere.

I dove in for more kisses but spoke between them. "I have—so many—questions, so much to say, but I can't stop kissing you."

"We have time." His hands got bolder, and I melted into him.

"For kisses— or questions?"

"All of it, and you must be exhausted. Most agents sleep a week after graduation."

I pressed my forehead to his, enjoying how he touched my body. "If you think I'm going to close my eyes and risk waking from this dream, you're nuttier than I am. And that's saying something." I might have hedged my bet on the dream thing.

"If you want me to stay, I promise I'll be here whenever you wake, but if you'd rather I go, I understand—"

"Shut up and kiss me." I appreciated Trey's discipline and his eagerness to follow orders—my orders. Sexy diligence. We collapsed on my new sofa.

"Wait. The body? How'd they manage the body?" I asked, propped on one elbow with a befuddled look.

"That's what you're thinking about now?"

"Um, I'm a woman. I can multitask. A skill you will probably learn to appreciate, you son of a rabbi. Wait, are you a son of a rabbi?" I let another question slip as more thoughts ricocheted in my brain.

"First, I'm a little afraid I won't be able to handle you if I ever have your full attention, but somehow that doesn't seem likely."

He chuckled when I walloped his arm, faking a pained look before he grew thoughtful. "Yes, my father was a rabbi who didn't make it out of the Soviet Union when my mother did. She fled, pregnant. She took the name Rabinovich and gave it to me. My father and his father were both named Alvah. The rabbis in Virginia took her in, and they made sure she became a citizen. She was lucky to have such great sponsors, and they kept her on at the synagogue until I returned from my final tour."

I rested my chin on his chest as he told me about his parents, but my head popped up again. "Tour? You were in a *band*?"

"Yes, Hattie. A Russian language death metal band."

"Shut. Up." We snorted at our own joking.

"Two tours. Stationed at Bagram. I was an airman."

"*Ah-ha*, you *do* speak Arabic." I gripped his chin.

"Yes, but in my defense, that was before we weren't lying to one another. If you'll recall, we were both telling our fair share of tales at that point, so—"

I bobbed my head back and forth, agreeing with his assessment. "So, what'd he say?"

"What did who say?"

"The guy in the food truck?"

"What guy?" His inability to hide his grin betrayed his ignorance act.

"*Trey*. If it was about me, say. Don't know if you've noticed, but I'm pretty thick-skinned. I can't imagine much that would shock me. Not easily flummoxed." I dragged myself off him and sat on my knees at the end of the sofa.

Trey cleared his throat and rose on his elbows, resigned. "He said—and this is a translation—and it's been a while—so—"

"Stop stalling. You know exactly what he said."

"He said, 'A redhead who likes dirty jokes? He should marry her.'"

I wrenched back and rolled off the sofa, officially flummoxed. "Oh. Well—*jeez*—that's not—"

"Something we need to talk about now?"

"Exactly." I found my beer. Warm, but I guzzled it.

"Table it, then?"

"Uh, yeah."

"Done." Trey sat with an apologetic look and a furrowed brow, leaning elbows to knees.

"I'm moving," I blurted.

"To Boston, I know."

"In a few weeks, less actually."

"I figured soon."

I ran my fingers through my hair. Already half-pulled from its elastic, the rest of it fell free.

"Wow, your hair got long. It's been up every time I saw you at— It grew."

The reminder he had seen me several times over the past ten and half months made my stomach tighten. He was nearly a year ahead of me, and I didn't enjoy playing catch-up.

"You wanna talk about my hair?"

Trey stood. "I wanna talk about anything you want to talk about—except maybe the body. That can wait." It was an attempt to lighten the mood, but it failed. "Or maybe you should sleep. This is a lot. Tonight has been a lot, these last months, this last year—and it would be understandable if you weren't feeling exactly clear-headed."

"What about you? Are *you* clear-headed?"

"Yes," he answered, not the least bit hesitant. "Less so when you're sitting in my lap, but *God*, I like it—" He pulled me to him when I smiled. "But I've had nearly a year to think and plan and imagine—" His mind-reading skills continued to impress me.

"Don't think I haven't imagined things too. Usually followed by a lot of cussing—at you. A *dead* you."

"That explains the near-constant ear-burning I've endured."

I scowled at his flippant complaint before pressing my cheek to his chest to avoid his eye, when I dared to ask the next question. "Do you know the Bureau has a language recruitment program out of Harvard?"

He tightened his grasp and cleared his throat. "I do." His heart thudded in my ear.

"Do you know there are openings in that language recruitment program at Harvard for F.B.I. language specialists?"

"I do."

"Did you know Bostonians proudly claim the nickname *Massholes*?"

"Yes." He kissed the top of my head with his breathy laugh. "My turn. Quid pro quo."

I looked up, eager to play another round.

"Do you know— while I haven't accepted because I—well—" He shrugged. "But did you know the Bureau is holding a spot for me in that language recruitment program at Harvard?"

My swift, two-handed shove packed more punch than I planned. What can I say? I don't know my own strength anymore. "You asshole!"

"Don't you mean, Masshole?" He grinned.

"I wish you had told me this an hour ago."

"If wishes were *fishes*..." He winked, and a new rush of adrenaline spread through me.

"Speaking of wishes," I rose on my tiptoes, kissing him. I spoke without releasing his lips, "let's go to bed."

"Oh, well, I didn't want to presume, but I have a bag in my car." His fingers found their way into my hair, tugging as our kiss intensified.

"Where's your car?" I slipped a hand under the hem of his t-shirt, finding the heat of his skin, the ridges of his tight torso, and the raised scar of the knife wound I had inflicted. I couldn't care less where he parked his damn car.

"In the alley, under the building. You got rid of the van, huh?" It seemed Trey Rabinovich was a talker, but I pressed my lips to his, my tongue asserting my mounting impatience.

I tugged on a belt loop, pulling him to the stairs, my eyes trained on his metal buckle. "Don't bother with the bag. Not tonight."

"You kept my sleepover stuff?" His sweet question included a hint of heartache as he held me close and kissed my temple.

"I did, but who said anything about sleep?" I grinned with down-turned eyes and poked his firm middle before taking two steps up the stairs. "You're about to get my full attention, Special Agent Rabinovich." My head pointed to the second story.

"I'm following you."

I jutted my hip. "'Cuz you like the vi—" My hungry eyes and bit-lip grin looked down at Trey. "Too bad you don't speak French." I winked.

"I do now—the latest addition to my CV. I got inspired, but my accent could use some work."

I gasped, mouth wide before I clamped my lips firmly shut and bolted upstairs, happy to hear quick feet in pursuit.

THE END

About the Author

Kelly Elizabeth Huston writes women-centric, genre-straddling fiction that always includes laughs and a love story. Sometimes there's heartbreak, a smidge of mystery, moments of suspense, and maybe a dead body... or two. Maybe. But above all, she hopes her protagonists are better for it in the end, and she entertains her readers along the way. She currently lives in Georgia with her husband and two nearly-grown sons, who are, hands down, the best cheer squad a writer could wish for. After spending a few years in the traditional publishing space, Kelly leaped to the indie side without looking back and is eager to dole out her book babies and get them read. She hopes you'll join her in the adventure. https://www.kellyelizabethhuston.com

Next in the *Found Families* series, we move south and if you enjoyed the gentle giant with a side of kickass sass Leo Kline, you'll be happy to see him again and meet his kid sister Sadie Jane, along with a quirky cast in a small coastal Georgian town that has seen some changes. *See Sadie Jane Run* hits shelves the latter half of 2024.

Also by Kelly Elizabeth Huston:
Tex Miller Is Dead
A Very Crowded House

Acknowledgements

Obviously, this book three in the Found Families series takes an even darker turn than *A Very Crowded House.* It makes sense to me because I like a little dark with my light. It's what I enjoy reading, and you know what so many credit Toni Morrison with saying…Write the book you want to read. Thank you for the permission, Ms. Morrison.

I also took a turn with a younger protagonist. Having some years on Harry, it wasn't always easy watching her flounder, but while she is so different from this writer, I related to that phase of life when you think you have yourself and the world all figured out, only to realize you aren't even close. We've all been there. Thinking we are definitely one thing when in truth we are definitely something else. *Knowing* we are ready for new things when we haven't done the work, or learned the lessons necessary for success. I hope that growth stage is as universal as my ego believes it is.

On the flip side, Harry's (and Trey's) allegiance to do right is admirable if not agonizing. I give her all the points there. I'm not so sure I wouldn't have caved. So, I guess I'd like to thank Harry for her own knack for discipline. She made it a better story.

There are also others to thank. The usual suspects who've been fans of this universe from word one (Mr. Kelly, Mom, Dad, Aly, Heather, Kyle Ann, and Michaela). Some new readers who have jumped in with repeated public praise. We writers live and die by reviews and every one of them helps. And, of course, my editor. Ash is always there to solve my comma problem and quick to nudge me for more or to use that delete key. She's rarely wrong, and she is an absolute *Kelly Whisperer.*

I'd also like to offer my thanks to Rachel Jagoda Lithgow. Rachel and I knew each other as teens and recently crossed paths again. She is a writer too but also has an impressive CV if you care to Google her. She guided me in some specifics of Jewish custom as well as confirmed choices I made regarding Alvah [Popov] Rabinovich the Third. Thank you for keeping it real, Rach!

See Sadie Jane Run

1
Sadie

I cussed when my head snapped back—the ridiculous veil caught in the door I'd slammed closed. Not one of the more genteel profanities my long-ago college boyfriend's mother informed me was appropriate for a lady to let slip from her lips, mind you. Polite society might abide the occasional *damn* or even *shit*, but beyond that, no one would approve of such a mouth. Naturally, I made it worse when, with a wink, I informed her that her son liked my mouth just fine.

I didn't even want to wear a veil—certainly not anything that long. Hell, I didn't want to wear a dress. *Shoot*, I didn't even want to get *married*. Then again, neither did Tristan. Right? So, we didn't. But there I stood, in a pitch-black room I didn't know, on *The Sapphire Selkie*, a riverboat casino I *never* would have chosen, with my *chapel-length* veil stuck in the door I just banged shut, trying to escape a banquet hall and the shocked faces of hundreds of wedding guests left in my wake. Wait, what was that look on Tristan's face? And why the hell hadn't he met me here yet?

Nope. I dropped a full-on *F*-bomb, then opened the door a sliver to gather the lace-trimmed tulle and eased the latch closed again.

Out of the dark, a chuckling snort startled me. My eyes adjusted to the lack of light with help from a dim glow that snuck through the round side scuttles on the boat's starboard. After freeing my tight curls from the veil's hair comb, I hoisted my organza gown to my knees, ready to make another run for it.

"Is that an invitation?" By the sounds of it, my hideaway pal had enjoyed the open bar before the ceremony. My fiancé called it pre-gaming, and since it was a midnight ceremony on a gambling vessel, somehow that tracked.

"Excuse me?" The southern drawl I tended to keep buttoned up doubled when I got frazzled or happy or drunk or... "Is that any way to talk to a bride on her would-be wedding day?"

"Shit." Chair legs screeched across the floor when the silhouette of a tall man pushed to his feet. "Sadie? Sadie Klein?" A faceless twang met mine.

I stepped deeper into the dark.

"I apologize. I didn't mean to—"

"Do I know you? Hard to imagine since I know all of ten people on the pages-long guest list— and I only like two of them."

The stranger laughed again. "It's Ellis, Ellis Holland."

I didn't speak, stunned but relieved I could hide my shock in the nighttime light.

"We went to high school together," he continued.

Still, no words would come.

"I was a couple years ahead of you in your brother's class. Leo?"

"I know my brother's name. Ellis?" I played dumb while desperate to keep calm. "Your name's Ellis?"

"You tutored me. In Calculus. How do you not rememb—People call me Dutch because my last name's Holland—"

"Yes," I interrupted. "How clever." Having little interest in any sort of small world reunion, I pushed ahead, knowing I needed help, seeing as my rogue bridegroom appeared to be a no-show. And I had no plans to stick around. But of all the people... "Two questions."

"Fire away, Sadie."

"How drunk are you?"

He didn't slur his speech, but what self-respecting southern boy did, no matter how inebriated he got? "Just drunk enough, I s'pose."

"Great. One floor down, at the aft of this too tall river barge, there are three twelve-foot, inflatable pontoon rescue dinghies with 10.0 short shaft outboard electrical motors." I met silence. "They're red," I offered when I realized my error. I have a tendency to focus on details few others find interesting or important or at all necessary.

"My apologies. Imma little drunk. Was that second question hidden in all of that?"

Adjusting to the environment, I'd swear I could see enough to register the handsome man's quirked lip. "Oh. No. Right. Think you could help me get off this hell-boat and pilot one of those puppies the two miles back to dry land, Mr. Holland?"

"Captain."

"O-kay. I'll call you whatever you'd like."

"No, it's *captain* one of those puppies, not pilot. You captain a boat, pilot a plane."

I waited a beat. "Ellis? Dutch? Oh, Captain, my Captain? Could you help out a runaway bride?"

"It'd be my privilege, Sadie Jane Klein." If he'd worn a hat, he'd have tipped it. Memories of small-town-living where everyone knew everything about you, including your middle name, washed over me and struck me dumb. A rare condition. Neither of us moved for a full three seconds.

"Uh, I'm assuming you mean *now*, darlin'?"

"Yes, Ellis. Now'd be good, but never call me that again."

Dutch rushed past me, opening the door a crack to see if the corridor was clear. Hall sconces highlighted his blue-green eyes and days-old beard. Sandy-brown curls, I recalled from our younger days, were gone, and now he wore his hair quite short, if not an all-out buzz cut. Unfastening his top button, he loosened his necktie while I stared at his chiseled profile. The man had aged well.

"Sadie?" It might have been the *second* time he whispered my name.

"Yes?" I jolted out of the chaos reigning in my brain but couldn't pull my gaze from his lips. A faint scar showed at one corner of his mouth. I winced, suddenly remembering how it bled all those years ago. And why.

"Isn't this boat going to move again soon?"

"Yes, out twelve nautical miles for the gambling to begin." *Oh, the irony.*

"So, we should probably hurry."

"Yes." My feet wouldn't move. Tristan should have been here by now. Hell, Tristan and I shouldn't have ever been here at all. *Son-of-a-*

"Are you sure?"

I met Dutch's narrowed eyes, bloodshot tinged. "Nevermore so." I hitched up my skirt again, grabbed the crook of his arm, and we bolted for the nearest stairwell, leaving behind the ludicrous veil.

I knew better. *Everybody* knows better. But as we fled the party at sea, buzzing through the humid night air, I couldn't help myself. "That was easier than I thought it'd be." I didn't say it *to* anyone. The high-pitch whine of the electric motor, splashing surf, and blustery wind demanded a near-yelled conversation, and that wasn't happening.

Nevertheless—I said it, even though I knew better.

Under the perceived circumstances, one might think our great escape should have included more than the uneventful run-in with an on-a-break busboy, a ladder that was a bit too narrow and a bit too steep for my bridal get-up, and a couple of troublesome sailor knots that slowed our freeing the dinghy. I'd never admit it aloud, but I couldn't have made it without help. It seemed my debt to Ellis "Dutch" Holland continued to grow.

Of course, the old chestnut about perception versus reality—well, it seemed to play a regular theme in my life. It wasn't a surprise no one had launched an all-hands-on-deck search for me. Dollars to dumplings, Tristan created some distraction to give me a head start, and as soon as I figured out how it all went so wrong, how I allowed that dumbass to get me into this mess— wait. Who was the dumbass?

My new cohort and I sped toward the socket string lights that seemed to twinkle along the faraway dock landing. They didn't really. The sea breeze made them oscillate, and the undulating tide beat out a rhythmic *clank* as moor chains hit the buoyed channel markers. For people who grew up in a coastal town, those markers, the lights, those sounds make finding your way, even at night, something like automatic. And I had no doubt Dutch would get me to shore. What would happen then? I hadn't a clue.

Halfway between the anchored riverboat and the berth, we found ourselves in the darkest part of the journey. Lights glimmered ahead and behind us, but out in the waterway, I could barely see my hand in front of my face. Barely.

Looking back at the *Sapphire Selkie* and the near-mistake I'd dodged didn't seem prudent, nor did staring at the man who looked like a mistake I might *enjoy* making. While I chastised myself for that impudent notion, the engine's whine, the wind, the splash of the surf—*everything* went quiet. Yep, I knew better.

My head hung low. "Ellis?"

The glow from the distant boat outlined the movement of the figure at the rear of the rescue craft. That figure didn't reply. I repeated his name, but my question was obvious.

"Can't say for sure, Sadie, because it's darker than a well digger's— *ahem.* I can't read the digital display, but I imagine the battery died."

"Yeah. I figured," I sighed. "Two things."

"You're big on that."

"On what?"

"Twos."

"What?"

"*Two* questions, *two* things."

You'd think my distress in the thorniest of run-ins at the most inopportune moment might encourage a milder manner—a less knee-jerk reaction toward the man who'd volunteered to be my liberator, but no. "Stick around, Ellis. Sometimes there's *three.*"

"Careful. I just might," he mumbled, but I caught it.

"Might what?"

"Stick around."

How had the night taken this wild turn? I faced the shore, hiding my smile. Not that it mattered on a moonless night. The choppy water lapped on the boat's bow, and I kept my eyes on the far-off marina. A chill racked my frame, and my grin nearly morphed into a laugh. I stifled it.

Finally, he spoke again. "You were saying. Two things?"

I paused to be sure I wouldn't let slip what I knew would be a maniacal guffaw brought on by the absurd circumstance—dressed in a $15,000 gown, stranded on an out-of-battery rescue dinghy in the middle of Booby Creek at o' dark thirty with the wrong man, a man I hadn't seen in fifteen years. A booby is a sea bird, by the way, and don't let the term "creek" fool you. It was big. I shivered again. "Please tell me this thing came equipped with paddles, and, more importantly, that you are carrying a flask."

The raft jostled, and I grabbed the nylon rope laced around the craft's hull. Dutch removed his suit coat and leaned to hand it to me. "Here. Put it on."

"That's not necessary but thank you." Hard-headed, I refused his kind gesture, already too indebted to the man.

"The flask is in the inside pocket."

"Oh." That changed things. I reached for the Fresco jacket, honestly eager for some warmth. "Aren't you the gentleman?"

"We'll see," came his quick reply.

I stopped short while slipping into the refined summer-weight blazer. Someone had expensive taste, and not just me. The sterling silver flask full of top-shelf Scotch further proved the point. I took a second healthy swig.

"And yes, we have paddles. Your favorite number. Two."

I stowed the booze in the breast pocket and extended my hand. "Well, hand me one, and let's get to shore."

"I will not. You're wearing a wedding gown, an expensive one, I'd guess. Not that I've taken much notice in our rush, but if I know Tristan Pembroke—and I do, it's pricey. No, you will not be rowing ashore, Miss Klein."

I opened my mouth to correct him. I was Dr. Klein, a Ph.D. in geotechnical engineering, but Dutch interjected before I could get the words out.

"Let me guess. Two things."

Damn, I wish he didn't make me smile like that. More stubbornness bloomed. "Three things, actually. I couldn't give a flying ferret about the dress, and how do you know Tristan?"

"That's only two things."

"Don't be an ass."

"But you said *three*—"

"No, that's the third thing. Don't be an ass, Ellis. Now how do you know my fiancé?"

"Oof. Hate to be the one to tell you this, but I'm pretty sure he's your *ex*-fiancé now. And I work with his father. That's why I was on the boat tonight. Work."

"Work? What kind of work?"

"Uh, I'm—kind of a—problem solver. I mean, security, sort of. I work—security." His reply lacked conviction as he stumbled over his words. Maybe he was drunker than I thought.

I laughed—couldn't help myself, but I kept it in check. "Hate to be the one to tell you this," I mimicked, "but after this show of disloyalty, I'm pretty sure you *worked* security for Tristan's father. Past tense." At some point, I might feel guilty about that dig when all was said and done.

"*Nah*, Mr. P and I are good. But thanks for the concern for my employment welfare."

I ignored his scored point. "Guess that explains why your name wasn't on the guest list. Since you were there for *work*."

"I dunno, Sadie. It was a pretty big list as I recall. Long. You remember *every* total stranger's name on that lengthy list?"

Dutch might have caught me in my earlier lie. Not so much a lie as an omission, a feigned non-recollection. Of course, I remembered Ellis Holland. How could I forget? No matter how hard I tried.

As if he read my mind, he continued, "How is ol' Leo these days?" The metal-on-metal clang got louder as Dutch made slow rowing progress toward land.

Opting to neither confirm nor deny his suspicions, I ignored his implication. "He's great. Really good. Lives in New York City. Queens. Recently finished grad school at St. John's. Their Physician's Assistant program. Works too hard and too much to make time to meet the man of his dreams, but he's happy." At least I hoped that last part was true. It had been a while since we talked and who the hell was I to judge him on work/life balance?

"So busy he couldn't make it to his kid sister's wedding? The kid sister he adores more than—"

I pulled out the flask again and busied my mouth with it.

"It's nice he's keeping the Klein family's medical tradition alive." Dutch softened his tone. "I was sorry to hear about your grandparents' passing."

My heart had barely stitched itself back together over the last year and a half, but I didn't show my pain. I wasn't a big sharer. My grandparents, Drs. Avigdor and Talia Klein, were the only parents I ever knew, and I supposed I should count myself lucky to have had them as long as I did. Still, the ache ran deep. Worse even, if I allowed myself to dwell on the loss, both of my grandparents and the mother and father I never knew. So, I didn't. I took in a big helping of sea air. "Yes, well, Mee-maw and Grandaddy raised us right, but it was too soon. I'm grateful they went together. It's the only way they would have had it. One wasn't long for this world without the other. Besides, physics says when the semi hit them, they never felt a thing. I think it bodes well, to be honest. Our parents went down together in an ocean storm, 'course, I was too young to remember, and our grandparents, in a car wreck. When my time comes, I hope it's like that. Fast and with the one I love." Why would I ever share that? Least of all with Dutch Holland.

More splatter and *clang* filled the void before Dutch spoke again. "Some might call it a curse, but you always did look at life a little differently." He took two more long, slow strokes before he asked, "Was the one you love supposed to be Tristan?"

"*No.*" My adamant reply came fast. "Never."

"Good."

"Why good? What makes that good?"

"If he was the one, and you still ran away, you'd probably be sad right now. And I don't want you to be sad. Not over the likes of Tristan Pembroke, anyway."

It had been a long time since Dutch and I'd known one another, and in the night's mayhem, wondering what memories of me he might have carried with him made my brain hurt. But I'd always been a runner. I ran *into* situations with little thought and often ran *away* if things got messy, then criticized every figurative misstep, coming or going. Now, there he sat, all these years later, acting like maybe he did recollect a thing or two, and being sweet about it to boot.

"*Hm.* Like I said, aren't you the gentleman?"

Dutch simply sniffed and kept rowing.

COMING LATER IN 2024